I0671502

Chocolatiers of the High Winds

by
H.B. Kurtzwilde

Clasp Editions
the romance imprint of

Circlet Press, Inc.
Cambridge, MA

Chocolatiers of the High Winds
Copyright © 2012 by H.B. Kurtzwilde

Cover Art Copyright © 2011 by © Kasia Biel | Dreamstime.com

Published by Clasp Editions,
an imprint of Circlet Press, Inc.
39 Hurlbut Street
Cambridge, MA 02138

www.circlet.com

ISBN 978-1-61390-050-5

For Robyn, my partner and treasure, for inspiring all within

Contents

Chapter 1: Runaway   7
Chapter 2: Legacy   13
Chapter 3: Salvage   20
Chapter 4: Grounded   27
Chapter 5: Expectations   33
Chapter 6: Deconstruction   40
Chapter 7: Crucible   47
Chapter 8: Fugue   54
Chapter 9: Barter   61
Chapter 10: Avarice   67
Chapter 11: Revels   74
Chapter 12: Primal   80
Chapter 13: Obfuscation   86
Chapter 14: Patience   91
Chapter 15: Exposure   96
Chapter 16: Examination   102
Chapter 17: Grounded   107
Chapter 18: Cunning   112
Chapter 19: Homegoing   117
Chapter 20: Tutelage   124
Chapter 21: Division   129
Chapter 22: Judgment   134
Chapter 23: Youth   140
Chapter 24: Distraction   145
Chapter 25: Median   150
Chapter 26: Groundless Confidence   156
Chapter 27: Simplicity   161
Chapter 28: Hypocrisy   166
Chapter 29: Absconded   171
Chapter 30: Shameless   176
Chapter 31: Reparations   181
Chapter 32: Acclaim   186
Bonus Chapter: Endurance   191
Chapter 33: Commerce   198

Chapter 34: Duty   204
Chapter 35: Desserts   210
Chapter 36: Adjustment   217
Chapter 37: Saunter   224
Chapter 38: Prodigal   229
Chapter 39: Entitlement   235
Chapter 40: Re-purpose   241
Chapter 41: Assay   246
Chapter 42: Fortune   252
Chapter 43: Swamplands   258
Chapter 44: Faith   265
Chapter 45: Retreat   272
Chapter 46: Anticipation   279
Chapter 47: Persuasion   285
Chapter 48: Intentions   291
Chapter 49: Deviation   297
Chapter 50: Establishment   303
Chapter 51: Commitment   312
Chapter 52: Focus   317
Epilogue   324
About the Author   328

Chapter One: Runaway

There was no point in trying to take in the scenery from a steam coach. The carriage rattled along in a shroud of smoke at high speed, but very low comfort. Each passenger fought his own private battle with motion sickness. The window seats were given to those who lost.

Despite the noise, smell, and shaking, Mayport Titus slept. He had made good his exodus from Ramshock's Academy for Young Gentlemen without detection by his personal watchdogs. Rest was necessary for the final leg of his journey. Somehow, he managed to get some before being jolted awake by the conductor's shout. Mayport grabbed his carryall pack. He had no idea what the man was saying, but felt he'd come far enough from Surat to get well and truly lost. The overcrowded coach gave little room for him to move. He tumbled from the side door, narrowly avoiding his own luggage being thrown down from the roof.

He grabbed his bags and scrambled well-clear of the carriage's tracks. Smoke and steam poured out of the engine, engulfing him in grime. The gears screamed, and the carriage thundered on its way.

Mayport hunkered in the tall grass and weeds until the dust had settled and he felt certain of his solitude. Only then did he get to his feet and examine the guidepost at the deserted crossroads.

Several bits of scrap metal had been fashioned into signs and fixed to a stone pillar. The squiggles were quite beyond his understanding. During his travels that intimidation had begun to wear off. He needed numbers, and found them clearly marked, directing the way to a farm village. Mayport stood there calculating distance and time. It would be foolish to change his plans so late in the game, and yet an opportunity stood before him.

He shook off his nervous hesitation and took up his bags once more. The difference in destination was only a few miles. The sun was high and bright, so he turned his back on the village road and marched off into the countryside.

Mayport wanted to keep a straight face and be dignified, even with only the rabbits to see. Instead, he found himself smiling, then laughing as he hurried along. The rolling hills were fresh and green and welcoming of his hard-won delight.

All across the pastures he saw cows making good use of the grass. In the distance, vast swaths of reeds rose up in a disordered jumble. Only a few houses were ranged about, but he knew somewhere a warehouse must exist. He had only to find it from ground level.

The first evidence was a plume of white, rising up to meet the clouds. Looking down into the dells, only then did Mayport realize his mistake. Above the trees of a distant park rose the banners of a European-style building that looked more whirligig than domicile. Mayport stared, finally realizing the miles he had to cover.

At least with the banners plain before him, he had no fear of losing his way even if the sun set. His bags were only three, but seemed to grow heavier as the afternoon wore on. Though he thought longingly of the comfortable village behind him, he stiffened his resolve and stayed on his chosen route.

He tramped over a pasture, dodging cowpies as he went. Wheels rattled from the direction of the road, and dust rose up like a pale shadow. Men on a pony cart rushed along, crying out as they went. Mayport ducked into the tall grasses near a stone fence.

A cow looked at him with benign curiosity as he huddled in the lee of the fence. Mayport laughed. "You would hide too, if you didn't speak the language."

The cow stepped closer to him. Its bulk hid him from the men on the road. He gathered handfuls of clover to keep her content while he waited.

"I haven't done anything wrong," he said. "It's not running away if you mean to go right straight home again."

The cow seemed disinclined to judge harshly where clover was concerned. Mayport kept company with her until he had his wind back, and had cooled down a little. Then he had to wait longer when the cart returned along the village road.

The cow turned away without comment and made her way to a path that linked the fields. Mayport took his bags and followed behind her when he saw that the path lay in the direction he wanted to go. As the sun made ready for its afternoon exit, he was glad of something more than the sight of the warehouse to guide him over the uneven fields.

The cow knew what she was about. As they went along to-gether, more cows came from the fields and joined the afternoon procession. Mayport did the best he could to stay off the muddy path, but his shoes grew soggy anyway. Eventually the path turned away from the banners Mayport sought. He said goodbye to his companion and went on his own way. As the sky put on its red and gold, the warehouse lit up as though a new star was housed within.

As he drew closer he could see motion in the light, and hear the steady sound of working mechanisms. He climbed stiles and found gates, all the while seeking out the shape of sails or even an anchor post. Only when the sun had set completely did he give up hope of seeing such a thing.

He tried not to feel disappointed. As an unannounced visitor, he could expect little. If his assumed host wasn't home, he had only himself to blame.

In his mind he began rehearsing his self-introduction. In his breast pocket was the weight of a thick letter he had been given to carry. In his youth, these fields and the shining house had seemed a kind of fairy tale, while his reality had been wholly his education. His friends from school were his only society, and even now offered the only help he might rely on.

Mayport didn't think himself a sensible boy, despite all efforts to persuade him otherwise. At age eight, he had gone away to get his education. At twelve, his parents had been lost on the high winds. The bank had a representative at school to watch over him in the person of one Costor Achely, who had been no more than fourteen when his grandfather bestowed his first account to tend. Costor's first goal in life was to make Mayport a man of means. Thus far, they had failed each other.

The moon rose full and bright as Mayport trudged on through the fields. He mounted the last stile between the pastures and the trees, then stopped to rest. He leaned against the wall, craning his neck back and back again to see if there was anything like a person moving inside the brightly lit house.

He set out across the grove of ancient trees, resisting the urge to turn back. Though he had neared, the noise of the tower seemed not much louder than it had at a distance. Windmill arms of metal and glass twisted and spun above the tree branches. Light and shadow cast ever-changing patterns as he went.

At last he came to a wide path of round, white stones. He could no longer deny the weariness in his limbs. But with every aching step his heart grew lighter, and some of his excitement returned. Mayport stood on the gravel and looked up at the house. The bottom stories were made of the local, sturdy mud brick. A few lights shone here and there. Only in the higher reaches did it become a vast, mechanical wonder.

He swallowed his fear and went up to the door. At the press of a button, warm bells rang out in welcome. Then, footsteps approached much more quickly than he expected.

A man in a smoking jacket of black and purple silk pulled the door open and opened his mouth to shout. He hesitated and then frowned. "Who are you?"

"My name is Mayport Titus. I'm looking for Jebediah Cully. I'm here to resolve the issue of this warehouse, and your disposition within the Titus Chocolate Company."

In an instant, the man's expression went from stormy to fair. "On my life, I never thought to see you here! What in the world has happened to you, poor boy? You're up to your knees in mud, come in, come in."

Cully stepped aside and soon had Mayport out of his muddy shoes and stockings. He was left to wait by the door while the captain hurried ahead to make a path. He looked around the place, astounded by the collection of oddities stacked all the way to the ceiling. Cases of trophies were crammed full of odd bric-a-brac that defied description. Bits of machinery and tools were mixed in with china figures and clumps of dried flowers. Between the shelves hung map weavings and painted star charts.

He leaned this way and that to get a better view of the ornaments. Deeper in the house he could hear Cully rushing to and fro. His legs ached, but he didn't dare to sit when the floor looked made of dust and debris. He kept his mind off the cold in his toes by trying to figure out the strange pictures on the walls.

"I'll have to write to that fool at the factory," Cully called down the hall. "He'll be afraid you've been carried off by kidnappers, or worse."

"I'm here on my own business, so it's none of his. What would be worse than kidnappers?" Mayport asked, amused.

"In his opinion, I would be," Cully said. "What in the world are you doing here? You're too young to have business of your own."

"I'm not," Mayport said, and frowned. Indeed, he wasn't. "How old do you think I am?"

Cully laughed, a warm, rich sound that seemed to wrap around Mayport. "I really have no idea. It won't matter way out here. You're as near to the end of the world as you can get without falling off the edge. Why have you come all this way, my dear boy?"

"I've come to assess the value of this outpost, now that the British East India Company has given up and gone home. What is all this junk?" Mayport asked as he followed Cully's nimble lead to the stairs.

"It's your father's. I didn't know what you'd want to keep, and he kept everything." They came together to a kind of den filled with books and more trophies, cluttered desks, and a table that was already set for a meal. "Look in the trunk behind that screen, see if there's something comfortable for you to wear."

Mayport went quickly to change. There were pajamas and slippers of soft, gray cloth. He peered between the cracks in the screen as he dressed, taking in the captain as he read the letters of reference.

Mayport had expected the broad shoulders and work-hardened hands, the silver beard and sturdy frame. He had not imagined brown eyes full of amusement, nor the expressive mouth, so ready to smile. He began to relax, and put his hopes in Cully's welcome.

The table was full of distractions, so Mayport hurried to present himself. Cully hardly glanced up from his reading. He merely waved Mayport on to enjoy the feast. Mayport smiled to himself, reminded of the so-absorbed professors who could sit for hours over a completely empty plate, now left behind at school. He pushed a few temptations into Cully's range, then sat down and tucked in.

Dining at Cully's table was an exercise in luxury. The velvet of the chair felt deep and plush enough to sleep in. Game meat was the main offering, but was surrounded by veggies and fresh, soft bread. Mayport lost himself in roasted rabbit, spring peas, and sweet, buttery rolls to the exclusion of all else. He followed that with a bit of a savory pie and tender okra. He marveled over the variety just long enough to taste it, then moved on to fruit pie.

"You have an appetite," Cully said in an approving way. "I thought I would have to bully and harass food into so scrawny a boy as you."

Mayport almost stopped shoveling down the berry pie to say he wasn't scrawny. He kept his eyes down and the spoon working. Cully could call just about any man scrawny, by comparison.

"So you've made it halfway around the world and no worse for the journey," Cully said. "Is that man Cane still hanging around as your chairman? He will have my skin if he thinks I somehow persuaded you to this mutiny."

"I'm not sorry," Mayport said. "He should have seen to my business before now. What are you doing out here, and what is this place? It looks like a stupa making a daring bid for flight. I thought you were stranded in the wilderness, not wallowing in the lap of luxury. I hope you can explain what you've done with the company's assets."

"You sound extremely resentful, young man," Cully said. "If you have something to say, speak up."

"Where's my father's ship? Not the one he crashed. The other one. The first one," Mayport asked. "Father went off on his new best ship, and the other was left here, under your care. She hasn't been seen in a port for quite some time. I want her back."

"She was decommissioned before the war," Cully said. "Don't be ridiculous."

"The British East India Company lost their 'disagreement with the local element' last year," Mayport said. "I was led to believe the first ship was lost in that war. Certainly, my father is considered dead and gone. He's been reported as 'apparently drowned' but nobody says where or how. Two ships, two captains, all gone but you, and so I must demand answers."

"You are very tired," Cully said. "I should never have kept you up so late, but that you needed your dinner. Well, you've had it, so you should rest. On up the stairs three more turns, and there's a room three doors down. It's dusty, but you'll survive. I was working, and I have to finish. We'll speak again tomorrow when you've had time to reflect on what you've done."

"I didn't do anything wrong," Mayport said. "I'm not out here on my own. My friend is coming, and we want answers. It's better if he doesn't get the idea you're trying to screw me. He can be very jealous about that sort of thing."

"Bed," Cully said.

That was the last word the captain spoke to him. He eventually gave in and went where he'd been told. He resisted sleep in a stubborn way by cleaning up a bit and ferreting out clean bed linens before he finally surrendered. As he lay staring at an unfamiliar ceiling, he wondered if all his efforts had been for nothing.

Chapter Two: Legacy

When Mayport woke the next morning, he was confused by the room he saw around him. Instead of the narrow cell he had lived in at school, he was surrounded by luxury. For a moment he longed for his old, rickety bed and shaky desk.

He climbed out of bed and went to the wardrobe, not certain what he would find. All his threadbare clothes were arranged within. Shelves and hooks were already overloaded before his belongings took up residence, but his stood out for being neatly folded or hung. He got dressed quickly, and discovered that his ruined shoes could be replaced with a pair of boots that were only a little too large for him.

He went out onto the staircase, and winced as his weight made the metal steps shift and complain. "Good morning!"

"Very late, by my reckoning!" Cully's voice boomed up from below. "Hurry on to eat. You've still got some explaining to do."

Mayport crept down the stairs, half-expecting to see the Chairman and his minions gathered at the table. Instead there was a sideboard to choose from, and a place set for him at Cully's side. Mayport took toast and built a sandwich nearly too large to bite, then went to stand behind his chair. "What do you want to know?"

Cully tossed his fork down and stood up from his table. "Bring that, and walk the line with me. I suppose I have some explaining to do as well."

Mayport put his plate down and devoured his sandwich as he trotted along behind Cully. He wondered what kind of line he had to walk. Images of rigging sprang to mind, but he dismissed them as improbable. Cully led the way out of the house and headed down to a row of low buildings to the south.

"I think I smell something burning," Mayport said. He scanned the horizon until he saw a smudge against the sky. "It's in the reeds, I think!"

"As it should be," Cully said. "They burn the sharp leaves off before they harvest, and were at it long before you rose. I might have gotten out of here with more cane than you can imagine, if I hadn't trusted your father's word."

"I should apologize for all that junk," Mayport said. "It must be dangerous, living like that."

"He left you more than just junk," Cully said. "You have an appalling lack of curiosity. Look around yourself and try to understand where you are."

"India," Mayport said. "Beyond that, I'm sure I'll never know. My friend Thiervy brought me to port, but his barge broke down. Without him, I should never have made it so far. He's sure to catch up with me before long."

Cully sighed loudly, then put on what he probably thought was a patient smile. Mayport could see his jaw flex as he bit back something he very much wanted to say. "Yes. You know absolutely nothing. Is that correct?"

"The Chairman has raised me like a mushroom," Mayport said. He swallowed hard at the bitterness which welled up at the back of his throat. He had come to associate that taste with any thought of the business his father had left on his plate. "I've been kept in the dark and fed shit. I'm ignorant of a very great deal, I imagine."

Mayport hurried to keep up with Cully's pace. In the distance he could see the smoke in the field and hear the lowing of cattle in harnesses. He hopped and skipped when he couldn't match Cully's stride, though he was aware this meant he was going along with a ridiculous bounce in his step.

Cully smiled at Mayport's excitement and said nothing when he ran ahead. Mayport found a fence to follow and climbed atop the stones. He jumped as he went along to the corral, trying to see over the gap between the low walls and the roof.

Inside the long, low buildings was a kind of bovine-driven mill. He had expected a terrible stench. Instead, the dusty sweet scent of feed rose to greet him. Absent too were the bowed backs, and the overall impression of misery he had come to expect of millworks.

"No wonder you holed up so far outside of town," Mayport said, breathless from all his leaping. "That can't be sugar. It's impossible to get now. This would be worth a fortune back home."

"You think it's all gone just because it's not in the stores?" Cully asked, surprised. "Well, go on then. This will be new to you. I bet you've never seen the fresh kind before."

Mayport laughed. "You're right. Of course there would be

plenty of sugar where it's grown. Is all this legal? Everyone from Holland to New Orleans is trying to get their hands on this stuff."

"This isn't the west," Cully said. "Go see for yourself."

Mayport jumped down from the wall and ran ahead to the corral. A gate stood open to let in the loudly-complaining cows pulling wagons. Just inside, boys waited to take control of their tossing heads and soothe them while the cane was unloaded.

From there the cane went to a whitewashed shed where the grinding took place. Aside from being far cleaner than Mayport had expected, the mill shed was more crowded as well. Boys scrambled to fill pails with the cane juice and carry them down to a hopper where all that sweet richness was poured.

Mayport stood there scratching his head, caught in a kind of vertigo. He breathed deeper, trying to hang on to a tag-end of memory that simply did not wish to come forward. He must have overdone it, because he choked hard on dust, and had to go lean against the wall. Cully came over to make sure he was recovered.

"How is this even possible?" Mayport asked, confused. "I don't smell anything burning here. How is it processed?"

"There's a solar boiler," Cully said. "Cakes travels better than juice, as long as there's a ship to carry it. There's cities all up and down that want all they can send. It's good for soldier's rations as well."

"These local rajas don't want to sell any more," Mayport said. "At least, that's what I heard."

Cully laughed and then ushered Mayport into a hot, wet room full of pipes and pumps of all descriptions. The hopper from the milling shed fed directly into the system. Teams of men were handling at least three different products all at once.

As Mayport stood and tried to understand it all, a whistle sounded, and the men seemed to relax as one. The work continued, but at a slower pace than before. Mayport felt safe in walking slowly about the place, taking in the line from all angles. At a tap, tin pails with tight-fitting lids were being filled with syrup and passed through a door to men standing about with small wagons.

All of them turned their gazes on the sky or the grass when Mayport tried to make eye contact. Instinctively, he did as well. Only when he'd come around to another mill did he realize what he had done. A hundred times he had looked the other way while black market transactions took place. He raised his head with an unexpected pride to know free enterprise existed out here in the wilderness as well.

At the very far end of the room, men were filling barrels with thick syrup. The smell of cloying heat was stronger at the barrel end of the room, so he hurried on to the storeroom. There, he was astounded to see sugar cakes of all kinds ranged out on shelves, as well as row after row of barrels.

"But how do they do it without a proper boiler?" Mayport asked. "Out here in the middle of nowhere, this shouldn't be possible."

"Your father thought it would be cheaper to boil the sugar down without fire," Cully said. "He took a couple of fellows and showed them the solar boiler on his airship. They copied the lenticular lens and here we are. There was never a shortage of sugar for your father's business. He just lost interest in actually supplying his factory."

Mayport walked slowly through the storeroom and tried not to gawp. Of the many miseries he had known at the Academy, hunger was at the top of the list. More than once he had taken foolish risks to steal a little milk while he worked. Even with that, he knew he was privileged and well-fed compared to most people of India.

"I remember this," Mayport said, but it came out sounding very confused. "Maybe not this exact place, but I've seen barns like this before somewhere."

"You sailed all over the place with your father, before you got old enough to educate," Cully said. "Maybe you were gone long enough to become a gentleman, but you didn't start out as one. Your father took these treasures in his own hands, and never trusted other companies to be daring on his behalf."

"I don't remember much about him," Mayport said. "I've been sent here by my principle at the bank. We suspect several acts of impropriety with the company's assets. Everything of value seems to have disappeared without a trace. You were the first thing to evaporate, along with the *Dutch Process*, headed for India. The records showed a warehouse here, so I came to see for myself."

"During the outbreak," Cully said, correcting Mayport's time line. "As to your ship, it is broken up and gone. You have only to thoroughly inspect what is stored in that warehouse to know I am right. It wasn't really much of a vessel to begin with."

"You're talking about that junk in the warehouse?" Mayport

asked. "That's what's left of her? What in the world happened? Did she crash?"

"Nothing so romantical as that. I broke her up," Cully said. "She might have been commandeered into serving the Brits out here. She would never have survived, and so she has not. At least this way her dignity will remain intact. Your father abandoned her to fate, as he did with you. He didn't educate you out of love. He didn't want to have to pay a manager if he had a son to do the work for free. He asked his banker where to send you, and off you went."

Mayport drew back from that harsh tone, and the sting of cold fact. "If it upsets you so, let's talk of something else, please. I think there may be some value gotten from what you've saved here for me. I'm afraid it's the last of the grand collections. Father never bought more than a shophouse or put real treasure aside. Chairman Cane had fun emptying and selling a warehouse full of oddities he'd brought home from all over."

Cully's jaw flexed again, and he swallowed hard. "If I am angry, it is at myself. I stayed here, hidden away with the rest of the treasure. I might have robbed you just as boldly, one piece at a time, if I had been left alone with it for long enough."

Mayport looked around at the storeroom again and felt very ignorant indeed. He had known about the sugar fields in a sideways fashion, but hadn't thought on them very much. His idea of making candy was the factory. It's filthy warehouses and harassed-looking laborers might have been a different world. Even if he once might have listed these lands as his legacy, the recent war had ended such a claim.

At last, he followed Cully back to the house, and into the den. By daylight he could see that this room was neatly ordered, if rather full. From a shelf, Cully took a wooden globe and set it on the desk. He turned an expectant look on his guest, then stepped aside.

Mayport studied the surface of the globe. Its lands and waters were detailed in decorative wood inlay. Most of the surface was brightly polished. As he spun it, he noticed patches that didn't shine quite as brightly as the rest. One of the rubbed spots was just above where his school might have been.

He found another rub south of ex-Spanish lands that were now part of the Confederation. It sat on a narrow spit of land that divided the Atlantic Ocean from a wide gulf. A particular point on the coast had been stuck with a pin several times. There were several other rubs, but that particular one drew him back again and again.

"This can't be right," he said, and leaned closer. "There's nothing but jungles and savages there. They chased the Spaniards out decades ago. I would have heard about a city there, before now."

"That's not a city. It's the mouth of a river," Cully said. He turned the globe and bent down to sight along it. "Only your father would have thought to go where the Spaniards had fled and see what he could find. It never entered into his head that other sailors didn't go that way because they knew things he didn't."

"But there was something to find," Mayport said. He fingered the spot on the globe and tried to resist his greedier urges. "It had to have been important to somebody, or why is it worn down so?"

"It is only important to you," Cully said. He spun the globe, and let out an exasperated sigh. "You are correct when you say your father didn't leave much behind. The Titus Chocolate Company is more of an idea than a real business. Every time your father came within hailing distance of success, he would be distracted and lose everything in some grand new adventure."

"What happened to him?" Mayport demanded. "I've asked and asked. Since nobody seems to know, I feel I should at least try to find him."

"He is dead," Cully said, with no sign of reservation. "I know the craft he was on. Even the slightest problem could have sent it plummeting. That's why I left him, in the end. I followed him on the seas, and later on the high winds, but that contraption! I could only despise it, for I knew he would die of loving it. The first vessel we built was security itself compared to what he tried to do. You're a fool to come hunting for it, as if it were something a sane man would risk to sail."

Mayport stared up at Cully, knew he was just being stubborn but couldn't manage to care. "I made it here, and came to help you. I hoped to find a ship and bring back some kind of cargo. I'll have to be satisfied with bringing you home safe and sound. Without some way to haul goods back, I'm completely ruined. They'll have me in debtor's prison the moment I return."

"You wouldn't last a week. The Chairman wouldn't let them have you anyway," Cully said. "Now, you've had an idea. That's just fine. What I'm asking you about is your plan. Don't try so hard to be like your father. It's the last thing he ever wanted for you."

"He wanted me to be a gentleman," Mayport said. "In that, I have already failed him. I must succeed where he failed, in business and in my responsibilities."

Chapter Three: Salvage

Mayport was deeply into a study of Cully's rutters when the sound of a siren whooping high above the warehouse broke his concentration. He knew what it was from hearing it all over the ports when he was traveling. This was the first time he'd heard an anchor-line warning in the still of the countryside.

He put the books away as a high-pitched alarm descended somewhere out in the fields. The strobe threw crazy patterns against the walls, then the light and noise ended in an anticlimactic thud. He hurried to the window. With the anchor strobe cut off, he couldn't see where the ship might be beyond the trees.

He opened the window and leaned out as he heard the thrum of the anchor line drawing taut. A disk like a pale moon slowly descended from the skies. In its glow, he could just barely make out the shape of a salvage barge hovering on the edge of the trees.

Mayport grabbed his coat and hurried down to the front door. He was halted by an arm catching him mid-stride. "Friends of yours?" Cully asked over the roar of the barge coming in to anchor.

"He might still be, if I'm nice enough to him," Mayport said. "I guess we'll see. It's only a barge, so they'll need rooms. I guess they'll just have to live with the mess too, while they're here."

"Your buddies have scared the daylights out of the farmers, and probably the cows too," Cully said.

"You ought to be singing praises to Heaven. You'll be going home, if I have my way. This little hidey hole might be a treasure trove, but it's no good to me out in the middle of nowhere." Mayport pushed his way to the door and hurried out ahead of the captain.

He ran to the edge of the trees and climbed atop the stone fence as the flat-bottomed airship came to rest on the grass. The red and black bladder of the sail began to lose volume as soon as the barge was on the ground. A familiar figure leaped over the side and hit the ground running.

Mayport ran to meet Thiervy halfway, hardly protesting when he was hugged near to breaking. He had half-expected awkward greetings and apologies. Instead he had the warmth of a trusted friend in his arms.

"I brought the craftsmen you need," Thiervy said. "The cost will be something else again. Father will take that barge back from me if I show my face in New Amsterdam after this. I'll have to squeeze you for all you're worth, or he'll beat me to a pulp for taking off with it."

"I hope you do," Mayport said, and leaned in tight against his thigh.

"I will, but later," Thiervy said. "Is that your captain? I thought he would be all tan and... um..."

"He hardly leaves the house," Mayport said. "No guests or occasions. I don't know why he leaves the light on. You're the first one to visit since I've been here."

"He must be quite mad, after being alone in this wilderness for so long," Thiervy said. "Anyway, it's too dark to show you my treasures. Is dinner over already?"

"No," Cully said before Mayport could answer. "Young Master Titus' guests will soon be welcomed in style. Would you and your crew like a beer while we wait, Mister...?"

"Thiervy," he said. "Joseph Thiervy, pilot first class, but here as a shipwright. It's an honor to meet you, sir."

"You're too young for a pilot," Cully said. "Where did you certify?"

"Charlottesville," Thiervy said. "I was at a rustic kind of school when I met Master Titus, but Father didn't like me coming home smarter than him. He brought me out and apprenticed me instead. Either way, I'm not much younger than most pilots. I'd better be a good one by now, or Father will have my hide for a coat."

"Don't call me Master Titus," Mayport said, not liking the teasing tone. "Why don't you both go ahead and see about beer? I'll stay and bring the crew on."

Thiervy let go of him but reluctantly. Cully turned and marched away into the shadows, with Thiervy tagging at his coattails and chattering a mile a minute. Mayport shook his head in amusement over his friend. The crew came down in good order, and were glad to hear news of beer.

Cully had thrown open his second-floor lounge and had lined the bar with foamy glasses. Thiervy was leaning against the bar looking quite satisfied with himself. Mayport went over to get his own beer.

"Victory already?" Mayport asked.

"Within hours at most," Thiervy said. "Or would be, if I wasn't preoccupied. Don't worry for him. He'll get his turn if he wants it with me."

"He's much in need of it, I think," Mayport said. "I have to be as lonely as he is. I would have taken after the locals by now, but they're mostly milkmaids and think too much of me. Where's the fun in that?"

Thiervy laughed, and slid closer to Mayport's side. "So. What do you need a shipwright for?"

"I don't need one," Mayport said. "I'm a spoiled brat and want one. Who's going to stop me?"

"You're fooling nobody," Thiervy said. "You've had me haul out supplies and craftsmen for a Hollander class vessel. You've found your lost ship somewhere around here. I didn't see her on my way in."

"She was never lost," Mayport said. "She's been completely disassembled, or so our captain claims. We'll have to sort through the junk Father left behind and get what value we can from it."

"Then you're not really just being a spoiled brat," Thiervy said. "You've got plans. I know you'll go back to New Amsterdam even if you're facing a judge. Cully might not let you go home if he knows the truth of what you've run away from."

"He's no more than a merchant, trying to get his cargo and head home," Mayport said. "I know he's as suspicious of the chairman as I am. I can't prove I've been robbed if I don't go back to make my case. If I manage to remain a free man, I'll need Cully more than ever."

"I'm sure he's open to persuasion," Thiervy said. "Better let him alone for a while, so he can get curious about what we're doing."

"You're the one that has plans for him, not me," Mayport said. "Happy hunting."

Thiervy ambled away to meet up with Cully again. The two of them stayed close through dinner. When rooms had been prepared, Cully personally conducted Thiervy to his quarters.

Mayport stayed up to play host to the rest of the crew, glad to make them feel at home. Cully certainly looked better for the company and the attention he was getting. Thiervy was sure to be better company than Cully had been getting in recent weeks.

Mayport made sure all the little details on their guests were handled, then went back to his own room. Only then did he realize he had spent all evening with his buttons undone and hair in a mess, with his pencil and pen shoved in among the tousled locks.

"You look as crazy as you are," Mayport told his reflection.

"You look delicious," Thiervy said from the bed.

Mayport tried to hide his surprise. "Finished with Cully already? I thought you had stamina."

"He only wanted to tuck me in," Thiervy said. "He's a gentleman. I shouldn't have been surprised."

"Good thing I'm not one," Mayport said. He pulled his shirt off and turned to face Thiervy. "I hope you don't expect me to behave."

Thiervy lifted the blankets back, revealing his perfectly nude body. He had gained quite a lot of muscle since the last time Mayport had seen him like this. He smiled at that familiar invitation and peeled out of his pants. He dove into his soft bed and wrapped himself in Thiervy's embrace.

He leaned in and claimed a deep kiss as he slid his knee between Thiervy's legs. Thiervy moaned into their kiss and rode eagerly against Mayport's thigh. Thiervy grasped at Mayport's ass, dragging him closer until his cock snugged down into the narrow curve of hip.

Thiervy tried to push Mayport over onto his back. By pure strength, there should have been no contest. Mayport stiffened his spine, then sucked hard on Thiervy's lower lip. Thiervy's whole body relaxed into Mayport's arms as he was pushed back against the pillows, letting Mayport have the control he wanted.

Mayport plunged his tongue into Thiervy's mouth again and again. He thrust his cock in a steady tease until Thiervy grasped his ass and pulled him down harder. Mayport laughed into their kiss and rode faster.

"I've never seen you so desperate," Mayport panted against Thiervy's lips. "Should I flip you over and make a proper welcome? You feel like you're on fire."

Thiervy worked a hand between them and clasped their cocks together in a rough grip. "You'd like that, wouldn't you? Do you think of it often?"

Thiervy's thumb curved around the head of Mayport's cock and toyed with the slit until Mayport yelped and twisted his hips. He leaned down hard and held still until Thiervy quit messing around, and began to stroke in earnest. Then he leaned in and caught Thiervy's ear in his teeth, holding him still for the ride.

"Do I think of you squirming on my cock?" he growled. "Sweating, just like this? Begging for more? Desperate to satisfy me?"

"Yesssssss," Thiervy hissed as he arched his hips up and drove harder against Mayport's shaft.

"It never once crossed my mind," Mayport lied.

Thiervy gave a surprised laugh, then pushed Mayport off him. He pulled the blankets down and Mayport stretched out on his back. He got comfortable against the pillows and tucked his hands behind his head, watching Thiervy in a rare moment of indecision.

Mayport spread his thighs and rolled his hips, letting his cock wag this way and that. Thiervy pounced like a starving man, pressing his wide-open mouth to Mayport's balls and licking all over. Mayport groaned and rocked his hips higher, chasing the heat of Thiervy's lips and tongue.

Mayport kept his gaze fixed on Thiervy's mouth as it turned red and puffy with his suckling. Thiervy lapped at and kissed every inch of Mayport's shaft. Then he dabbed his tongue at the head, lapping up the drops of fluid there.

Mayport reached down and fisted his hand into Thiervy's thick, dark hair. He tugged only a little, and Thiervy opened wide to take him in deeper. He kept steady pressure on Thiervy's hair while Thiervy bobbed his head up and down, swallowing and gasping as he licked and sucked.

"Come on, you can take it deeper. You out of practice or something?" Mayport arched his hips, thrusting his cock in a little deeper into Thiervy's mouth. Thiervy yelped in a muffled sort of way, but managed to take what he was given.

Thiervy wrapped his hand around Mayport's balls and tugged gently, easing their tension as Mayport thrust deeper. Mayport held Thiervy's head steady and fell into their familiar rhythm. He thrust just deep enough to feel it was too much, but not so rough as to overwhelm that generous mouth.

Mayport gasped and moaned as his cock seemed to swell and throb. Thiervy squeezed less gently at his balls and Mayport yelped. He twisted them both over onto their sides and hooked his leg over Thiervy's shoulder, pinning him easily for the taking.

"Touch yourself," Mayport said, breathless as he drove faster into the yielding grasp of Thiervy's throat. "Let me see. Do it!"

He felt Thiervy shift around, then his cock was vibrated by a lusty groan. He lifted his head and could see Thiervy tugging roughly at his cock. Thiervy was staring up at him, though his eyes were glazed with pure and burning need.

Mayport reached down and traced the curve of Thiervy's lips with his thumb. The tender flesh stretched and relaxed as Mayport slid in and out. Thiervy groaned, then somehow managed to smile around Mayport's thrusts.

Mayport groaned in answer, whole body going tense as he pushed in deep, then froze as raw pleasure welled up in him. Thiervy swallowed and swallowed, throat milking Mayport's cock. His balls quivered then he howled out his satisfaction as he came.

Mayport jerked and jolted as he poured all his need and lust down into Thiervy. "Swallow it, oh fuck, so damn good!"

Thiervy groaned as he gulped, then his whole body shivered between Mayport's thighs. Thiervy broke out in goose bumps all over as he pumped his come onto the sheets. He leaned back, re- leasing Mayport's cock with an obscene popping noise.

Thiervy kept his mouth open, and Mayport saw the last of his seed being swallowed down. Then Thiervy grinned, extremely pleased with himself. Mayport pulled him up onto the pillows again and dove in to kiss that swollen smile.

They clung together for long, breathless moments. Then Thiervy sat up and made to crawl out of the bed. Mayport caught him by the arm and tried to pull him back down.

"I can't," Thiervy said, and pulled away.

"But we were just getting started," Mayport protested.

"I agree," Thiervy said. "But for tonight, we're done. My crew is here. I have to be in my own bed if they need me."

"What are you so afraid of?" Mayport asked. "Why would they care?"

"They wouldn't," Thiervy said. "You're the one that seems to care so very much. Don't be so demanding. You don't really want me to sleep here anyway."

Mayport pulled the blankets up and got comfortable against the pillows. "I wasn't planning on sleep."

"I know you're not, but I am," Thiervy said. "There's work to- morrow, even if you sleep through the whole morning. That wreck of yours will never fly if you keep me preoccupied."

"I wish you wouldn't be so practical," Mayport said. "You're more fun when you're being irresponsible."

Thiervy finished pulling his clothes on and came over to kiss Mayport. "I promise to be extremely impractical with you very soon."

Mayport felt his mouth pull down into a pout. "I can tell I'm going to have to compete with a boat for your attention again. I should have remembered that before I had you come out here."

"Yes, you should have," Thiervy said. "You'll understand better once you have one of your own. Are you sure you're not interested in telling me where we're going?"

"New Amsterdam to start, but I hope it's only a beginning." Mayport rolled over onto his side and propped his head on his hands. "Apparently, there's a place called May Port somewhere in the south. I could show you on a globe, but that's the most I know about it. There's something there that my father knew about, hence my ridiculous name."

"I never thought your name was ridiculous," Thiervy said. "It sounds nice to me. Like a safe haven, someplace I'll always be welcomed."

Mayport smiled. "You've got that much right. I'm glad you're here. I need somebody to be practical for me, even when I fight against it."

"Don't count on me for that," Thiervy said. "If my working hours weren't at risk, I'd have you tie me to that bedpost and carry on for the rest of the night."

Chapter Four: Grounded

Mayport woke quite rested and invigorated. He only recalled why he was feeling so fine and high after he had washed and dressed. Then he rushed to the window to make sure all was not a fond dream.

In the field, the salvage barge was at anchor. The crew had thrown open the doors to the warehouse and were carrying out loads of stuff. Even with so little progress, Mayport could see piles of wood and rope, pipes and other gear wedged in among the garbage. Heaps of castoff goods surrounded the barge in piles that grew as the men emptied the warehouse. Thiervy was standing atop his barge, surveying the labor with easy confidence.

Mayport wanted to climb out and shinny down the building, then run straight for the work site. His stomach rumbled, reminding him of the hour. He resisted his impulse and went down to breakfast like a gentleman instead. He was surprised to find Cully lingering by the table.

"At last you appear," Cully said. "It's no good sleeping late when there are working men about. They'll get the idea they're employed by a lazy fellow. Your friend Thiervy seems to know something about vessels. I told him to begin by emptying out your warehouse. When they see what's in there, they'll be sure to think they're working for a madman."

Mayport filled his plate and sat, eager to bury his misgivings in a hearty meal. "Maybe I am. Or a foolish one. I was so looking forward to all this. Now I'm not sure I've done the right thing."

"That's quite a deep thought for breakfast," Cully said. "What has caused this sudden change in your resolve?"

"I was thinking of a time at school, about some foolishness one of the students fell into. I was only fourteen, but he was close to graduating," Mayport said. "I suppose a young man likes to think he's not a fool."

"Oh, that's only the start of it," Cully said, with a mock-serious expression. "Some go so far as to claim a kind of native wisdom."

"At least I don't have that vanity," Mayport said. "Still, I'm worried about myself. I didn't know the boy this happened to, but everyone knew what he did. He hadn't been a frivolous person, and his grades were good. I suppose that's why it was such a shock to us all.

"He seemed suddenly to have the means to offer treats to the younger boys. Those his own age told rumors of wilder indulgences. I thought they were only bragging. I'm sure you can imagine where this tale leads.

"He began to make a habit of expensive clothes, even as he began to ignore his lessons. He fell in with the kind of fellows who help to spend what they never earned. Within a matter of months, he had been ruined with debt and a collection of minor civil offenses. Officers came for him, and he was taken to the courts."

"Did they ever discover where his sudden affluence had come from?" Cully asked.

"He had only been given a larger allowance by his family," Mayport said. He shook his head, still confused by the whole incident. "His family tried to intervene, but it was beyond their control by then."

"They ought to have rescued him from himself before the city had to notice," Cully said. "He might have turned thief. Or worse! He might have become a banker."

Mayport laughed, but was still troubled. "If I were ruining myself now, would you stop me?"

"Yes, I would stop you. You still haven't explained how you intend to pay for this crew you've hired," Cully said. "The materials alone will cost rather a grand sum for a boy who never worked a day in his life. Are you expecting someone to come along and pay for all this?"

Mayport took a worn-out leather purse from his pocket and held it up. "There's something to be said of having a pirate for a father. Every week the bursar had something for me. I suppose I should have spent it. If I had, I wouldn't have even thought to call Thiervy out here. I think that's what made me remember that boy from school."

Cully opened the purse and fingered the coins before answering. "You earned what you have in a way he did not. That may be enough to make a difference."

"I didn't earn it," Mayport said. "It was given to me."

"You earned the having of it now," Cully said. "You might have squandered it all. Time gives more than opportunity for frivolity and self-indulgence. You might have felt assured of your future wealth, and thrown these away on nothing."

"But I never can be sure of my future," Mayport said. "My fortune is in the hands of a man I don't trust. He might be ruining me now, and I can't stop him. I've never felt wealthy, or privileged. I suspect that by the time I come into my own, it'll all have magically disappeared."

"I may have to credit you with a small amount of wisdom," Cully said. "I imagine you were squirreling these away out of resentment and a stubborn nature, rather than true restraint. Perhaps you only wanted some hope of independence. But steward your wealth you have done, and faithfully. I will not forbid you spending it now as you please."

"Thank you," Mayport said. He was surprised at how his voice shook. He swallowed hard, trying to accept the protection he felt coming from Cully. "I don't think I was really being wise, or resentful. More than one boy at school had set his cap to gain glory and leisure through eventual inheritance. I found them to be rather gruesome."

"You've set your cap to own a ship," Cully said. "That might have a more gruesome end than you imagine."

"But what'll I do with her once I have her?" Mayport asked. "I can't sail. I can't navigate. I'd be as useless to her as I would be to a real lady."

"First, learn to love her. Discover her needs. That will make you a useful man to her. It will also make the real ladies quite jealous of her charms," Cully said. "Many young men would be quite upset with me for this kind of oppression. Be careful you don't set yourself apart by being both wise and industrious at your age."

"I have a friend at home who expects both of me, and never mind my age," Mayport said. "I should go see about Thiervy. He had so much planned, I'm still in confusion over it all."

"Keep him on his ledger every step of the way," Cully said. "If he gets you excited, he could make you agree to anything."

Mayport laughed, knowing very well the ways Thiervy had with persuasion. Then again, Thiervy also cultivated the agreeable habit of ignoring his excesses in the cold light of day. Once, Mayport thought Thiervy cruel for pretending nothing ever happened between them. Now, he was only grateful for that discretion.

As he ambled down to the work site, he marveled at the array of equipment that had been brought. Engines of all descriptions encircled the barge. Long rows of junk were being laid out side to side. To him it seemed the whole lawn was being eaten up by garbage.

He began to walk the rows and saw that there was a method to the process. Moreover, what he had taken for wads of cloth, chunks of wood, useless masses of rope and pulleys were being untangled and organized. It was taking all of Thiervy's crew just to pull out all that had been stored away.

Thiervy soon spotted Mayport and bounced over to him. "You made it sound like a fool had run her aground. She's been completely dismantled. We'll have a real job getting her back into one piece, and that's before we try to caulk and rig her. Then we'll have to get creative about finding a boiler as well. I'm not sure we can do all that here."

"Are you trying to tell me there was an entire ship in that warehouse?" Mayport asked, trying to sound like he was at least marginally informed of the job he had set.

Thiervy laughed. "I didn't recognize her either until we started sorting out the salvage. I don't think I want to know what undid her caulking in the first place. She'll have to be pegged back together, out here in the middle of nowhere. I have men enough and tools, but we need time to do this right. That's the only thing to suit the *Dutch Process* herself."

"Surely she can't just be stacked up and sealed," Mayport said. "She was destroyed. Are you sure she can be made sound again?

"I'll know more when we have her completely laid out," Thiervy said. "She might have warped and cracked if she hadn't been sheltered like this. The lady kept her figure, as far as I've yet seen. She only wants some new pretties to wear. Then she'll love you forever. I just can't understand why he did such a thing."

"You're not cutting corners are you?" Mayport asked.

"No!" Thiervy said, affronted. "I'd never call work finished until I've made her sound enough for my own soul!"

"Interesting standard," Mayport said. "Will you prove it?"

"What do you mean?" Thiervy asked, suspicious.

"I have no idea where I'm going," Mayport said. "I could point on a map, but nothing more. You're the best pilot I know."

"I'm the only pilot you know," Thiervy said.

"I think you're not completely satisfied, stuck on your father's barge," Mayport said. "Are you really certain it suits you?"

"Don't play on my ambitions," Thiervy said. "I'd rather be my father's pilot than give myself over completely to a gentleman's word. The wide sky is more than enough for me, even if I'm only a working dog."

"You give me too much credit," Mayport said. "Everything I have in the world, I'm spending on the Process. I'll take to the high winds because I must. If a friend came with me, I might even get to return one day."

"I heard rumor you were actually quite well-off," Thiervy said. "It made me wary of you. Our dear Costor used to dog you like you were made of solid gold. What happened to your fortune?"

"Only a gentleman's luck," Mayport said. "It could just as easily turn around one day but it won't all by itself. I have to make it change. I want to, and will."

"We have a long way to go before you set yourself against fortune's whim," Thiervy said. "I won't be satisfied until The Dutch Process is fit to match the stories. She was untouchable once, and will be again when I'm done with her. She'll really be quite a feather in my cap."

Mayport saw something like passion in Thiervy's eyes. That, at least, could be trusted. He went some distance from the work site and tried not to hinder Thiervy's efforts.

Mayport stretched out on the unbroken grass and watched the shipwright's work. As they chipped away the piles of parts, they took measurements and put beams in place to receive the massive, heavy timbers. Two poor souls bobbed up and down, working a pump handle twice their size to keep the boiler full on the power hammer.

The equipment was a mishmash of copper and rubber construction. He had no idea how a runabout like Thiervy had gotten hands on such materials, and certainly wasn't going to ask. Though the tools had a questionable history, they all appeared to be well cared for in their new life.

At some unseen signal, the men organized to select the hand-hewn blocks and set them in place on the frame. He could see that each one was unique, carved to serve in just one place on the vessel. The pieces were locked together with thick tongue-in-groove joints and the ship's own weight, and snugged together with deep, final sounds. He thought of that same thing happening in other direction, somewhere on a lonely sea.

"You missed lunch." Mayport rolled over and saw Cully standing above him. In one hand he held a heavy-looking basket. He sat down by Mayport and looked at the *Process* while Mayport rummaged for a snack. "I thought I'd never see such a sight again."

"What? The *Dutch Process* being made sound and whole again?"

"No. A young Mister Titus watching over her with pure love and pride in his eyes." Cully sat down and found something to nibble on as well. "We'll never get her out of here. We should just load her up on the barge and go home. Damn the profit margins."

"What happened to her?" Mayport asked. "Thiervy said he couldn't understand how she got stripped down like that."

"She's a lady of luxury," Cully said. "Hand built by men who never believed she would work a day in her life. Your father would have saved himself time and trouble sticking to sails and the sea. He had her built instead, but never forgave her for the little ways she disappointed. Then he commissioned *Coverture*, and moved on to his new love. I thought he would be unable to let her go to a new master, though he had no use for her. But he gave her to my care."

"Was the *Coverture* ever found?" Mayport asked. "I know he was aboard her when he was lost, but the documents only said he was 'apparently drowned' so… it's possible he survived."

"The Coverture was lost in open ocean, and could not be recovered. Your father might only be lost officially, but to any kind of sailor it is accepted that he is dead and gone," Cully said. "He was only a very tall boy out to have adventure so he could make his mark and get a seat among the spice barons. He never doubted that the call would come. He thought he had conquered the sea, but then again, he also thought he had conquered the world."

"All this time, I thought he died doing what he loved," Mayport said. "He was only a man who died with his ambitions disappointed."

Cully reached out and rubbed his back. "If you've got a drop of sailor's blood in you, it came from your mother. We'll know soon enough which you take after."

"I never thought of that," Mayport said. "Maybe I can go my own way, instead of being a miniature Corey Titus. The more I learn of him, the less I can admire his daring. If I succeed where he failed, perhaps I can do without his genius for grand devices. I think I should like very much to find out."

Chapter Five: Expectations

Thiervy hadn't intended to start an avalanche of work by hunting up a saw. He'd done the reasonable thing, looking in what Cully called a tool room downstairs. What he found sent him running for Mayport. Together they cut the lock on the back doors of the warehouse and swung them wide open. They were both curious about what filled up the bottom floor of the warehouse.

Mayport forced the door open and jumped back, not a bit surprised when tottering piles of junk spilled out. "How embarrassing."

"Some of this stuff will be very useful to you," Thiervy said in a scolding sort of tone.

"Not thrown together like this, it won't be," Mayport said. "How are we ever going to figure out which goes with what? It's impossible."

"This can't have all been brought here at once," Thiervy said. "Even packed to the rafters, your lady couldn't have carried it all. He must have hidden things away a little at a time. I wonder if he even knew what he had stashed away in here."

"Sometimes I wonder if he didn't keep an extra son somewhere in case he needed one later," Mayport said. "Cully's right. He never threw away anything that might one day be useful to him."

Thiervy laughed merrily. "Well, you'll never haul this stuff out of here on her. Maybe you can get something in trade that she can carry home. She's built for speed and secrecy. That cargo's full of enough hide holes to suit a rat. Tell me the truth of what you want with her."

"Isn't it a little early for you to be jealous of her?" Mayport asked. "She's not even built yet. There are things I feel I must do. I need her, in order to do them."

"I'll write your new estimates," Thiervy said, but sounded dissatisfied. "I bet whatever you're planning will be more damaging to your reputation than any pleasure cruise could ever dream of being."

Mayport couldn't deny it, so he only laughed. Thiervy went

back to his crew. Mayport watched only a little while before returning back to find tea.

He found Cully in his little oasis of order and cleanliness on the second floor. He was lingering over a tea table and obviously expected Mayport to join him. Mayport took the cup he was offered and settled down to a plate of tarts. For a time, his worries were lost in a world of tender, sweet berries and flaky crust.

"You do seem to have everything here," Mayport said as he chose a chicken sandwich. "It makes a fellow feel wanted, to be fed so well."

"There's one thing missing, and you seem determined to get some," Cully said. "Are you absolutely certain you want to risk your life over something you've never even tasted?"

"I've tasted it," Mayport said. "I can barely remember it, but I did. This isn't about my personal pleasure, though. If there was a fortune to be made from the stuff in my father's time, I'm sure there's still one to be made on my watch. I can't do it alone, no matter what the reward might be. I know how lucky I am to have friends who will help me."

"Just what is that Thiervy to you?" Cully asked. "He seems a little free with his flirtations."

Mayport licked his lips slowly, trying to think of a polite way to state the plain truth. "I've been terrible to him. I'm lucky to still be his friend. He knows I'm a snake and plays with me anyway. He doesn't even seem to mind that, in the end, I always bite."

"Does he know you're the next thing over from worthless in your fortune as well?" Cully asked.

"Yes," Mayport said, and struggled not to blush. "We have a friendship, and nothing more. Don't imagine more complications than I already have."

"Yes, you do have quite a crop," Cully said. "You're far to the east of what jolly old England says can be sailed. If you can get a cargo of poppy or sugar, anything at all that proves you were here, you'll be a made man in the colony unions. Moreover, you'd be proven fit to take control of your own destiny. I imagine that ship out there fits in with your plans of being welcomed home an adventurer and hero."

"I hadn't thought of myself that way," Mayport said, concerned. "I can't claim to be going out to open new trade routes. Father did all that before I was even born."

"I can tell you're not as wise to the world as is needful," Cully said. "Our Chairman, Cane, is probably in debt as deep as he can wallow by now. He might sign the papers, but it's you going to the debtor's prison if all fails. Your father pulled that trick twice, then ended up in a prison where he didn't speak the language. You're too young and pretty for that, but it's what you can expect of that dried-out old cuss your father called a manager."

"It's beyond my control," Mayport said. "I have what I have and not one penny more. If Thiervy can make something of his wild promises, we can have real hope. If that vessel was even a fraction of what the tales said, he'll get us up and home again."

"Us and what crew?" Cully asked. "The men who were with me found new captains when the pay stopped. It wasn't a difficult choice for them. They stayed long enough to help me take her apart. I didn't want her pressed into service if things got hot in the north, which they did."

"They might have left thinking you a coward and a fool," Mayport got up and stretched. "Perhaps you want me to think of you that way. I have only gratitude to offer, for your loyalty and vigilance. And also for the excellent tea. I'm going for a walk."

"Be careful of the village if you go that far," Cully said. "They'll sell you your own hair, and make you think you got a bargain."

Mayport set out across country toward the village, glad to have a distraction from all the confusing choices that lay before him. He waved to Thiervy then turned to angle across the pastures. As he hurried on, he felt the kind of relaxed confidence that usually led to mischief.

He made much better time back to the crossroads than when he had arrived carrying luggage. He glanced back at the top of the last rise before the road. The warehouse cast a shadow over the work crew. Mayport felt the weight of his responsibility settle on him. He took a deep breath and hurried on his way.

He worried over Thiervy all the way to the village. He wished he could be completely honest with everyone who was only wishing the best for him. His fingers tucked deep into his vest pockets, and he traced the line of a thick belt that lay under his clothes. Even if Cully had taken his meager collection of coins, Mayport might still have made his way back home.

He walked to the village feeling distracted and burdened. Worse, he felt too obvious in his somber clothes and expression among the brightly dressed and energetic villagers. By chance, he found himself mixed in with the crowds of a market.

The smell of the place was intoxicating. Exotic spices blended with fresh fruits and toasty-scented flatbreads. He could recognize peppercorns and ginger, but the variety of spices far exceeded his knowledge. A sun-browned woman enticed him with a slice of pure sweetness cut from a fresh sugar cane.

Mayport's fingers twitched toward his pocket, but he managed not to dip into his purse for a coin. Walking on down the row, he found men drinking tea and smoking deeply of a water pipe. He walked on by, certain that compared to the least of these men, he was a pauper. Everywhere he looked, he saw gold. Not in heaps and bars, as some liked to say in stories, but in a flash on the finger of a pretty hand, or glinting against the swell of a throat.

"English! English!"

Mayport turned at the shrill call. The woman who had given him the sugar cane was tugging a man along by the arm. She parked the man before Mayport and looked at him expectantly. Mayport folded his hands behind his back and tried an inquiring smile.

"You English?" the man asked, seeming proud of himself for speaking first.

"I am Confederalist. I know English." Mayport had heard opinions on whether or not he could actually speak English. The British fellows he knew thought probably not. "I'm here for a ship."

"Oh, Cully, yes. Very sad about him." The man put on a very sad look indeed. It went away just as quickly as it had appeared. "You come for sugar?"

"Perhaps." Mayport frowned. "I have to see about the ship first."

"Yes, always the ships." The man looked up at the sky as if wondering where they might have all gone. "Such a lot of sugar. So very few ships. You are a special man."

"I don't think you understand," Mayport said.

"Of course understand. You are here for ship. Very special man," he said. "I am Devegoda. Come, tea…"

"Oh is that the time?" Mayport asked, though he wished his voice hadn't been so shrill. "I shall be very late. Good day."

"Wait, look, such a lot of sugar…"

As Mayport hurried past the stand where the woman had given his sample, she stood ready. A thick cloth was tossed aside. Under it lay a treasure that caught Mayport as surely as El Dorado had called out to other men. Even the air seemed sweeter for all that pale, brownish temptation.

"May I try that?" Mayport asked. His voice sounded too needy even in his own ears. "I do have to hurry on."

Devegoda wrapped up a few lumps in a twist of cloth and let him go with a hopeful smile. Mayport swallowed again and again as he hurried back to the farmhouse. No matter how he wished otherwise, the sun was getting on before he could trot up to Thiervy's side.

He pulled out the cloth and unrolled it in triumph. "There, see? There's plenty to haul back, a surplus in supply I mean. If nothing else, we can cargo in the barge and..."

"How did you find this?" Thiervy frowned at the brownish lumps, then chose one out. He held it at arm's length for a moment, then popped it into his mouth. At once he shivered, and a warm smile lit his eyes. "All right, I know places this would sell to."

"Idiot, it's for me," Mayport said. "I need that ship, and all of this we can carry."

"You sound burdened, my friend," Thiervy said. "Calm down, your lady will be well as soon as I can figure out this crazy boiler we found. There's linen and wax enough to caulk. She'll be happy to take you anywhere you want to go."

"New Amsterdam," Mayport said. "What about the weather? Can we make it back faster than we would over land?"

"Yes, of course," Thiervy said. He took a few more sugar lumps and smiled wider. "Did you know your ship is kitted out like a whorehouse? I never saw anything like the fittings he's got stored away in there."

"Are you serious?" Mayport asked. "I thought that was all furniture for the collection in there."

"Cully says all that fancy stuff in there is from the Process. It looks crazy, and worn out. It can't possibly have all fit and still left room for a decent cargo."

"I'll find out what's going on," Mayport said. In the golden sunset, he could see plumes of dust drifting up from the open door. Cully was in the front hall, busy with a broom. Mayport was surprised to be able to see the plain stone floor exposed to light. "You must be relieved to have this cleared out a bit."

"I thought I would be," Cully said. He looked a little confused even as he finished sweeping out the dust. "Instead, I'm feeling as jumpy as a cat in a dog pen. As long as all her stuff was under me, I felt like this was home. Maybe I was being a coward, pulling her apart like that just to keep her from being pressed into service or worse. She's my home. There wasn't anything else I could do."

Mayport wanted to chuckle over Cully's distracted tone, but managed to keep a straight face. "She didn't end up in flame and ashes, nor you either. For that, I am grateful. Now. You're not really serious about putting all this furniture on her, are you? We can't possibly need half of it, even with a crew aboard. You said these were my father's things. What in the world are they doing way out here?"

"They must have been his," Cully said. "Some of it, we found in a few hidden cargos I hadn't seen until we pulled her apart. The rest was... all over the place. He must have loved it, or he wouldn't have carried it around as he did."

"Or it might have just been trade goods," Mayport said. "I'm sure it will turn more of a profit than the bare bit of gold I have, here."

"You can't really mean to give your father's things to strangers," Cully said.

"I am my father's," Mayport said. "A few chairs more or less won't make a difference. I doubt even one stick of this was anything special to him. It would have been cared for better if it was."

"Do what you like," Cully said, but sounded unsatisfied. "At least lend a hand with the sorting. From what you say, she'll soon be your home as well."

Mayport went meekly to his task and soon was lost in the confusion of treasures. Some were lovely, others grotesque curiosities, and no two things alike. A harlequin collection of furniture was weighted down with bolts of cloth, boxes and bags of random souvenirs, each looking dusty and neglected. Not one item showed any sign of having been the personal belonging of Corey Titus.

There were few genuine valuables in among the bric-a-brac. He made a great show of saving the ones he found, for Cully's benefit. In the end, Cully withdrew to cook his burdens away. Mayport sucked on sugar to keep his throat clear of dust as he carried on alone.

When he was weary and exasperated, Mayport finally gave himself a break. He dropped down into an overstuffed chair and looked the room over. All he saw around him was ruin and chaos. Other than Cully's kindness, he seemed to have been left little else.

In stories and childish memories, Corey Titus had stood larger than life. Mayport had only halfway believed the tales. Now, he had to face the facts and see that perhaps the whispers of madness and pride weren't far off the mark. He decided then to stop trying to make sense of what his father had intended, and take his bearings by his own heart.

Chapter Six: Deconstruction

Thiervy made every use of Cully's expertise to hurry work along on the *Process*. The work hours were exhausting, and they had little to offer in the way of comforts. After such a show of professionalism, Mayport could do nothing but go ahead with his plans. Even with that, he had to navigate the misgivings coming at him from all sides.

"I don't want to seem disrespectful," Thiervy said in a nervous tone.

"Toward whom?" Mayport asked.

"Captain Cully," Thiervy said.

"Oh, him." Mayport frowned up at the shambles that the *Process* had become. "He's not the captain of anything just now. What's on your mind?"

"Is he sound to command?" Thiervy asked. The thread of real fear drew his voice high and tight. "The things he's done to that ship is pure insanity. He acts proud of it. The artillery alone is a suicide waiting to happen."

Mayport laughed, too loud and too hearty, at Thiervy's sincere concern. "I thought you were a master shipwright. You spoke admiringly of my lady. You pilot that barge yourself. You said you designed and built it, as well."

"I carry fuel, and cram my crew in like sardines. Even with that, she's not light enough to take cargo. Your vessel, such as she is, comes near to being paper-thin. How could she ever survive what will be demanded of her if we get her off the ground? I don't mean to insult your sweetheart, but neither do I intend to let her kill you. Where in the world did he get such crazy ideas?"

"My father," Mayport said.

"Oh." Thiervy looked even more uncomfortable, then lifted his chin and met Mayport's eyes once more. "I mean what I say. Unless there's some reason to fly without real weapons, this vessel of yours is a death trap."

"Wouldn't that explain why it's grounded out here in the middle of nowhere, pulled apart and abandoned by all but her

captain?" Mayport asked. "He said he was a coward and wouldn't
be privateer for either side of this most recent war. I don't believe
a word of that, but I think you're on to something."

"Maybe he just couldn't stand to see her proven incapable of
battle," Thiervy said. "Let's forget these old men. Come to Charlotte
with me. I'll build you something much nicer, and we can piss on
our fathers from the beams."

"No, that's not possible," Mayport said. "That vessel will sail
back to New Amsterdam, crammed full of sugar. That's what I
mean to do, whether you see sense in it or not."

"You really mean to chase after him," Thiervy said. "You don't
doubt him, no matter what you know to the contrary."

"Not for a moment." Mayport folded his hands behind his back
and gazed up at the *Process* once more. "You know I'm not rich.
This vessel is all I have to call a home in this world. I need it to do
what it did before, but better. All I ask is that you have faith in
yourself. I know you can do what you have set out to achieve."

"I didn't know you were in that kind of trouble," Thiervy said.
He sighed, then drew on his stubborn, clever look. "From here to
New Amsterdam, carrying cargo? Those are the terms you have to
meet?"

"Yes," Mayport said. "Costor smuggled me out of town when
we found out what Cane had done to me with debt. I'm not supposed to go back until he sends for me. I find myself impatient,
and Cully's style suits me. He might be prone to take pointless risks
in extreme situations."

"I am too," Thiervy said. "It's better if we don't try to hurry
back. Slow and steady still fits your bill."

"I'm really in no big hurry to get back," Mayport said. "For all
the obvious reasons."

He was grateful that Thiervy left the deeper humiliations unspoken between them. It was bad enough to have a proud name
and no fortune. Worse to be called a fraud and a thief, threatened
with prison for a debt he was certain he didn't owe and positive
he could not pay. His only hope was to prove that the *Dutch Process*
was a real ship, actually capable of doing her job, and not just a
hustle concocted by a mad adventurer to scam investors and insurance salesmen.

Mayport had very little sympathy for the salesmen. He was even
less enchanted with the business manager who had allowed things
to get to this desperate stage. He quite relied on Thiervy's steady,

pragmatic nature to keep him from true peril at the mercy of his father's mad invention.

In the end, it took days of work to re-assemble the inner workings of vents and pipes, whirligigs and makeshift arrays that constituted the engines and rigs. Thiervy had the satisfaction of proving the steam-driven guns did not work. Though it proved a theoretical point, it left him completely without defenses on a craft that would soon be carrying a fortune in exotic goods.

They solved the problem by sending Thiervy off in the barge with a load of trade goods. He came back with breech-loading cannons that had never been intended to fly. The weight of the weapons and their ordinance outweighed the steam-gun system Thiervy had rejected, but had the advantage of being able to strike a target with lethal force, as the previous guns had not.

At last they tethered the Process to Thiervy's barge and set out to move her to the coast. Mayport leaned against his locker and watched the crew sliding the engine lenses into the sockets. The forward fans turned and complained as the lens array heated up air to fill the various bladders and balloons.

Mayport climbed the ladder up onto the loft deck. The stiff breeze caught him by surprise. He looked out over the railings and saw that they were already aloft. The wind picked up considerably, telling Mayport all he wanted to know about their speed.

He glanced up into the rigging, comforted by the shadows of men in long coats and strong boots. As the air grew cooler and the breeze whipped by, he was glad that so much of his skin was protected from the elements in his heavy sailing clothes.

Below, the lines strained and twisted as the barge and the Process struggled to match speed. The split crew worked seamlessly, making excellent time across country. He was certain the noise and startling vision of their passage would not be appreciated by the locals, but could spare little regret for their plight.

"We're sailing due east," Cully said. "See if you can spot the city from here."

Mayport squinted over fields and expanse of fallow land. "No, I can't. Maybe I should have paid more attention on my way here. I might recognize something."

"Not likely, from a steam coach," Cully said. "You would have circled around miles to avoid the river bogs. No, it's best that you see this now. A city, even a nation, is absolutely nothing up here. You can't see it, even if you're looking."

"No wonder it took days to come so far," Mayport said. "I was so focused on what comes next, I didn't think about going back. Much less what things would look like from up here."

"This is only sailing," Cully said. "We're not even above the clouds. You weren't afraid of this until you realized perhaps you ought to be."

"It was different on the barge," Mayport said. "Joseph never acted scared of his own vessel."

Mayport stayed well back from the railings and looked up into the rig. His heart stuttered in his chest as he caught sight of blue sky above. The balloon and sails were thin as yellow shadows. Through that pale scrim, he could clearly see clouds and birds above them.

His belly wobbled and he swallowed hard. Nobody paid him any mind as he edged closer to the railing. Though the sight of ground and the swift breeze unnerved him, it was better than seeing what he was dangling below.

"Just breathe easy," Cully murmured. "It's the motion that makes your belly twitch. It will stop as soon as you get used to it."

"What if I don't get used to it?" Mayport asked.

"You won't want to go home by any way other than steam coach," Cully said. "That boat is too expensive to just be a toy. If you can't play with it, I doubt you'll want to have it."

"I understand," Mayport said. He swallowed again, and made himself smile. That fixed expression made his breathing come easier and he began to relax. "I may need longer than a few hours to be sure about all this."

"Try not to throw up between here and the coast," Cully said. "Everyone does sooner or later. Try for later."

"I simply didn't realize how thin the sails were," Mayport said. "I've seen it, but I didn't understand."

Cully glanced up, then smiled. "The bladders are nothing to worry on. You're in a jigsaw boat miles above dry land. If you got in trouble up here, there's no chance of help. You have to trust your ship and crew. There's nobody else."

"You're right to be so careful of me," Mayport said. "I might not like freedom. I might be weak and useless, stupid and incapable. I might need to be kept in like a maiden, the way our Chairman Cane wanted. If that's the case, I'm going to need more proof than a wobbly belly."

"What do you really think about yourself?" Cully asked. "You act bold as the cock of the walk."

"Never try, never know. I haven't been allowed to try much, so far," Mayport said. He turned and gingerly rested his weight against the railing. The beam seemed to give slightly under his weight, but he might have imagined that. He wrapped his hands around the rail and held a little tighter. "If I'm not more hindrance than a passenger, I suppose I'll have to be satisfied."

Mayport looked up as shadows passed over them. Some of the crew were in the rigging, doing he knew not what. Thiervy ambled over and pulled a lifeline loose, then secured it about Mayport's hips.

"It's a lovely day. We're taking her up to speed," Thiervy said. "Now that my passenger is secure, anyway. I thought I would have to set the lens myself, but they finally caught the angle. Might as well run the engines while we can."

"I should go and see," Mayport said as he reached to unfasten his safety line. "I didn't think you would run them on so short a trip."

Thiervy caught his wrist and re-attached the line. "You're not going to fool around with those engines. For one, you're not kitted to be in those engine rooms. For two, you should see what this boat can do before you get fancy about how she does it."

"But I want…" Mayport began.

"It doesn't matter what you want," Cully said. "Thiervy is the captain of this vessel, such as she is. You obey, you respect, and not any other thing. Is that understood?"

Mayport looked up into two pairs of eyes that would accept nothing but complete compliance. He swallowed his protests and hoped his inward defiance didn't show much. "Yes, I understand."

"I suppose they did teach him something at that school," Thiervy said to Cully. "He knows when to shut up, at least."

"It's a start," Cully agreed. "Let's see how far it goes when he is the master of the vessel."

"I hope that will be a long time off," Mayport said. "I know I'm ignorant of… everything… to do with this plan of mine. I can only hope my friends will haul me back from the brink of disaster, if that's where I take myself."

"I'm afraid we're well beyond that point," Thiervy said. "Perhaps you'd better have a try at being the spoiled businessman you don't want to be. Nothing else is going to get you out of this mess your daddy left behind. Come on if this isn't excitement enough for you. I'll show you where it's safe to go."

Mayport followed after Thiervy until they were deep in the empty cargo gondola. It was the largest and lowest-slung of them all. It was also useless weight, until Mayport did his job better. There they were completely alone, if in the dust and dark as well. Thiervy hauled him in close for a bruising kiss. Their hands were savage on each other, stripping away only what was necessary to grasp at flesh misted in sweat.

"I should have dragged you in here last night," Thiervy grunted as he went to his knees and began licking at Mayport's cock. "I thought it would be another day or two before we were ready."

"We'll make up for lost time," Mayport said. He pulled Thiervy up to standing once more, turned him and braced him against the wall. Thiervy moaned under the rough handling and spread his legs a little wider. "So hungry for me. I don't know why you starve yourself so. It's not as if I deny you."

Thiervy only lifted his hips higher, and looked back over his shoulder. The heat in his eyes was all impatient demand. Mayport smiled and pressed closer, ever eager to indulge Thiervy's sudden whims. He stroked his cock slowly against Thiervy's ass, chuckling as his cheeks flexed and relaxed. He leaned down to bite and suck at the back of Thiervy's neck. The scent and taste of his flesh over-whelmed good sense. He thrust hard, bearing down on Thiervy until he yelped and squirmed against the bulkhead.

Mayport groaned, every muscle in his belly and thighs burning with effort as he held Thiervy in place. He sucked hard at the side of his neck, biting and pulling until he was sure he tasted blood. Thiervy went soft and easy in his arms, moaned plaintively and yielded as Mayport gasped through a few short, sharp strokes.

Mayport tried to catch his breath, but Thiervy chuckled, making his cock throb and pulse. "We could hang for this. Did you know? It's naval law. Cully could say swing us, and nobody would mind."

A delicious shiver twisted Mayport's spine, and he began again to thrust once more. He pinched and slapped at Thiervy's thighs and ass, forcing him to buck and squirm. Thiervy slid down against the wall, so Mayport braced him up with an arm around his chest. He felt Thiervy's skin turn to gooseflesh, and thrust harder as his lover cried out in triumph.

The dark cargo swayed, making their union a rough and

uncontrolled thing. Thiervy struggled for balance but only managed to drive himself harder over Mayport's cock. They wavered
between falling and standing, but neither cared. Danger and pleasure fused to make Mayport's body sing with pure need and
claiming.

Thiervy squeaked and shivered as Mayport pumped hard for a
few moments more, then fell gasping against his back as pleasure
burned out too fast and sharp to truly satisfy him. They ended up
in a sweaty pile, hurrying back into their clothes with long-prac-
ticed hands. Mayport laughed, thinking that they really had not
grown up at all.

"Seriously, we can't again until Gibraltar," Thiervy said. "I didn't
believe it until I saw a man die that way. No more of this until
we're very sure of Cully."

"This was your idea," Mayport said. "It always is, and then you
treat me like I'm the one who can't be controlled."

Thiervy laughed, then kissed him one last time. Mayport tried
to hold on to the taste, hoping it would somehow linger and keep
him warm.

Chapter Seven: Crucible

Mayport lay in his bunk, blinking slowly in the darkness. His hands were curled into aching fists. It took all his willpower and concentration to make them relax open again. Even then, the ache did not relent.

The pain in his body had woken him from much-needed sleep. Around him, rows of hammocks swayed heavy with resting bodies. The smell alone should have been enough to knock him out cold.

He turned onto his back once more and dozed off. When morning rouse finally rolled around, he was among the handful of youths that got a hard whack across the legs to start the day. Even the youngest dared not complain as they scrambled to the water taps for a cold scrub.

Mayport endured it all as he had in his days at school. Instead of cleaning mud off a sea of boots, he was fetching and carrying for every craftsman and the port crews. Scrambling all over the half-loaded craft had taught Mayport to give up all attempts at benevolence or kindness.

Cully and Thiervy had chosen to make the most of the loading time and continued work on their uncertain vessel. The seasoned and skilled crewmen were the ones sleeping late, and who would soon want their breakfast. Mayport grabbed buckets and filled them at the taps, then hustled his load over to the cook shed.

One woman stood above the fray with a heavy hand and unforgiving eye. "Fill that barrel all the way to the top and not a finger less!"

Mayport emptied his buckets into her water reservoir and kept moving. He knew it made no difference who was threatened or thumped. The rule went for all the young men and boys on the work site. Discipline and thumps would only grow harder once they truly set sail.

Much as he might like to resent and bully the younger boys, he was firmly caught in the middle. The men above them all knew that Mayport held the purse strings. They had decided to see him as Cully's trainee, and held him responsible for the gaggle of boys that worked with the port crew. Given the resources they had at their disposal, the maiden voyage was probably going to be a disaster.

Mayport loaded dishes onto the waiting breakfast trolley and pushed it out of the kitchen shed. Whatever the chef's faults might be, she never disappointed at the table. Mayport bumped into Cully's cabin and began to quietly lay the table. Another boy came in to put hot water in the pitcher, and accidentally rattled the mirror as he turned away.

"Titus!" Cully bellowed from his bed.

The other boy fled the scene, leaving Mayport to apologize and finish preparing the shaving stand. He hurried back to the breakfast and managed to have the places set before Thiervy came in, scratching and yawning as he took up his place at the table. His face was already smooth, and his clothes were clean and neatly buttoned. Mayport felt sorely outclassed with his untucked tails and limp neckerchief.

"I believe they bring your shave water first," Cully said. "Isn't that backwards precedent?"

"I'm the one that whacks 'em in the morning. They best see to me first," Thiervy said. "I'd love to see all these heavy pipes actually carry hot water where it's wanted before we lift off. There's no point in having steam if that doesn't give us any power."

"We'll get that squared before we lift," Cully said. "The main point is to get these gun crews up to scratch. It's a long, hard drift from here to Gibraltar, and no telling who we'll meet. Sit, Titus. Hurry up."

Mayport sat perfectly straight on his chair and said his thankyous before he began to eat. He used all the best manners he had endured at the headmaster's table. Any mistake was sure to be noticed and punished. This sudden change in climate had everything to do with the fact that the *Dutch Process* had proven herself an airworthy vessel.

His mind felt soft and bruised from all the facts that had been beaten into it since arriving at the port. The complex exercise of intimidation and blackmail that had been buying his sugar seemed like child's play compared to what Thiervy and Cully had done to him since they began loading the ship. After a few days living with the crew, he began to understand why they had both taken on a prickly sort of propriety once they were underway.

Worse, Thiervy had stopped yielding to the temptation of

having Mayport sleeping so nearby after that one fleeting indulgence. Certainly, they were too tired to care much about getting even more hot and sweaty at night. Mayport understood clearly that the offer was off the table and would be until Thiervy changed his mind again. He could hardly complain, since he'd done the same thing to Thiervy more than once, and with less reason.

Though neither Cully nor Thiervy was particularly warm to any individual on the crew, they had every man's best interest firmly in the forefront of their thoughts. Mayport's first duty was in the lowest reaches of the ship. Boys were packing in a multitude of sugar cones according to Thiervy's precise instructions. Mayport tied his neckerchief over his face to avoid breathing in more sugar than they managed to load.

He knew that Cully was up in the rigging somewhere, resetting the balloons to take on the new weight. Thiervy was probably keeping his word to the accursed plumbing, now that he had seen what the Process was supposed to do. He had taken to cursing Corey Titus's name in time to his hammering.

As he was re-organizing the sugar brigade to take on the fourth cargo, word came down the line for him to find Thiervy. He passed off his command to the next senior boy and trotted up to the engine room. He found a cluster of men around Thiervy, who was head and shoulders inside a gear box.

"Get in here," Thiervy bellowed, and moved over so Mayport could wiggle in beside him.

Mayport got down on his knees and squeezed through the narrow access. He peered at the inner works and wished he had some hope of seeing the sense of it. Then he looked at Thiervy's hands. One sleeve was caught in the teeth of a gear. The other hand was too slick with grease and blood to turn the shaft back.

"You see the problem?" Thiervy asked in a perfectly even tone.

"Yes, sir. I've got it." Mayport grasped the gear-back and hauled with all his strength until Thiervy's sleeve slid free. The white cloth was streaked with black and red. The only wonder was that Thiervy's arm hadn't been chewed up and sheared off. "We have to tie that up, at least."

Thiervy tried to hide the trickles of crimson while Mayport backed out of the access. As he stood to help Thiervy up, he felt even more aware of the half-dozen men around them. When Thiervy marched away without shouting at anyone, the others only looked relieved.

Mayport followed Thiervy back to his cabin, washed his hands and found some bandages. Thiervy stripped to the waist and let Mayport look him over. The bruises and gashes only showed how much worse things might have been.

He cleaned and dressed the wounds, then stood waiting to see what else was wanted. Thiervy looked him up and down. "You know why I sent for you when others might have helped."

"My father designed this thing," Mayport said. "I'm putting people's lives at risk, going on as he did."

"This could have been my arm, in less than a second," Thiervy said. "I don't keep a surgeon on my crew for ballast. You need to go home and let the professionals bring your cargo to port. Cool your heels in the pokey until we come get you. It's not as if you can't trust us."

"I can't trust the winds," Mayport said. "There are more lives than just this crew hanging on to this crazy scheme of mine. Even if this works, I'm only just getting started."

"I thought you'd put up more of a fight than this," Thiervy said. "You're a rebel and runaway, a debtor and a scoundrel. You ought to have lit out for home as soon as we put you on the crew, much less set you to work."

Mayport wanted to answer, but managed to keep still and quiet. He might have reminded Thiervy that their headmaster had many of the same ideas. Discipline had been no joke. That same discipline helped him keep such foolish remarks to himself.

"Back to work, then," Thiervy finally said.

Mayport kept his smile on the inside until he was headed back down the cargo ladder. Soon he heard Thiervy cursing Corey again, and felt that all was right with the world. Indeed, life had been getting better as more and more of Corey's wild ideas had been traded off for cargo.

By listening carefully to Thiervy and Cully's rants against his father, Mayport had learned a great deal about his vessel. The majority of their work had been to rip out supposedly-automatic or safety-enhancing gadgets that didn't work, or actively prevented access to key parts of the engines. Dangers such as the narrow accesses into the gears had been left in Heaven's hands, as Thiervy's accident had proven.

Now the cargo lines were open to the crews, and work was progressing well. He satisfied himself that the boys had things under control, then went up onto the sweeps deck for his first glimpse of sunlight for the day. He saw the nimble form of Cully up in the rigging, but dared not tilt his head back to watch. The Captain was passing judgment on Mayport's work below, based on how the Process responded above.

The rigid envelopes were being deployed and rigged to support the upper gondolas. The fans below turned slowly, filling them with cool air. The crew took meticulous care of the fabrics as they unfolded the support struts and tented out the envelopes. Cully had one of his officers going along the keel spine under each envelope, inspecting lines that would support half the crew as they lay asleep.

The upper non-rigid balloons fell open and he sighed as their shade cut off the unforgiving sun. The engine crew called all hands to the fan wheel, so Mayport hustled along to help. Some agile soul carried a soft duct up above the rigid envelopes and passed it through the belly-net under the white balloon. Mayport squeezed in with the others on the fan-wheel and spun the blades until they whined with their own speed.

"Titus!" Cully bellowed down. "Is cargo five packed?"

"Near to it, sir!" Mayport shouted back.

"Get off that wheel and move the sugar!"

Mayport slipped out of his place and hustled on the ladders again. He climbed down onto the engine deck, then took the heart-stopping trip down into the cargo gondola. The promise of being caught in a net if he fell was fine here on the ground. He could only imagine how his limbs would shake if he had to make this journey once they were aloft.

He dropped down into the cargo gondola and trotted along the line to count bays with neatly stowed crates and cones. The fifth hold was indeed filled. Cargo six was being loaded with a multitude of foodstuffs, from hardtack to lively ducks and sweet-smelling melons crammed into straw packing.

The satisfaction of seeing that task finished was overshadowed by grim reality. He dismissed his laborers and went to clean up once more. The grubby work clothes were put aside in favor of more respectable garments.

He took a sheaf of papers from a bag hung up beside his hammock. He managed to climb up to the command gondola before the bells rang out the hours. Cully noticed his red face and breathlessness, flicked his ear for being unpresentable, and moved on down the line. No man onboard was spared that unwavering regard.

Because he could report a complete inventory of the cargo load, he was left with just a throbbing ear. The reports from other areas were equally promising. From all over the array of hot air envelopes, balloon rigs, engine compartments, even down to Mayport's cargo bays, the *Process* was ready to set sail. Cully looked up at the sky, then nodded once, as if accepting advice from the Almighty.

"We'll cast up within the hour, gentlemen," Cully said. "Unless our Mister Titus has anything against it?"

Mayport kept his mouth shut, and expected the rest of the crew would as well. To his surprise, Thiervy had something on his mind. "I think it should be a little more clear exactly what Mister Titus' position is, before we set sail on this mad adventure."

"I should think it's rather obvious," Cully said, eyes still fixed on the blue sky above.

"I mean to say, in the chain of command," Thiervy said. He gave a cautious glace to the rest of the assembled crew. "In case of emergency, if there should be reason to…"

"Second mate," Cully said, loud and clear for all to hear. "If he can't cut it, he'll go below with the crew like any other man would."

"Yes, Captain," Thiervy said. "Thank you."

Thiervy stepped back but still looked uneasy. Then, nobody had time to feel or think anything, for being busy with the captain's orders. The fans were turned to inflate the lower ribbed envelopes, raising the last gondola from dockside and porting it to its place in the rigging. Thiervy's barge was lifted up with it, on nothing more than balance and thin air.

Mayport hustled up and down the ladders bellowing warnings against stowaways. Then Cully sent the crew scrambling to haul in the counterweight lines. Soon, Mayport was alone on the command deck with the captain. "What am I to do? I'm in no way fit for an officer, even on so makeshift a vessel as this."

"Keep your word," Cully said. "Obey my commands, instantly and without question. You're in the worst berth on this rig, so don't think I'm doing you favors. You'll be pestered night and day for all kinds of junk these men will want out of the cargo. Don't make friends. They'll only use it to get extra fruit rations later."

"I understand," Mayport said. He swallowed hard and reminded himself of all the times he'd had to keep control over a class full of angry, homesick boys. "The only confidence I have in myself is completely groundless."

"We will make do, Mister Titus," Cully said. "We'll make a complete change of crew in Gibraltar."

"We'll have to," Mayport said. "What little we have is really Thiervy's. He might decide to drop off at any port we find."

"It would be better for you if he did," Cully said. "I intend to make you fit for the position you have. The fewer men on this vessel who knew you as a landsman, the better off you'll be later."

Mayport said nothing, and soon was too busy with Cully's brusque education to worry much on that suggestion. As they took the *Process* aloft and began to test her rig, the weight of his responsibilities came down on him once more. He put his focus and trust in his captain, knowing that all their lives now depended on the will of one man.

Chapter Eight: Fugue

When the *Process* finally got underway, Mayport had an hour's worry that he might become useless cargo. A trans-oceanic flight in the southerly season was no joke for an experienced crew. As a shakedown cruise, it was a nightmare.

An hour was all the time he had to think. After that his days were lost in an endless haze of sleeplessness and urgency. He ran messages to all parts of the vessel, relaying orders from Cully. When he wasn't scampering up and down ladders, he was doling out goods for the crew. That his position was held in universal disdain became apparent within the first few days of the voyage.

Time and again all hands were roused in all sorts of weather. Merciless winds whipped between the gondola decks when the sky turned against them. When the skies were clear, it was all the crew could do to repair what had been damaged by the weather. More than once, he heard Thiervy and Cully debating the use of the coal boiler, as though the captain still did not trust what had obviously been keeping them aloft in such foul rains.

The *Process* had not grown any less haphazard for all that Thiervy had done for her. The coal fire added an element of danger to the list. Though Thiervy had admired the theory behind the previous engine designs, it was impractical on a number of points. Mayport couldn't imagine the *Process* being set down every night just because of a clever idea, and was glad Thiervy had been able to build solution.

Cully remained displeased with Thiervy's innovations. He was even less happy when the gun crews were put through their paces. He disliked the smoke, the noise and the sudden jolts that sent the whole of the rig swaying and complaining. Gibraltar was the captain's only happy thought, and so his bitter mood held on until at last they had arrived.

As Cully had predicted, most of the men Thiervy had recruited chose this opportunity to signal their intention to depart from their mad adventure. Mayport could hardly blame them. He doubted they had been told that they would be flying a deathtrap back, and wouldn't have believed it if they'd known the whole truth. Thiervy stayed on and kept the crew in line, though muttering about hauling his barge home in such a luckless craft.

Mayport was in no position to question his choices. The first thing the crew had taught Mayport was that his vessel was not among the illustrious creations called 'ship.' The more he learned of those fine vessels, the less he admired what he had. The sturdy, tall and pampered ladies of kings' navies were objects of pride with good reason. Though there were a handful of soot-belching steamers here and there, most were squatty craft with more brawn than elegance to them. His own lady stood somewhere below and to the side of even those lowly yet seagoing vessels.

What she lacked in prestige, she made up for in relative luxury. The *Process* was less cramped than the average merchant vessel. Her owner was obliged to pay extremely well, to account for the risks men took just to sail on her in the first place. Mayport was still left with the impression that no amount of pay could make up for the indignity of sailing on so awkward a conveyance.

Together, Cully and Thiervy managed to keep discipline over a crew of the skilled and the desperate. Some were at home with the new artillery. Others knew everything there was to know about rigging, and were persuaded to bend their craft to suit the *Process*. The rest were wind-tanned and salted down to the bone. Making for the Americas seemed to be the only attraction their voyage could offer.

When they set out once more, the first two weeks were pure torture. Mayport gave up trying to learn the names of the crew. He got on well with the irritated bellow he had learned from hearing Thiervy chivvying his men. Endless rounds of rigging, unrigging, sewing canvas flues and keeping the decks dry made for days full and busy, leaving little room for discontent.

His first chance for a little rest came when Thiervy happened to be on watch while Mayport was only making sure his men didn't get so drunk they swung over the side without a lifeline on. To his surprise, Thiervy caught him by the collar and pushed him at the nearest ladder. He was so accustomed to sudden, strange orders he simply began climbing.

They scrambled up and up again, along ladders and up veils of knotted rope, crossing above the hot air envelopes and engine gondola. They arrived at last on the square perch that sat above it all. Thiervy hung an arm around Mayport's hips as they looked out north and west. Far below, the Process cast a shadow like a faint stain on the face of the ocean. Mayport took a deep breath and tried to forget his own failures.

"You are one brave little landsman," Thiervy said, and chuckled. "Half this crew wouldn't come up here if they weren't afraid of a beating. What in the world made you do it? Have you got any idea how far up you are?"

"I guess not, or I wouldn't have obeyed you," Mayport said. "I never thought about defying you. I thought you were giving orders."

"That's a rather unusual change in you," Thiervy said. "What do you want a sailor's life for? I don't see a glimmer of passion in you, for this ship or anything other than this mysterious business of yours."

"That's no more than good sense," Mayport said. "If I let my passion show out here, I could be hanged for it just like you. Owning this tub won't save me from the law. Then add the two hundred or more prying eyes, and an equal army of lips to go telling tales once I'm home... I can't put you at risk. I assure you, my restraint is only an expression of my need to protect you when I can."

"We are a pair," Thiervy said, even as he edged out of Mayport's reach. "You're too old to take up this kind of life. Every man here took to the sea when he was a boy. Even the ones who think they're on no more than a glorified kite knows better than you about how to handle her. If your business is so important to you, stay home and run it."

"I can't," Mayport said. "I told you the reasons why."

"Not all of them," Thiervy said. "I don't hang my hopes on knowing the full truth about your intentions. If there was some reason to think you weren't completely mad, I might sleep better at night."

Mayport sighed, then stared out over the glittering blue of the sea and the soft azure of the sky above. If there was a truth to be told, it was hidden from him in miles of contracts, charters and account books. "Did you really hear of my father before you met me?"

"Yes, of course," Thiervy said. "I thought he must be some kind of genius."

"And now that you've seen his handiwork up close and personal?"

"Pure madness," Thiervy said. He looked down at their vessel and laughed. "I thought this thing would be some kind of dream machine. Everything automated, setting rigs with the pull of a lever, perhaps delivering meals with the press of a button. That's all myth, I see that now. And to think this was only the first one he built and launched! It's almost like he didn't learn a thing."

"I think he was not mad, but proud," Mayport said. "In the beginning, I'm told it was all quite straightforward. The goal was to produce fine confections from the best ingredients he could get. Then he had some kind of disagreement with his suppliers... wars and pirates and everything else that can change the way trade flows. He took it all personally, as if the world were conspiring to stop his grand plan. So, thinking he was smarter and better than everyone else, he decided to operate his own imports as well. After that, it only took pride to make him a madman. He simply could not grasp that the world was not under his particular control."

"And now here you are following after him," Thiervy said.

"If I had any other choice than to pick up where he left off, I would take it," Mayport said. "I may even submit myself to debtor's prison, if this voyage goes much worse than it already has."

Thiervy only looked confused. "You do sound rather unhappy, my friend. These men are counting on you to be the gentleman they think you are."

"Far be it from me to disappoint all these expectations," Mayport said. "I wish I could remember what it tasted like. At least then I would know if it was worth all this trouble."

"You can't remember the taste of chocolate?" Thiervy asked. "I thought you must be a fiend for it, the way you've driven yourself trying to make some."

"The Titus Chocolate Company became something of a farce, once Father got wrapped up in these rigs of his," Mayport said. "We haven't produced so much as a wafer for some time now. I was an idiot. There's the stone cold truth, and you may laugh at me for it. I listened to men I did not know and should not have trusted, because I thought somehow I was so special in the world, nobody would dare to misuse me."

"Now we come to it," Thiervy said. "You were defrauded somehow? I thought you were very clever. You certainly sound like you are."

"I thought I was being taken care of," Mayport said. "I knew in an intellectual sense that I was heir to a rich company. I never realized how well off some men would be if there was a company and no heir to bother over. I'm a coward, and a fool. I ran when I should have stayed to fight."

"This was a tactical retreat," Thiervy said. "You've regrouped, armed yourself with... well, it's sugar. Not much in the way of weapons, but you seem to think it will make a difference."

"Do you know what the difference between a real company and a pure fraud is?" Mayport asked. Thiervy looked confused, and didn't offer an answer. "A company tries to make things. A fraud says it makes things, but really doesn't try at all. If I try and fail... that's just normal business. If I don't even try, then I am a fraud from the start and deserve what will happen to me. I would like to at least demonstrate my sincerity, if I can't show any kind talent for business."

"This conversation went over my head a long time ago," Thiervy said. "Try to talk sense, please."

Mayport smiled instead, and eased his hand over to press against Thiervy's. If he had talked himself hoarse, he might have been able to explain. His situation was all too humiliating, even without his only friend knowing every detail. The banks and the insurance companies were arguing over who owned the biggest chunks of him, and if they had to stay connected. Mayport was being sheared like a Merino sheep, close to the skin and down into it if necessary. Worse, he knew it and felt powerless to stop his own destruction.

"I am afraid," Mayport finally said. "Perhaps if I'd simply learned to sail a ship instead of keeping my nose in books all these years, none of this would have happened."

"Don't be a damned fool on top of the rest," Thiervy said. "Even if that was true, becoming a sailor at this late stage won't help. You have to be what you are."

"That's what I'm afraid of," Thiervy said. He slid his hand down over Thiervy's and twined their fingers together. "What if I can't? You know what they say about men like us. I can't love a woman. How can I love this vessel or anything else worth having, if I can't do that much?"

"You love me." Thiervy sounded completely confident, and didn't even glance at Mayport to judge his reaction. Mayport was glad, since he was frozen on the spot, with blood pounding in his ears and rushing to his cheeks. "Look down there. Ships. Lots of them. We must be getting on to the coast. I'll have to report them to Cully. I think seeing the sunset will do you good."

Mayport stayed where he was, glad of the chance to enjoy

some peace and quiet. He opened his shirt and stretched out on his back, soaking up the little bit of sunshine left to the day. Above, the clouds gathered and thinned on the breeze, stretching out to the west.

The sunset was spectacular, and did much to balm Mayport's dissatisfaction. Once the last edge of the sun had dipped down beyond the horizon, Mayport felt the first chill of evening. He fixed his clothes again and went to the ladder to climb down. Only then did he realize his situation.

The ladder down to the highest gondola was rapidly disappearing into shadows. At once, he was aware of the empty air between himself and the sea. He swallowed hard and looked around the albatross deck. Without shelter or provisions, he might have been on a deserted island high above the sea.

Exposed to the elements, he could only expect a miserable night if he stayed where he was. Descending the ladder in total darkness offered a different kind of risk. His resolve wavered between the two options until the night was total and the stars looked down on his plight.

He might have called out for help. He felt Thiervy would come back for him in time. The thought of being rescued seemed less attractive than a cold and lonely night in the open air.

Smoke from the coal fire reached him from somewhere below. That scent and a few tiny lights were all he had to aim for as he sat on the edge of the ladder hatch. He grasped the highest rung and stretched out, reaching with his toes until he found a hold and began to climb down.

He kept his gaze fixed on the mast before him and went by feel alone. Every muscle in his body was drawn tight with fear. Even his fingers wanted to rebel against clinging to the rungs, though his life depended on it. Time and again he cursed his own cowardice as his fingers shook and his muscles tried to freeze.

The dark seemed total as he crept along. The wind tossed his clothes around him as if trying to strip him naked. His legs burned and his breath felt icy in his lungs.

He was sorely tempted to stop at the crew's gondola and spend the night. Its tiny pool of light in the darkness seemed like a perfect welcome. He made himself go on, creeping down the ladder to the engine gondola and down again to the command deck.

At last his boots found solid wood. He locked his knees to keep from crumpling up right where he stood. Breathless and aching, he stumbled back to his cabin. He flopped down on his bunk and stared at the planks above him until the haze of effort and terror faded, leaving him adrift in a fog of exhaustion.

Chapter Nine: Barter

The voyage across the Atlantic remained in Mayport's memory only as sustained shocks to his mind and body. The weather turned cold early and stayed that way. The engineering gondola had been a narrow haven to reanimate fingers and toes. Even with such torment behind him, he looked on the open port with true fear.

The Dutch Process herself made an inconspicuous return impossible. Worse, they came on a mist of their own coal fire, steam and flints of frost freezing and stripping off of the hull. Cully ordered the crew about the business of anchoring with complete disregard for their shocking state.

In the narrow streets around the port, he could see curious faces turned up to watch their passing. Mayport leaned out and called the thoroughfare names until they arrived at the warehouse district. One block of buildings were set about a bricked yard. There, Cully let the anchor lines fall.

The whole facility was silent and abandoned. Mayport hung over the side of his gondola and scanned windows for any sign of light. He caught but one glimmer, and that only when some figure within moved aside. That was enough to send Mayport scrambling for a veil to climb down to the paved courtyard.

He stopped inside the door to dust the ice and snow off his coat, and called out "Is the factory not in operation today?"

"As you see," Cane called back from where he stood on a catwalk above the warehouse floor. "What in the world are you doing here?"

Mayport's smile was automatic and insincere. He felt himself stand up very straight and tuck his hands behind his back. He rocked to and fro on his toes, trying to look as careless as if he'd only returned from an afternoon stroll. "Captain Cully thought you might be worried for me."

"Don't play the naughty boy to me." Cane was at his most severe in an instant. "You've gone off and imposed yourself on that poor old man. Tell me you didn't cajole him back to the helm of that death trap. How could you be so ridiculous?"

"You manage a factory with no production. I think you will not be the person to scold me for being ridiculous." Mayport mounted the iron stairs that spiraled up to meet the catwalk. He walked straight past Cane into the office he usually ruled over. Within, a man lay on a leather sofa with a hat over his face. The stale smell of wine and sweat rolled from him as if to fill the room. Mayport went and took a seat behind Cane's desk. "Tell me this isn't our secretary."

"I have no intention of allowing you to simply walk in here and play the dandy gentleman with me," Cane said. He reached out and thumped the sleeper on the leg until he woke. "There is no way under Heaven we will allow it."

Mayport arranged himself more comfortably on his chair and put on a bored expression. When he slouched just so, he could see the crew still hard at work. He counted crates as best he could and tried to calculate his worth as it mounted. While he watched, the sleeper managed to sit up and remove his hat, revealing the ruddy face of Van Luten.

"You're a young fool to come here, Mister Titus. Most men who get out of my grip are smart enough not to walk back into it," Van Luten said. "Your father regretted crossing me, and you will too. Now do what your guardian says, or I'll put you exactly where I said I would."

"If that were probable, I would not be here," Mayport said. "If you look down in the warehouse, you'll see I'm not as alone as I was when I left. Any one of those men will drag you both out of here just for the fun of hearing you squeal. Would you like to behave with dignity or not? That is the only choice you are being offered."

"You've been disappeared for so long, and you come back like this? Van Luten, go get the block guard. We'll have him arrested right now," Cane said.

Van Luten lurched up and went waddling down the stairs. Mayport let him reach the warehouse floor, then shouted an order down to the crew. A couple stopped what they were doing, collared Van Luten and sat him down out of the way. Their stern eye and rough hands were enough to cow the loan broker.

Mayport watched with a sense of pride to see his men so well disciplined. He turned his attention back to Cane, studying his thin face and waning body. His clothes and jewels looked fine and bright, but could not hide the paling of his hair and skin. Mayport had expected to feel fear when the moment arrived. Instead, he felt as clear and cool as the wind that so recently had tried to shatter him.

"What have you to say for yourself?" Cane demanded, clinging to the last shreds of his authority. "You ought to have left school when I sent for you. Instead, you disappeared and now come here under these circumstances of want and… and…"

Mayport smiled, realizing that Cane had also anticipated this moment between them. "You must have imagined this differently. Was I supposed to be penniless, forlorn, abandoned to the world, with only you to rely on? Was this supposed to have happened long ago, when you stopped sending me my tuition? As you see, my circumstances are quite fine, and I want for nothing. This is no thanks at all to you and your services. Therefore, they are longer required."

"You are nothing but a boy," Cane said. "You can't possibly intend to manage things all on your own. You need guidance from an experienced hand. Perhaps I was a little cruel in my methods, but my intentions were for your improvement."

"I am not a boy," Mayport said. "You misunderstand my absence completely. I didn't need to be here to see what you'd done to me and my estate. There was always someone watching over me, even all those years away to school. Did you never for a moment wonder if perhaps someone else had also been told to look after me while Father was out running loose?"

"You can't mean Cully," Cane said. "He's not the sort at all."

"I mean the bank," Mayport said. "I never belonged to you or Cully or any of my father's friends. I belong to the bank. I've been treated as collateral against his loans for years now. They have seen carefully to their investment. Here I am, returning dividends. You and your sharks have taken chunks from my hide, I won't deny it. But you have not found the nerve or means to strike a killing blow."

"What in the world have you hauled back with you, child?" Cane asked, confused and angry both at once. "Where did you go, and what has been done to you, to change you so? Once you were a cheerful, willing boy. Now you've turned hard and cruel."

"It's sugar," Mayport said. "More than you've ever seen in your life, and all mine. Not a penny of debt is owed against it. This shop is once again a going concern, and I won't have you ruin it for me."

"I am the manager here until you are twenty-five years old," Cane began to sputter.

"Only if you do your job, which you did not, and cannot do," Mayport said. "Very well. We'll make this a matter for the courts."

"Idle threats," Cane said. "You haven't got the means to try."

Mayport started leafing through the account books, thoroughly tired of the conversation. As he read, Thiervy came to update him on the cargo transfer. He looked at Cane, then seemed to realize who he was facing. "Is this the one I get to kick out of here?"

"The very one," Mayport said, though this was the first he'd heard of such a scheme. "And the fat one downstairs. Into the mud and ice, if you can manage your aim."

"He looks a little fancy to get dirtied up," Thiervy said.

"Have you ever borrowed money just to buy a new suit of clothes?" Mayport asked.

"No, never did," Thiervy said. "I didn't know banks would loan out for that kind of thing."

"Banks don't," Mayport said. "It's a sad story, what happened to our Mister Cane. He's not the first, but he hasn't yet realized what he's done. You see, if I had died or disappeared for long enough, he'd be a very rich man. He counted on it."

"He should have killed you himself then," Thiervy said. "That's the only way to count on a man going down and staying there. Why'd he let you run around like you have been, if he had reason to see you in the ground?"

"I've known this man all my life, but he has not known me," Mayport said. He finally found the booklet he was looking for among Cane's collection. "What I'm about to do is see him ruined, humiliated and imprisoned. I wish I was angry, so I could blame this on rage."

Thiervy came to look at the books Mayport was reading. "These are the business accounts?"

"Yes."

"Here's bills for clothes and wine and… good God. How can one man owe sixty florins to a single baker?" Thiervy began to show signs of the anger Mayport wished he felt. "Give me the word, my friend. I can make him pay up. I have the belly for it, if you don't."

Mayport traced row after row of plain embezzlement with his finger and sighed. He took out a pen and found ink, then began carefully annotating all the pages that listed Cane's debts. Thiervy watched in confusion as Mayport wrote his name again and again, then added up the total. "He will starve to death if I do what you suggest. It's slow murder, but the end is the same. I should be proud of myself for hesitating over this."

He gathered up the book and waved for Thiervy to bring Cane. They went down together to where Van Luten sat against the warehouse wall. Mayport opened the book and pointed to the total he had calculated. "I'll buy this debt from you at twenty percent. You've made a bad investment. Take what you can before you lose your life to this deal."

Van Luten grinned his rotted smile and tried on a false humbleness. "You'll forgive me saying so, but that's a very deep discount. Now if we could perhaps discuss terms more reasonable to a man of business..."

"I could just have my men kill you, bury you under the bricks and forever wonder what became of you," Mayport said. "I could do as you intended, call the block guard, and see what the law says about what you've been doing to this doddering old fool. You've much more to lose here than your interest. You may have imagined you were only bleeding a babe dry in me, but you were mistaken. Shall I show you how much, or do we have a deal?"

Van Luten smiled a crooked apology to Cane, then accepted a pen to make the sale fast. Mayport handed over the coins and put his purse away, feeling sick at how cheaply a man's life could be bought in fair and open trade. The lender was back to cursing Mayport's bargain before he had made it out the warehouse door.

Mayport stood still, staring at the line of men unloading the Process until the sense of nausea passed. None of them looked directly at him. After a time, Cully came over, looking wary of Mayport. "The port master came to see already. You're looking at a cold, hard tax but he'll take it in goods. I don't think you can fancy your way out of paying him. He knows you've got the only cargo of sugar to port in nearly two years. He might not take your gold if you offered it."

"Make sure to get my receipt," Mayport murmured.

"Yes, Master Titus," Cully said.

Mayport wanted to frown, or crack a joke about the title. Something in Cully's eyes didn't let him take that liberty. He glanced at Thiervy and saw a similar kind of wariness. Cane himself stood in a head-down sort of attitude, already looking defeated where Mayport had never before dared to defy. He put his hand in his pocket and felt of his purse, then walked out the way Van Luten had gone.

Thiervy followed him, with Cane in tow. A couple of the gunners peeled off the line at Thiervy's gesture. Mayport led the way out of the warehouse and into the streets of New Amsterdam. He kept his chin raised so that his head was tilted slightly back. He breathed slowly to stay perfectly calm in appearance.

He knew where to go, as everyone knew who had ever feared the debtor's prison. The dread for him was as terrible as if he were the one being led to account. The sponging house was but a few blocks away from the warehouse district, but he ambled on in no hurry to arrive.

The block guard welcomed him cheerfully, recognizing at a glance what business he had come about. He took Cane away and made accounting with Mayport by asking "Should he be kept to his own devices, or are you to be called upon?"

"Give him everything," Mayport said, knowing his own cruelty as he did it. "Anything he desires, let him have. Account it to me as he goes on, down to the half penny. If he wants to spend on his grandchildren, let him. They will be gotten and brought to survive with him, the full seven generations."

Thiervy made a surprised noise, and Mayport turned to stare at him. Thiervy started, then bowed his head. The guard gave a nervous laugh and made a note on his ledger. "Did you take some particular dislike to him, young Master? That's a sharp steep interest."

"He's paying the price of betraying Mayport Titus. I do not care who knows of it." He turned and walked out, belly tight with disgust, but face as still and smooth as glass.

"You're a frightening man," Thiervy said. "What would Costor say if he knew what you were doing?"

Mayport barked a laugh. "Who do you think told me how, down to the last detail? Cane would have let me starve to death in there if I'd come back alone. In our dear Costor's opinion, I have been far too merciful in my coup."

Thiervy laughed, and slung an arm around Mayport's shoulders. "I understand it now, why you were so desperate. No wonder you were too ashamed to tell me. Don't hide these things from me, my friend. I prefer your endowments to your dowry."

Chapter Ten: Avarice

At the door of the bank, Mayport did not allow himself to hesitate. Just as he had strode into church early Sunday morning, Monday found him calling again with perhaps more reverence. He presented himself to the clerk and was pleased to be shown in at Mister Achely's office.

This was a junior Mister Achely, but the consideration was all the same to Mayport. He put his hat under his chair and sat, smiling in triumph. "You won't believe who sailed into port with me. I told you I could bring him back."

"You can't have," Costor said. "When can we meet? It's been too long for so old a friend."

"I came to ask you for lunch. If all goes wrong, I'll not be at liberty to dine." Mayport reached down into his valise and took out the balance books. "Nothing is resolved, my friend. Cane filed claims on insurance. The brokers turned around and filed suit on me for fraud. It will take more than a warehouse full of sugar to unravel this mess."

"Where is Cane at present? Run south the moment he saw you alive?"

"I put him where he meant to put me. In the poorhouse." Mayport wanted to duck his head and let his shame show, but instead sat back and smiled as if he was proud of himself. "This was all your idea."

"I never suggested you put your manager in the debtor's prison! Why in the world did the wardens listen to you and take him?"

"It's a fair cop," Mayport said. "I bought some of his private debts off a shylock and bounced him down the road myself. I won't let him starve, but he's not bleeding me any drier. You should be proud of me for taking an interest in my fortune."

"I shall have to hire someone to replace him," Costor said, still trying to sound disgruntled. "You didn't really bring Joseph Thiervy home. His father will beat the starch out of him. He's been swearing to ever since that boy lifted a barge and disappeared."

"He's in port, and delivered the barge back this morning. There was plenty of gold to go with it. Nothing else will matter as much as a profit," Mayport said. "If I'm wrong, I will take full responsibility for him. It's my bad influence that set him wrong when we were only boys."

"I'll hold you to that promise. I feel you will have to keep it. Thiervy will never take responsibility for himself." Costor folded his hands together, and turned to look out the window. "Had you been more plain about your concerns, I could have saved you this safari. I think you did all this to please your friends, and now expect to be forgiven your faults."

"I know what little plans you hold in your heart, and I mean to help you." Mayport fished through his pockets and came up with a pouch of red silk. He handed it over and watched with pleasure as Costor opened it and drew out a cord of carved sandalwood beads. Tiny figures of animals and men of all sorts gave a sweet scent to the chill air. "Your Bess might make a necklace of them. I saw men praying with them, and thought the resin very pretty. Of course I thought then of your lady, and how she dotes on exotic perfumes."

"As always, a faithful devotee. Go find Thiervy and meet me at my club."

Mayport made his promises and carried a smile out into the streets. Seeing Costor looking determined gave him hope. Now, he was able to look forward to his day with real pleasure.

He walked down to the sail maker's district and caught up with Cully. "I'll need Thiervy for the rest of the day. Should I send a boy with your lunch and supper?"

"Yes, thanks. You're welcome to all of Thiervy, if you can find the elusive young cuss. I haven't seen a whisker of him since he went on about that barge. My pay packet was settled out, did you know? Am I to be on my way?"

"I hope not. Some things are beyond my control. The banker, Mister Achely, will be the one to say for certain."

"I will hope for the best." Cully tried to smile, but his eyes betrayed a hidden worry. "That friend of yours was looking for a fight when he left. I think you knew."

Mayport bowed in thanks, then went to find Thiervy. He was eventually located in a small, cheap bar where he held court with empty glasses. Mayport took one of the available chairs and waited for Thiervy's eyes to focus on him. One was swollen and would

H.B.Kurtzwilde   69

probably close up if not cared for. Mayport knew better than to let Thiervy realize his wounds had been noticed.

"You're not in jail?" Thiervy asked in as neutral a tone as he could manage.

"You started too early on drowning your sorrows," Mayport said. He put a coin on the table and took Thiervy by the elbow. "Costor is having us to lunch. You'll have to clean up or they won't let you past the door. Time to give them a gentleman they can see, I'm afraid."

As they stepped out into the street, Mayport got a better look at Thiervy's face. It was bruised on one side, and flecked with dried blood. Thiervy tried his don't-care smile despite the split lip, and shook his hair forward. "Father let me live. He knows everything, and isn't exactly unmarked for our disagreement. His fury will be enough to kill me, like slow poison."

Mayport had long ago said his final word on Thiervy's father. He concerned himself with steering them back to the factory. On the command gondola, Thiervy cleaned up and put on clean clothes. Mayport held up his side of the silence until Thiervy was fit for their leader's company.

They stood before the mirror and made the last touches to their attire. Then, Mayport could see the changes. Both were tall, but now they matched in strength as well. A proud smile came to his lips, and he pressed it to Thiervy's hair.

Thiervy stepped away, disgruntled all over again. "You three, sometimes I could have hated you. There wasn't any reason at all to raise my eyes up from the work at hand. I don't know why you had to pick me out from all the other boys. It's not like there was much to recommend me."

"I thought our late Frenchman made this clear at the time: You're not the sort that would understand why even if we told you," Mayport said. "Stop fighting against your betters. You're up above yourself already. Make it look good."

"I've been disowned! You think there's a way to make it look good? I might as well have been born a bastard!"

Mayport felt his mouth go soft as his face lost all expression. He looked at himself in the mirror, the way his body assumed a relaxed pose in a natural-looking reflex. Once upon a time, he would have drawn up tense, fist at the ready. Now, he only looked beautiful and bored. "Like that."

"You know I didn't mean you," Thiervy said, half-whining.

"You make anything look good, no matter how improbable."

"Then stop telling me it can't be done," Mayport said.

He acted as the tugboat once more to get Thiervy back up to Costor's end of town. Hauling Thiervy along to endure a good time reminded Mayport of earlier days. Costor would know the situation at a glance, and have all the best remedies to hand.

"Good lord, who have you been brawling with now?" Costor demanded as they took their places at his table. His eyes went to the last empty seat by reflex, then he shook himself all over. "Your father found you out? Who has betrayed you? I'll see them broken within the hour."

"I betrayed myself, so rest your revenge," Thiervy said. He slouched on his chair and hung on to his stubborn look, marring his appearance far worse than the bruises did. "I was tired of waiting. I thought getting this over with would make me happy."

"You wouldn't know what to do with yourself if you were ever happy," Costor said. "Neither would the rest of us."

"That's much, from a man who has happiness in full measure. Where is our darling Bess? I thought you must surely die if you lose sight of her."

"I do a little, each time. She knows nothing of our woeful plight, so we won't worry her yet. Now, real food for our adventurers, and after, to business."

Costor seemed bent on emptying the kitchen into his friends. Now and then an appreciative noise was thrown his way as thanks. Mayport knew that the others were missing Gasteau, who somehow had managed to stuff himself with both hands while complaining nonstop. The table was less crowded without the girl or two who would have followed their friend to dine, but was less lively without them as well. Even now, their meeting felt like a table with a leg gone missing.

When Mayport felt stretched thoroughly all through his middle, he sat back with a contented sigh. "Tell me all is failure. I could take it without a flinch just now."

"Alas, you are not paroled from your responsibilities to society," Costor said. He signaled for another bottle of wine and poured round. "Indeed, you come out a hero, though I know you will not believe me."

"Has no one else broken through to the Indies?" Thiervy asked, sounding excited. "We took so long, I thought we must have been passed by."

"The seas have taken back more than many this year. More buxom ladies than yours have given up farther south. With your return, it is certain that the Indies are open to Dutch vessels by steam, if not by sail."

"He's assuming you'll sell the sugar and pay your debts." Thiervy snickered loudly, then hiccuped.

"That sugar is mine," Mayport said. "It's not for ladies to make their jellies. I would be ruined by sundown without it."

"You truly mean to go on with your father's disease," Costor said, sounding disappointed.

"You do with yours. What would you have me do? Turn merchant seaman?"

Thiervy recoiled from the scorn in Mayport's voice. "What's wrong with that, exactly?"

"You spent months telling me how badly I am suited to it," Mayport replied. "List the reasons. You have, many's the time."

"Is that true?" Costor asked. "What happened?"

"Nothing." Thiervy poured again, but did not drink. Instead, he used the bottom of the glass to mark circles on the tablecloth as he spoke. "Not one damn thing. He presented his authority, kept discipline, obedience, and steadfastness. The crew hated him, but that's what a second mate is for. I told him every day he was abysmal. He never complained or gave up trying. It's no difference if I lie to him. He only believes you anyway."

Costor let his last plate be cleared away before he took out his dreaded portfolio. "The value of your company has gone up by quite a lot, for a start. If you chose, you could stay here like a gentleman and send your ship to get your infernal beans. You've taken control of your business and turned a profit."

"Only if I sell that sugar," Mayport said.

"There will be other sugar," Costor said, trying to persuade.

"That had been the story since England got her hand bloodied. No. I trust what's in my warehouse more than another man's daring. It's an asset, not merchandise."

Costor's jaw tensed, his eyes went cold and sharp, but he said not a word. Instead, he turned that baleful gaze on his papers and began to drum the table with his fingers. Thiervy and Mayport kept quiet, grinning at each other all the while. An abacus could not have been so coldly calculating as their dear, ruthless Costor.

"Very well, Mister Titus. Have things your own way for now.

You delay my marriage another year by this caution. I could wish you had learned restraint another way."

"But I've done something terribly clever that I don't understand, and so you will forgive me?" Mayport asked.

"As ever you did." Costor closed the portfolio and turned a perfectly cheerful expression on Thiervy as he opened another bottle of wine for the table.

Thiervy and Mayport could only smile back and enjoy his good mood. Many people would have bet with confidence that Costor Achely did not have a good mood to his name. More than one young dandy had taken him for a kind of oyster, and dared to approach Miss Bess. They went so far as to assume her attraction to Costor was of the calculating sort.

Who would have guessed that the blue-eyed slip of a girl had picked Costor out as her special pet, and kept him? He had been so flattered, from the age of sixteen he had set out to return her compliment. She ruled him with a diet of stern expectation and gentle petting. For each of his little successes, he had been rewarded with her faith in him redoubling, as well as her respect and love.

For this reason, Costor had bullied his brothers into joining her worship. They had lost their most devoted slave to their idol, the young Frenchman called Gasteau, and yet worked hard to fill his place in her world. Mayport had to admit that her elegant tyranny had done his manners a fine turn, if not his preferences. In no man could he hope to find the refining qualities carried in her soft and graceful hand.

"We will not be forgiven if we are late to be received at Bess's parlor," Costor said. "You are to port some ten days. Let me make the time fly by for you, as I used to."

"But we cannot borrow your coats as we used to," Thiervy said as they stood to follow Costor. "The seams would never manage it."

Costor looked surprised, then reached out to feel Mayport's shoulder. "What in the world was done to you?" He tried to sound pitying, but came through as jealous.

Mayport stepped back, casting an envious glance at Costor's still-slim figure. "I sailed from here to India, my brother. When I'm put back at a desk, you'll have nothing to covet of me."

Costor didn't look satisfied, but led them out of the club into the waning afternoon. New Amsterdam was only beginning to offer up its delights. They held on to each other in the merry glow of good wine in better company. For the first time in months, Mayport felt the comforting protection of the only family he had ever learned to love.

Chapter Eleven: Revels

The longer Mayport stayed in port, the more he relied on the hope of leaving again. That knowledge gave spice to the endless parties, and urgency to his work. Costor's confidence had made him relax, when in fact the battle had not yet been joined.

By night, the three of them stretched the limits of Costor's wardrobe. By day, they went around to quiet, dusty offices and bargained for Mayport's life. His friends being both confident and intimidating; he escaped a date with the jailor.

He had assumed that a large-scale assault on the off-market competition would make Costor happy. Three different loan sharks packed up and ran, after his visits. Two insurance brokers paid up on the claims related to Corey Titus' estate. Even without touching the sugar, Costor dragged Mayport back into the black.

That one element to a man's character, solvency, was the key to doors which he must be able to open. Despite this, Costor was not pleased. No matter how hard he squeezed his prey by day, his exaltation was always gone before the evening dances had begun. Such changes were not unknown to Costor's temper, but they were irregular. At last, it was pretty Bess who gave Mayport the answer to this riddle.

"I know you're stealing these from my Costor," she said, caressing the sleeve of his coat as he squired her about the dance floor. "Why does it look so different on you?"

"I have no idea what you mean," Mayport said. He knew the lie was too obvious, so he spun her fast, making her forget fashion for laughter. Soon it was Thiervy's turn to steer, for little Bess needed all her squires once the dancing started.

Mayport flopped on a sofa beside Costor, to be watered and fed. "So you're jealous. Is that it? What has that girl told you now?"

"Does she need to say a word?" Costor asked back, disgruntled.

Mayport turned to watch what Costor was staring at. Bess and Thiervy moved over the floor together, relaxed and light in their steps. Her white gloves lay in contrast against the burgundy velvet of his jacket. Mayport squirmed as he realized how she caressed his shoulder and arm.

"Maybe she doesn't know she's doing it," Mayport suggested.

"She does it to you as well," Costor said. "How can you not know?"

"I simply never noticed," Mayport said. "Anyway, it's harmless. She doesn't want what we're selling. Couldn't have it even if she did."

"You are mistaken on all of your assumptions," Costor said. "When are you going to show me this ship of yours?"

"It's not really a ship. She lacks quite a lot, and looks like nothing but junk on the ground."

Nevertheless, Costor insisted. When his schedule permitted, he came to the factory. Gondolas were scattered all over the courtyard. Sails and rigging lay on the factory floor, or was hanging off cat-walks. Cully's voice alone made order from the chaos.

Costor walked around to have his look, then sidled up to Cully. "What if I wanted to come along for the voyage?"

"Climb that!" Cully barked without even glancing at Costor. One broad finger pointed straight up at the knotted veil, which hung down from the catwalk above.

"I'll give you a boost," Mayport offered while Thiervy dissolved into wild laughter. "It's not so bad after you've done it about five hundred times."

"What in the world came over him?" Thiervy asked between whoops.

"Miss Bess likes our broad shoulders too well," Mayport said. "He wants some of his own. I don't think he can do without his desk and Bess long enough to get them."

"If it wouldn't kill him, I'd say bring him along," Cully announced. "He looks pale and thin. What did you say he does to earn those fine goods he's wearing?"

"Banker," the three friends said together, all of them aware of the embarrassment showing in their tone. Costor cleared his throat, then lifted his chin to meet Cully's gaze. "My grandfather was Mayport's guardian, and the responsibility got handed down the line. I've known him since we began school together."

"Running off to sea is no way to win a lady," Cully said. "Even if she's won, she might be un-won by the time you got back. You'd better stay here, guard the women and gold. Let us useless men take risks, and be ready to comfort us when we return."

"Do it quickly and I'll make you a godfather," Costor said. "But first, I must measure and account for this treasure you've brought."

Mayport led the way into the warehouse, bearing a lantern to send the rats scurrying. Even now, the vast store of sugar did not seem real, or his. The value of it was enough to let him live at leisure for a time. The prospect was tempting, but his ambitions were still far ahead of his means.

Costor went up and down the rows of stacked goods, marking things off on a list as he went. "I understand your concerns about supply. I'll do everything I can to protect what you have. If it comes down to responsibilities and this plan of yours, I would choose to sell."

"What could happen while I'm gone, to strip my storehouse bare?"

"With me standing watch, nothing," Costor said. "I want to emphasize that I can, not that I will. In your absence, there will be nobody but me to answer for you."

"That's how I want it."

Costor shook his head as if amazed. "I don't think you have the first notion of how valuable you are at this moment."

"I don't need to. You know, and that's what matters," Mayport said. "Anyway, if I don't come back, you're my beneficiary. Make sure the kids go to a better school than we did."

"Don't make jokes like that," Costor said. "These places you want to go might as well not be on the map. The Spaniards did everything they could to conquer those lands and failed miserably. It brought an empire to disaster."

"But I don't want the land, or the gold, or people to do my bidding," Mayport said. "I don't care who they pray to, or what they do to each other. They've got my beans and are known to part with them on terms. I'll go and arrange them, and come right straight home."

"We shall trust one another a little longer, and see what fortune finds us," Costor said. "Send word ahead the moment you reach any of the Confederated states. I won't give you much in the way of coin to take south. You'll do better in those jungles if you haul trade goods."

"Any particular suggestions on what to take?"

"I am only a banker," Costor said, as if such beings were not their own pantheon in New Amsterdam. "If you need a clerk, you should hire one."

"He can clerk," Cully said. "He did fine on his own, and without the local lingo to help. He's a skinflint too. Don't worry on giving him coin to carry. He'd sooner part with his own blood than gold."

"I'm glad to hear his education was not a complete waste. Thiervy, I want a word with you about this invoice for your services."

"No," Mayport said. "I made that good with my own money. It's paid, and he's not giving it back."

"You can't cure him of his generosity, no matter how you scold," Thiervy said. "Most of that was owed to my father's company. As he says, it's paid and gone. At least my father got a thin taste of what he lost in me."

Mayport didn't like the bitterness he saw brewing in his friend. Only work made him stop growling. Though he stayed his post in the revelries, he did not find refreshment or pleasure in them. More than once he went away with Costor and Bess, only to escape the lovebirds to his own distractions.

At last, they could not ignore the truth of Thiervy's nighttime prowls. He arrived at a supper party with as many bruises and wounds as he had started out with. His swollen visage was so appalling, even Bess would not dance with him.

While Costor and Bess took a turn on the dance floor, Mayport took Thiervy away into a corner. "Did you meet with your father again?"

"Only in the metaphorical sense," Thiervy said, stubborn and angry. "At least I need no excuse for not squiring a lady. Who would have me in this condition?"

"Only me, but you run away every night," Mayport said. "Let's go to a club. Those two get on fine without us, and we're both eyesores tonight."

"We can't go to a club together. There's no mystery as to why I've been expelled."

"We'll go where we please, since you like a fight anyway," Mayport said. "Why not a club?"

"It's all right if we're with Costor. He has Bess, and it's a kind of shield," Thiervy said.

Then Mayport understood, and laughed at Thiervy. He leaned in closer just to watch his so-bold friend slink a few inches away. "Stand still. Don't pull away from me. Do you understand?"

"Yes," Thiervy said, then clenched his lips down into a thin, hard line.

Mayport resumed his lazy observation of the dance floor. "I never thought I would see such a cowardly flinch out of you. Look at these people. I could buy half of them outright, if I cared enough to make them respect or fear me. Costor says…"

"Money isn't going to solve this problem," Thiervy said, on the edge of losing his patience.

"Costor says they feel it more than I do," Mayport continued, unperturbed. "You feel it, and so hide at my shoulder. He feels it, and lets me do as I please when he'd rather pin me and thrash sense into me again. It has to be the money, for it's all I have. I asked him how to keep you safe. He told me to make enough money so that nobody could tell me what to do."

"And just what does that make me?" Thiervy demanded. "Kept as well? Bought, like any one of these fools might be?"

"Don't be stupid. You can't be bought. Why do you think I did it?" Mayport smiled while Thiervy's expression went from stubborn to surprised to sheepish and back to stubborn once more. "I mean to paint your name up on the shingle before we leave, but your behavior is making Costor resist the notion. Don't you want to be partners? Lately, I wonder if you've changed your mind."

"By the time we get back, every door in this town will be closed to us," Thiervy said. "It's Costor that keeps us from being barred. These fine friends of yours won't hesitate once they smell blood. You've seen them turn on men before. We'll be no different."

"Which one of these men will refuse a profit over what your father thinks of you?" Mayport asked. "Do they really respect his opinion so very much? He drinks his friends' cellars dry, leaves his sons to do his labor, and brings shame to the bride that stooped to marry him. Don't take up his vices just to spite him. Besides, we can go elsewhere to re-open the shop as easily as we can here."

"We?"

Thiervy's voice was faint with surprise. Mayport kept his eyes on the swirling skirts as they opened and drew tight in the turns of the dance. His smile seemed intended for everyone, but he glanced over at Thiervy. His friend stood very still, eyes half-lidded, ruined mouth almost the heart-shape that Mayport loved so to kiss. He was not going to repeat his opinion that Thiervy belonged to him particularly and always would. He had made himself clear on that point long ago.

"If I want to, we can take this whole factory somewhere else, right?" Thiervy demanded. "If I want to go south, back home to Ma's people, you'll get me out of this cesspool. Won't you?"

"You had better decide before we start production," Mayport said. "The machines can be moved, but once we start, we'll have

to stay still for our men. Choose before we get back, and I'll do
things exactly as you say."

"Costor won't like this promise."

"I probably wouldn't like some of the things he's promised
Bess," Mayport said. "We understand each other very well. He
won't get in my way."

"Anyway, I don't see why Costor deserves so very much. Why
do you admire him so? He's hardly the sort you notice. Did he really get you in his first account portfolio?"

Mayport held his smile, patient as a stone while Thiervy's contempt wound out of him. "There's no shame in me admitting I
admire the better man. He's sincere and obedient, loyal and thrifty,
trustworthy. I've come to no harm in his management. Gasteau
would have had a happier, longer life if he had cherished a little
admiration of our Abacus."

"Let's not talk about Gasteau," Thiervy said. "I'll make a daring
bid for freedom with you, but change the subject."

Mayport agreed and they slipped out together. Gasteau had
made a quartet of their trio at school. They had taught him English
out of pity, thinking him ignorant and lost. He had taught them
everything else, in a proud Frenchman's style, as soon as he had
the vocabulary to correct them.

His demise had also been in French fashion. In a fight over a
prize not worth having, he'd taken things too seriously. What had
begun as a flirtation ended in blows. The few witnesses had blamed
an unlucky fall for his broken skull, but the end was the same. All
his youth and promise had been made sacrifice on the altar of a
pretty Polly who might have been bought for a pot of beer.

Mayport tried to shake off his lingering disappointment with
Gasteau. This proved impossible, with Thiervy chasing after his example. In a fit of caution, Mayport went to the wine shop to pro-
vision their night. They holed up together in the factory office,
which yet served as Mayport's lodgings.

Thiervy was in too much pain to bear much kissing, though
he pretended not to be at all hurt. As they shared the wine and
Mayport cleaned and bound the wounds again, he found himself
longing for the high winds. Mayport put his friend back in his
cabin after he'd lost his fight with the wine. Again the urgency
welled up in him, the need to get up and away to somewhere else
that would look on him as a stranger.

Chapter Twelve: Primal

Though Mayport would have liked to ignore the truth of Thiervy's maudlin suppositions, facts were on the pilot's side. He didn't like to feel as though they had been chased out of town. After all, they had not planned to stay, but worked diligently to launch their southerly journey. He did bow to reality far enough to speed his plans ahead on the purchase of cargo, and made sure Cully was satisfied with his crew.

Thus it was with little repining that they went aloft from the factory courtyard. Cully's wants for his crew had been settled. Thiervy's engineering had been refined, refitted and made as near to reliable as such a contraption could be.

Weather was against them for the first leg of their journey, from New Amsterdam to the Carolina coast. Rain, mist, bad winds, and chills of all kinds buffeted the crew every mile of the way. The only men not constantly losing their meals over the side were the ones who could not force themselves to eat.

They stopped to resupply at a town squeezed between a pale, blue-green water and mosquito-ridden, marshy salt flats. Firm and solid and in no way rocking to and fro, Mayport blessed its every pebble for the brief time they were anchored there. Thiervy was in a fine mood over the performance his vessel had given him.

He dragged Mayport down to taste the waters of a new expanse. Together they stood on a shell-crusted beach and looked west. The water tasted the same as had the Atlantic Ocean, the Indian Ocean, and the Mediterranean Sea. Thiervy stooped to draw a picture of the coast in the sand so that Mayport could see that he was tasting a gulf for the first time.

"We would have to be in Europe to stand on a beach and look west over the Atlantic," Thiervy explained. "To the north, this is lee of the Confederated states, until about the middle. After that, it's all tribes and warlords. Cully swears he knows where he's going, though he hasn't got a rutter to show for this route. If there was anything worth having, the Spaniards would have fought harder to keep it."

"You can't trust a Spaniard's courage to tell you what's valuable," Mayport said. "What's the language like over there?"

"Your guess is as good as anyone's. It depends on who you meet. There could be a few Catholics still clinging to their missions, but I doubt it. The few white men there are on the run, cutthroats and thieves."

"What does that make us?" Mayport asked.

Thiervy laughed, and glanced around before he leaned in to take a kiss. At last his lips felt soft and strong. Mayport did not feel his lover wince at their embrace, so he parted his lips and sucked at Thiervy's tongue. At last Thiervy stepped back, and checked the coast for spies again.

"It makes us merchants, and no loss to anybody if we never return. I have some Spanish if we need it, but it might not help. I despise the thought of lining some Jesuit's pockets just to make an honest trade. They're worse than taxes for squeezing a man." Thiervy spat on the sand. "Maybe if we have to, we can work a gentleman's trade. A fellow posted out so far might be hungry for good company."

"Anything to widen the profit margin," Mayport said. "I know for a fact your ass would trade well, if only you would keep your face pretty instead of fighting."

"If the Devil offered to sell to you cheaper, would you take it?" Thiervy asked.

"Yes. Satan's got more reason to care what I do than baby Jesus. I don't worry much on that anyway. There's all kinds of superstitions about this bean I'm after. In my hopes and dreams we'll find savages who are willing to sell at any price. If I fail here, I fail for the last time."

"Don't be so dramatic," Thiervy said. "You're doing all this because you want to. If it doesn't work out, you'll think of something new to try. You know this could have been anything. Camel imports. Rum. Tulip bulbs. If your father had gone in for the flower mania, would we be in Holland right now?"

"No, I don't think so," Mayport said, but was uncertain.

"Then don't worry if this doesn't work," Thiervy said. "You have other prospects. Other hopes and dreams. This is an adventure, and not bound to succeed."

Thiervy's practical assessment made Mayport feel confident again. Moreover, the weather turned fine and let them make good speed toward the setting sun. A few days of good sailing led them to the coast they wanted. There, all sense of self-assurance disappeared.

The land itself was a green and closely-woven place. They cruised south along the coast for several days, taking on fresh water where they could and trusting Cully's memory. He would peer at each inlet or sweet-water creek and point out the ways it wasn't what he was looking for. At last he found a tiny creek that met all his criteria.

They sailed west again, following the river for another week before Cully found a port landing. To Mayport's surprise, none of the natives seemed terrified or even particularly interested in their arrival. As their vessel drew down to anchor, Mayport saw the reason why their arrival was not remarkable. Here and there tiny European boats were tied up and unloading cargo.

"They can't be regular merchants," Mayport murmured as he pointed out one boat to Thiervy. "There's too many weapons for that, and not enough crew. Is this a pirate's port? I thought those were further south, and on islands."

"You read too many news journals," Thiervy said. "You asked once what being here made us. Nobody's supposed to come in to trade, and exports are supposedly still under the auspices of Spain. We're going to ignore all of that and take what we want. Since we have our own vessel, we're smugglers. Does that shock you?"

They anchored on a sandy strip of land near the river coast. Cully sent his two officers to scout the area while the crew got the gondolas settled in. As soon as they reached the main path in the village, Mayport was struck by the familiarity of the place. Individually, the scents and sights were completely new to him. The populace was the same hard-edged mix he had learned to expect of ports. All of it thrown together and stretched out before him, chaotic and busy, seemed as familiar as his own pillow.

Thiervy followed his lead as they wandered past fruit sellers and fishmongers. At last they came to a man reclining under an awning behind several bowls piled high with pastes and seeds, powders and roots of all kinds. Mayport stood still and breathed deeply, picking out the sweeter flavors from among the spices.

The man stirred, then opened one eye to assess Mayport. He grunted in an inquiring way, and curled his lip when Mayport could only offer his request in English. The man turned his head and shouted into a shack that stood a few paces away from where he rested.

An old woman came shuffling out and eyed Mayport up and down. She argued with the man under the awning, but he only waved his hand at a nearby kitchen shed, and then closed his eyes. The woman carried on her argument even as she took up a bowl and began gathering items from what the man had to sell.

Mayport kept a hopeful smile on his face as he followed the woman to the kitchen shed. With a cylinder of stone she began grinding and crushing together herbs and berries and pods. In the heat of the day, she was soon sweating with her efforts. The bubbling pans on the hearth added their part to the humidity.

When the bark and twigs were finely ground, the woman added them to a pot of boiling corn. She stirred and crushed the brew as if taking a personal revenge on it. At last, the brownish-yellow slop was strained into a bowl. It swirled around, thick and appetizing as a potter's muddy wheel water.

The bowl was thrust into his hands, too hot for the sticky blaze of the afternoon. Mayport didn't give himself time to think before he took a deep drink. It was far too bitter, spiced in wild conflict to his distant memories. A vast disappointment welled up in him as he tried to savor what he had come so far to find. Only in faint hints did he find anything to relish. Even then, he did not know which root and leaf he was tasting. He forced a smile. "Good! What is it?"

"Shouldn't you have asked that before you drank it?" Thiervy asked with a chuckle.

The woman stared at both of them, then shouted something to the man under the awning. He opened one eye and looked at Mayport. The other eye opened, and he rubbed them. When he saw that Mayport yet stood there, he got up and hurried down the street, calling out as he went.

Several men came out to meet him, and they turned as if to advance on Mayport. Thiervy grabbed his arm and yanked hard to get him moving. "I don't know that this is a welcome party."

"I doubt that it is," Mayport said, and they broke out into a run.

The Process lay not far from the village. They managed to reach the veil of knotted ropes hanging down from the still-hovering command gondola. The village men came and gathered at the anchor line, shouting up at the ship in what seemed like friendly tones. Still, Mayport had no intention of going back down until he had some idea of what he faced.

"What did you do to stir them up?" Cully asked as he peered down over the side. "They don't really look hostile, but they surely were chasing you."

"I drank some chocolate," Mayport said. "You know how superstitious these people are about their drink of the gods. It's here, though. They still make it the old way, but right out in the street. If they don't have what we want, they will know who does."

"You certainly are bold as brass," Cully said, then laughed. "They might go away to talk you over, but they'll be back. You'd better stay below until they're more certain of what they want with you."

Thiervy grabbed Mayport by the back of his neck and marched him down to the officer's cabins. They heard Cully calling a general respite for the entire crew. A hurrah went up, and Mayport laughed at Cully's sudden change of plans.

He was pushed into Thiervy's cabin, then grunted as he was shoved back against the closed door. Thiervy leaned in close, hands already making quick work of Mayport's clothes. "If I was superstitious, I'd say you cast a spell on these poor people. You walk into town and everyone does just what you want. Look at me, I'm doing it too. You're a witchy boy, Mayport Titus."

"Blame whatever you want," Mayport happily agreed as he stripped Thiervy bare. "I never thought to need a reason to get you on your back. Any opportunity will do for me."

They were standing so close, Mayport could feel every shift in Thiervy's body. He leaned in tighter, head bowing until his cheek lay on Mayport's shoulder. They stood still together for a moment, then Mayport seized Thiervy's hair and tilted his head back for a kiss.

Thiervy laughed and let Mayport muscle him over to the bed. He sat on the edge and leaned in to lick wet swaths up and down the length of Mayport's shaft. The heat and coolness made Mayport shiver and thrust. As his efforts became more desperate, Thiervy sat back and spread his thighs, giving Mayport a confident smile.

Mayport pounced on him, and his whole body relaxed down into the bed. With very little effort, he got Thiervy stretched out and began to taste him all over. Savage bites and sucking kisses left bright marks on sun-browned flesh. Mayport lapped at each mark, savoring the shift from sea salt to heady musk as Thiervy began to sweat.

"Do it do it do it do it do it," Thiervy chanted as he dragged his hands up and down Mayport's back. The rough calluses scraped at him, making him arch down and away. "Please, for fuck's sake, man, I need you so much."

"Let me sleep here tonight," Mayport said, nipping harder at Thiervy's throat. "Nobody will notice or care. Just one night."

"Don't make me choose between what I want, and my duty," Thiervy warned.

Mayport growled and seized Thiervy by the hips, then rolled him over with a rough twist. Thiervy ended up half-off the bunk, one knee on the deck and the other caught in a blanket. Mayport leaned over his lover and bent his knees, thrusting too hard as he searched for a good angle. Thiervy squirmed, so Mayport bit hard at the back of his neck to settle him down.

A surprised yelp was muffled against the bedding as Thiervy bucked under Mayport. That helpless struggle presented Thiervy's ass perfectly. Mayport skewered him and he howled, thrashing against the bed. His hips rolled and dropped, rose up again, and fell, never quite yielding to Mayport's cock even as he thrust in deeper.

Mayport laughed and rode harder against Thiervy, reveling in each gasp and cry. He slid an arm under Thiervy, grasped his cock and stroked. He expected to be able to tease his lover for as long as he liked, making him mindless in the edgy pleasure.

Thiervy was beyond any kind of control. He pounded down into Mayport's fist, rose up with all his strength and slammed his ass back over Mayport's cock, racing to the finish line with everything he had. Mayport tried to slow down, back off, drag the pleasure out like a thin quivering wire between them. Thiervy would have none of his teasing, and rode harder, driving them both to the breaking point with his unrestrained desire.

Thiervy's ass squeezed hard and fast around Mayport's cock, spurring him on in his taking. His balls drew up tight and throbbing, then he shivered, and groaned, pouring out all his passion in a white-hot instant of pure satisfaction. Thiervy's cock pulsed and twitched in his fist as thick jets of come splashed over his fingers.

He didn't give Thiervy a chance to catch his breath before he hauled them both up onto the bunk. Old habit guided their limbs to a comfortable embrace. Thiervy fell asleep between kisses. Mayport lay awake to watch him breathe, feeling confident that all his hopes now lay within his grasp.

Chapter Thirteen: Obfuscation

Thiervy looked down on the beach feeling quite lost in his position. As Cully had predicted, the village fathers had changed tactics with the sunrise. A clutch of maidens had chosen this bit of riverside for their morning baths.

"You have to go down," Thiervy said. "That would be the normal thing to do. They would dangle their sons if they thought it would work."

"I don't want... well, in the broader sense... I'd rather avoid distraction." Mayport stuttered and blushed. "You'd better come with me. I'm hopeless."

"You've got Cully fooled into thinking you know how to clerk. What do you need me for?"

"You want me alone with nymphs running around loose? Perhaps one of those down there can persuade me." Mayport knelt to make a final check on his sample pack. "Look on the bright side. We might get into a fight. Won't that be fun?"

"Not with these odds. You'd better negotiate for a few doxies to come aboard. The men are already taking numbers." Thiervy holstered an extra brace of pistols and put on a don't-care smile. "I think those mermaids might do you some good. You look nervous."

Mayport didn't bother to deny it. At last he saw a portly matron who sat in the shade of a low tree. He strode down the gangway and went to join her. Thiervy tried a greeting in French and got a rotten, mistakenly lascivious smile in return.

She asked a question and arched a coal-black eyebrow. Thiervy said: "She asked if we're Christian. I thought you knew French."

"Play like I'm dumb, then. Tell her we're not Christian." He watched her eyes while Thiervy translated, and saw her suspicion change focus. She took a battered cross in the Spanish style out of a pouch. Both dark eyes stayed fixed on Mayport as she cast it onto the sand, spat on it and stamped it down for good measure. He copied her blasphemies without hesitation, and gave his best smile.

"You're a scary man," Thiervy said.

"I may never get another chance to be so honest," Mayport laughed. "Our hosts aren't bound to have a good opinion of Christians. They probably won't care of the difference between you and a papist. I don't mind to take their side, since they won fair and square. Maybe their gods know something ours doesn't."

"I'll see about doxies for the lads." Thiervy made delicate inquires, and Mayport showed samples of his goods. "Any medicines to trade? They've got wounded or similar, maybe from a battle nearby. Who could they have been fighting?"

"Anybody who wants this good spot by the river." Mayport went back aboard to the cargo. One of the many squirrel holes was crammed with cotton batting and bottles full of tinctures. He took a small brown bottle from the store and bolted it closed again. He wrapped the bottle in a scrap of blue silk and carried it back to Thiervy. "Trade well on that. It's sovereign stuff, from India. Fit for use on any battlefield."

"You really would make enemies of kings," Thiervy said. "Are you sure of taking this risk?"

"I think we're safe from the Spanish for now. Ask about the beans. Ask for any food at all." Mayport sat down in the shade beside the matron and made a pretty arrangement of silk and beads on the sand. "Go on. This isn't a shop. We'll be here a while no matter how well we trade."

The woman called to her girls and gave orders. Some went to the village. Others went laughing up to the gangplank to meet the cheering crew. Cully's voice rang out among the rest, giving orders of his own to control the merry chaos.

A band of men came down to the river. The eldest among them made a greeting and sat on the sand. Pretty girls came to attend him, each carrying a flat woven tray full of treasures. Mayport examined slender black pods, breathing in the scent of vanilla. Enough of those pods could make his voyage a success, if not his business. Melons and corn would help see to their crew. He puzzled for a long while over a yellow squash, sniffing its stem for freshness and wondering at the fragrance.

He drew his knife and cut it open, exposing a hollow of wide, flat seeds. He examined them closely, then tossed them aside. "If they have them, they haven't brought them. I'm not sure the pods can be stored fresh. I've never heard of such a thing."

"They gave you some in the village," Thiervy said. "They must have some to offer."

"I'm not sure of what I had in the village. It was almost like boiled coffee, but it wasn't what I came to find," Mayport said. "I know what they do to the beans. I've just never seen it done and might not know it if I saw it. I know a rat couldn't eat the beans like they come, but that's true of cider apples as well."

The old man put on a proud smile as the girls returned with more woven trays. There were several kinds of dried beans offered, and a dozen more squashes. Potatoes were brought in a rainbow of varieties. Mayport chose out the things he could persuade the men to eat, and showed his interest in the vanilla as well. In his heart he was disappointed, even seated before an exotic buffet.

"There's nothing. I must have been mistaken," Mayport said. "Chocolotle was more than a fashion, here. The Spaniards stole it from a king, for a king."

"Lie to them," Thiervy suggested. "Tell them you're the chocolate king of New Amsterdam."

"Don't be ridiculous," Mayport said, though he couldn't help laughing. He faced the woman and said "Cacao. Chocolotle. For Titus Chocolate."

The old man reached out and grabbed a boy by the wrist. He gave instructions, then launched the boy toward strangers. Mayport sensed a kind of danger in the scene, but the boy only took him and Thiervy by the arms and dragged them to follow along.

He led them down a slick path to the water's edge, and up around the curve toward the village. They saw again more boats being unloaded of pods and other goods. Much closer now, Mayport found baskets packed brimful of cured beans. He wanted to touch and taste, but was taken past the landing too quickly.

They followed the line of porters with cargo to sheds where the goods were stacked and sorted. The baskets of dried beans were lined up to be carried away elsewhere. One corner of the shed was dedicated to the yellow pods, but it seemed a makeshift arrangement. Women and boys struggled to split the thick husk, and children scraped the milky pulp out as quickly as they were opened.

The pulp was dumped into jars which men came to carry away. Mayport followed the little boy as he eagerly waved them on. In another hut, the jars were arranged in rows. Little girls went about the place with sticks, stirring the white slop in the jars. The smell was sweet and wretched, as if the thick soup was spoiling in the heat and humidity. Here and there the girls chose jars to be carried away once more.

Mayport and Thiervy picked up a selected jar at the little boy's urging. They carried it to a place where woven mats had been spread out under the sun. The boy took up a rake and urged them to pour the pulp out onto the mat. Only then did Mayport realize the change that had happened under care of the little girls.

Instead of white mess, shiny brownish beans poured out onto the mat. The boy raked them out to cover the whole mat, then moved the fellows on to another mat. They went on together until the whole heavy jar had been emptied so the beans could fully dry. They carried the jar back to the shed, and the boy smiled proudly.

Mayport sat down in the shade and put his head in his hands. "This is terrible."

"What's wrong?" Thiervy asked, confused. "That's it, right? Cacao, these little beans, just like you wanted."

"These are only dried," Mayport said, and rubbed at his eyes. "If you've got any idea how to roast these, grind and press them, make them be chocolate like they think of in Europe, I'm all ears."

"You don't know how to make it?" Thiervy demanded, incensed and not without reason.

"Not from this," Mayport said. "I'm not even sure how my father found out. Chocolatiers are a dime a dozen in Italy and France. Chocolate makers... they're scarcer than hen's teeth, and it's worse since the Brits got beat down."

"I know where there's plenty of Frenchmen," Thiervy said. "Don't worry about that. If your father figured it out, you can as well. The real problem is getting these things back where they'll do some good."

"Those beans are going somewhere," Mayport said. He turned to look at the lines of porters that led out into the thick jungle undergrowth. "These people aren't doing this for fun. They might be slaves, for all we know. What they aren't, is surprised to see us, or startled to speak French. What if those trappers down on the delta got here before the Dutch did? Wouldn't our Costor be surprised? He's sure it's going to be Dutch ingenuity all the way, with the rest of Europe reeling from wars."

"If they're getting here and buying this, they're not selling it on to anyone else," Thiervy said. "But I never heard of a Frenchman giving up a pleasure once he'd found it. I bet I'm French enough to suit them, even though it's only half on my father's side."

"If they've decided to sell to the French, we'll be French for a while," Mayport agreed. "You're the one with the silver tongue. You talk them into selling, and I'll pick up the tab. Just like going to Saturday market."

"Were you serious about not knowing what to do with these things once you get them?" Thiervy asked.

"Oh yes," Mayport said. "Quite serious. I have no idea what those machines do, back at the factory. Everyone who knew, or built them, has gone. I suppose my father imagined he would be the one immortal who could know everything and tell nothing. Once again, he has been proven entirely wrong in his opinion of himself."

"This is not news," Thiervy said. "You figure out what has to be done to these things, and I'll make those machines do it. We could stop by to see my uncle on the way home, and you can hunt a Frenchman willing to sell his secrets. That won't be hard at all."

"It may be easy to buy, but it will take time to learn," Mayport said. "I haven't got three years to apprentice with a chef. Worse, I don't think a chef will ever work for me. Not after what happened to the last fellow."

"I thought we agreed not to talk about Gasteau," Thiervy said, impatient. "I move that rule be extended to his brothers, father, cousins and all kin. You just don't know how families can be about spilled blood, back home."

"Nobody blames you," Mayport said. "I owe that family more than just guilt for their son. You have no idea what they were promised, and how little they received."

Chapter Fourteen: Patience

Mayport lay in the breeze of a backing fan and sipped at a cup of wine. He looked to be at his leisure. The mask of indifference hid a weight of despair.

For three days he had been caught in a trap of indecision. From his vantage point, he could see canoes coming and going from the port. The display seemed designed to fire his frustration.

Thiervy had lost patience with Mayport's hesitation. By the second day, he was ready to take by force what Mayport could not yet get in trade. Mayport refused, and Thiervy had decamped, impatient with Mayport's delicate sensibilities.

Thiervy came from the harsh and unforgiving Confederated States. All vices and most atrocities took place in those lands as a matter of course. Violence was screened by the opulent elegance of the landed gentlemen. Thiervy felt that suppression was more efficient than persuasion, and saw no sense in Mayport's ideas.

Mayport was from nowhere. He knew better than Thiervy how a stranger must sidle and whisper if he meant to have his own way. Thiervy saw only the river port. Mayport saw the thick forest and knew it for a fortress, which defended a mighty empire.

Somewhere to the north and west, a king sat on his throne. His many treasures included the bleached skulls of Spaniards who had seen the world as Thiervy did. The fate of those expeditions had been discovered long after the fact. Tales of victory spread by the Azteca north and east, on the trade routes they employed.

Mayport lay watching the river traffic, finding no charm in ambition. He might have destroyed the port village with just his small crew and weapons. He had no doubt that the forest would reveal its defenders if he tried.

His reputation-by-complexion was one of warfare, disease, and defeat. Only the toothless old woman would acknowledge him. Her trade made her indifferent to the risks of contact by day. At night, the port village was silent and still. No houses stood near the bank. As yet, Mayport had not discovered where the people took their leisure and rest.

A shadow fell across his face. Cully stood over him, looking amused. "You don't look defeated. Thiervy thinks you're ready to give up and go home."

"He doesn't know what to do," Mayport said. "I told him about this fellow named Cortez, and now he's mad at me for even coming here. I'm still thinking how to go."

"Are you getting anywhere with that?" Cully asked.

"I have thought of six plans that will not work," Mayport said and smiled proudly. "Should I worry about Thiervy? He goes wild sometimes, and we do have the guns."

"He took off into the woods with one of those doxies. That should take the edge off his mood." Cully swatted at mosquitoes, but seemed cheerful. "I'm proud of you for not marching in there like a white devil. The men would have followed after you, like Cortez and his fools."

"I came to trade," Mayport said. "What would I do with a village even if I took one?"

Cully laughed, loud and merry. "You are mad, young man. I'm glad it's my kind of crazy."

"What would my father have done in my place?" Mayport asked.

"He would have wasted more than a year on these rivers. I know, because he did," Cully said. "He talked a fellow into being his guide. He imagined he could go around to farms, buy the goods or the farms themselves. I have no idea what befell him in this jungle. He came back lean and confused, but had his beans. I stayed right here waiting, though I thought I would only get word of his death."

"He did that every time?" Mayport asked, impressed.

Cully shrugged a couple of times. "He says this is a savage land ruled by murdering bastards. As far as I know, he never knew much about them."

Mayport chuckled quietly. "He didn't know much about anything, did he? Not about ships or sugar, not these people or the ones back home. These folks aren't afraid of us. I'd say they're at least as clever as those fellows in India."

"They look like monkeys," Cully muttered, unconvinced.

"You look like a bear," Mayport said. "I could put on feathers and dance like a chicken. Don't be so superstitious. It discredits your intelligence. If they're murderers, they're being patient about us."

"Your father thought they were only simple creatures, so

maybe you've got the right idea," Cully said. "How can you know better than him, when you only sit here and drink?"

"I sit here and nothing happens," Mayport said. "Savages would have attacked and destroyed us out of fear. They might have worshiped our ship out of superstitious wonder. Since they have not I am willing to believe these are reasonable."

"How long have you suspected this?" Cully asked, surprised.

"I never thought otherwise," Mayport said. "Savages would not have madams who speak passing French. My problem is convincing our hosts that I am reasonable as well."

"Gifts fix everything," Cully said. "I told your father that, but he never tried. He said generosity would paint him as an easy mark."

"The reverse is true," Mayport said. "I had better try Thiervy first. He goes crazy when I don't have answers to his questions."

"Keep him happy," Cully said. "You'll never get home again without him to baby that engine along."

Mayport finished his wine and fetched a few pickled limes. He went to sit by the old woman to wait for Thiervy. He gave her a couple of lime quarters and won a gummy smile. When Thiervy arrived, he had a girl with him who only looked confused. Mayport recognized that look as one Thiervy often provoked in women who expected to be screwed.

"Vocabulary lesson?" Mayport asked in a genial tone. He offered the limes and Thiervy accepted, but didn't look placated.

"I have nothing else to do," he snapped.

"You do now," Mayport said, and held up the bottle of wine he had brought. "Show me where you went, if it was quiet and private."

Thiervy accepted the bottle and helped Mayport to his feet. Without a word he led Mayport into the forest. In the cool shade, they broke through the underbrush and came to a narrow stream. A hard-packed path followed its twisting bed.

At last they came to a mossy patch where a mighty tree had fallen. Sunlight cut down through the leafy canopy. Thiervy went and sat on the moss. He looked annoyed but soothed himself with the limes and wine.

"I came here with no plan. I want to thank you for being so patient with me," Mayport said, beginning the buttering-up of his engineer. "I couldn't have known what to do until I saw this place for myself. Father made mistakes, but he had time on his side."

"I assume this apology means you've figured things out," Thiervy said. "I can't wait to see what you decided."

Mayport smiled at Thiervy's sullen attitude. He went and sat beside Thiervy, and took his hand. That simple contact lit something up in Thiervy's eyes. He leaned in closer and claimed a deep kiss.

Mayport sighed, and sucked at the sweet taste of Thiervy's mouth. His soft lips went hard and demanding. Thiervy's hands closed on Mayport's shoulders, and bore him down on the broad trunk of the fallen tree.

A moment's thought was spared for bugs and splinters. Only that, and then Mayport was pinned down by the warm and urgent heat of Thiervy's powerful body. Mayport made a surprised noise, then relaxed before the force of Thiervy's passion. He undid all his buttons and ties so that his lover wouldn't tear them off and lose them in the detritus.

Thiervy growled at the sight of bare skin and bent his kisses to taste. Mayport moaned as teeth sank into his nipple. He lifted his hips, stroking his firm cock against Thiervy's hip. His whole body throbbed, and he squirmed. Thiervy rose only a little, and yanked at Mayport's trousers. When they were tangled at the tops of Mayport's boots, Thiervy flipped him over.

Mayport laughed and curved his bare belly over the trunk. Its broad surface stretched out before him farther than he could reach. The crushed mosses and leaves made a sharp scent, spicy and wet, as he wriggled, then he smelled lavender, and looked back over his shoulder.

Thiervy gave half a roguish grin as he brandished a vial of oil. "You never remember. It's a good thing I plan ahead."

Mayport laughed, but shivered at the same time. "It's usually your ass getting chafed, so I can see why."

Thiervy poured oil down the cleft of Mayport's ass. He spread it up and down with his fingers, stroking rough to make Mayport lift his hips. Mayport undulated, rolling his ass back against rough fingertips. Thiervy teased him, prodding and rubbing until Mayport cried out, helpless and burning with need.

"Please, I need you, please, deeper," Mayport gasped.

Thiervy chuckled, low and lusty, then thrust his finger deep into Mayport's ass. He humped desperately, back and back again, trying to force Thiervy in deeper. His whole body ran with sweat as he struggled, spread out and aching before his lover. Thiervy smacked Mayport on the ass and then stepped back.

Mayport lay as still as he could. He felt Thiervy's eyes on him. He shivered, reminded of more furtive moments when he had lain still for Thiervy's observation. When these passions were on him, the mere touch of Thiervy's gaze on his flesh made him feel loved and possessed right down to the bone.

Then all thought was burned from him as Thiervy's weight came down on his back. His prick leaped mightily as Thiervy drove into him, confident of what Mayport would surrender. Mayport yowled like a wild creature and scrambled to seize his own cock.

"God your ass is still as tight as the first time," Thiervy groaned. "I should ride you more often."

"You could," Mayport grunted, then threw himself back against Thiervy's weight. "If only you didn't love my cock so well."

Thiervy shoved at Mayport's back, thrust harder, silenced him with rough taking. Mayport tried to hold in his cries, but Thiervy knew all of his tricks. His thighs made loud slaps against Mayport, making his whole body rock to and fro over the fallen tree.

Mayport's chest and belly were raked mercilessly by the bark and moss. His nipples burned, but he couldn't care. His spine undulated, every muscle straining back against Thiervy's surging cock. His own shaft pulsed and jerked in his fist, an instant away from the release Thiervy tried to drive out of him.

Mayport laughed in triumph as Thiervy lost control first, and roared out his pleasure against the back of Mayport's neck. He felt Thiervy's cock pulse inside him, pumping hot come in deep. Only then did Mayport relax, let his thighs twitch and his balls rise up in ecstasy. He groaned under Thiervy's sweaty weight as he shot his load on the tree.

Thiervy lay panting and laughing for long minutes before he finally rolled over and set Mayport free. He helped Mayport turn and sit, then saw the deep scratches on Mayport's chest. He had the grace to look ashamed, and knelt to help clean and dress Mayport once more.

Mayport leaned back on his hands and let Thiervy do what he wanted. Aftershocks of pleasure made him twitch at every touch. Through slitted eyes he watched the shadows under the trees, and basked in narrow shafts of sunlight.

"Wait." Mayport sat up fast and snatched at his open shirt. "We've been seen."

"Too late now," Thiervy said, and smiled. "Don't be afraid. Nothing bad will happen to you because of this."

Chapter Fifteen: Exposure

Thiervy remained unconcerned over Mayport's panic about being seen together. He offered no doubt that they had been careless and caught. He was fearless, in ways that seemed unnatural.

"Don't act ashamed," Thiervy said, exasperated with Mayport's anxiety. "If you are ashamed, act indifferent. I'll need an inventory list of trade goods tomorrow morning, so get to work."

Mayport had licked his wounds in the cargo hold and slept on the deck, choosing mosquitoes over body odor. Cully found him there, heard why, and set the crew to scrubbing their gondola clean again. Mayport's time with the baseboards was halted by an order to open the cargo.

Thiervy himself stood in the dim hold, arms crossed over his chest. He frowned down at Mayport. "Are you over your little vapors now?"

"Yes, I'm sorry," Mayport hurried to say.

"Good. Get your cheapest goods and come on with me. I got something to see with your own eyes," Thiervy said. He turned to go, then hesitated. "Also, don't expect me to apologize for stealing your fancy oil. There's better use for it."

"You'll admit I'm the one that brought it. It's for young men to get for their sweethearts. I don't even know if they do that way here." Mayport made packs of cloth and beads, small tin works and perfumes. He counted the flower oils twice, and was pleased that Thiervy had only taken one vial.

"I don't think you'll worry much on their courtship once you see what I've seen," Thiervy said.

Mayport hurried to follow Thiervy down the gangplank. The old woman had company under her shade tree. A broad-shouldered man with a full, round belly sat beside her. On this day, her girls were unusually quiet and subdued. They were busily tending pots used to pour brown liquid in endless cascades. Some were tending cups among young men who were hanging around in the tree line.

Mayport stayed on his feet, kept his hands behind his back and spoke only when spoken to. The man made no introductions, but immediately began barking demands at the woman. She put on a forced smile and spoke to Thiervy, who sat up very straight and answered in the negative.

Everyone stared at Mayport. Thiervy cleared his throat. "Am I your slave?"

"No," Mayport said, and laughed. "Who could keep you, even if they owned you?"

Thiervy laughed, but he didn't look completely pleased. The words were passed around the circle and a question came back again. "Why were you in the forest yesterday?"

Mayport laughed in surprise, and blushed. He liked the direct curiosity, but hadn't expected it. "Thiervy is my friend. I love him."

"Is that true?" Thiervy asked for himself.

"You're the one who told me so," Mayport said, still laughing. "Go on and tell them. They might take pity on crazy people."

"Let's begin with the lesser truth," Thiervy said, eyeing their opposites with suspicion. "They'll get your life story in this bargain if they can."

Thiervy said his piece to the woman, and she hesitated. Mayport tried not to fidget while he was studied and discussed. At last he was given a cup, and a small amount of the cool, earth-colored drink to enjoy. The girl pointed to the frothy cup and murmured a word very near to 'chocolate'.

Mayport tried the pronunciation out, but only got laughter from the natives. He kept his smile on and asked "Why is it called that? What's in it?"

The old man laughed, and gave a mocking answer. Thiervy was amused at his tale. "The White Devils called it a temptation from Satan. I think they almost believe we're not Spanish."

"I doubt if that little detail matters much," Mayport said. "If the Spanish were here, I'd trade with them, too. I'd turn around and sell to the Dutch as fast as I could. I just need cacao, as much as I can get."

That word caught on and was repeated a couple of times. "You're not here for gold?"

"I like Dutch gold," Mayport said. "To get that, I need cacao. Do you know where I can get some?"

"How much?" Thiervy prompted.

Mayport pointed at the cargo gondola where it sat landed on the riverside. "I would fill that if I could. A plantation could do it in a season. I'll just have to take what I can get."

Their hosts sat and argued for a long time. She grew passionate, stood up and stormed away. Thiervy pulled Mayport to his feet and made him follow into the woods. The youths in the trees got out of her way. Thiervy kept them tight in her wake.

"Did we piss off the wrong person?" Mayport asked as he trotted along.

"You know that fellow. He tallies the taxes down by the port." Thiervy said. "If you wanted less, he might have just siphoned it off and pocketed the difference. It would have been cheaper for our poor souls."

"And I'm the one that's called a tightwad?" Mayport laughed. "Were are we going? There's nothing but trees for miles around."

"I think you're about to see what I wanted to show you yesterday," Thiervy said.

"What, again? I thought we were going somewhere."

Thiervy dragged harder at his arm, so Mayport stopped teasing. He went along willingly, though the thick, wet heat made him long for the back-draft fan. In the distance he heard the sound of ax on wood. The dim shade of the forest grew lighter, then fell away at a bright clearing. Crews of men worked to push the tree line back. Beyond their clearing stood a town of blazing white and brilliant color laid out in neat rows, like a grid.

Mayport gawped, and Thiervy laughed. "They must be some kinda civilized. This town is planned better than New Amsterdam herself."

"New Amsterdam hasn't got a plan. It just happened," Mayport said. The breeze freshened, bringing the perfume of a thousand flowers with it. Mayport scented something stranger, and hesitated. "Is there a slaughterhouse nearby?"

"You'll want to scream and cry when you see it," Thiervy said. "Don't, if you can help yourself. Christians may slaughter in conquest and war, but at least we don't right in the town square."

"Of course we do, right next to the prison," Mayport said. He swallowed hard, and with that could taste what he was smelling. "At least that's where we keep it now that witch finders and inquisitions are out of fashion. What's your point?"

"They're sacrificing people to their gods," Thiervy said. "I guess the tribes weren't lying about what happened to Cortez and all the rest."

"You've seen it yourself?" Mayport asked. "Human sacrifice?"

"Saw it? They're proud of it," Thiervy said. "Mass is one thing.

This is pure death worship. Should I be glad I'm an abomination in the sight of God? That should keep me off the menu. My heart would taste sinful, right?"

"Sure," Mayport managed. He took Thiervy by the hand as they hurried to catch up with the woman. The townspeople drew back from them with surprised, angry sounds. "Don't eat or drink anything if you can help it. You never know what they think a proper Mass is."

Thiervy looked a bit green around the edges but managed to nod. They hurried through a market square, and Mayport saw what Thiervy had meant about the native pride in their atrocities. A tiny grove of trees was the site of a thousand sacrifices. Flowers and the altars of the dead made the place brilliant with beauty and gore. Mayport turned his eyes back to Thiervy, full of apology he dared not speak.

"Cortez was a fool to even try," Thiervy muttered. "Without some amazing luck on his side, these people could defeat anyone. What would an enemy's life matter after this?"

Mayport nodded, and squeezed harder at Thiervy's hand. The smell of the gods' grove faded behind him, giving way to dust and the scent of endless flowers. They grew in every nook and cranny. Bundles were shoved in together on flat baskets. Bouquets floated on narrow fountains of pure water, which flowed here and there. On every surface, the eyes of their gods looked over their faithful.

For a moment, the childish parts of him quaked with fear. He recalled again the first moment when he had dared to disagree with a minister in the privacy of his own mind. The carvings around him were baleful, daubed with the offerings of the faithful, and nothing that inspired devotion. In this way he found familiar ground with his experience, and manged to hold off raw terror and panic.

They came at last to a stick-and-daub wall that stood square with the street. Its wide-open gates revealed a yard full of brisk business. Dried goods from maize to spices were being carried in bushel baskets in all directions. A row of fine warehouses backed into the yard. Beyond them Mayport saw the broad white walls of another grand palace.

The old woman marched through the lines of workers with much side-stepping and irritated complaints. At the door to a warehouse she presented herself, and sat down in a narrow strip of shade. Thiervy squatted, watching Mayport's back while mutters spread through the lines about the interlopers.

They stood back-to-back out of reflex, and were therefore facing the wrong ways when a man came to the door. His voice was a booming bass not suited to keeping secrets. The woman fussed and bullied until at last he gave instructions to one of the workers. A bushel basket was delivered to him, and he summoned Mayport with an impatient gesture.

They squatted down by the basket and the man took out a copper coin. The Spanish markings gave away its origins, so Mayport handed it back with a sneer. The man lay it on the ground, and then measured dried brown beans. Mayport laughed outright and pushed the coin aside. He chose out a couple of beans and chewed them, then spat the pulp out. The taste of root and wetness lay at the heart, leaving doubts in his mind about quality.

"I wouldn't buy red beans that dewy," Mayport told Thiervy. "I can't imagine what they'll do if I roast them. They might blow like popcorn."

"Is that something your daddy taught you?" Thiervy asked.

"I know it don't taste right," Mayport drawled. "There must be plantations. They can't be gleaning this from the wild. What the hell did my father get into with these people?"

"Robbing kings is the least of his adventures. Are you sure you don't want these?" Thiervy asked. "It's the closest you've come to what you wanted."

With regret, Mayport refused the beans. Thiervy looked ready to explode with fury, but the woman soothed him. "Our friend the headman here has something else to show."

This time a half-dozen baskets were brought. The headman went along with his Spanish coin to show the price. Mayport was amazed by the precision of his reckoning and wondered if he understood the value correctly. He took out a silver coin, though it was Dutch and of more recent minting than the Spanish copper. The headman sent for scales, made his own reckoning, and portioned out the beans according to his value.

"No wonder the women never drink it," Thiervy said, and whistled low. "Who could ever afford it?"

Mayport took his coin back and made up a measure of colored glass beads. He compared out silk and his oils, then smiled at the headman. Gold and silver were all very fine, but were found around the world. He offered value in scarcity, the only wealth this man was likely to appreciate in him.

"Bring me an umbrella please, and ask Cully for a basket lunch," Mayport said. "This is going to take a long time. We're buying money, I think. If I try to pay in coin, the conversions will give Costor a stroke."

"Are you sure you'll be safe here alone?" Thiervy asked.

"I'm not sure they'll let me leave until we've made a bargain," Mayport said. "They'll probably take my entire cargo and send me back half-full. I'd rather not owe them for lunch as well."

"You want Cully to know where you are and what you're doing," Thiervy said, and laughed. "You can speak plainly to me. They don't understand a word of English."

"Don't be so sure," Mayport said. He looked around the warehouses, and what he could see of the city beyond. "They know much more than anyone imagined. We'll deal fairly with them, and get screwed on the trade this time. If I get out of here with my life and the cacao, we'll have done very well for ourselves."

"I'm glad our lives still come before the beans," Thiervy said. "I risked mine to help you. I expect you will be extremely grateful to me for this."

"It's your company too," Mayport said, very stubborn on this point. "Remember that when we reap our rewards."

Chapter Sixteen: Examination

"It would be best if the cargo hold was scrubbed before we load," Mayport said when Cully took a break in shouting at the crew. "I'd rather not see our prize rot in transit. Not to mention what the smell alone could do to our product."

"You seem confident of getting it," Cully said. "I thought it was all up to these savages. I must admit you are not a wildly ambitious boy. If you were, you would have sold these goods where they're worth the trade in gold."

"You spent too much time with my father," Mayport said. "He could have saved himself time, trouble and expense if he had put off his self-importance for a while. The man I'm waiting for isn't a savage. He's vain and powerful, wealthy and worshiped as a god. If my father had more mind than ego, he would have cut a deal instead of adventuring on the rivers."

Cully shook his head in disbelief. "You two young bucks can really talk to them. It's amazing."

"It's French," Mayport said. "As soon as I get home, I'm going to find out about that. I'd reckon those Cajun fellows have been here and gone more than once. No wonder the rumors say that the nobility of France still sips cups of chocolate, despite the Spanish having supposedly blockaded this coast. I wonder if my fool of a sire ever even tried to speak plainly with these men, or took them for lively monkeys as you seem to do."

Cully shrugged a couple of times. "I guess I don't know. You keep surprising me. I'd almost take it you find men of your own kind more savage than these fellows."

"I know my kind much better. These ones will at least kill you in the square, instead of sneaking up behind," Mayport said. "One day I'll snatch failure from the jaws of victory with my broad view of what is human. I do not think that will happen here."

Cully laughed. "What could these creatures do that might threaten us? Your confidence springs entirely from the bores of our guns."

"They outnumber us," Mayport said. "They could starve us, or

sacrifice our hearts. I'm willing to wait a while to see if I find my
fortune or my fate here."

"They must worship devils, or be them," Cully said.

"That's the trouble with worship," Mayport said. "Even if you
give all yours to God, you must assume that the Devil is just behind
him. I have trouble with that, and so must consider myself beyond
the scope of redemption."

"What do you believe in?" Cully asked.

"My friends," Mayport said. "They're not perfect, nor powerful.
I can count on them in times of need, and they on me. Forgive the
blasphemy, but that makes them more reliable than anything I've
yet found under a church roof."

A shout came down from the upper reaches of the rig. The
news passed down the line and Thiervy came running. "There's
something going on in the woods. All kinds of people are coming
to the port."

"Ready the arms, but keep them out of sight," Cully said. "Man
the rails and look sharp."

Mayport could say nothing, and only hoped the men didn't
lose their heads. A wild shot or even a threat could ruin his hard
work. Cully had his men well in hand, but they were all as superstitious as any other sailor. There was no way to know how they
might react if the local devotions were made plain to them.

Mayport heard drums while the men were still arranging the
guns. He had his own pistols ready, but was more concerned about
his cargo. The cadence of drumbeats was slow and steady, giving
the crew plenty of time to get nervous.

At last they saw the first of the parade. Men carried timber,
flowers, and yarn to the riverside, set them down and went back
the way they had come. Mayport went down the gangplank to wait
for Thiervy to join him. In the distance, they heard screaming, a
lone voice in the jungle.

"You look nervous," Mayport said.

"Can't you imagine why?" Thiervy asked.

"No," Mayport said. "They must have decided to trade. Why
else would they have come?"

"To rob and murder us," Thiervy said. "What are those posts
for? Those screams don't sound promising, my friend."

"Their sacrifices don't scream," Mayport reminded. "Anyway,
they're in their own land. Who are we to think we know so much
about what they're doing? Accept your ignorance, my friend. It

will prevent you making these strange leaps of logic."

A man came with the same old madam who had cultivated an acquaintance with the ship's crew. She shouted something up, and Thiervy argued with her. Only when she insisted did he finally translate to Mayport "She wants us to carry our goods down to the beach and leave them there."

"Do it," Mayport said.

"They will steal everything and set us on fire," Thiervy darkly predicted.

"It's mine to burn, so do what she says."

The bales and crates of goods were unloaded on the riverside. By then, the main body of the natives' procession had arrived. At its heart was a beautifully decorated cage bedecked with colorful paint and bright flowers.

Within the cage sat the source of all the screaming Thiervy had worried over. An ape-like creature braced itself with limbs and tail as the cage was carried down to the cargo. It protested in full-throated, furious howls. The natives sat its cage among Mayport's trade goods, and then retreated.

Others came and erected a temporary shelter of boughs and posts, which shaded cage and cargo alike. Strings and flowers were arranged all around, and the natives returned back the way they had come. The woman called again to Thiervy, who pretended cheerfulness in his reply.

"We're to leave things as they are for three days," Thiervy said, and glanced up at the sky. "I hope it doesn't rain again. She said they'll feed the god. Do you suppose she meant the monkey? It's all to be sure we didn't curse the goods or something like."

"I'd think it likely they're trying to find out if it's full of the pox," Mayport said. "Never mind. There's nothing that will hurt that monkey, much less a god. If there was, we would be dead now of curses or disease."

"I feel bad for the monkey," Thiervy confessed.

Mayport laughed. "That thing probably gets more respect than we do. Get the crew off the cargo gondola and tell them we have a few more days to go. I don't want their religious convictions to screw me up. They might destroy the shelter, monkey and cargo if they intended to please God."

"I'll do my best," Thiervy said, doubtful. "Secrets don't keep on ships. Even a crate like this one."

"It's not a secret. Just don't take this seriously, or they might start thinking," Mayport said. "Keep a lid on this powder keg, and I'll make you a very wealthy man by and by."

Thiervy kept his word and did his best. The crew took the news with grudging patience. They made a betting pool over whether the monkey would survive. The regular offerings to the loud and discontented creature provide a sort of entertainment three times a day.

Cully watched the proceedings with a critical eye. "You mean to say if we do this and play nice, they'll trade to us? We could be home within a month. Before Christmas, if the weather doesn't put us to port in the Confederated states."

"Yes, I think this will do to make nice with the locals," Mayport said. "Do you suppose my father ever tried? It wasn't very hard."

"You have the patience of a stone," Cully said. "He would have rather tramped this jungle for weeks than sit still for three days. I hope this works. Though, if it does I won't be happy. It would mean he risked his life to no purpose, and lost it that way as well."

"I risk everything, but I hope it is to some purpose or will be," Mayport said. "I will try this. If it doesn't work, I'll try something else. If I've got the patience of a stone, it may be my fortune."

"He had none of that to trade on," Cully said.

Mayport made a surprised noise. "Really?"

Cully nodded. "He was full of contempt and always in a big damn hurry. That's why you came as such a surprise to me."

Mayport felt oddly flattered, though he wasn't sure Cully meant to give compliment. He felt like he was on the edge of disaster even as the days passed by. The caged god seemed to suffer no ill effects though he complained nonstop for hours at a time.

At dawn of the fourth day, the procession returned. This time they carried the trade goods away and brought baskets of beans. Then Mayport had his own rituals to observe with scales and cargo manifest. The crew was snappy with the work, sensing a chance to escape the muggy heat of the riverside. Before long they would be full of brags on how they would comport themselves once they reached a civilized land.

Thiervy oversaw the engineering crew as they prepared the Dutch Process for its journey north. Mayport was scrupulous about packing the cargo for balance rather than efficiency. Like his crew he longed for the dirty streets of a port town where his grasp of English might bring him a beer.

The cargo hold was filled about halfway when they were done.

Mayport looked on the cache as a challenge as much as a success. He kept his worries to himself, certain that neither Cully nor Thiervy could solve the problem. They had their hands full with the hard work, which would carry them all safely home.

He wished he might send a message of thanks to whatever king had accepted his trade. He could not, for no more visitors came. He had to assume the best thanks would be to clear out as quickly as possible. Cully ordered the hot air envelopes filled, and the gondolas set to lift off for their voyage north.

Mayport watched, a useless passenger, as the gondolas were guided back into formation. The sight inspired a profound longing in him. So majestic was her beauty, he wished to accomplish her promise. The name of Gasteau stood out in his mind as his next necessary prize.

"Captain Cully, I have made a decision," he said when he had the chance in all the busy work of the deck. "We must make our port in the Confederated States, if you can get us that far north."

"Eh?" Cully turned away from his crew and faced Mayport like a storm coming head on. "Why's all that? We had a course straight back home from here."

"I have lingered too long about my business," Mayport said, and contrived to look ashamed. "These southern airs have made me forget what we face. Let us not try against nature, since we have won out against man."

"Again, I must suspect you of some wisdom," Cully said, but didn't look pleased. "Are you sure it won't ruin your whole scheme?"

"I think it may improve us greatly, though our Mr. Achely is certain to squawk," Mayport said. "Savannah will be our port. The crew may go to the Devil there without fear of arrest. Then again, our Thiervy has something like relations to either visit or avoid, when we arrive. I myself have avoided business there, but now I may have some confidence in addressing it directly."

Mayport's hopes for a swift return north proved groundless. The winds and weather were against them all the way back to the eastern coastline. There, they put in to a lovely cove just hours ahead of a vicious storm. The gale kept them battened down for a long day and night. Its howls gave voice to the frustration locked tight in Mayport's heart.

When at last the rain and winds slacked off, they were all grateful to be set free. They came out into a world of battered mangrove and fallen trees that clogged the little cove. The sky hung low like a gray blanket that threatened to smother them anew. Cully surveyed the sky with real worry in his eyes.

"That came awfully late for these waters," he said. "Blowing off the wrong direction, too. Things might be a lot worse as we go north."

"Should we sit pat, or push on?" Mayport asked.

"Let's wait and see if we have a choice," Cully said.

"Who stowed these struts!" Thiervy bellowed from somewhere over the side. "Find him and flog him, Captain! We're landed!"

Cully ran for the nearest ladder, with Mayport hot on his heels. The mud flats under the mangroves sank Mayport to his knees. Cully yanked him to better footing and hurried on down the row of ported gondolas. Thiervy was still doing a filthy tour of European languages when they found him, mud all over except for teeth and the whites of his eyes.

Mayport saw the torn-open compartment and wondered if struts were the real worry. Somehow a limb had slammed into the gondola's deck and worked open a gash. "Thiervy, these were stowed right. That storm, it must have..."

"This fucking *basket* of yours isn't made for real weather!" Thiervy shouted. He seemed to only be hunting a target for his curses. "Strings and sticks ain't what you want in a spot like this! Once they're broke, you're stuck. Can't patch in like sail cloth, you know!"

Mayport looked at the mess of envelope veins, then up at the torn hull. "What about this... um... Thiervy, I'm seeing a rather large and gaping hole in the hull. Did you notice?"

"I can fix that!" Thiervy snarled. "Wood everywhere! I think I hate your father!"

"Mutually, my friend. Get the rig up on deck and take your carpenters to work. We can creep back up to Savannah if we must." Mayport yanked down a few planks and made a firmer place to stand. "Get out of that slop. There's no telling where it's been. Your mind may have gone strange in the storm."

"There's no point in patching this if those struts are broken!" Thiervy struggled with the mud until he was breathless. "Help me out of this."

Mayport frowned down at Thiervy, half inclined to leave him stuck in the muck. The opportunity to lecture was a rare one, but somehow he managed to resist. He helped Thiervy up onto the planks and shook his head over the still-sputtering volcano of Thiervy's temper. "We must be thankful we were not scattered or shattered completely. Put up catwalks first. The crew will need to move about, and this mud flat is no joke."

Thiervy gritted his teeth, forcing words out directly into Mayport's face. "I will not be grateful for even one thing about this disaster. Do something about those struts until you know nothing can be done. When you are resigned to reality, we will abandon that gondola and go on north."

Thiervy stomped away, came to the end of the plank, stuck again knee deep in mud, got himself loose and finally managed to clamber back aboard a gondola. Only when the way was clear did Cully sidle over and raise an inquiring eyebrow. Mayport was embarrassed of Thiervy's mad ranting, but had become accustomed to the way he blew. "He's not thinking right. I need to figure out about those struts, I suppose. They've been destroyed somehow, it seems."

Cully grunted, and pulled at the corners of his mouth. "There's not much to it, really. I'm sure the plans are folded up somewhere in my chest. Find your best whittlers and carvers, promise them the world in a bottle, and turn them loose. This isn't the first time I steered this ship fit to shatter every envelope strut it's got. This is no more than a half-dozen to replace."

"There, I knew he wasn't being sensible," Mayport said. "If you could help that much, I'll manage the rest. I imagine you'll have enough on your hands with all the crew going stir crazy."

Cully clapped Mayport on the shoulder, then began shouting orders even as he began his journey back across the mud to a ladder. Mayport crawled onto the damaged cargo, hoping desperately for a miracle. He saw baskets of cacao being shifted out of the way. He turned on the hop to find space in other holds for their prize. By the time his cargo hold was squared up for repair, the envelop struts had been hauled onto the deck.

Mayport stood on the narrow ledge that served as his command post. He strolled to and fro as the men worked. Their nimble fingers picked the narrow laths apart and re-set hemp cords. The skeleton of their rigid envelopes lay twisted with narrow ribs dangling from frayed tendons. He understood Thiervy's moment of panic, but could not allow himself that same luxury.

He could only stand still and wait for more expert men to pass judgment. His impatience only looked normal, but he somehow managed not to shout. A rushed or nervous hand might make worse what was already damaged. He took comfort in the fact that the ruin was not total. By following Cully's mechanical drawings, he was able to pretend he was somehow fit to the commands he must issue.

To his relief, his opinion wasn't solicited. By the time Thiervy came up to check, the men were cutting struts to replace the broken ribs. Thiervy clapped Mayport on the shoulder and smiled proudly.

"I should have had more faith in you," he said. "You'll have those struts fixed before the hull's sound."

"I never lifted a finger," Mayport said. "You should have had more faith in your captain and crew."

Thiervy laughed in surprise. "Every time I think we've made an officer of you, I'm proven wrong. You would never have survived an apprenticeship, nor your honesty neither."

Mayport laughed, and left his post in Thiervy's more capable hands. He went below into the cargo, where Thiervy had contended with the gondola hull. The light pouring through the side was more disturbing than the usual stale-smelling darkness.

Thiervy drove a team of carpenters like devils were on their tails. Mayport pitied them their pace, but dared not question the urgency. His worry was over the bushels of cacao that might have been exposed to rain or seawater. He put them all together and marked the baskets as questionable, but hoped they would dry and be just as well.

The crew in the hold cried out to heave-ho, and the light grew dim once more. He was surprised at the sudden change, wondering if the men were going at it very fast, or if he had spent more time with his beans than he knew. He went back above deck to check the sun, and found the men rushing with a kind of infectious urgency.

Cully was chivvying the crew to set the full rigging, though they had hours of work still to go before the Process could be launched. Thiervy stood beside the Captain, with a spyglass aimed at the horizon. He called out speeds every few minutes, and sounded worried. Mayport joined them at the railing and peered out to sea.

"Is your cargo square and stowed, Mister Titus?" Cully bellowed.

"Right and tight, Captain," Mayport shouted back, though they were close enough to shake hands.

Cully spared him a surprised glance, but did not question him further. He had orders aplenty for every hand, including a dangerous command to the gunners. Mayport could see them preparing the breech-loading guns even as the engines began to turn and fill up their unbroken envelopes with air.

"Let them come. It's the wrong day to slow me down!" Thiervy cried.

"Keep your calm," Cully said to Thiervy. Then he turned and cursed at every man he saw moving slowly. With his next breath he was back to calm interest. "Mayport, you might want to go below."

"I'm not tired," Mayport said. He scampered off to collect Thiervy's rifles and pistols, as well as Cully's and his own. He carried them back to the command portion of the cargo gondola and settled down to prime and load them all. "Thiervy sounds excited. Are we in for some kind of fight?"

Thiervy laughed at Mayport's innocent inquiry. "Look here at our enemies. I doubt they expect anything other than a wild welcome."

Mayport took the spyglass and looked where Thiervy pointed him. A single sail stood out against the sky. Its white triangle was at the lead of several smaller boats. The claptrap flotilla struggled through the shallows, making straight for the cove where the Process lay. The shift of the tide made the cove a maze of floating mangrove and narrow mud flats.

"Are they fishermen?" Mayport hazarded.

"Salvagers," Thiervy answered. "Or will be once they get here."

"Don't they help wrecked ships?" Mayport asked, still confused.

Thiervy laughed, once again caught by surprise over Mayport's ignorance. "They're vultures. They'll finish a crew off and haul the goods as salvage if they can. These islands are full of 'em. If the fishing turns bad, they turn pirate. They'll carve us up like a landed whale, or would, if we couldn't defend ourselves."

Mayport handed the glass back and began to double-check their weapons. "It's not that I don't trust your word. I've never heard of such a thing before. What makes them think they can get away with it?"

"We're apparently drowned," Cully said, again quiet just for his officer's ears. "That's to say, if we were a seagoing vessel, we would have no way out of here. If we had broken up on rocks or a reef, they'd let the sharks have us. A fellow can't be expected to risk his life on a dying man."

"But they'll risk their life to rescue the cargo," Mayport said. "These mangroves aren't going to dash our brains out any time soon. We're in no immediate peril, other than them."

"You've struck it right, my friend," Thiervy said. "I know you like to hope for the best in people, but you're in no position to be generous. Even if there was law to protect us in these waters, it's Spanish law and we're criminals to them. We're on our own."

"I don't hope anything of these fellows," Mayport said. He peered through the glass again to be certain. "Those are European style ships. I know precisely what to expect of men like that."

Mayport knelt and cradled his rifle on the railing. Thiervy calculated the range and put a restraining hand on Mayport's shoulder. "You'll never strike from here. It wouldn't matter even if you managed to warn them. They're coming straight for us, and must have seen the guns already. I assumed you would want to avoid a fight."

"I would, if we were only scrapping for fun," Mayport said. "I don't suppose I can avoid having fun once the smoke flies. They'll never get close enough to attempt a boarding until after dark. That will put us at a vast advantage."

Chapter Eighteen: Cunning

Mayport lay flat on the deck, wishing desperately for a mosquito net. The storm, which had thrashed them, had bestowed more clouds on the coast. Cully worked the crew at a fever pitch, one eye on the approaching salvager ships, the other on the sky.

Mayport wasn't the only apparent loafer. A pair of men lay low on each gondola. Though the foreign boats drew close, they made no hails to the crew above. No vessel, including their own, flew colors declaring an affiliation to any country. Matters were as Thiervy had predicted; they were on their own.

The cold reality of being a smuggler had settled at last on Mayport's heart. To a stranger, his vessel looked like a half-dozen broken shapes strewn against the mangroves. Though she was sound, the teetering rigs and rigid envelopes looked nothing like what a seaman thought of as travel-ready.

The gondolas might have passed for fishing boats at a distance, but even that was being generous to their craft. The mouth of the cove was clogged with sturdy little vessels filled with browned and hard-eyed European men. Mayport kept both eyes on their progress, aware of the treachery such men traded on.

The largest boat tacked to and fro along the wash-out channel. The *Process* had flown over the maze and set gently down on the narrow rise below the mangroves. Thiervy had taken odds that there were no navigable lanes to their snug port. He was up in the rigging like a bold target, certain he was out of range from any guns they might be carrying.

The sun had nearly reached the water by the time the sail of their main vessel had crept past the mouth of the washout. The haze of gold on the water dazzled Mayport's eyes. He closed them to clear the green phantom shadows, and looked again. The sail had frozen in place where he had seen it last. He blinked hard and rubbed his eyes to be sure. The slender mast danced a while, then settled to a cockeyed two o'clock.

"You owe Thiervy a bottle," Mayport muttered to himself. He rose to a crouch and looked closer with the spyglass. He could see dark figures rushing about, mere shadows in a cutout play against the crimson sky. He put the glass away and stood to shout across to the command gondola. "They've run one aground! Stuck fast in the mud! The other boats look to still be coming! You reckon they know something we don't?"

"These waters!" Cully bellowed back. He came across the cat-walks with a quick, light step surprising on a man his age and size. He took a look at the salvagers and gritted his teeth. "Tide might make enough difference."

"We've got them fooled, though," Mayport said. "They'll imagine that we sailed in here, and that they can do the same. For all we know, they'll all get stuck before they get close enough to do any harm. They might expect to sit still and wait for us to come out tired and hungry."

"Let's hope they get lazy," Cully said. "We can just sneak off in the night. That would be a story for telling. Makes me feel a little sorry for them, though. Keep eyes on them and sing out if they make even one move against us. Did you learn anything at that gentleman's school of yours that might be helpful here?"

"I learned not to be afraid of making mistakes," Mayport said. "Maybe I'll learn I was wrong to blow these bastards to smithereens. I still mean to do it, if they don't back off my boat."

"There, I knew you weren't the coward Thiervy imagined you to be," Cully said, sounding proud. "What made him think you wouldn't fight? From what I know of you, a hopeless fight is just what you love best."

Mayport looked up, surprised. "When have I ever fought in front of you?"

"For your company, and your vessel, just to have them," Cully said. He looked up at Thiervy in the rigging, then pulled at the corners of his mouth. "You fight hard and steady for everything you treasure. I just can't figure why he thinks you're a coward."

Mayport cleared his throat and tried not to look as embarrassed as he felt. "Because he knows I care for him."

Cully laughed as loud as a cannon boom. "What that boy imagines! Painting you a coward, just for that. It might make you a fool, with it being him and all but... it takes real courage to even breathe such a thing."

"I'm not afraid of making mistakes," Mayport repeated. "I'll take the consequences if I must. It's better than living as a coward and a liar. I'd sooner die an honest man."

Cully laughed again, and then left Mayport to his post. Mayport might have set another man to watch the boats and gotten some rest. He wasn't so loyal that he would lay still in the open sun out of pure obedience. The closer the sun dipped to the horizon, the more anxious he became. By keeping his own watch, that anxiety would not pass like wildfire through the crew as rumor and speculation.

He watched the distant boats with naked eye, trying to estimate what the crew could really see. The shadows were indistinct, and held no secrets. Longboats had been sent out to try unsticking their vessel. Two boats plugged away at the mud spit, but a third drifted ever away from them, back toward the mouth of the washout.

Mayport struggled with his reckoning and began silently to curse. The rowers were fresh and made good time. He fought against itches and yawning and distraction, one eye on the sun and the other on the boats. As the bottom of the sun's disk touched the sea, the longboat and smaller vessels began to slowly drift back to the stuck sailboat and the narrow channel between mud spits.

"Don't be stupid," Mayport muttered. "Don't come up against me, you scoundrels. I got no choice, but you do."

They heeded his superstitious warning for as long as the sun shone. When it had set, he saw them move as one. The longboat skimmed past the mud spit, poking ahead with a pole as it came. The still-stuck sailboat lit its lanterns as purple light crept down the sky, eaten up by a black and starless night.

Mayport jumped when Thiervy flopped down beside him. "All for nothing, I suppose. They're stuck fast and will be until morning."

"The others aren't stuck," Mayport murmured. "They're sneaking past the mud while you watch the lanterns sit still. They'll be here in an hour or two."

Thiervy squinted out into the darkness. "I'll have to take your word for it. I was busy getting those soft envelopes deployed and couldn't watch."

"How fast can we get out of here?" Mayport asked. "They'll be expecting us to have to pass them, won't they?"

"We need more time than we have, as it ever was," Thiervy said. "Normally I'd say we need six hours, to be sure none of the balloons rip or pull loose. Do we have time to eat?"

Mayport wanted to say no, shout his fear to the absent stars, harry and drive the men until they were safely aloft. Instead he nodded and turned his attention back to the shadows. The crew was sent off in shifts for the only meal they had been given since breakfast.

The officers tried to keep a calm front, but their men were not idiots. They ate fast and rushed back to their stations. Mayport assumed they understood the presence of danger, if not the nature of the threat. They finished the rigid rigging as if their lives depended on it. Then Thiervy shifted as many hands as he could get to the engineering gondola.

Mayport went to the center of the command deck to check the breech-loading cannons. The crews stood by their weapons, proud of perfect preparation. They looked excited, and wanted only for a target. He stayed close to man the shell cache as Thiervy's rigging drew taut and hauled a hot air duct up to the main rigid envelope on the command gondola.

Mayport kept an anxious eye on the shadows of his own crew. The sounds of their labor came in creaks and groans as cables shifted to allow the expansion of the rigid envelope. Minutes felt like hours, but Mayport enjoyed the wait. The uncertainty was better than what he dreaded out on the water.

The lapping of sea against the *Dutch Process* was an alien, confusing sound. Against its chaos he found order: the rise and fall of synchronized oars. He stole forward to his watch post and felt the hair stand up on the back of his neck. His balls tightened as real fear gripped at his heart. In the pale cast of lanterns on the water, he could see the whiteness of wet oar tips, and the bristle of a half dozen muskets or rifles.

Cully cried out in a French far-removed from Thiervy's delicate tones. The threat was returned in a mélange of tongues that turned the night primal. Thiervy whistled, and one of his men sent a Chinese rocket flying. The sky lit up a hellish red, and a cry rang out from below. Above, teams shouted and hauled away on the lofting levers. The command gondola shuddered, then settled again on the mud.

The crew of the Process knew not to look directly at the flare, but hurry on at their work. In seconds, the supports were in place and the fans began to turn. The moment of confusion was enough to panic the men in the boats. Guns discharged in the night, though they might have struck only thin air.

Mayport saw them as clearly as in broad daylight, and called the range to his gun crews. His hands had already full-cocked his rifle, even as he brought the sight to bear on the memory of a shape on the sea. He fired, heard a surprised cry, and held his breath while smoke billowed from his weapon. The metal felt hot in his hands as he set it down and took up another.

The world shook under the boom of a breech-loader, and the *Process* jumped with the recoil. Mayport laughed, and could not hear his own voice. His hearing had been lost in the rapid explosions. Darkness and smoke made him blind as well. The fate of their target remained a mystery until wooden splinters flew up in his face.

He fell back and rolled, came up under the railing and fired at random. He drew a brace of pistols and let fly with those as well. Like sound, pain seemed a distant thing. He re-loaded right where he lay, then scrambled to another hide to search for a target.

The deck leaped under him, and he tumbled away from his cover. He caught the stock of his rifle musket between his knees and held on to the pistols. The jolts turned into swaying and Mayport slid again, this time to the center of the command deck.

"Why aren't you firing?" Mayport bellowed at the sergeant. "We still have a line of sight!"

The man shouted orders to the gun crews, who were still scrambling back to their posts. They ranged the weapons again and the guns gave their deadly shouts to the night. In an instant the command deck was lost in a white-out of smoke. Though Mayport was standing among the guns, he felt more than heard their booming.

The command gondola yanked hard at the rigging. Men cursed and shouted as the craft swayed and pulled free of the mud. Fans drove a draft down, clearing the haze of smoke in a mighty gust. Someone sent up another flare, and lit the night in poisonous green. The flare revealed splintered dinghies, broken men, boats tossed aside or retreating to deeper water as the *Dutch Process* rose up and poured damnation down on them all.

Chapter Nineteen: Homegoing

Mayport lay in his bunk, aching all over but very merry. His collection of cuts and bruises were mere decoration compared to his left arm. A splinter twice as long and wide as his finger had pierced his shoulder. He hadn't noticed it much until it was gone, yanked out by the coldly practical Cully.

Two of the crew had died. One had hanged in the rigging and the other broken by a plummet to the engineering deck. Another lay moaning of burns that seemed determined to kill him at last. Mayport tended his own wound and showed proudly to himself that all his fingers still moved. Beyond his own nursing, his good hand was chiefly occupied with the rum bottle.

He had been relieved of his office and returned to the rank of passenger where he belonged. A better man for the job was called up from the crew, and seemed grateful for the advancement. He gave tender care to Mayport's cargo. As cargo himself, Mayport could only be grateful.

With wounded men growing ill, Cully had every reason to become grateful for their shift in destination. Thiervy was anticipating their port with a Confederalist's stoicism. In Mayport's experience, any Confederalist who went a step further north than he had to bore a kind of suspicion upon return. After dragging Thiervy halfway around the world in both directions, he was returning the sentiment.

The port lay just north of the Spanish colonies on the peninsula. They might be received with a cold welcome or an open keg, depending on the mood of the place. Thiervy was full of tall tales brought secondhand from his mother, who was in every degree a lady of particular depth and experience. Mayport marveled at Thiervy taking the time to spin yarns for his entertainment. He would have attributed it to the handy bottle, but Thiervy had none of it in his visiting hours.

The weather was nothing but disagreeable even when they brought the Process to anchor. When at last Cully let him try, he was able to get up and about very well. The fresh air stirred a powerful longing in him. His impatience grew stronger as Cully argued by megaphone with the port authority over their docking allowance.

He elected to break the Process down and let the crew go where they may. He would not have housed them in a massive, teetering death trap any longer than he had to. The docking cost him a little, but he had no intention of remaining aboard at all. Thiervy had already persuaded him on that point.

Cully went with the command gondola. Thiervy brought the engineering down. Mayport was put with the cargo, reeled down and anchored like a playful bird on a ribbon. Before he ever made it from dock to dry land, delightful smells wrapped him up from all sides.

He made himself walk past the nearest saloons and inns. They were too near the port and unfamiliar to him. He suffered little guilt for leaving Thiervy behind to his labors. Without discussion, he knew where Thiervy would go as soon as he was set free. The only regret was that Costor was not able to join them. Mayport had committed the directions to memory, and so could pretend confidence as he rushed through the jumble of offerings the town presented.

The streets of the city were crowded with traffic and slush. Mayport jogged across a broad thoroughfare and plunged fearlessly among narrow, twisting streets. Here, the complexion shifted from fair to dark, but the business changed not at all. He hustled past the many shops until he came to a bright blue door that stood between tall, sparkling windows. He mounted steps and hurried across a wide, shady porch that harbored men as they enjoyed their bottles and mugs.

From the size of the crowd beyond the blue door, lunch was still being served. Mayport squirmed in among the masses and forced his way through to the bar at the back. He hollered an order over the din of the kitchen and was coldly refused. He tried ordering in Thiervy's name and got a whoop as a reply. The kitchen crew parted and Idora herself came up to the bar.

"You brought one of our boys back home!" she cried. Her smile was as if a long-lost son had found his lonely way home. "You're too fine to be squashed in here. You go out back where the rich folk eat."

"Yes, ma'am," Mayport agreed, glad to be allowed to dine in the first place. Confederalists boasted a social system that could lay a cold, hard ban on a man in an instant, never to be appealed.

Mayport shoved through the crowd and out through the back door. There, a broad porch was set up with long, wide tables of rough planks and benches of same. The seats were full, but there seemed always room for a couple more. He staked out enough bench and table for two, and craned his neck watching for Thiervy.

He came around the side of the building and climbed over the porch rails to claim his seat. Mayport gave him plenty of room as Thiervy reached for everything at once. The center of the long tables were filled with a harlequin set of bowls and platters which sat protected under domed screens that kept the flies off.

Thiervy snatched Mayport's plate and loaded it to breaking. Mashed potato and squash were lost under gravy and buttered biscuit, green beans and sweet corn, stewed tomatoes and slabs of fried fish. A boy from the cellar delivered a spring-cold jug of water to go with their jug of cider. Mayport leaned his elbows on the table and devoured everything, lost in the world of pure contentment.

Idora came out to make sure he stuffed himself silly. She replaced the biscuit with crispy cornbread soaked in honey and butter. Mayport was only grateful. He had been educated among the young gentlemen of the Confederate states and counted himself as one. The native blood of all shades had their opinion of his origins. Chief among those ideas was that he did not know what good food was, and he had to be helped along.

"I got a question for ya," Thiervy said as Idora dished stewed okra and tomato over rice for the whole table. "You got anything like a room I could rent? I got to go see my uncle. I'd rather to tell him he can find me somewhere that I took with my own coin."

"Is he talking to you all again?" Idora asked.

"He might to me, since my daddy turned me out." Thiervy drank deeply from his glass. "That's why I got to go see him."

"You can have the back corner, unless y'all are gonna share a while," she said. "For two, you can have the front rooms. They got their own porch up there."

"We'll take the one with the porch," Mayport said. "I don't know for how long. The crew's pretty beat up and worn out, but I have to go on up to New Amsterdam when the weather breaks."

"Too cold for me up there," she said, and shivered. "You ought to bring your business down here. I'd fix you such a pie as you never had, if you could get me the powder for it. I mean to say, if you're chasing after your father's coattails and all, I could."

Thiervy blanched, but Mayport said "I will."

She seemed satisfied with his promise, and went back to rule over her kitchen. Thiervy went on eating, but complained around his food. "You can't just give that stuff away. You ought to treat it like gold dust."

"Some of it's for me," Mayport said, and dug in again with his spoon. "I've never heard of a chocolate pie before. What do you suppose it is?"

"Delicious. You're right, it will be worth the cost," Thiervy said. "I wonder if I can say the same thing about going home but... I don't feel like I have much choice. Ma's home folks picked the school I went to. I'm not sure I can say thank you without lying."

Mayport laughed, but didn't reprimand Thiervy for his ingratitude. "They'll never know you were here if you don't go tell them. I won't turn you in to the relatives if you don't want to."

"If it was just me, I wouldn't bother to be polite," Thiervy said. "I got someone else to think of, so I better try to pretend I know how to be a gentleman. You won't tell the truth on me, will you?"

Mayport shrugged a couple of times. "I guess not. I don't know how you stand being loved for a lie, though. I'd rather to be hated for the truth."

"Like I said, if it was just me, I wouldn't care to be polite. Ma wants to run off on Daddy and I mean to help her," Thiervy said. "If her brother won't help her out, that's fine with me. I still reckon I better go ask."

"I hope he's the kind that doesn't mind a sensible woman," Mayport said. "Some men are funny when it comes to their own sisters. His wife might get ideas on him after something like this."

"He doesn't have a wife," Thiervy said. "Other than that, he's as traditional as they come. He might throw me out just for asking the question, but then I'll know for sure that he's a fool."

They finished the cider together then went up to inspect their rooms. They found two wide, sunny rooms that opened onto a narrow walk above the porch. Each room boasted a bed and chair, small table and separate wash stand. To Mayport, it seemed palatial, clean and smelling of Idora's kitchen. He lay down on a bed and was perfectly content.

Thiervy paced the walk until a boy came up with another stone jug. Mayport watched his shadow through narrowed eyes, counted his steps when he passed beyond the window and returned. Now without a jacket, then without a shirt, he monopolized the jug and took his measure of the town. Mayport turned onto his side to ease the sudden tension in his pants. He cleared his throat loudly and Thiervy turned around, startled.

"Who were you expecting to see?" Mayport asked with a grin. "Bring me all that energy if you're not going to do anything with it."

Thiervy corked his jug, then stooped to pull his boots off. He stalked across the room, watching Mayport unknot his muffler. He stretched out as his throat was exposed, fingers spreading his collar wide. Thiervy growled, then pounced at Mayport where he lay.

Mayport rolled to the side, though his shoulder complained. He caught Thiervy's arm and used his momentum to drag Thiervy forward. He looped his muffler around Thiervy's wrist. Thiervy looked surprised and annoyed, but didn't reach to undo the knot.

Mayport took Thiervy's kerchief and repeated the knot on the other side. He moved the pillow and stood back, watching muscles in Thiervy's back flex and relax. Though he lay nearly still, Mayport knew a profound struggle was at work under Thiervy's skin.

Mayport's balls throbbed, and gave a sudden, sharp complaint of pure need. He eased his trousers a little, then leaned down and slid his hands under Thiervy's belly. Between warm skin and the mattress, he made quick work of buttons and buckle, then stripped Thiervy bare in a long, slow series of tugs. Thiervy wriggled his hips this way and that, helping Mayport get him naked.

Mayport walked slowly to collect the chair, and took his time crossing back to the door. He set the chair back at an angle under the doorknob and rattled it a bit. Thiervy jumped against the sheets, testing himself against the bed frame.

Mayport pulled his own belt loose and tested the doubled weight against his palm. Thiervy squirmed, then lifted his hips up from the sheets. Mayport grinned, still enchanted by all the contradictions wrapped up in his lover. A warm bloom of pride burst in his chest, that somehow he was the thing that could occasionally tame Thiervy's wild impulses.

He stroked the smooth length of leather against Thiervy's ass and thighs. Thiervy undulated, moaned, welcoming everything and wordlessly begging for Mayport to begin. At last Thiervy was able to lay still, and Mayport brought the leather down, slowly at first and gentle with pale, cool skin. Thiervy's ass turned pink and lively with very little encouragement. Mayport stepped back a little, and brought the belt down harder, making red lines rise up in a cruel ladder.

Thiervy gripped the bed frame in both fists and groaned into the mattress. Mayport tossed the belt aside and yanked impatiently at his clothes. His cock writhed and jerked as he hunted out the oil. Not for the first time he wondered if Thiervy was truly beyond caring. He fisted his shaft slick and hot as he came back to the bed.

He crashed down on his knees between Thiervy legs and pushed them wide apart. He spread Thiervy's ass wider in his hands and thrust against quivering flesh. Thiervy bucked and screamed, every powerful muscle in his body flexed, giving up his pleasure to Mayport's cock. The clenching heat was nearly more than Mayport could take. He slapped at Thiervy's squirming ass, then seized his hips and forced him to be still once more.

Mayport leaned down on Thiervy, trying to keep them on the bed as he thrust hard against Thiervy's rebellion. Their bodies ran with sweat and oil, smacking together in obscene harmony. Mayport held on tight to Thiervy's hip with one hand, fingers digging in deep enough to bruise. With the other hand he struck mercilessly at pale and striped flesh alike, driving Thiervy this way and that until his ass churned wildly, pulsing around every twitch and throb of Mayport's cock.

Thiervy's cries grew hoarse, and his struggles began to slow once more. Mayport eased off of him and reached down to grab at his thighs. He managed to catch Thiervy behind the knees and lifted them up toward Thiervy's chest until he was forced to push his ass higher and kneel with his head still pressed to the bed. Thiervy whimpered and squirmed delightfully, but barely resisted being put into the new position. Mayport sat up on his knees and stretched his shoulders, finally free to draw back to the tip of his cock and relieve the aching heat. He plunged in hard, angling down a little so Thiervy would howl and bounce, lost in pure pleasure.

Now Mayport need not hold Thiervy still at all. He stroked at his own body while Thiervy rode him with eager undulations. His cock throbbed luxuriously, some of its urgent demand eased by the warm grasp and pull that came with every move Thiervy made. He rode the squirms at a leisurely pace, letting his smoldering passion draw them along. He breathed deep and let out low groans while Thiervy's shouts grew high and desperate.

Mayport's balls crept higher, making his ass twitch and clench. His thrusts grew irregular, so he withdrew, sat back and tried to catch his breath. His whole body burned. Thiervy growled, a dangerous, disappointed warning.

Mayport got up and untied Thiervy's wrists. With a nudge, he sent Thiervy scrambling to turn over. Beyond all possibility of shame, Thiervy lay on his back and lifted his legs high. His powerful thighs trembled and tensed as Mayport petted them. Thiervy reached down and spread his ass wider, propped himself up a little on his arms.

The invitation was as obscene as it was irresistible. Mayport seized Thiervy at the back of his knees and yanked, turning him sideways on the narrow bed. His head hung down off the far side, and he clutched at his ass, spreading wide again.

Mayport prodded gently at Thiervy's ass, enjoying the sight of him squirming in thin air, desperate for more. He eased his way back in, cock quivering and begging for release. He took his time, gasping through the agony of pure need, taking another inch or two, then withdrawing again to the tip. Each slow invasion made Thiervy relax a little more. Mayport lifted him up at last, hooking knees over shoulders to drive in those last inches.

Thiervy yelped, hands leaping to his shaft as Mayport thrust again. Thiervy's ass clamped down hard as he stroked his cock. He shivered all over and came, spattering his belly and chest and fingers. Mayport kept riding those convulsions until his own thighs ached and his knees quivered. He grunted and rode his own pleasure, pouring all his love out in shouts and spasms of delight.

He sank graceless to his knees, ending up with his cheek cradled against Thiervy's thighs. Through half-lidded eyes he saw Thiervy, glittering with semen and sweat. He sighed with pure contentment, proud and satisfied with the love he had made his own.

Chapter Twenty: Tutelage

Mayport looked at himself in the mirror and wondered how long he had been across the gulf. His freshly-shaven face and neat hair looked foreign to him. Months had gone without civilized company. Cully might have made issue of that on the Process, but was himself no spokesman for gentility.

Thiervy was the one to insist on being polished up and made Mayport go along as well. He was still steaming under the barber's towel, but Mayport was ready to go have his boots shined. They had gone dirty and dull in his trunk, unused for so long. As he sat, a boy came to offer him a choice of cigars.

For a moment he stared, dumbly marveling at such riches. He licked his lips and glanced at Thiervy, then chose trios of cigars from the boy's selection. He tried not to begrudge himself the indulgence. Thiervy's pleasure would be excuse enough later.

When at last the barber had done his best, Thiervy looked fit and fine, full of sun-kissed vigor that had long gone out of season in the city. He smiled at Mayport's hair, now cut clean of sun streaks and cropped close all around. Neither of them looked prosperous, but now they had shed the pure neglect of their lonely stay abroad.

They went out into the street together, and Mayport handed over a cigar. Here they could walk without fear of coaches, steam and horse alike. They had no choice but to seek out the fairer parts of town to find a barber that would serve them at any price.

"We could have gone like we were to see Uncle Jesse," Thiervy said as they headed west from the port. "His valet would have spit-shined us for free. Plus, he might have thought we were pitiful."

"Trust me more than that," Mayport said. "You're the one that wanted to give the impression you know to use soap once a month."

"I saw men die on a pagan altar. That don't wash off." Thiervy shivered at the memory, then ducked his head down. "I might rather be back down there as the solo on Sunday morning than go show my face at my momma's house."

"You wanna tell me what I should be afraid of?" Mayport asked.

Thiervy shook his head and hurried on. He seemed to know all the streets, though the houses were quite nice. He turned down a narrow alley that ran behind kitchen gardens and vine-gripped walls. They stole through a graying wooden gate and into an orderly garden that lay to rest in the cold.

Thiervy went up and rapped at the kitchen door. A coffee-colored face answered, and withdrew quickly. Fast, scolding words poured out in a thick accent that Mayport couldn't understand. Thiervy took him by the elbow and steered him through the side yard, then up the broad front steps onto a whitewashed porch. The tall door was opened at Thiervy's nervous rapping.

The fellow at the door took their hats and left them to be led through a series of sitting rooms. In the last one they found a tall fellow standing near a hearth where a merry blaze danced. He was slender and fit to overreach Thiervy. He was not broad or as deeply muscled as his nephew. Instead he had the pale, fine complexion of a gentleman as well as the chestnut eyes and hair that Thiervy boasted. His smile was a thin, cool shadow of the family reputation.

He crossed his arms and tempered his expression to benign interest. "Well, young man. Let's hear it."

Thiervy blushed around the ears, but held on to his cocky grin. "My father always hated you, and now he hates me. I came to see if we have anything else in common."

"Your mother," Jesse said, serious as a stone. "I let you in even though you abandoned her up north. Who's this long drink of water you brought along?"

"My boss," Thiervy said, and betrayed his own frown. "My friend. Mayport Titus, my uncle, Jesse Peel. He's my mother's brother. I might have mentioned him, or not. I don't remember."

"Maybe once or twice," Mayport said. "It's not possible to keep up with your whole family. If your daddy don't like him, I guess he's probably okay."

"Is that truly the way you judge a man's character?" Jesse asked.

"It's in your favor, so for now, yes," Thiervy said. "What did you mean about abandoning Ma? She's in her husband's household. That's hardly the same as left in the gutters."

"Your mother is a very traditional lady," Jesse said. "Be grateful you have no sisters to suffer your father's tyranny. He would ruin a girl child, and may destroy his wife if she isn't helped."

"You're talking about coming between a man and his wife," Thiervy said, concerned. "There's more than just the law that would stand against you on general principle. This isn't exactly what I thought of as a welcome."

"Fair enough, but remember that I welcomed you," Jesse said. He spared a brief smile for Mayport. "Can you ride a horse?"

"Not that I'm aware of," Mayport said. "I imagine Thiervy will prove me wrong about that by and by. I rely on his common sense in such matters."

Jesse led them to his library and settled at a small table. Mayport offered a cigar, and was bent to light it when a servant appeared as if conjured. Mayport was badly startled, and went to take a seat by the window. He managed a polite thanks when she brought him a cup of hot tea, but could not hide his horror at her plight.

Thiervy and Jesse looked embarrassed at Mayport's bald shock. The silence drew long between them, even after the slave woman had gone. Jesse blushed red at the collar, and begged Thiervy with his eyes to explain.

"You see, they're counted as property," Thiervy said. "Grand-father mortgaged them instead of the land. Now, we couldn't be rid of them if we wanted to. The banks would hunt them down like a wandered cow if we sent them north. Can't hardly find a way to feed 'em, and can't get what's owed if we sold 'em."

"You didn't have to tell him all our little secrets," Jesse grumbled.

Mayport looked into his cup and made himself sip again. For the first time in his life he knew the cost of that warm sweetness, and what a man must do to earn such luxury. The tangle of Thiervy's relations had always been quite beyond his understand-ing, and this made them no clearer. "I thought your grandfather was a shipwright. I don't mean to know your secrets. I do have to go look special to a couple of fellows today. Would you rather I went on a while?"

"I think you'll be asked favors if you stay," Thiervy said. "He's full of big ideas for me, so I'll meet you back at Idora's by and by. What do you think Cully will do if he needs us?"

"Die of shame for wanting help," Mayport said. He had Jesse Peel marked for watching. Every now and then a fellow came along who tried to turn Thiervy against himself. "If we're lucky, we'll unsling some cargo this very day. We'll send a boy along after you if you're wanted."

Mayport left Costor's card on the calling plate and set out again into the winter garden. He wondered at the solemn silence and turned slowly, studying the blank windows. He backed away from the house, watching for what he knew would come, and finally saw in an upper window. The twitch of curtain that let him know his watcher wanted to be seen. He listened to the silence more closely, and caught again the undertone which had always plagued such places: fear. There seemed to be a competition on among the rich old families to pretend that perfection was common and everyday.

Mayport enjoyed the hospitality but had begun to take after his father's habit of not staying long. The tea warmed his belly as he hurried through the streets. Savannah was the town that had been spoken of at length by Thiervy and Gasteau. If not for the Academy, the two boys would have never met. They had a nation in common, and differed in every other particular. Where Thiervy was coldly practical and devilishly focused, Gasteau had let knowledge and life fill him up in languid gulps regularly imbibed with men of all kinds.

Mayport had only to find a matron at a street shop to ask after the name. She was able to suggest two different shops, one a farrier and the other what she supposed a very wicked kind of bakery. Mayport couldn't help but smile with delight at her suspicion of all things foreign. Again, that understanding of fear flowed between them while she filled him in on where he wanted to go.

The streets were crowded with haphazard shops and leaning stalls of all kinds. More than a few previously-prosperous dens of innocent vice stood empty or re-purposed. One of the more childishly splendid shops was still in business. The scents of flashy dough and creamy delights yet freshened the air. Mayport hurried inside to be seduced before he gave up on his wild plan.

If the senior Gasteau was undone by the untimely loss of one of his sons, it showed not at all. Mayport knew the plump and genial face gave a mask to one strong man of definite opinion. The chef noticed Mayport immediately, and came to usher him to a spindly chair and table painted white and glossy to go with the glass and brass of the shop. Mayport had no patience for mystery, and so introduced himself before he dared to sit.

Chef Gasteau seized on Mayport, squashed and kissed him, then hauled him out of the cafe and back into the kitchen where he was pleased to meet the current Madam Gasteau. She stood at the head of a table laden with sweets to be iced and decorated. Beyond her domain was a brick-walled bakery, where the ovens blazed and filled the whole shop with the smell of the chef's secrets.

Each table and workspace was tended by yet another Gasteau until names and plump faces blended together in Mayport's mind. At the end of the introductions Mayport had been fed small tarts, a warm cookie and then sat down at a very small table near the cool breeze at the back door. The chef sat down across from him and sang out in French until a warm pot and tiny cups had been delivered.

Mayport recognized the aroma at once, coffee prepared in the Italian style. He sipped at the warm, creamy froth and sighed in satisfaction. "How in the world did you get it? Where are you finding sugar? Everyone in the north swears there's no such thing going anywhere these days."

Chef Gasteau laughed heartily. "Spain never stopped France from doing what she liked, and won't start any time soon."

"What about cocoa?" Mayport asked.

Gasteau sat his cup down gently. "Now that, I would do quite a lot to have again. You can't taunt an old man. Out with the truth at once."

"I have the dried beans," Mayport said, trying to contain his excitement. "I need to know... more than I do. Perhaps we can make a trade? I promise to be more sensible than my father was, and more generous."

Gasteau hesitated, then nodded once. "Come again in the morning, with proof of these boasts. If things are as you say, we'll try once more. I won't take you at your word about being sensible. I knew your father too well to believe such a lie."

Chapter Twenty-One: Division

Mayport might have known that Chef Gasteau did not suffer from the problems that the Titus Chocolate Company had faced. His heavy figure had more to do with familial devotion than personal inclination. The conspiracy was to make the chef a useless creature under his own roof. The family had decided that Mayport would be a harmless distraction and, therefore, adored him.

The lessons began with illustrations of the difference between dried and roasted cocoa beans. He had imagined that the machines back at the factory would know what they were about when it came to such things. One day in Gasteau's kitchen made him understand the craft very differently. He could only be grateful that he had not voiced his supposition to the chef.

Gasteau seemed to know what Mayport had imagined, even if he never said a word. He was also aware of Mayport's ignorance and the dangers it represented. To Mayport's relief, his instruction was conducted without insults or humiliation at each mistake. Gasteau satisfied himself that Mayport could memorize by rote any lesson he was set, even if it was in French and to exacting standards. With that established, he poured his secrets out to Mayport with no question of repayment for his kindness.

Gasteau began by roasting some of Mayport's cacao. Beginning with the dry raw beans, the goal was to make chocolate by hand, using only what could be found in the kitchen. With ideas of heavy machines in his mind, Mayport thought he was being given an impossible task. Such exercises in futility were not unknown to him, so he settled in for the long haul.

Gasteau lost no time in proving the exercise to be entirely fruitful. Mayport hardly cared for the relative value of the beans as they were measured out for roasting. The work soon became a pleasure, with him stuck in with the other boys on mortar and pestle. His relative strength made reducing the roasted nibs very easy. He was soon able to produce the texture Gasteau demanded, and was moved on to the press where his muscle made a real difference.

Gasteau produced delicacies one after another, each more

decadent that the last. The chef had a wealth of tricks with pastries and cakes, sweet creams and hot drinks. For even the simplest magic to work, Mayport had to remove as much oil as possible from the cacao so that a fine powder could be put to use. Not one bite made it beyond the kitchen doors.

No matter how the press groaned and the pestles whirled, all their work produced very small amounts of the precious oil and powder. Several batches came near to ruination, with only Gasteau's experienced hand able to salvage the mess. Too little pressure in grinding, too much on the press, a little water where it didn't belong or none where it was wanted, any variation at all could mean disaster. Mayport wondered how much of his father's wealth had been lost by such simple mistakes that no clever machine could prevent.

All the while that Mayport worked, his mouth was being tutored as well. Sweet crackers were dipped in a kind of sauce, little chunks of chocolate were baked directly into cookies, smooth pours of chocolate were converted into delicate fans to sit atop custard. Each hour showed him a new facet to the object of his business. Though he enjoyed the lessons, he could not help the bitter taste that came with realizing how untutored he was in this most vital subject.

He had a suspicion that his friend the younger Gasteau would have been just as ignorant. He had a heart like an abacus, and little patience for physical work. Even where his temperament matched Costor's, he had not the depth of focus required for real profit. His tenure at the Academy had been to make a clerk of him, and make his English sound less imported. He might have been hiding surprises, but Mayport had his doubts. He could only wonder at two fathers, so ambitious and proud of their own knowledge, who thought their sons too fine to go on as they had.

At the end of each day, Mayport was sent home with a little treasure box made up of the Gasteau's delights. Somehow, the shop stayed open and operating, but Mayport never knew how. He remembered only tortes and patty cakes, hot sauce laced over whipped cream, and the moist, fat cake that had made an end to a full two hours of grinding. Mayport trotted through the streets to Thiervy's uncle's house, where the loyal boy continued to visit each day.

This afternoon would not let Mayport fake the somber mood of the house. He galloped up the back steps and banged the porch door behind him to announce his arrival. He scooted through the kitchen and out to the fairer parts of the house. Thiervy and Jesse were sitting as they always did, facing away from each other over cold cups of tea. Mayport skidded onto the scene and burst out laughing.

"What?" Thiervy managed, trying to hold his poker face.

"You look like you're playing Quaker Meeting," Mayport said. "I hope the weather is still bad. I'm having the time of my life."

Jesse pointed to the window, where fat flakes of snow squeaked against the glass. "You just came in out of the weather. Did you not notice?"

Mayport shook his head, gleefully unconcerned at his own ignorance. "Know what I did today? Made chocolate. I brought you lots, and for your uncle, too. I always mean to share, but it doesn't make it home somehow."

"So you finally made some?" Jesse sounded skeptical. "How can you have a company if you're only now learning the trade? You need a manager, my boy."

"I had one. That's why my training has been delayed." Mayport sat on the arm of Thiervy's chair, leaving his shoulder to Jesse. "You be proud of me, then. It might be the only perfect food in the world. Even the Frenchmen say so, and they should know. They'll eat anything."

"That's what worries me," Thiervy said. He opened the box and sniffed at the treats. Then he made a selection, daring the cocoa cream puff, and hazarded a taste. After that first bite, he put all suspicion aside and began devouring everything in the box. "Don't bother to taste, Uncle Jesse. Not worth it. I'll just take care of the rest."

"I tell you, men do not belong in a kitchen," Jesse said. "You're too obvious, my boy. I can't imagine why you haven't been restrained before now."

Mayport put on a blank look, and opened wide, innocent eyes at Jesse. "What do you mean?"

"We're partners," Thiervy said at the same time.

"You've made him a partner in your business?" Jesse asked, astonished.

"Well, why not?" Mayport returned his attention to Thiervy. "Our friends have saved us from disaster again. We would have ruined everything if we had just turned those machines on and let them run."

"How much different can it be from a corn mill?" Thiervy sounded worried. "I thought we had only to grind them and be done."

"If you're his business partner, you've only gotten half-shares in his troubles," Jesse announced.

Mayport turned to frown at Jesse. "Don't prod and poke at me, good sir. I have no idea of pleasing you. Insult as your nature insists. You shall not shame or alter my intentions."

Jesse's nose wrinkled up sharp and disapproving. "I mean to advise you. I'm not ignorant of your game, young man. If you will only do as I say, you might find yourself safer."

Mayport looked around the orderly, quiet home and shivered. "I appreciate your meaning, but safe doesn't enter into it. There's risk involved when a man does what he set out to do, come hell or high water."

"That's no reason for Joseph to take part in your risks," Jesse said.

"Who?" Mayport asked, utterly confused.

Thiervy slapped Mayport on the knee. "Me, you idiot."

"I know what he's done and said to his father over you," Jesse added. "Have you no idea what he's done to himself?"

"None," Mayport said. "I have no relations to suppress and organize me. If I should fail, you may have your laughing day. I assure you, my ruin will not be his."

"What did you mean by bringing this creature here?" Jesse demanded of Thiervy. "He's a catamite and a huckster. You made me think he was a gentleman."

"I made you think he was rich. That was all you wanted to know about him," Thiervy said. "His discretion is imperfect, but so is mine. As is yours. The two of you have more in common than you would be happy to admit."

Jesse went pale and drew back into his chair. "I don't know what you mean!"

"You fool nobody," Mayport said. "A man your age, with your resources, ought to have wed and bred by now. You never leave the house, so courtship can't be on your mind as it should."

"Who's to say I never will?" Jesse demanded. "I've not found the right lady yet. Anyway, I have no immediate need. My intention was to settle my lot on my favorite nephew."

"And give me the same gift of debt and shame your father has settled on you," Thiervy said. "I can only hope I've somehow changed your mind. You'll face a lonely long time here if you turn me away now."

"I never proposed anything so drastic," Jesse said. "I hoped you would be wise. My own example might have guided you."

"Failing that, your money might have forced me," Thiervy said, then glanced up at where Mayport still sat perched on the arm of his chair. "You may claim success. Your example has been considered in all that I have done. What is it that you expect me to do, to be more like you?"

"Be careful," Jesse said. His voice dropped to a conspiratorial whisper. "Keep yourself very safe, always."

"Live in fear," Thiervy said. "I can't. I won't. I don't care that I could die for being who I am. Nothing changes me, least of all money that isn't there to give. Stay here and be afraid for me, if you think it will help. I have a business to run."

Mayport laughed, feeling quite lost in the conversation. If they were arguing, it showed not a speck on their faces. Only in the bitter choice of words did the fact of anger make itself known. Mayport gave Jesse his most charming smile. For once, this genuine expression did nothing to soothe.

"I will keep the door open to you," Jesse said. "I hope when you return you will be wiser, but I think you will also be a sadder man. You've broken your mother's heart once. I won't make it be twice."

Thiervy laughed now, and Mayport couldn't keep quiet. Jesse's grim expression took on a sour frown, so he tried again to smooth things over. "I wonder if you imagine that Thiervy caused a scandal back home. There was some about his father's ways, but he hasn't been shut out. Even so far north, where he's almost a foreigner, they say not a word against him. I think they never will."

"You care so little about opinion, I doubt you know what is said about you," Jesse replied. "Men like you cause the most trouble for real gentlemen."

"But I won't," Mayport said. "I can be as hypocritical as the next fellow. I prefer to be honest, and take the pains that come with it. There alone do you and I differ."

Chapter Twenty-Two: Judgment

Thiervy stood in the center of the factory work floor shouting orders and looking quite at home. Their journey north had done much to restore him. The weather had settled to standard winter cruelty, daunting to Mayport but predictable to the likes of Captain Cully. Thiervy's coal-fired engine had made all the difference in getting them home once Mayport had been pronounced presentable by Chef Gasteau.

He gazed fondly out at the ported shell of the *Dutch Process*. He would have preferred her sleet-slicked decks to the desk he manned. Thiervy had made his point that Mayport's education had prepared him for just this task. He was, nonetheless, unhappy with spending his daylight hours in pursuit of understanding his father's intentions. The Academy had made Mayport expect something like accounting books. Instead, he had reams of ramblings, real plans mixed in with fanciful dreams on page after page of repurposed ship logs.

Cully had taken responsibility for unloading the *Process* and preparing her to lay still a while. Thiervy had made it his business to explore the factory itself and was having the time of his life. He had composed a little tune that he sang as he went along, of improvised verses against the name of Cory Titus. The warbling melody reminded Mayport of India, a welcome memory in the frozen New Amsterdam noon hour.

The engineering crew was being courted by Thiervy. He offered a job held down by gravity, if uncertain in its goals. His reports on the factory equipment had led to general hilarity. The merry few who accepted a situation asked for permission to curse the company's founder and were exclusively granted the privilege.

Cully was astounded by the easy conversion from sailors to landsmen. Mayport suspected that the engineers had followed their love to the sea, and relished the chance to follow it back to dry land. With the ship's crew stowing the *Process* piece by piece, Thiervy's pet team had a good time inspecting and dismantling the various contraptions on the factory floor. For a bit of variety, they undid the damage done to a small oven when some bit of claptrap had been connected with it.

For Mayport's part, he could only draw a very annoying conclusion from the documents he had found. The machines below would never be sorted out to serve their intended purpose. The main drawback was that they had no single purpose among them. Cory Titus, in his infinite enthusiasm, had attempted time and again to devise just one machine to do all the work required to turn raw beans into cocoa powder and butter. When Thiervy came up to inform him of their progress, Mayport broke the news with as much tact as he could muster.

Thiervy went to the window and looked down on the work floor. "Your father's besetting sin was a lack of perspective. He must have had no patience or real talent for design. It's as if he built a machine, didn't like it, and started over from scratch every time he tried to equip this place."

"I wonder how much cacao he intended to process," Mayport said. "You could put the entire warehouse through one of those things in a day."

"You could if they worked," Thiervy agreed.

"You were very confident in tearing the *Dutch Process* apart," Mayport said. "You risked your life to prove your ideas were right, and we came to no harm for it."

"I knew something about airships, and more about sailing," Thiervy said. "I know absolutely nothing about what you're trying to do. Still, I imagine I'll be able to make something of all this, if only scrap for sale."

"Certainly there will be that," Mayport said. "I need a thing that grinds, and a thing that works like an olive press. We'll want to control the grinding very carefully, and be able to get the pulp out and into the press. We'll have to be careful about capturing all of the cocoa butter off the press. It's as valuable as the powder itself."

"I can do that," Thiervy said, once again completely confident in himself. "I'll need time and a free hand, but nothing more. Your father made this place far more complicated than it needed to be."

"Just like the ship," Mayport said. "I suppose he had no time for simplicity, but I think we must try to be wise."

"Never mind the ambitions of a spoiled man," Thiervy said. "Let's be practical, since we can't be grand. Our little vessel could never live up to what he had in mind anyway."

"That means his couldn't either," Mayport said. "Instead of

scaling back the factory, he built a whole new ship. Why was there nobody to stop him from this madness?"

"He was rich," Thiervy said. "Nobody's trying to stop you, for that very same reason. Now, tell me the truth. Are you rich again now that we're home, or are we still putting on airs?"

"We're not poor," Mayport said. It was as far as he would go on that topic until things with the factory were more certain. "Money can't solve these problems anyway. I think we get on pretty well without it, even with needing to puff ourselves up in polite company. I mean to make you comfortable and safe. Real wealth is measured in time, and that I can't guarantee I will have with you."

"Why not?" Thiervy asked. "I'm not going anywhere."

"I had to catch up with you before," Mayport said. "If you run again, I might not be able to find you again. You're very good at being in places the maps don't mark."

"A map wouldn't have helped you find me," Thiervy said. "I wanted to be a pilot and an engineer so that I could sail the hell away from my father. I worked and studied harder than you can imagine. I forgot all about you, along with everything else I left behind."

Mayport shrugged off that cold confession. "You remembered quickly enough when I found you again. I think I can keep your attention better this time around. At least I know enough to realize it's worth keeping."

"What you did smacks of obsession, the same as your father's," Thiervy said. "His obsession became a legend, which is fine for a dead man. Do you want immortality, too?"

Mayport licked his lips, nervous of admitting the truth out loud. "I want to finish what I started. Reputation means nothing if a man has no standards. That's the same reason I came to find you. My tenacity is the only legendary thing about me, but it serves better than obsession."

"You'd better not hang your hopes on me making you a better man," Thiervy said. "If anything, the effect will go in the other direction."

"I'm willing to take the blame for anything you do," Mayport said. "What if I wanted you, right here and now?"

"I would say no." Thiervy gave an acid smile. "There are laws and they apply to us both."

"Try denying me and see what happens," Mayport said as he

stalked across the room. He straddled Thiervy's knees, pinning him to the chair. Thiervy stiffened and drew back. He glanced at the windows that let them look down on the factory floor. "Say no to me. Tell me to stop."

"We will go to jail or worse if we're caught," Thiervy said.

"Say no." Mayport leaned in and kissed Thiervy's brow.

"Stop," Thiervy rasped. He squirmed hard between Mayport's thighs. "You can't do this."

Mayport went on kissing Thiervy, light brushes of his lips over eyes and hair. If Thiervy meant to stop Mayport, all he had to do was stand up. Instead, his head rolled back and his eyes fluttered as Mayport tasted the quickening pulse at his throat.

Mayport feasted on Thiervy while his hands worked fast on buttons and ties. He pushed jacket, vest and shirt down off Thiervy's shoulders all at once in a tangle. Thiervy snarled as his clothes twisted tight around him. The sound of his protest was lost in another plundering, sucking kiss. Thiervy's tongue jabbed up into Mayport's mouth even as his hips hitched and pumped up away from the chair. Mayport stood up, wiped the sloppy kiss from his chin and hauled Thiervy up and over the desk.

"No," Thiervy rasped, tense all over in an instant. "I said stop, now I mean it!"

Mayport stepped back to ease open his own clothes. Thiervy didn't move, and after a few tense heartbeats, he relaxed again. Mayport smiled as he caressed the warm skin that had been bared across Thiervy's back and shoulders.

Thiervy might have stood up, walked out of the office and out of Mayport's life forever. Sometimes he did. This time he lay still after his little show of defiance and meekly parted his thighs as Mayport stripped his pants down to his knees.

Mayport took his time stroking the taunt curves of muscle that lay offered before him. Every inch of Thiervy's skin quivered with heat and need under his touch. Mayport lost himself in pulse and low sighs as his hands went though the familiar routine of taming his lover's passion.

When Mayport thrust in, Thiervy cursed his name, beyond any kind of control. Mayport only laughed and thrust in deeper still. "Shout at me all you like. Nobody will bother to see what the matter is. They're used to you cursing me and my father by now."

Thiervy groaned, and his whole body drew up tense once more. Mayport laughed as Thiervy's ass flexed and fluttered around his pulsing shaft. He held on tight as Thiervy bucked and struggled against him. Once, Thiervy could have muscled his way free. Now his rebellion was futile, and drew out into long, rocking strokes of his ass over Mayport's shaft.

Mayport seized Thiervy's cock as he leaned down to kiss and bite at the back of Thiervy's neck. Together they rode the tide as Thiervy struggled between resistance and yielding, not to Mayport, but his own desires. Mayport stiffened his spine and resisted the urge to thrust, withholding what Thiervy craved so desperately, waiting again for a moment of total surrender.

"Please, please!" Thiervy gasped out at last.

Mayport growled and let go easily, driving his cock with all his strength. His thighs trembled with the heat of Thiervy's ass, and he leaned in with all of his weight. Thiervy stuffed his fist against his mouth as Mayport bore down on the throbbing, sensitive spot buried deep within. His belly rippled and tensed, relaxed and then his whole body shuddered, beyond his control. He swallowed his own cries of delight as he poured out all his need and love, burning in the pleasure until he was left weak and gasping, safe in his lover's embrace.

When Mayport next opened his eyes, the candle was low on the spike. He helped Thiervy up and offered a sheepish smile. Thiervy looked triumphant, but contrived to pout as he righted his clothes. They collapsed together on the sofa, full of the covert satisfaction so familiar between them.

"Is this how it's to be?" Thiervy asked at last, trying to sound offended instead of eager. "Turning me over your desk? You're the kind of boss my mamma warned me about."

"I said I would take the blame. You work for me. Call for help. I'll confess." Mayport sat at his ease on the sofa and enjoyed a contented smile. "If I had a house to keep, would you even come? You've seen everything else I was left. You can't still imagine that his home was any better."

"Whatever it is, it's your home now," Thiervy said. "I thought that would have been sold before you got back to stop Cane."

"I am assured that he tried," Mayport said. "It was certainly mortgaged beyond all reason. This isn't the life I wanted for you. Say the word and we'll leave it all behind."

Thiervy sat bolt upright on the sofa. "We've got work to do, but I said I would help. Don't sound so lonely to me, Mayport Titus."

"I almost hoped you would give me an excuse to run away," Mayport said. "If you mean to stay, you have to put your signature to it. I can't be made to take all the responsibility. I don't have a hope of doing well on my own."

The candle sputtered out and left them in warm shadows filled with only each other.

Chapter Twenty-Three: Youth

Mayport crept up the back steps of the shop, certain the treads would break under his weight. His morning had been a confusing assault by the legal profession, conducted in Castor's office at high volumes. In all the blustering, he had spoken no more than five words. His sole occupation had been to sit still wearing a fine suit and a blank smile.

Costor thought he knew what Mayport wanted, and the pressures that would make them happen. Mayport had been surprised and dismayed to find himself the possessor of a tired and dirty Dutch-front shop-house on a quiet street between a butcher and millinery. He had managed to dare the steps, but could force himself no further.

Mayport might have postponed this homecoming if his nerves had not given him that moment of resistance. He worked the key, patient with a lock that had never enjoyed its lot in life. He shoved with all his strength and the door moved the few crucial inches that let him squirm inside.

Not much had changed. That came as both a sorrow and a relief. He sneezed as he stepped carefully along the narrow footpaths allowed through the storage room at the back.

He smelled rat or mouse, probably both and worse, but pressed on in the dusty half-light. By some primal instinct, his toes knew where to seek out the next bare patch of floor. On all sides stood piles and packets, cabinets and jumbled bits, all of it covered in inches of dust. Mayport let his eyes slide over the mess without taking in too-familiar details.

He made his way through what he assumed might still be a kitchen, and out into the tarnished remains of a shop. The glass he could still see was black. The floor and every surface was piled high with oddities. He sighed and turned his back on it all, fumbling his way back to the kitchen for the stairs.

The narrow, twisting steps had enough space for his toes between piles of papers and drifts of books. The upper landing was dim and crowded. Six doors stood shut, each with barricades of unknowables that prevented them being opened again.

He worked his way to the front of the building. A narrow strip of grimy window allowed a band of light to pierce the shadows. He knocked piles and stacks down until he could see, then clawed his way to the door he wanted. It creaked against the doorjamb, then popped free and swung in, bringing Mayport along on a slide of linen rags.

He gasped, shocked to find open space on the floor of a neatly-ordered room. The dust was thick on the little bed and desk. A rag rug lay before a hearth. Shelves were home to faded toys and a few childish volumes. Mayport took a hesitant step forward as something moved the coverlet of the bed.

He snatched at the corner of the blanket and pulled it back, then dropped it at once. A family of mice had made a nest of the bed. Mayport stumbled back against the wall and clapped his hand over the horrified sounds spilling past his lips. His legs went weak and he sank down to hide his face against his knees. He closed his eyes and tried to deny the facts of what his home had become.

"Titus! I heard a shout. Where are you?" Costor called out from below.

"My room," Mayport answered, trying to sound confident and failing completely. "Don't bother, you'll never find your way. I'll come find you at the club later."

"The devil you will!" Costor shouted back.

Mayport stayed where he was, marking Costor's progress by the sound of falling objects. He was cursing on every breath by the time he reached Mayport's door. He took in the mouse nest and Mayport's miserable crouch, and finally came to the end of his invective.

"What is this mess?" Costor demanded. "Is this what those creditors meant about this place being worthless?"

"It was like this before any creditors came along," Mayport said. He made himself stand, and busied his hands with his hand-kerchief. He tidied himself up and forced a smile. "My father would have kept things as as they were when I left. Cane tried to unload this mess, but who would want it? I would have saved my-self a great deal of trouble if I'd let them take the place."

Costor surveyed the scene in dismay. "Good God! Why didn't you stop me?"

Mayport smiled sheepishly. "You looked like you were having a good time."

Costor turned slowly, staring down the piles. "You would be surprised who might be interested in this sort of thing. Don't look so blue, my boy. I got you into this and thought I was doing you a favor. I won't leave you alone."

Mayport shrugged a couple of times, then ducked his head down low. "I hoped that this place would be better if I was gone. That's why I asked to go to school. I was always such a distraction. I shouldn't have let myself hope for anything of home."

"I think you'd better come out of here," Costor said. "The smell alone could drive a fellow crazy. I'll have someone come and see if this should be sold or burned."

"I appreciate the offer, but shouldn't I deal with all this myself?" Mayport asked, confused. "You always want me to take more responsibility. When I found the *Process*, she was buried under a mountain just like this. You've seen the warehouse and factory for yourself. Thiervy thinks it's mostly junk, and that's what this is."

Costor slowly shook his head, astounded. "I never imagined it could be like this. You say it was the same when you lived here? I thought that mess at the warehouse must be Cane's doing."

"Not a bit of it," Mayport said. "You know the whole truth about my father's fortune. Surely you wondered where it all went."

"Not here," Costor said, clearly offended on a fundamental level.

"Oh yes," Mayport said. "Do you remember how he used to send me clothes at school? The master had to write to him and explain about how children grew up. Otherwise, he might have sent me little boy's costumes forever."

"How embarrassing," Costor said, shaking his head once more. "No wonder you loved that place. Compared to here, it must have been a paradise for you."

"It was clean, and so was I," Mayport said. "If people had any idea about all this mess, they wouldn't have eaten his chocolate. If the Titus Chocolate Company has a secret, this is it."

"You're not trying to live up to your father's legend," Costor said. "This is nothing anyone would want to repeat."

"I have to do much better than he did, if we're to be a going concern," Mayport agreed. "We will succeed in all the ways he failed, including the defeat of this horror. I'll do it with my own two hands if I must. Now that I have a power, I'm putting a stop to this insanity."

"I wish you had told me what you intended from the start,"

Costor said. "I could have found you a little place, and had it ready."

Mayport laughed. "If I had known from the start how I meant to do any of this, I would have told you. I'm not keeping secrets. At least, I don't mean to be. I do not know how to begin, or how this might end. I only know that I will not give up, as he used to do to everything he began."

"We'll go in sloppy and come out sharp," Costor decided. "This doesn't have to go perfectly. We can even lose money on it, as long as it gets done. This place will be worth something then, so it will count as an investment."

"If you say so," Mayport said, and cast a despairing look around his room. "Don't let Thiervy see this, please. He's seen the warehouse. He won't set foot in here if he knows how bad it is now."

"Just as you say," Costor agreed in his gentlest tone. "Won't you come away with me now? You really do look like you've seen a ghost."

"I think I have," Mayport said. "Isn't that what happens when things aren't laid to rest?"

"Is the warehouse really the same as this?" Costor asked. "I thought it must all be things for... well... whatever it is you fellows get up to."

"I really don't know," Mayport said. "How could I possibly know? It must be done, and I want it done. I mean to do it, truly, I do."

Costor took him by the elbow and steered him out of the shophouse before he said another word. He leaned Mayport against the alley wall and frowned down at him, at his most stern at the first opportunity. "You are not to go back in there until it is clean and safe. I want to see the factory as well. Are you still living on that ship of yours?"

"Sort of," Mayport said, and shrugged a couple of times. "I got used to it. It's small, but it's clean and..."

"I want to see this for myself," Costor said. He nudged a little to get Mayport moving down the alley.

They went together through the cold and found Thiervy hard at work. He, at least, had managed something useful with his share of the surplus. He presented an inventory and state-of-repair list for the artifacts in the factory. He joined their expedition in the warehouse to keep an eye out for parts he still wanted. His chatter distracted Costor from Mayport's mood, and let him keep quiet.

Their stroll through the storage was enough to wind Thiervy up good and tight. "It's just like that place Cully holed up in! I wonder how many of these places there are?"

"Let's hope we've found the last of them," Mayport said, kicking at loose scraps in the dust.

"One in India, three in New Amsterdam," Costor swallowed hard. "It seems unlikely this is the end of it. There are a couple of other places down the seaboard. At least they're paid for."

"It will be the same," Mayport said, resigned. He forced a smile and threw his arms out wide. "Behold the wild and exotic treasures of Corey Titus, gentleman adventurer. Surely one of the world's wonders, and all mine."

"You might as well laugh. It's better than seeing a grown man cry," Costor said. "Titus said something about finding the Process in similar conditions. I'd like to see where the two of you are living."

Thiervy came up short, surprised by the demand. "Since when do you care how we live?"

"Now will be soon enough," Costor said. "I think I finally know why my grandfather gave me this account. It's a nightmare. Buy, buy, buy, never sell, even these parcels of land and useless buildings. He must have needed the youngest of us to outlive our client's obsessions."

"I owe him a great deal for his foresight," Mayport said. "I won't stand in your way, if you have any idea where to begin."

"Don't look so frightened," Costor said. "You're no the first young fellow to inherit a lot of useless junk. I only need you to tell me what you mean to use."

"There's not much here that can be of real use," Thiervy said. "I'll do my best to save what I can."

"Don't worry on that," Costor said. "We're not trying to save this crap. I'm trying to save these buildings before they're chewed to pieces around us. We should all be glad that our Mayport doesn't care a pin for any of it. There won't be much left when I'm done."

Chapter Twenty-Four: Distraction

Mayport admired the broad expanse of fine wood grain that was his desk. Costor's clerks had descended on the premises to secure the company paperwork once and for all. Thiervy had been seduced away by the prospect of small precision machines. Wanton destruction reigned on the factory floor. At last, Mayport felt like he was off to a good start.

The desk, office, factory, and warehouse were no longer his personal responsibility. Mayport locked the door to the office behind him, certain he would not lose another hour to its dim confinement. The crowds of people bustling through the courtyard paid him no attention. They were each intent on discovering some piece of his inheritance that might be carried away and made useful.

The Dutch Process alone was not for sale. She was waiting to be moved out to a proper home, which Thiervy had secured for her care. Mayport's narrowed horizons meant only good things for her future as a useful working vessel. If not for that fact, she might have been destined for the auction block along with the rest of Cory Titus' harlequin legacy.

Mayport had more pressing matters for his attention, no matter the phenomenal estimates some giddy gossips had made. His attention was all on his cocoa, and keeping his smile in place. He had expected no more than a cold toleration from his neighbors. He would have been grateful to be left alone with the few tools Thiervy had been able to provide.

Instead, proud little Bess wanted to show off her Costor's success. She would hear no arguments to the merits of the claim. Her order for parlor chocolate had to be satisfied, no matter how primitive his working conditions. Mayport could only wonder what she thought chocolate was, and hope his efforts didn't disappoint.

He found her snug in her father's expansive townhouse, arranging flowers in her mother's drawing room. The strange scent of hothouse blooms made the warm air thick with sweet perfume. "Don't tell me a word if you only have excuses. I've been as patient as I can be with you. Every young lady in town is dying to see me embarrassed of my Costor at last."

"That will never happen because of me," Mayport said. He produced a pair of hammered tin boxes. One was full of finely-ground sugar. The other was an offering of priceless cocoa powder. He had nothing to sell, and wouldn't have taken her coin if she'd offered it. "I could show one of your fellows how to blend this, if you like."

"Once, this home was so fashionable to serve cocoa," Bess said with a sniff. "Take it to the housekeeper if you've come early as your own delivery boy."

Mayport made his farewells and went out of her elegant home, glad to have avoided disgrace. He found Costor among his fellows at a little restaurant catering to New Amsterdam's flourishing legal trade. The regulars of the establishment were at full volume of severe advice.

Settled in at Costor's side, Mayport swallowed his jealousy with his wine. Through some arcane knowledge, Mayport's return meant Costor had the wherewithal to make his most heartfelt acquisition. He let go his stubborn determination to have a similar security in his own life, and settled his hopes on Costor's future happiness.

A little, stout fellow ran in and out with notes for Costor's eyes only. Though the wine flowed freely, Costor grew more and more serious as the luncheon hour waned. At last, he drew Mayport away from the crowd to a quiet table in a private room.

"You are not completely without property, so don't expect me to let you go," Costor said, at his most severe in an instant. "It's like you knew all along, that the whole estate was nearly worthless. How could you know, when even I am surprised at the losses?"

"How could I live in that place and truly expect riches?" Mayport asked back. "Hearing other people talk about him was like listening to fairy tales. Wasn't I a lucky boy, to have a funny, rich father who flew around the world making candy? I wondered how long people would go before they realized there wasn't any candy."

"Then you always knew there wasn't any coin either," Costor said. "I hope it's a comfort for you to know he wasn't a complete fraud. He spent more than he made, but not so very much more. I'm sure he meant for you to have everything he ever acquired. That was apparent in the orders he left."

"You're a breath away from apologizing for him," Mayport observed. "Don't embarrass yourself. As for his intentions, they were meaningless. Who would want or need all these things? If he had thought of me, I would have been left with capital and a reputation for diligence."

"You're earned both for yourself, so be satisfied," Costor said. "The bank itself is responsible for some of the damage. It seems we have come to some terms over our Mister Cane in all of this. I should have wondered why so few of your father's things were being sold to support you. Instead, I was suspicious of how much he wanted to dispose of. It was a drop in the bucket, compared to what was needed."

"No matter how his deficiencies came to be, he turned embezzler as quickly as circumstances allowed," Mayport said. "I don't know how he means to excuse himself."

"He may have been doing the very job he was hired for," Costor said. "Safeguarding the treasure."

"There was no reason to guard it from us," Mayport said.

"Of course there was a reason," Costor said, impatient. "It wasn't supposed to be sold, you silly creature. Your father meant for you to preserve his things exactly as you found them. That's what Cane was told, so he ought not have touched so much as a broken button."

"If he was stupid enough to take pay for such a ridiculous job, we can't be surprised at his complete idiocy," Mayport said. "I am disappointed over all this, but not a bit surprised. Let's leave it where it belongs, now that it's all settled."

"How can you be so calm?" Costor asked, bewildered. "You should have been at least a comfortable young man, if not a gentleman of leisure. You should feel robbed, at least a little."

"I never imagined as much for myself as other people did," Mayport said. "You did the same thing, even with the accounting right in front of you. Now, you look a little sober. Let's dress and go to Bess before your lawyer friends can dose you again."

Costor's home was a broad, deep, warm and sturdy warren full of thick, comfortable Achelies. Somehow, Costor's man could find coats and shined shoes in the chaos of all members setting out. Though Costor's intentions were the cause of the uproar, the man himself hardly figured in the day's preparations.

They made it out a side door and into a little tramp carriage to fetch Thiervy and Captain Cully. The two working men had a healthy laugh over their delicate transport. Once aboard, they were glad enough for its comforts in the afternoon traffic.

"Have you asked her father, or do you mean to make an end to your whole life tonight?" Cully asked Costor.

"I asked long since," Costor said, and blushed over the admission. "I had trounced another lad who insulted her ribbons. The only possible way to explain why was to make my confession."

"You must have been a child," Cully said, surprised. "How can your parents let her hold you to it?"

"They didn't," Costor grumbled. "I would have been engaged years ago, but it took this long to prove I knew my own mind. My father and hers insisted that I must make good in my portfolio. Our Mayport has been working as hard for this as I have."

"How could I dare to argue?" Mayport shrugged a couple of times. "Anyway, we're here. Don't let even your sisters slow you down this time. Our Bess has been Princess Patience long enough."

They squired him to the door and set him adrift among fawning relations. Cully went to make a place with the cards and brandy set. Thiervy wanted to avoid the dancing, and so they paid due admiration to the buffet together.

Thiervy sipped at his cup of French-style cocoa, and at last found something to admire of Mayport's craftsmanship. Bess had not been boasting when she spoke of past indulgences. Mayport took his time over his own cup, but drew more pleasure from the excitement around him. On every tongue was a compliment to the little treat he had provided for so auspicious an hour.

The assembly was called together for the formal announcement of Costor's intentions with Bess. The two made a formidable pair, each representing a form of strength unlikely to waver or wane. Mayport looked on, proud of his friend and comforted to know he could rely on such constancy.

Thiervy watched the little ceremony without comment. He urged Mayport out of the way as the couple was mobbed by well-wishers. "We'd better break for it before we get crushed. There's got to be a quiet spot somewhere."

They found a corner in a study overflowing with gamblers who wouldn't care about their conversation. Mayport let himself be sat at a window, and waited for Thiervy to bring drinks and cigars. He couldn't trust so serious an attitude on Thiervy even under the best of circumstances.

"Is something on your mind?" Mayport hazarded.

"Recently, you offered me something." Thiervy hesitated, then rubbed at his eyes like he was confused. "Hell, you're offered me all kinds of things. I don't know how to say which ones I changed my mind about."

"You've always turned me down," Mayport said. "It would help to be specific."

"I don't either always turn you down, but I don't mean to argue," Thiervy said. His shoulders went tense and stubborn as he stared hard, waiting to see if Mayport wanted to fuss anyway. "You can't just take the blame for me. I won't stand for it."

"Let's not get caught," Mayport suggested, suddenly mindful of their near company.

"I feel like I'm giving in to you, no matter what I do," Thiervy grumbled. "I won't work for you, nor accuse you like a... I won't! I should have said yes when you wanted me for your partner."

Mayport drained his glass and lingered over the smooth taste of his cigar. He leaned back in his seat, stretched his leg and let the toe of his shoe rest against Thiervy's. "Are you saying yes now? I want to be absolutely clear."

"Yes." Thiervy looked Mayport in the eye and smiled, half acceptance and half challenge just like always. "You're not the man I thought you were."

"In my case, that's a good thing." Mayport smiled back, then nodded at the room in general. "I simply can't imagine what has changed your mind."

"My mother," Thiervy said. "I have to get her away from here somehow. There's nobody else in the world who cares, except you. I finally realized, what I have with you is so much better than what she's suffering."

"Let's just carry her off, then," Mayport said with a smile. "You're a good son whether you like it or not. I want to be one, too. That might not be possible for me, and I understand that. If I can't, all my hopes hang on being good to you."

Chapter Twenty-Five: Median

Among his friends, Mayport suddenly found himself as the most reluctant of adventurers. Costor's promise to liquidate what could not be made useful was somewhat hampered by Thiervy's broad areas of curiosity. Mayport let them sort their own matters and kept his eyes on familiar things. He had his way in the long-neglected chocolate shop, a challenge he felt prepared to tackle with no idea how to finish.

He was left alone with empty counters, windows that had been left unwashed for most of his life, and floors that wouldn't have passed Cully's exacting standards. He armed himself with brooms and buckets, then rolled up his sleeves and got started. With Gasteau's example firmly in his mind, he cleaned until his muscles burned with raw vitality.

He was on his knees dealing with the rough wood floors when his holystone came within inches of wide skirts. He looked up, half-expecting little Bess come to scold over the state of the place. Instead, he saw where Thiervy had gotten his tall, strong good looks. Mayport smiled, and stood to offer his introduction.

"I had the thought that you may have been left on your own in certain respects," said Missus Thiervy. She looked neither at him, nor the mess around her, but seemed to gaze into some distant, beautiful world made for her eye alone. "Would it go too far if I saw about a staff for your kitchen and upstairs?"

"I would be grateful for any help at all," Mayport eagerly accepted. "Without a few ladylike hands, I'm afraid we'll lack quite a lot here."

"You seem to be doing without ever a gentleman's comfort," Missus Thiervy said with a soft, distracted smile. "You must let me make you home convivial, as much as business can allow."

"I enjoy a convivial business," Mayport said. "Cleanliness and order are the first priority, but after that you may have your way. Shall I conduct the grand tour?"

She favored him with a brittle smile and he hurried to lead the way. Though much had been done to improve the upstairs

quarters, he could only see what had not been done. He had taken
a large room at the back, over the kitchen. Thiervy preferred the
broad windows facing the street at the front of the second floor.

In between lay the hall that had once been a canyon of discards.
Now, doors stood open on rooms bare of any furnishings. Costor
had disdained it all, but had not thought to offer a solution about
choosing appropriate replacements.

The dining room below was but halfheartedly furnished. He
and Thiervy preferred to dine at the little stalls that stood on corners in all directions. Missus Thiervy gave a disappointed sigh over
the little home kitchen, then raised her chin in a familiar, stubborn
expression.

"I shall do what must be done, for decency's sake," she said.
"Perhaps I was too quick to speak of entertainment. A young man
like you has no idea about such things."

"I know what any gentleman should: pay the bills you send to
my fellow at the bank," Mayport said.

Missus Thiervy gave a short, sharp laugh. "You would do better
than some men, if you can do that. I'll try your boasting only a
little, but I have expectations about my child. Living in squalor is
not among them, if it can be helped."

"I'll take any help at all to make him happy," Mayport said.
"Without him, I won't make it to the summer. All I know to do
for him is keep him in tools and sailcloth."

"Is that what you're doing?" she asked. "Keeping him?"

"No, of course not," Mayport lied with total sincerity. "He'll
be out of port again with the season, if not sooner. If he wasn't
here, he'd be holed up at a port house and no use to anybody. I'm
not ignorant of his vices, but neither will I leave him to struggle
against them all alone."

"Don't mention to my son that I was here. Let him think that
you've managed all by yourself," she said. "I doubt he'll wonder
to ask."

Mayport nodded, suddenly awkward under her languid gaze.
She had no more instructions, and made her farewells without taking much notice of him particularly. He stood amazed as she
picked her way down the rickety kitchen steps as if drifting along
just above them. Her violet silk skirts disappeared around the corner of the building. The dull street hardly seemed fair enough to
have recently been the backdrop for her elegant presence.

Mayport sniffed the air to catch the lingering scent of her

perfume. Without that trace, he might have dismissed the en-
counter as his own vivid imagination. Despite his reputation, he
was not accustomed to sudden, secret visits and plans.

His attention after was absorbed with indulging his every
childish wish about the little shop-house. He relied on Gasteau's
example in the matter of the workshop. He felt no need to innovate, when his circumstances were so far beneath the standard.

As predicted, Thiervy never thought to ask how his room became furnished and his wardrobe filled. All of his attention was
on the battles he fought with Costor in the warehouse and factory.
It was all Mayport could do to make Thiervy understand that the
workshop was ready for his attention.

"When did you have time to do all this?" Thiervy asked, astonished by gleaming glass, brass and marble. "What in the world
could it possibly need?"

"Haven't you been getting ready?" Mayport asked back. "We
talked about this weeks ago. I need small batch machines. You said
you could make them."

"I can," Thiervy said, but sounded uncertain. "I will. When do
you want them?"

"Yesterday," Mayport snapped. "Have you nothing but fool
with rust and dust all this time?"

"Well, Costor's selling everything," Thiervy said. "If I don't
claim a thing particularly, off it goes."

"That's what I asked him to do, or his fellow more likely,"
Mayport said. "I thought you understood your share, and here I
am disappointed. How long must I wait?"

Thiervy looked embarrassed. "I haven't even begun. You acted
like you had a lot of work to do here first. I never expected you to
be ready so fast. You might have told me I was running out of time."

"You live here," Mayport said, beyond all patience. "There's
nothing in that warehouse worth keeping if you can't do your
work. I hope this will put an end to your idiocy with that mess
and do what you're fed and housed for!"

"How can you sell everything you have without even looking
at it?" Thiervy asked. "Are you so spoiled that all your father's treasure means nothing to you?"

"They meant nothing to him!" Mayport shouted. "Just like me,
and Gasteau's father, and the rest of the world. He didn't get all
this stuff because he wanted or needed it. He liked anything he
could buy. None of it means anything to me."

Thiervy was only incensed at Mayport's careless attitude. "There's some very nice things, useful and valuable. You're just throwing it all away for what pennies you can grab."

"Wrong. I'm getting pennies because of Costor," Mayport said. "I would have thrown it into the harbor weeks ago. We have bigger problems than that useless nonsense. Now, what about my mill and press? Can you really do it, or was that nothing but big talk?'

Thiervy stood shocked into silence by Mayport's demands. At last he had the grace to look embarrassed, and bowed his head. "I don't mean to ignore my work again. I don't know how you can let it all go without looking. I think it's fascinating."

"I don't have time to be fascinated," Mayport said. "My father didn't, but he let himself be anyway. I'm ready to start work as fast as you can keep your promise. Do you really prefer to moon over his oddities instead?"

Thiervy kept making annoyed remarks, but finally understood that Mayport meant business. When he was sure that all of Thiervy's attention was on their immediate need, he went to the warehouse to survey his stock. The cacao was fragrant in the dusty air. His worry was that it had never been in robust supply and might never be.

Costor's man came to offer an inventory of all the things Thiervy wanted kept aside for curiosity's sake. Mayport struggled against his frustration once more. "This is ridiculous. It's like a disease that can't be cured. Did he say what he means to do with all these things?"

"He said they could be useful somehow," the clerk said. "We could take another shed where we stowed your boat if you mean to rent this place."

"I won't take on extra expenses to eat up what little profit we may gain from this place," Mayport said. He signed the documents and looked around the factory floor once more. "Perhaps I lack ambition."

The clerk laughed in a quiet, sincere whisper. "I wouldn't worry about that if I were you, sir. What you lack in ambition you make up for in tenacity."

Mayport stood in the courtyard and looked again. He saw bare floors and open doors where before there had only been chaos. Whatever ambitions had driven Cory Titus, he had lost sight of his goal. To Mayport an imperfect and small success would be more valuable than clinging to such spectacular failures.

He walked through the streets of New Amsterdam, wishing wholeheartedly for a more friendly climate. He might have gone home and waited for the clerk's reports, but followed the impulse to go look for himself. He found the *Process* under Cully's care, stowed in a more dignified fashion than her recent hideaway.

"I wondered if you'd fallen off the earth with that frog of yours," Cully said over a warm handshake. "Let's get coffee on the right side of you."

Mayport sat gratefully at Cully's ever-bountiful table. "I think Thiervy has caught a touch of my father's fever. I've put him to work in the shop, but you know it won't work for long."

"This weather won't last forever," Cully said, patient as a stone. "Quick as spring, we'll carry him south again and get his mind on being useful."

Mayport smiled in gratitude. "You're right of course, but I can't go along next time. His dithering has put me weeks behind. Time is the most expensive commodity, and that's what he wasted."

"You can trust him to go and come back again," Cully said. "He wouldn't abandon the *Process* for any temptation."

"She carries temptation enough to keep his attention." Mayport grinned as Cully shifted uncomfortably on his chair. "What's your game? You're made Thiervy and I wonder more than once, but you've never been that bold."

Cully blustered over Mayport's sudden interrogation, then settled to red-faced muttering. "You will insist on imagining that you're so very original. Do you think your father went his whole life without a friend such as your Thiervy?"

"I..." Mayport hesitated. "I never thought about it."

"Try." Cully crossed his arms over his chest and put on what he probably thought was his patient smile. "I can't tell you to leave that boy alone without being a hypocrite. I'm not sure I mean to leave him alone myself."

"Don't restrain yourself on my account." Mayport took a few more pickled olives and studied Cully anew. "He'll want to be done with me over this workshop before long. At least I know you'll bring him back home where he belongs."

"You seem pretty sure that home means you," Cully said.

"It does," Mayport said, all confidence. "He'll make you think whatever you want. I don't warn you against enjoying it. I only say, don't believe it."

"If he's such a good liar, how can you trust him?" Cully asked.

"Sometimes he talks like you're the Devil's own man."

Mayport laughed, and then took more wine. Part of him was bitter and jealous over what he imagined to be inevitable. The rest of him was all tired resignation. He couldn't change what he needed, or the price he would pay to get it. His only hope was to find a way to forgive what could not be avoided.

Chapter Twenty-Six: Groundless Confidence

Thiervy had the last laugh over Mayport's scattered attention when he finally ordered Mayport to abandon his grindstone until something better had been devised. Missus Stevens and her endless row of daughters declared Thiervy the genius of the age and forgave all his faults. Thereafter, Mayport bore the weight of their suspicions.

He was judged a dullard for, though he was male, he admitted total ignorance of Thiervy's profession. His own work was close to the Stevens's area of expertise. Again, he being male, they were entitled to give their opinions. Foremost among his sins was want of a wife.

The peace of his house might have asked for him to yield, but his conscience could not let him take that cowardly if comfortable escape. Once, he had borne the jeering predictions of a confident young Gasteau. He had known all the ways a man like Mayport could fail in his ambitions. At the time, he had indulged in the luxury of imagining all the merely proper French pessimism.

Mayport, banished from the workshop at home, spent his fretting times down at the docks. All his worry focused on the whalers as they came and went. Their smell was all rancid destruction, and the men toiled on in misery. Mayport took in their fate and wondered if he had the nerve to join their hardened number.

The afternoons he spent working the press. He began to find the textures and scents he desired, though he had very little material to work with. The precious oil came in streaks and traces, not at all like the robust cocoa butter of Chef's kitchen. Though each effort brought him closer, he still fell far short of the standard.

Certainly, he could not create the filled cookies and masterly tarts that Gasteau thought of as mere practice. He contented himself with the local favorite, though its true creation was far beyond his meager skill. The local ladies were forgiving of quality, for lack of any better options. He took the various M. Stevenses as his trustworthiest judges.

Though he was offering his house help the most expensive delicacies in the city, he got nothing but the rough side of their notions. Every cup was rejected until even the youngest accused him of ignorance on French chocolate as if she were the next Miss Bess. He was forced to the conclusion that their Dutch idea of French chocolate rather differed from Chef's.

Mayport then had to stalk the valets at Bess's parties until he found the fellow who manned the cocoa pots. His hawk-eyed study of the task nearly sent the fellow mad, but Mayport had no choice. Without witnessing the process himself, he couldn't know what the clever ladies of New Amsterdam had looked on as improvement. To his surprise, their cocoa was milk, sugar and air, with chocolate treated as any other rich and bitter spice.

He let himself forget all considerations but satisfying his kitchen girls. Despite his promise to Missus Thiervy, he refused all social invitations. Even Costor's appeals were heard with only half an ear. Mayport was glad that his friends didn't question his new obsession, for he could not have easily explained his fascination.

There was a precision to preparing each delicate cup that he hadn't previously appreciated. Gasteau had tried to influence his attention to detail. It was Missus Stevens' laughter that finally made him focus. All the charms of France would not help him until he had mastered what the matrons thought of as chocolate.

That type of detail had been the sort of thing Chef Gasteau could not give him. In the proud Frenchman's style, he went through the world teaching all of God's creatures to appreciate his work. Mayport had been taught a different kind of charm, in a more homey place. He worked diligently to adapt his skills and adopt the native customs.

When at last his offering won Missus Stevens' prim smile, he smiled back with real amusement. Never would she of the stiff mourning bonnet accept any comparison between herself and a half-naked madam on a primitive beachhead. Nevertheless, Mayport wished that the two ladies might somehow be introduced.

Thiervy accepted his cup and Mayport's achievements with the carelessness that came of expectation. His own promises remained half-realized, though his effect on the workshop was extreme. His notion was to drive a wheel of stone at terrifying speeds, with flowing water to keep the works cool. Mayport looked on the prototype with real misgivings.

"I need more time to make it safe," Thiervy apologized. "This could get hot, crack an axle, who knows what else until we try it? I won't risk you that way, so please be patient."

"I'm not the impatient one," Mayport said. "Bess and her set want things their own way. Do you imagine I can make them sit still forever? Their fathers will fund my rivals just to shut them up."

"Go out and be charming, then. They're desperate to wait on you, no matter the pretense." Thiervy frowned at his creation. "It will be ready when it's done. I can't change that, so they'll have to be good and sit still."

With that much bad news, Mayport had to go face Costor and the rest of the Achelies. He was no stranger to their dinner table. With his recent frustrations, he felt that chilling change had set in among their various opinions.

He was lucky to be held in any regard at all by the Achely family. That they overlooked much in his character told him that his particular fortune would not make a difference in their warm and hearty home. Their help was all for his benefit, out of a good-hearted kindness not often found in their profession. Yet for all their generosity, he had seen them let proud men suffer for their own folly.

After dinner, he sat down with Costor and his brothers. Over cigars and brandy, he made a clean breast of his misgivings. "Thiervy can do the job, only he hasn't. He's built something as impractical as the *Process* herself. I don't think he grasps the urgency of our situation."

"Give him credit for making progress at all," Costor advised. "He's the only man in town who has any idea at all what you mean to do. Are you really risking your health down at the port every day? I've heard many a fellow ask."

"I don't know if it's every day," Mayport admitted.

"Thiervy isn't much of a problem if you're being foolish," Costor said.

"I'm not being foolish at the port. I'm thinking. There's nothing else for me to do until Thiervy has a result," Mayport said. "I've never had reason to doubt him before. Maybe that warehouse full of junk did something to his reason."

"He's nothing like what your father was," Costor said, struggling to repress a smile. "If he's getting anything done, it's with the junk he saved. He hasn't drawn a penny from the clerk."

Mayport bit down on a dozen arguments and made himself

nod. Costor's brothers were all nodding along to his advice, too. Their little meeting had less to do with Mayport's plight than Costor's future. That fate was vital to more lives than just Mayport's.

"As to the port, I like watching the whalers come and go," Mayport said, trying to be reasonable with Costor's worry. "I've stood worse weather on a deck. Don't be such a nelly, I won't come to any harm."

"Suppose you did," Costor said. He cleared his throat and glanced sidelong at his eldest brother. "Have you any instructions that should be written down?"

"Just give it all to Thiervy," Mayport said, and shrugged.

"In lump sum?" Costor laughed outright. "Is he to be your sole beneficiary? You can't be an embarrassment to fiduciary responsibility anymore if you die rich. I suppose I can't stop you from failing your filial duties. You have no practical experience with them."

Mayport smiled over Costor's disappointment in him. "If I have responsibilities, they'll make themselves known long before my health wanes. As to long-lost relations with greedy intentions, you must protect Thiervy against them. I can't imagine who might have a claim on me."

"You should stop imagining and think," said Benton Achely. Again, the brothers exchanged a sort of sly amusement. "Some relations come at birth, and others are acquired. Until recently, we were charged with protecting you from any such influence."

"Carry on with your job then," Mayport said. "Who would arrive at this late stage?"

"Your partner's mother must certainly be able to rely on you," Benton said, very final. "At least, there's a suggestion that she might. Would you prefer to deny your duty to her, or bow to tradition in this small way?"

"Oh," Mayport said. He squirmed on his seat, feeling every Achely eye burning the truth from him, as they had always been able to do. "Well, she offered to arrange the house help, for Thiervy, you see. I said to send me the bills, and hope she did. If you're getting other bills from her, pay them by all means. I doubt her worthless husband forgives a penny's frivolity in his household expenses."

"There, you see?" Costor crowed, and turned a proud smile on his protege. "You wouldn't begin to understand what these fiends imagined. You've done a poor, lonely woman a kindness, and long before any of us thought to do it."

Mayport shivered, wondering if his offhand trust had carried more meaning than the moment implied. "I meant what I said, Mister Achely. If I have a duty, I want it done, with bells on and ad infinitum. I'm certain you're more than able to attend this matter in full."

Days later, as he stood watching the whalers come and go, he had time to wonder what secrets were being kept from him about gentle, elegant Missus Thiervy. At last he resolved to ask the most reliable source in all of New Amsterdam. He brought home a bag of apples for Missus Stevens and sat down to hear her wellspring of gossip.

"That Thiervy came into port like he owned the place," she said, dismissive as only old blood can be. "For a while, he did his best to make it so. The neighbors thought he must want for a bride, but six months on a child arrived. That was the first we saw of his sons here."

"But his mother," Mayport protested. "Why would she send a little child alone?"

"The wife was brought later," Missus Stevens said, frowning at the interruption. "After another boy, oh, it was two or three years before she set foot in this town. She wasn't shy, either. She thought she'd married a widower, but others knew different and said so. The boys came long before Missus Thiervy, and I never did see a veil clapped on her."

"I'm not sure you're making anything clearer," Mayport said.

"Why, she was too young and fair to be mother to those who'd come before," Missus Stevens said. "She was so pretty a Confederate belle, we were astonished she would have come north for such a man. It was nigh on eighteen months before your friend came along, so you have to think... well! She was heartbroken until he came to give a little light. After he was sent to school, her little candle went right out."

Mayport thanked her, and left her to her apples. Costor had imagined him better than he had really been, but the end was all the same to Missus Thiervy. Still, Mayport smiled over the knowledge of this new duty. It added a rosier color to the warmth he felt when Joseph Thiervy was near.

Chapter Twenty-Seven: Simplicity

Mayport's housekeepers were never happier than the day Thiervy finished the roasting oven. No longer was their kitchen invaded by low commerce. Their home was quiet only when they had things their own way, so Mayport was just as proud.

He lost himself in the daunting task of roasting all the stock he had left. More than once he longed for even one of Gasteau's sons to help him. The one he missed the most would have been no help at all with the task at hand. Mayport wished for him just the same.

As he worked with the oven, he admired Thiervy's cleverness. His design had ended up somewhere between a Franklin potbelly and Gasteau's massive brick edifice to precision baking. It was small but Mayport wasn't baking dozens of loaves each day. For his purposes, the style was perfect, but he wondered over some of the features.

He might have moved the entire contraption, if Thiervy's crew had helped him with the lifting. That was startling enough, but the theme continued as more machines were prepared. Compared to the magnificent but useless equipment of the factory, Thiervy create mechanical artwork in miniature simplicity.

Somewhere along the way, steam power had been abandoned in the workshop. Even with that nod to safety, the new designs were wonders of productivity. As Mayport learned to operate his new toys, be began to suspect Thiervy of real genius. He had imagined that Thiervy paid no attention to Mayport's efforts. In each new contraption he found evidence that Thiervy had considered every detail of his labors.

The mill was a stone and brass sculpture of balance and elegance. Mayport could pour in roasted beans and work a treadle to turn the millstones within. He could produce a batch of mash for the press in hours and still have the strength of his arms to rely on.

The press took his efforts to extract cocoa butter beyond what even Gasteau's kitchen could achieve. With unexpected riches on his hands, he had to make quick arrangements to store the precious oil. At last he understood the sheer number of glass jars that had been found in the warehouse, but too late to save them.

"There, I knew you would sell something we needed later," Thiervy said with a triumphant little laugh.

"That's a sight better than buying two thousand things we didn't need in the first place, so be proud of me," Mayport said. "I have the coin to buy them. Costor isn't grumbling over the expense, and he would."

"At least we know why your father had jars in the first place," Thiervy said.

"You sure changed your mind about my father once you got your feet on the ground," Mayport said, annoyed. "Maybe we should go for a spin on the *Process* so you can remember how brilliant he wasn't. You made those jars useful, not his having them."

Thiervy had the grace to look embarrassed. "If I understand him better, maybe I'll figure out what you're so mad about."

Mayport shook his head, tried to swallow his own laughter and failed. "What am I so mad about? My father was this kind of fool and coward, and you don't know why I'm angry?"

"Well!" Thiervy stepped back, surprised. "Costor wasn't worried about the expense of jars, but he does worry on you. What do you do out there watching those whalers? Everyone knows you do it."

"I think about you," Mayport said, though he tensed all over from admitting the truth. "You can't stand on the ground and be sane. I could give you a good life here, but I think it would make you crazy."

"I'm not bound to go whaling while you work," Thiervy said, all contempt. "I've got work enough here to keep me busy a while."

Mayport patted the side of his excellent new press and smiled proudly. "You don't mean for this to stay here when the *Process* flies again. You'll have a clever way to bring it along right and tight. I bet some of these fixtures are to make it run without me pushing."

"You'll need it," Thiervy said, as if this were the most obvious thing in the world. "Smaller is better, you said so yourself. Capacity can be..."

"I see my pilot means to take me with him when he goes." Mayport crossed his arms over his chest. "Were you going to invite me, or put me in with the luggage?"

"I thought you would want to go," Thiervy said. "Why would

you want to stay here? You didn't want to come back, but had to. You can go, any time you like. Of course, I know I have to go. That's exactly what I want to do."

Mayport looked around the bare bones of the shop, and breathed in the smell of Missus Stevens idea of a simple dinner for two hardworking young fellows. The austerity of life aboard the *Process* could only contrast with the homey new atmosphere they had created. Only to Mayport did their peaceful domesticity seem a lie.

Thiervy reached out and seized Mayport by the shoulder. "I don't mean to lose this. You've given up more in two months than most men ever own. If this is the one thing you want to keep, I'll help you."

"It's not this place I want to keep," Mayport said, leaning into Thiervy's touch. "There's custom here, folk who know what to do with what I sell. That's got a value of its own that I can't get in most places."

"Then leave this here, and some fellows to run it," Thiervy said, still confused but hunting solutions. "I don't see why these women should mean you can't go where you like."

"I still have to learn the best ways to use these machines, before I can tell a man what he should do," Mayport said. "These traps of yours don't run themselves, and can't taste for me. There's more to what I do than you've imagined, much as you obviously know."

"I'll go on to finish the *Process* then," Thiervy said. "I can make better plans, now that I know what she's facing. We have to be ready when the season turns, whether you sail with us or not."

"Don't imagine that I mean to send you away," Mayport said. He drew Thiervy closer and claimed a kiss, despite a lack of closed doors to protect them.

Mayport kept regular hours like a proper shop keep after that, to prove he meant what he said. Thiervy ran the crew on ship time. To keep peace and company, they abandoned Costor's set to their indulgent hours. Their labors were made to fit men who worked merely because he chose to do so.

Mayport's little shopfront shone bright from Missus Stevens diligence. She made it up like a salon, having only Missus Thiervy's ideas of business to please. Having no better solutions, Mayport bowed to sheer force of personality.

With such a welcoming storefront, Mayport was soon entertaining customers from the better kitchens in the city. As a lowly proprietor, he hardly expected to host the ladies who would eventually offer the fruit of his labor at their tables. He was gratified by the eager patronage, and proud of making an honest profit.

He fought the urge to tuck the profits away for future need. Some part of him wanted to keep a little treasure safe, though that was one thing he could not do. More troubling was his sudden resistance against suiting himself instead of what his fellows expected. Though he tried time and again to make himself deposit all with Costor, the errand remained undone.

He let himself ignore this new-found anxiety. Over time, he was surprised and delighted with its evolution into a little handful of silver. His experience with coin went in the opposite direction. Had anyone known of his private delight, they would have thought it more fitting of a pirate's chest.

Costor came by to marvel over their wonders on his own, and still Mayport said nothing of his purse. The young banker was too distracted by Thiervy's inventions to wonder or ask. "I had no idea you were so far along in production. We should have had an event to celebrate your grand opening."

Mayport rubbed at his eyes, tired by the mere thought of a gala fete. "It's more than word got out and cooks came to find me. The last thing I need now is more publicity. They're buying up my cocoa and sugar as fast as I can blend it. My stock has to last until spring or the doors will close forever."

Costor folded his hands and frowned at Mayport. "Sell your stock out, crazy creature. Don't argue with me. Do as I say, as fast as you can."

Mayport shifted uncomfortably, full of anxiety he couldn't ignore. "What if I never can get any more?"

"Then I'll force you to retire and be a gentleman, as I have always threatened," Costor said, annoyed. "You can't go on imagining that you're anonymous and unremarkable. Dozens of ships are insuring themselves to repeat your feat come the spring."

"Let them try," Mayport said. "It's simple enough if a fellow is brave, strong and crazy. If one can do better than me, I'll pay him to do it and leave me at home."

"What if the men who can do it better are Cully and Thiervy?" Costor asked. "Can you send them and stay here where you belong?"

Mayport was so surprised, he laughed loud and hard. "Of course. Thiervy wants me to go with him. He's done everything he can to make me, except ask."

"Then let's be finished with this talk of you failing out of the merchant class," Costor said. "I can offer you good news, in one respect. Most of the shippers mean to bring sugar and rum. You're the only fellow who will risk his life for cacao."

"Maybe I'm part French," Mayport said. "The Frenchies down southern way are doing all they can to bring in every bean they can find, cacao and vanilla both."

"Interesting," Costor said, in the tone that implied he meant to make a great deal of money very soon. "You're doing well. Don't be so afraid to succeed."

Mayport knew he would get better advice if he were more honest about his worries, but kept his secrets anyway. The drawing rooms of New Amsterdam asked only for his cocoa powder. They might not have known what his precious cocoa butter was, even if he offered it. Though he understood the rarity, the jars of oil were useless to him.

There was one person who could have made something of what Mayport had created. He had no idea what delicacy might come of the venture. He recalled Gasteau's dreamy description of long-ago days when he mastered the art of blending a peculiar English recipe for something solid and fascinating with milk and vast amounts of cocoa butter.

He had waxed poetic about its delights, and lamented at length the loss of such rare ingredients. Mayport mounted the treadle of the grinder and set the millstones turning once more. It was all very well to dream of Gasteau's creations, but the making of them would take all the labor he could give.

He focused once more on the work he had set himself. The smell of cacao permeated his hair and clothes, like a ubiquitous perfume. When the sun set, he lit the lamp and went on grinding. He could not allay his fears, but could escape them in long hours of steady effort. As his muscles took on their familiar burn, he set his focus on a new, unattainable dream.

Chapter Twenty-Eight: Hypocrisy

Mayport woke slowly, stretching his toes out to test the weather beyond the covers. The coming of spring made rising an uncertain thing. He might have met a humid morning, or a river of half frozen mud, depending on how the winds blew.

The kitchen below him was quiet. Missus Stevens had been persuaded to keep Sunday for herself. She had bragged of the privilege to other ladies of her profession. He gave her no reason to think he was generous out of purely selfish motivations.

He rose and dressed for Sunday services. Thiervy was already in the kitchen raiding the broken meats when Mayport came to get his share. "You look like a young man going courting."

"Am I not?" Mayport asked. "I will walk with you to church and sit beside you as well. Your family knows all about me and have encouraged me in their own way. Do you refuse to be escorted?"

"You could make anything sound honest and sincere," Thiervy grumbled. "Have you no shame?"

"Of you? None at all," Mayport said with a sniff. "Nothing could make me. Not even your scolding."

Thiervy laughed, but it was a nervous sound. Mayport almost suggested playing hooky from church. He could easily imagine Thiervy's outrage, not from his own piety, but because of what he imagined other people would think. With that being the case, he did what he had promised to do and never showed so much as a blink.

The church was crowded and the vestibule slick with mud from so many marching boots. They took seats with the other bachelors and put on expressions of stern reserve. Mayport ignored the sermon, and instead surveyed his superiors in the rows toward the front.

From Costor's gossip, Mayport knew of secrets the merchant families concealed. There were few fellows left who could claim total innocence and honesty. Without being told, he knew their shield from the law was made of diamonds and gold.

He wanted to sneer at their hypocrisy, but knew he could no longer sit in smug judgment. Despite opportunity and instruction, he was compelled beyond all reason in the matter of Joseph Thiervy. His only comfort was a cold one: the knowledge that his father had been similarly inclined.

He turned that nugget of information in his mind while the minister droned on. He assumed that Captain Cully himself had once been intimate with Corey Titus. He could see the attraction, but wondered at how things had ended.

His feelings toward Cully were a knot of curiosity, respect, and shame. Regardless of the personal matters, a man like Cully ought never to have been abandoned in a garbage dump. Nevertheless, Corey Titus had done just that, and left nothing to show that he intended anything different.

Mayport knew that the resumption of salary and the restoration of *The Dutch Process* was inadequate. Worse, he could offer no better. His guilt and regret were not enough to make him reduce Thiervy's fortune to make up for his father's failed responsibilities.

Without real knowledge, he tried to learn from his father's mistakes. That endless study had been the sole occupation of his Sunday morning. He kept his thoughts far away from God, and assumed the consideration was mutual.

He fixed his gaze on the back of Costor's head and let his bitter jealousy creep out from the hidden place in his heart. By some luck or curse, he had to watch Costor and Bess be celebrated at the least opportunity. He dared not even smile kindly at Thiervy in public, though he despised his cowardice. Discretion had no valor, when his every instinct was to stake his claim in a final fashion.

If he had been any other man, he would have dragged Thiervy back home directly following services. Certainly, the proper place for a young gentleman was at the patriarchal table once the bell had rung. He looked on as a polite squabble broke out over which household had the claim on Costor and Bess.

At the height of the ruckus, Mayport and Thiervy drifted away into the slow, sleepy exodus of the faithful. Bright sunshine and fresh air came as a real blessing after being penned in for so long. Mayport strolled down the street, away from the genteel neighborhoods. Thiervy hesitated, then came away after him.

"Shouldn't we tag along with the Achelies?" he asked, his old anxiety putting an edge in the question. "You know this isn't safe."

"You certainly look like you're up to something," Mayport said. "Stop skulking along, froggie. Nobody knows what you mean to do unless you tell on yourself."

"I have never known a creature like you," Thiervy said, exasperated. "Men of similar persuasion, I have known in plenty. Not one has ever dared the way you do."

"You have terrible taste in men." Mayport paused to regard himself in a warped window reflection. "Still, I find your attention flattering. How can I not feel admired, when for my company alone do you abandon your machines?"

"What will you really do if we're caught?" Thiervy asked.

"I will put out my pistol and kill the bastard," Mayport said with a laugh. "Someone would have to break into the house to catch us, these days."

"Some might wonder why we live as we do," Thiervy said.

"Sometimes, I wonder. I hate that hallway between us every night. It's enough to make me miss school, when I could be closer to you if I wanted," Mayport said. "For answers, these are wintering quarters and you'll abandon them when your spring voyage begins. I assume you mean to lie. I only say 'Joseph Thiervy is my partner.' I like the way it sounds."

"Even that isn't the whole truth," Thiervy said. "You're a good liar, for such an honest man."

Mayport laughed, and was glad when Thiervy gave in and smiled as well. They were being very foolish, carrying on as though they were still schoolboys and invincible. Soon enough, Thiervy would spook and shy off of their constancy together. Mayport encouraged their hooky-playing from propriety with everything he had.

The weather was fine enough for the hawkers to line the square in front of City Hall. From them he got a bag of roasted nuts, and honeyed fruit on sticks. Thiervy chose roasted sweet potatoes and sausage on a bun. Thus fortified, they made their way home sharing bites of their treats along the way.

The house was still and devoid of Stevenses. Therefore, there was nobody to be shocked when Mayport seized Thiervy on the stairs and claimed a kiss. Thiervy made a surprised noise, then yielded as Mayport leaned in with all his weight.

The scent of Thiervy's skin drove Mayport mad in an instant. He bit and sucked at Thiervy's mouth while he hurried to loosen the cloth at Thiervy's throat. He licked the still smooth skin at

Thiervy's jaw, then buried his mouth against Thiervy's pulse. He bit and sucked hard, savoring the heat and that particular flavor which came only after he'd made his mark.

"Wait, I don't always keep my collar closed," Thiervy said, a moment too late and already breathless.

"You'll have to now," Mayport said, very pleased with himself. "I know who you have to show off to, and mean to deny him everything I can."

Thiervy pressed his leg between Mayport's thigh, rubbing too hard at Mayport's cock. He'd thought he was already up for this, but his shaft writhed with aching vitality at that one touch. Thiervy leaned in slowly, and whispered against Mayport's ear. "Are you jealous?"

"Yes," Mayport growled, an honest sinner to the last.

"Show me." Thiervy bent his knee and stooped down to wrap his arm under Mayport's ass. All that muscle slid between Mayport's legs as he was drawn up to ride about Thiervy's hips. He held on and resumed his tasting, as comfortable as he had always been with gallant kidnap.

Thiervy carried him up the stairs and down the hall to his own room. He flung his cargo on the bed. Without hesitation, Mayport began stripping out of his Sunday best. Thiervy stood with his arms crossed over his chest, watching the hurried show.

Thiervy shook his head and chuckled. "I don't know why you still surprise me. You were always like this, from the first day I met you."

"That's not true," Mayport said. "I knew you for a long time before you found out I was like this."

"And you truly do not mean to change?" Thiervy asked. Mayport couldn't tell if he was teasing or not. All of his attention was on Thiervy's broad hands moving from buttons to buckles, just as fast as Mayport's had been. "Aren't you afraid I might hurt you one day? It's not like I never have."

"No," Mayport said. "I'm not afraid of it."

Thiervy left his trousers abandoned, bundled up around his boots, but brought his belt along. He stood over Mayport and his smile turned hungry. "Do you remember how I used to like it? Would you still..."

Mayport reached up and found a grip on the bed, then lay still as Thiervy wrapped the warm, soft leather belt around his limbs. Once the loops were tight, he bucked hard, testing his weight against the frame. Already, Thiervy was on him, making an oily mess of his cock and balls.

Thiervy planted one hard, broad hand on his chest, and leaned in while he straddled Mayport's hips. Mayport groaned as his cock was seized and pressed firmly against Thiervy's ass. He struggled to draw breath and lay still for the one moment Thiervy needed to pin him down completely.

He tried to buck his hips, but was just as helpless as he had always been to Joseph Thiervy. Wild cries poured out of him as Thiervy began to ride in long, slow, tormenting strokes. Thiervy grinned down at Mayport, eyes burning with the kind of passion that had only one name.

Mayport answered that feral smile by thrusting up into Thiervy with all his strength. His balls felt hard and hot, pulsing with raw need as he bounced on the bed. Thiervy's ass clenched around his cock, each flex spurring Mayport on in his reckless taking.

Thiervy rode him hard, back bent and belly rippling as he took Mayport's shaft deeper and deeper. His cock bounced and waved merrily, so close and yet tantalizingly out of Mayport's reach. His cock writhed, ensnared completely in the trap of Thiervy's desires.

Mayport thrust and bucked until his body burned. Thiervy let him tire himself out, then resettled his weight over Mayport's hips. He stretched and smiled down at Mayport again, confident in his conquest. Then he began to rise and fall over Mayport's shaft, impaling himself in rough, relentless strokes.

Thiervy grasped his own cock and began to stroke hard and fast. With his free hand he seized Mayport's hair and pulled him closer. "Open up."

Mayport licked his lips and put his tongue out, desperate for just one more taste of his lover. He thrust back against Thiervy's stroke, and Thiervy shouted in triumph. Hot jets of seed spurted from his shaft, spattering Mayport's cheeks, lips, and tongue.

Mayport moaned, whole body quivering under the convulsions of Thiervy's pleasure. His cock throbbed, thighs twitched, and Thiervy squirmed as Mayport came hard and aching, lost between memory and the moment.

Chapter Twenty-Nine: Absconded

Costor stood against the wall of the workshop watching Mayport contend with the cocoa press. "It would seem like you could hire a fellow for that."

"Will you fellows leave me no honest work to call my own?" Mayport asked, exasperated. "You stand there with vest buttons strained near to rebellion, and wonder why I bother."

Costor tried to tug his coat forward to cover his buttons, and found that garment lacking a few inches. "It's my spring wardrobe. I have some of winter to melt off, still."

"One spring will come when it doesn't melt at all," Mayport predicted. "Ask your father, he would know. Anyway, a fellow like me is fair enough to work this thing. I'd bet Thiervy has the same idea you do, but with an engine instead of a man."

"I thought he was all wrapped up in the *Process*," Costor said. "He's acting like spring took him by surprise. Where do you plan to send him? I need to contract your insurance."

"Take lots, I have no idea where he'll end up," Mayport said. "The Confederation first, at least. He has to make a delivery and see how the weather is down south."

"That's not enough of a plan to take out a policy," Costor said. "Come now, ask me along. You know this might be my last chance."

"If I had a reason to drag you away, I would," Mayport said. "Without one, your Bess will never smile on me again. That's a knot even Captain Cully couldn't unravel. You're in uncharted waters, as far as adventures are concerned."

"If I can get away you won't say no," Costor said. "At least give me a wink and a nod."

"You have my word, much as it will help you," Mayport agreed. "I suppose just the run south with passenger and cargo changes what you can do about my insurance policy. There's a profit in these pots, if we get it to the right man."

"I've never seen oil like this, but it smells like a fortune," Costor said. "It'll be worth five fortunes, once Chef Gasteau has his way."

Mayport smiled and agreed until he had packed a tin of cocoa for Miss Bess and sent Costor away to enjoy his raptures. Costor could anticipate a fortune for Gasteau's genius, but Mayport foresaw a backache.

He finished his morning work and set out early to find lunch on the street. The Misses Stevens had been disappointed of ladies fair and covert assignations, which they had colorfully supposed together. They disapproved of obstinate bachelorhood in a young man of fortune, and punished via cuisine.

He carried paper packets of fried fish and French bread with him to the shop where Thiervy and Cully worked. The door was thrown open to the sunlight. The vessel within was stripped down, exposing her inner workings. He stood staring at his ship, undone by the sight of her in such a dire state.

"No, don't faint!" Cully bellowed from above. "She'll be right and tight by sundown Friday, or I'll know the reason why!"

Mayport let one of the crew boys take away the lunch packets, hardly distracted by eager fingers. He walked the length of the vessel, admiring her new, slim lines and winchette rigging. Small machines were set in place of ten strong men, and were less likely to be drunk when wanted.

"I didn't know you meant to visit," Thiervy shouted from somewhere within the engineering gondola. "I'll find you in a moment."

Mayport sat down with his lunch and waited to truly listen to his partner. Thiervy had been talking nonsense about the *Process* for weeks. The words hadn't stuck, and probably hadn't conjured up such radical changes when Mayport had bothered to hear them. In the face of what Thiervy had wrought, Mayport felt mean and low for pestering over the cocoa press.

Thiervy hurried up, beaming with pride over the half-gutted vessel. "Isn't she beautiful?"

"She's beyond everything I imagined," Mayport said, all honesty. "I see you've done something clever about the crew's quarters."

"I scuttled it," Thiervy said, with a grin. "She won't be as tall or grand, but she'll sail better so. I used to imagine how it was done, operating a ship's rigs by levers. Your father's ideas were sometimes good, but he always failed to execute with standards."

"You've done the job better than what we had," Mayport said. "Thank you. I couldn't be more proud of her if I tried."

Thiervy's mouth drew down in false irritation. "She'll get the job done, that's for certain. The Captain had his way about a few things, but that's Cully for you."

"Costor means to come along," Mayport said. "I came to see about putting him with the crew. I can tell I'm behind the times somewhat."

"I think the trip will do him good," Thiervy said. "At least, he'll come to no harm in the Confederation. I won't risk him overseas, no matter how he begs."

"I'm sure he'll be sensible, even about his adventure," Mayport said. "Let him have his fun, even if he goes too far. He must have lots bottled up to spend by now."

Costor received the news of his acceptance with delight, and closed himself up with his secretary to plan. Captain Cully took charge of the young explorer, in as far as cataloging the larder. Fresh poultry featured heavily in the dining plan, and so again they had livestock to tend in the cargo.

Mayport stowed his cocoa oil in the narrow aft holds. Thiervy had caused the cargo gondola to be refitted for carrying several small lots at once, instead of vast and vulnerable bays. Beyond his own particular interest, Cully had taken on cargo lots to move south, and stood the risk with his own coin.

His goals showed him to have an eye for quality and workmanship. Those same tastes dominated the interior of the passenger gondola. Instead of a crew hold and narrow officer's cubbies, there were luxuriously appointed quarters. The men were so proud of their work; Mayport dared not ask what the furnishings had cost him.

By previous standards, each room was expansive. A sort of abbreviated wash room was shared between two apartments, offering hot water and privacy previously unknown on the vessel. The common mess was a more practical affair of bolted-down furniture and no carpeting. Mayport began at once to anticipate the delights Cully and Costor were diligently devising.

When the *Process* was finally ready to go aloft, poor Costor nearly lost his nerve. His farewells were nothing short of festive, but at last their friends had to take their leave. Costor watched them go, then looked confused.

"Will it really be months to go and come back?" he asked, uncertain. "It's not so long by steam coach. Perhaps I should..."

"A coach goes directly there and back," Mayport said. "You won't be tied down to one path, so take advantage of the freedom."

Thiervy and Cully leaped to their stations, chivvying their machines, but Costor still looked confused. "I didn't see your luggage come aboard. Shouldn't we wait?"

"Don't be ridiculous. I'm not going," Mayport said. "Mind Cully and don't fall off."

Mayport hurried down the gangplank and stood back with the crowd to see them off. From the ground, the Dutch Process looked fragile. Her narrow hull and fanciful rigging defied the expectations set by whalers and merchant vessels on the sea. She stood proud and splendid against the spring sky, at last as majestic as stories had once told.

Thiervy bellowed from the pilot's chair, and the few crewmen aboard leaped to station. Mayport recognized Thiervy's pet engineers by their precision handling of the rigging. Not one man went aloft, but the envelopes deployed and heat fans began to turn at once.

The throb of the fans echoed like a heartbeat. The golden-colored shrouds and rigid envelopes spread above like fish skeletons under a silken veil. The ladies gasped, and the gentlemen grumbled with envy as she lifted free of her moorings. Her shadow passed west over New Amsterdam, and then she was only a receding shape against the sky.

Many of Costor's friends gathered to congratulate Mayport, and tried to make him an excuse for wine and speeches before dinner. He declined gracefully and retreated to his workshop. Here he found a cold hearth in the kitchen and a pot of corn mush that had gone stiff on the stove. The absence of dinner or any of the various Stevenses made him feel at last how alone he had made himself.

He went to his room and tried to repair the damage done to his wardrobe by the mud and the crowds. He could do nothing about his tired eyes and nervous jitters. They were the only thing, for a man who intended to be daring.

He walked out alone as always but far more lonely than he had been since India. The streets were thick with traffic, but not enough to slow him much. He arrived at the Thiervy residence far ahead of sundown and settled in by a gatepost a few doors down. Mister Thiervy's wagon had already returned from the dockyard, and his pony buggy stood at the door. Before long, the man himself appeared and drove away, as solitary a figure as the one who watched him on his way.

Mayport strolled across the street and knocked without hesitation. At sight of his card, the man at the door showed him to the parlor. Missus Thiervy sat at a little sewing table, looking as much a permanent fixture as the gas lamps. Mayport bowed low and smiled at her.

"Madam, I am going south by steam coach very soon," he said. "This may seem sudden, but I have reason to hope you might come along with me. Would this very moment be too soon to effect a gallant kidnap?"

Missus Thiervy favored him with her too-familiar smile. "Mister Titus, I began to fear you would never ask."

Chapter Thirty: Shameless

Mayport had at first worried about taking care of Missus Thiervy. He had imagined she would be preoccupied with anxiety, and in need of guidance. However, she took the lead in her own kidnapping, making use of him in terms of signature and sovereign coin with casual grace.

Her similarities to her son did not stop at the physical. She was quite sensible to her husband's faults, and eager to fail him as a wife. It seemed the only way to protest his various and particular failings as a spouse and parent.

"He may be clever, but you're the practical one," she said after hours of silence at his side. Together they had gone by steam coach to the northernmost rail terminal to wait for their overland egress. "He always knew a hundred reasons why it wasn't safe for me to leave."

"There was one good reason why it wasn't safe to stay, and that wasn't likely to change," Mayport said. "I couldn't think of myself as a gentleman if I sat on my hands and waited for you to ask for help."

"That's the very thing I was talking about," Missus Thiervy said. "Why should I have to ask permission to come and go?"

"I certainly agree," Mayport said. "You'll find me quite reliable in that opinion, no matter what your circumstance."

Missus Thiervy turned her head a little and studied Mayport anew. "I heard a story that you met my brother."

"I don't suit him very much," Mayport admitted. "I can play humble if I have to, but not for long or very well."

Missus Thiervy laughed and patted his hand in a forgiving way. Then the rail yard crew began organizing the southbound train of coaches and carriages. All opportunity for quiet conversation was lost. Their hired steam coach was put up front with the other engines. Mayport took Missus Thiervy to board a passenger carriage that was more a traveling hotel than practical conveyance.

At last the line was cleared for southerly travel, though by then Mayport and Missus Thiervy were settled into the carriage's observation parlor. She set about charming the waiters and discovering the extent of luxuries they could provide. Mayport smiled on everything, and nodded when she explained him as a son's friend acting gallantly in his place.

Mayport let her say and do anything she liked. Her tastes would have shocked the innocent boy he pretended to be. His youth and carelessness had the weight of gold behind them, and lent all the heft they needed among strangers. Missus Thiervy was so easy to please, making her unhappy out of social convention was a cruelty beyond his ability.

At their southern destination, Mayport rented a shed and stored their cargo as one lot. The steam coach he had used to effect his escape went north again, contracted to a new renter. Missus Thiervy waited patiently at his side, and watched as all her worldly goods were locked away with his grinder, press and all. She sighed, and looked at him with patient expectation.

"Would you like a carriage to take you to see your brother?" Mayport asked. "I'll need time to find a suitable lodging, but a hotel for a night or two should suffice."

"You really mean to keep me?" she asked, faint with surprise.

"I didn't spring you from one prison to put you in the old one," Mayport said. "Of course you must see the way of things and decide for yourself, which you prefer."

Missus Thiervy looked startled by Mayport's assertion. "Well... but surely you would advise and..."

Mayport blushed, embarrassed on several fronts. "Let me be more plain. I am merely your son's partner. You owe me no explanations, and I have no permission to give. For advice, I go to your son or Mister Costor on my own account. I would do the same for you, but you'll learn more if you ask for yourself. I rather doubt a woman of your wisdom needs the guiding hand of a spoiled boy, which I am by any comparison."

Missus Thiervy took her turn to look embarrassed. Then, she stood up very tall, reached out to straightened Mayport's clothes and nodded once as if satisfied. "Very well, young man. I shall go to my brother on my own while you see to your business. See to it well, mind, and come report to me at the Merriweather for a very early dinner."

"Yes, Ma'am," Mayport said, startled again by her resilience.

She put her hand out for a few coins, then conjured porters for her lesser luggage and set out on foot. Mayport stood still and watched her go, admiring her confident and elegant self-possession. He wondered at men who imagined she needed or desired a cold separation from the world as all other creatures knew it.

He called first on Chef Gasteau and had a few private words of conspiracy he had dared not share even with Thiervy. Chef reacted to his notions with a craftsman's curiosity over tools, which gave Mayport hope. It almost went without saying that Gasteau had a cousin very nearby with interests in his very trade, but lacking in certain resources.

Also from the endless cousins came other possibility of a very small cottage, entirely unsuitable but at such a reasonable price... well, Mayport was in no suit to refuse. He took the details as part of his loot to the Merriweather after Chef had put him back to proper use for the afternoon scrub-down. Though he had prospects, nothing concrete could be said about his efforts.

"Oh well," Missus Thiervy sighed. "We are much the same. My brother means to keep me like a maiden for fear of whispers I've turned vixen. Did you ever hear such? Well, you would have, raised down here as you were."

Mayport laughed at her sour bluntness. "What would you do if you could?"

"Plant onions," she said, and forced a smile. "I'm good at it. They grow up and everything."

"That doesn't seem like much to ask," Mayport said. "I have a request. Hire our help for us as you did up north. There are some things I do not tolerate, no matter how long I've lived next to it. This comes in turn for the things I allow. By any reckoning, it's going to be called my home."

"You simply don't care a bit for what people say, do you?" she asked.

"I care very much," Mayport said. "What if someone could say of me with total honesty that I abandoned a lady to her hideous husband? I knew him to be a monster, Madam. Whatever they say of me, I did not commit that common sin of omission. I am shameless, if that's what you mean."

"Shameless isn't the same as blameless," she said. "Why did you do such a thing?"

"Your son, my partner and friend, wasn't there to do it himself," Mayport said. "The reasons for his absence are convenient, but blameless. What more needs to be said? You've come to prepare for your son's arrival, as have I. Don't worry so, or take stock in borrowed trouble."

"And in this way you explain absconding with a married woman?" She shook her head. "You're as innocent as a child. He will know who helped me and come with whatever excuse he conjures. You are right that he is monstrous. Where did you get the nerve to provoke him not once, but twice?"

"If he comes, the truth of my position will be obvious. I'll do for him what I always promised I would, and with more reason than ever," Mayport said, then smiled brightly. "I walked by this cottage our Chef mentioned. I could have the garden patch turned if you can find your onion sets. There's a good sunny spot for them."

She laughed, as if giving up all responsibility. "You'd think a little thing like onions couldn't ruin a marriage. A kitchen garden, something useful to remind me of home, was what I wanted. So, you see, I did it on my own one day, or ordered the work done. He didn't notice at first, but when he did! He said it was shameful for a lady to grow onions like a slave. That was the first time he beat me like a slave for acting like one. The next day he made the fellows put roses instead."

"Madam," Mayport said, when her eyes wandered away from his. "I am sincere in my protection of you. I have never met your husband. If any stranger molests you, I won't know who it is until after a fact. I have considered it on all sides. I won't care much if I do swing from ending that vicious fool, so let him come on."

"You speak lightly of violence, for a boy," she said. "What makes you think you know what you're talking about?"

"If you worry about me taking a beating, don't. It has happened before, many's the time." Mayport let his careless smile go, and bowed his head. "I *have* seduced your son, and face death for that. It's a worse fate than if I'd seduced you instead. The risk for me is all the same in both cases, and I know my duty."

"Bold child!" She shook her head slowly. "You seem so natural, you make me forget who I've turned to. But you're an honest sinner, which is more than most."

"You deserve my honesty, which is also more than most," Mayport said. "Nevertheless, be more mindful of my true character. You have rid yourself of one worthless man, and can do the same to me."

She frowned at him. "I like you better when you let me think of you as a wide-eyed innocent."

Mayport smiled again, and kept the rest of his opinions to

himself. There was no doubt that her husband could easily guess who had robbed him. That cuckolding seemed unlikely made very little difference, considering the way Mayport had taken up with the same man's son instead.

The weight of his pistols at his back were a cold comfort. He knew the passion of Thiervy's violence toward his father, but felt it lacked a certain depth of intention. Under all of this lay an old truth, that Mayport craved his chance at the beast.

His soberest reflections relied on the hope that no chance would ever come. He turned his thoughts to a more constant kind of revenge, this lasting success of his ventures. Missus Thiervy settled on the cottage, though she dismissed his notions on her patch of earth there .

Her tastes were simple, and her nature so easy to please, it was a pity she had been so shamefully neglected. He made a game of gathering gifts and treats for her as they prepared for Thiervy's arrival. The *Process* and her cargo were barely on his mind, for worry as days turned into weeks, and she made no call upon the port.

A message arrived at last that she had been delayed by weather, but no news of whether she had forged on. He took to prowling the docks by day, and busied himself in his rented shed each afternoon. He dared not rent a workshop until the fate of his vessel was assured.

Despite all his fretting, word of her sighting came when he was at his most relaxed, at his barber's shop. It took all his restraint not to leap up half-shaved and go to watch her come on. At his barber's edged insistence, he went to meet her in a high state of cologne, and still had time to watch her fold neatly into a single mooring, safe at rest.

He went aboard at once, found Thiervy and confessed all that he had done. Cully and Costor listened, but none could believe him. Only a light and lilting call from the docks convinced them of his perfect candor.

Cully studied her elegant figure, then blushed and turned away. "I can't even look at her! What were you thinking, you young fool?"

Thiervy laughed at Cully's sudden guilt. Mayport smiled at his partner, understanding all in an instant. "I told her I wasn't ashamed of you, and she never said I should be. So, you finally caught your captain and didn't swing for it, Joseph Thiervy. I hope you're satisfied."

Chapter Thirty-One: Reparations

Mayport reclined at his ease on an unused machine, watching Thiervy at his most hectically inventive. After Mayport had boldly surmised an obvious affair, Thiervy had demanded a change of topic. Mayport had yielded, and instead took up a pulpit full of unreasonable demands in the matter of cocoa and machinery.

Captain Cully and Chef Gasteau had carried off an ecstatic Costor on a sort of landward pleasure cruise. Wild stories of a monster balloon run amok came to port from counties around. They might have made a tidy sum on penny tours of the *Process* if the crowds had their way. Missus Thiervy had been asked to tea with renewed acquaintances, by virtue of proximity.

"I don't... I just don't know *what* to tell them," she said, even as she tried in vain to tidy Thiervy's shed workshop. "Chocolate! I've never seen the stuff, so can't sing its praises. Those that have, well! They talk about it like it's good enough to marry."

"We will remedy all anon, your child's genius willing," Mayport said. "I have threatened you with guests and I mean to follow through."

"You see, I simply must," Missus Thiervy said, half apology and half happy anticipation. "They knew me before ol' Mister came along, and want to be proud of me for something."

Mayport nodded in time to her running details of the local gossip. They could not directly praise her for getting shut of one born fool. There were too many young girls who might begin to admire her good sense. Instead, they had settled on admiring her son. They could have cared less what he did, but were desperate to know what it was they liked so well.

Mayport wanted very much to show them, but had made up his mind about one thing long ago. If all they wanted was chocolate to drink in their parlors, he wasn't about to break his back for them. Thiervy bent over his worktable, angling delicately with his file to remove a nib from a grinder gear no wider than his thumb. "I say the principle is sound, if nothing but a novelty. In practice, you're as mad as your father. Who would want such a thing?"

"Just me, after a hard day's work," Mayport said. "It's a toy for my leisure hours. There's more than many who, like your own mother, haven't had the chance to become enchanted by our vice. You said you'd do anything I wanted if I would stop asking about the captain, and I have. Hurry on."

Thiervy muttered at his little masterpiece of engineering. A wee coal fire made it all go. A child might have tended it, so it could be thought of as Mayport-proof. The project had gotten quite beyond the mill-and-press tool he had proposed.

The scale of the thing had confounded Thiervy, once he had finished his design. The first test had been a shock to Mayport, coming in the form of a syrup as thick as tar and twice as bitter. Thiervy had cheerfully called his failure a mere error in ratios. He stubbornly insisted that he intended to ruin a small fortune in nibs over the thing to make Mayport see his point.

That point had lain somewhere west of chemistry, a terra incognita to Mayport. When Thiervy stood back at last, Mayport got up and approached the machine with no small trepidation. It hummed and whistled like a living thing. Mayport's role was a far cry from what he had endured with Chef Gasteau, and yet he could not help but long for the pestle.

He followed the instructions Thiervy had written out in checklist fashion. He measured water into a reservoir, milk into another, a precise measure of nibs in one hopper, and another of sugar. The coal fire glowed on the tiny grate, and the boiler sang its frantic tune. Mayport drew a lever back to set the timer going, and sprang as far away from the machine as he could.

The contraption jolted on the table, sputtered and whirled and gobbled up everything in the hoppers and reservoirs. The smell of the coal smoke overpowered the rich aroma of cocoa butter and warm milk. Liquids within the pipes gurgled down the ever-narrowing path until a thin stream of black goo drizzled into a stone jug that sat waiting to collect it.

Warm milk flowed from another tap to fill the same jug brimful. Mayport took up his dasher and tried once more to blend the two. "You can do all this and I'm still a-mixing at the end. I think you forgot what I asked you to do."

"The dashing is the fun part," Thiervy said. "There, look. Isn't that the very thing?"

Mayport studied the foamy, brownish liquid, then went on beating it to his will. "It's nothing like, and won't taste it, either.

You must have a screw loose, and not in this trap of yours."

"It does so look like the very thing we had across the gulf,"
Thiervy argued. "If it doesn't taste like raw mash and mud pots,
that's because I'm brilliant."

Mayport poured the mixture into teacups and dared to sniff it.
The milk was not scalded, nor the cocoa chunky and bruised. This
time, the syrup had blended smoothly with the milk. Mayport
sipped, and breathed a sigh of pure pleasure. A moment later, Missus Thiervy repeated the sound.

"Well, no wonder they were crazy for it up north," she said. "I
presume this is better. You boys look pretty proud of yourselves."

"Yes, ma'am," Mayport said, and smiled bright for Thiervy.

She finished her cup at one go and stood up. "I'm to dinner at
Fairlain's tonight. I won't make you boys go. Her cook's a devil,
and you should celebrate. I'll find my own way home with the
buggy."

Mayport smiled and nodded for her as well. He knew that at
least a driver would be on hand, if not a few fellows for incidentals.
Thiervy went to change his clothes while Mayport closed up the
workshop. Only when he was alone with the contraption did he
realize the scale of Thiervy's success.

He went at once to repair himself for the evening, and met
Thiervy at the door. "Shall we dine early?" he asked, even as they
stepped out together. "We can have the evening to ourselves."

"You're nothing but a troublemaker," Thiervy said, without a
moment's resistance.

Mayport shivered with delight, and smiled proudly. "I've begun
to enjoy your scolding. Does that take the fun out of it for you?"

"It gives me something else to scold about," Thiervy said. "Take
me someplace lively, with music. I can't begin to explain why I'm
so pleased, but I feel like celebrating."

Mayport slung an arm around Thiervy's shoulders and steered
him in the right direction. His whole body went warm, and not
from the fine weather. Whether Thiervy remembered or not, they
had started out just like this. Neither of them had learned why
Thiervy's mind sometimes behaved badly and forced him to pure
misery. The sunny moods were just as strong as the stormy ones,
and so Mayport learned how to like them both.

They found space at a rowdy, Spanish-speaking place that
smelled of onion and pepper. Mayport said 'si' to anything the
pretty serving girl suggested, and they ended up with a fine spread

and a tall pitcher of sweet wine. Thiervy managed a few bites before resorting to his ever-present notes and drawings.

"I almost forgot to tell you, I figured it out," Thiervy said, sounding dangerously serious all over again.

"Is it really important?" Mayport asked, wary of the tides. "I don't feel like thinking businesslike."

"It's about you," Thiervy said. "Don't look so! You'd think I made you swallow a live frog."

Mayport nodded hard, then resorted to the wine to keep him warm. "Do tell."

Thiervy returned to his notes once more. Mayport tried not to worry that the pile he had looked particularly thick. "What would you do if I asked you to buy me a house?"

"Die of shock," Mayport replied without thinking. He hesitated only a moment, then squared his shoulders up against the back of his chair. "Let's go find one tonight."

"Listen to me!" Thiervy insisted. His hand fisted up around the papers, and he calmed himself by smoothing them again. "Listen to me, please. It's horrible, and I've taken after my father in the worst way."

"Tell me you have to marry a girl," Mayport said, and drank his cup dry. "Just say so. It's the very thing, if you've done what I think you have."

"I should have," Thiervy said, and bowed his head lower. "I've tried very hard to be a scoundrel. Now that I've succeeded, all I want is to be a good man somehow."

Mayport scratched his head and tried to see his way through the riddle without forcing Thiervy speak plainly about his sins. "You don't have to tell me why you suddenly want a house. All you've ever looked on fondly for a home was a pilot's chair. That's why I gave you one."

"You can't think I'm ignorant of how I abandoned my mother," Thiervy said. "I left her there, alone, and never could think of a way to help her. I didn't really try. Now, you hear how people talk, and you know my uncle. I thought she would go home to him, but I can't stand it! He helped choose my father in the first place! I have to do better this time. I need a place for her to call home, not some cheap cottage rented off French furstealers."

"Yes," Mayport said.

Thiervy stared at Mayport, like he was expecting something

more. At last, he shook his head and sighed. "I had so many ways to convince you. There's nobody on your side to be embarrassed. You've got so much to give, and like to. I've been practicing."

"All you had to do was ask," Mayport said, and shrugged a couple of times. "I'm sorry to deprive you of a good proof, since you've thought it all out for me."

Thiervy sat still for a long time, still unbelieving. "Uncle's right in a lot of ways. We can't expect to live peaceful and honest here. I would have picked just about anyplace else, until I saw my mother so happy with her friends. I'd never seen her like that before, and it liked to have broke my heart."

"I had no intention of giving her back to that fool anyway," Mayport said, irritated. "I've never had a mother like her. If you didn't want her, I was going to keep her for myself."

Thiervy looked shocked to hear his mother spoken of as a collectible, but didn't really argue. "She's strong in some ways, and utterly helpless in others. She's a mess with the household accounts. She's adorable to try, but nobody ever made her do math since she was wed."

"That's as near to a sin as anything I ever heard," Mayport said. "Anyway, let her try. We can afford mistakes on the scale she makes them. I've seen her fret over pennies. Neither did she forget to bring every jewel and chain she ever got by way of apology from that idiot you have to call a father. If she had time to think and plan, she could do without us very well."

"I don't want her to," Thiervy said.

"Then we'll go on as we mean to about your new toy," Mayport said. "Once that's done, we'll set Costor on whoever has the house we want. I used to hope you'd find a port to call home. I didn't dare think it might happen this soon."

Chapter Thirty-Two: Acclaim

The cottage taken by the Titus Company gained a reputation as a palace of unknown wonders. From it came forth Missus Thiervy, an icon of the citizenry, if a bit reticent for her station. Within dwelt the fellows of the company, creatures of mystery to the last. Mayport postponed the ceremonial welcoming of the neighbors until Costor had exhausted his curiosity about the port town, its surrounding lands, and the citizens thereof.

When their dictator of taste had at last been permanently installed, he made free with opinions on every topic. His collusion with Missus Thiervy over a guest list marked the beginning of his conquest. That steady focus on society left Thiervy and Mayport free to devise wonders and entertainments for their guests.

The cottage was too cozy a venue for the extravaganza Costor planned. He made free with his resources, and soon secured them an invitation to Missus Bradley's mansion for the fete. They were far out of season for a ball, but the polite population seemed willing to overlook the irregularity.

Costor took a little townhouse for his own, anticipating the arrival of Miss Bess and her sisters. He had suffered badly without his helpmeet-to-be, and managed to gain her assistance for the venture. A party was no such thing without her fair grace.

Thiervy hid out in his workshop, keeping secrets from everyone over his invention. He took every complaint seriously. Over days, his cocoa machine grew quieter, and less apt to violent expulsions of scalded milk and ruined beans.

Mayport let the fellows go on as they wished. His daily labors involved a crowd of daring Frenchman, and their lust for gold. Cully drew up maps and wrote rutters out of his own records. Within lay the knowledge necessary to unravel the knots that held Mayport at the mercy of failed commerce.

Without fanfare, a few boats set out to the west, others to the east. Mayport could not count the times he had heard his father wail against such ventures. His attempt to avoid such risk had led him to build The Dutch Process and later the Coverture, on which he had perished.

Mayport couldn't afford such grand schemes of avoiding the mundane. He paid ahead to set men to sea. If they never returned, the loss was life on top of gold. He dared not entertain such morbid anxiety, and put his faith in the smuggler's will to profit.

He might have sent Cully west to lead the voyagers, but Miss Bess won out over cocoa. She came south under his watchful eye in that grand conveyance, bringing all her clever gentility as a matter of course. Costor worked to shield her of the obvious Confederation realities, but she was too sensitive to ignore the matter.

They took care to employ only free men, though the expense was extreme. What Bess could not countenance, they could not employ. Missus Thiervy called her a prig and snob for her sensibilities, thereby embarrassing Thiervy to the bone.

Uncle Jesse appeared very late to voice his opinion in the matter. "You fellows are just begging to take a long walk off a short gallows. Bad enough that you ruin yourselves, but you take my sister along, too. I'll soon be mentioned in your schemes as well!"

"Take no notice of us," Mayport suggested when it seemed blood would not argue with blood. "Speak out against us if you like, and we'll take no note of you. Only do not try to stop me, or share in my inevitable success."

"These people are farmers and sailors," Jesse hissed of his neighbors. "It's not the right time to display yourself so. Perhaps when you're older, things will be safer."

"I mean to do this now," Mayport insisted. "You think only of your own dark imagination. You're a coward, so I can't take your advice."

"You are risking us all over your pride!"

"Yes!" Mayport shouted. He rose from his chair and went to stand by the window. He resisted the urge to loom over his semiuncle. "I will risk everything for my pride and Joseph Thiervy. Nothing could persuade me from it, least of all a skulking, spineless slaver like yourself."

Jesse sucked his lips into his mouth and bit down, staring daggers at Mayport. After a moment he said "Son, you just don't know what you're messing with."

"Whatever it is, it don't scare me a bit," Mayport insisted. "I see what a life of fear is, just by looking at you. A man might as well be dead, before becoming what you are."

"We're just the same," Jesse said. "I've got sense enough to be discreet. That's how I got to be so old. I use my wits."

"I think you were born old," Mayport said. "If you only come as a Cassandra, consider me warned. I won't lie and sneak to get by as you have. I'd rather be an honest dead man than a living liar."

"You can't change the world, you young fool!" Jesse shouted.

"I only have to change myself!" Mayport shouted back. "You think you're the first old boot to try and scare fear and hate of myself into me? I won't have it, nor anyone like you whispering that poison to my Joseph! You'll never be the man I take after, even if that makes me a young corpse this very night!"

Jesse was rendered speechless with rage. Thiervy and his mother tried to contain themselves, but at last gave up and laughed. With that sound chasing him, Jesse retreated from their home. Missus Thiervy chose to chalk his abandonment up as shyness. Mayport was disgusted by his cowardice, but kept quiet about it for the peace of the household. Without doubt, he was the head of their crazy operation.

The whole exercise seemed unreal until he and Thiervy moved the cocoa machine to Missus Bradley's house for final testing. Rumor of their invention spread faster than a horse could trot. By nightfall he found himself the master of much expectation. He dressed high and fine, though Thiervy stayed true to his own black, unremarkable wardrobe. They stuck close until the first guest arrived. Then Mayport left Thiervy to his machinations and turned his own charm up to full blast.

He greeted strangers with a perfect smile, squiring Missus Thiervy about the place while Thiervy soothed his one true love. She knew every face and kept Mayport on a steady keel. Their guests offered no curiosity about the reason for the party, showing all the genteel reserve of new money and recent advancement in the world. Mayport felt at home for the first time in months.

Costor and Bess led the floor in dancing. They knew all the latest steps, and showed them to any who asked. Within the hour, a regular ruckus had been raised. Mayport stayed his post instead of joining in, but his guests were captivated. Rich manners and refinements would not have gotten him so far with his neighbors as did the unseasonal feast and the local and secretly-blended rum punch.

"These people have no idea who you are," Bess whispered when she finally came to catch her breath. "Is that a worry, or was this your intention all along?"

"Give me time," Mayport said. "I'll have to be remarkable,

sooner or later. Our Joseph can hardly stand being looked at. You must help me keep him safe."

Bess nodded and smiled all the brighter for her mission. She flitted away again to gush her curiosity and stern expectation of Thiervy's cocoa machine. Mayport waited for her to collect Costor from the brandy and cigar set, then led the party to a side parlor, where that very creation remained in smokey obscurity.

Thiervy set his machine going as natural as breathing at a word from Bess. "I've invented something for the weather here," he said, by way of excuse. "It's nothing like what you had at home."

Bess clung with one hand on Costor's arm, and the other on Mayport's. Her courage was obvious in the face of Thiervy's whirligig. When she was presented with a cup of milk and syrup, she accepted with characteristic aplomb. "I do so love fresh novelties!"

The company and guests watched with breathless anticipation as she sipped. Thiervy blushed from collar to ears. "It's too bitter, I know."

"It's so original!" she said, all honesty. "My chef would be proud to serve this and the device is... entirely unique! Where may I acquire one for my Costor's lounge?"

With that simple question, other ladies came forth to taste. Thiervy shrank behind his machine as usual. Mayport was left free to sing his praises without interference. To his delight, most questions were about the machine, not the chocolate itself.

Mayport could hold his own in matters of craftsmanship and ease of use. The omnipotent team for the opposition arrived in the form of Chef Gasteau and family. They came up to the buffet all dressed in white, blue and red, the image of ex-French gentility.

"You would know better than I would," Mayport murmured. "It's just as you said, but coal-fired."

"That smell!" Chef complained, and not without reason.

"It's my very next priority," Thiervy said, the first words he had ventured among company.

Chef Gasteau condescended to taste. His family went along after, each expressing startled good cheer. Mayport recognized the look from a time when a nursery child had delivered a rather clever song at the top of his voice. He blushed to see that indulgent pleasure come his way.

"It's not me," Mayport hurried to say. "I only held him to the standard you set. This is what came of it."

"This is the Joseph you sing about?" Chef asked.

"Yes, uh..." Mayport hesitated, and blushed even deeper. "Do I?"

"Oh yes," Missus Gasteau assured him. She drank more deeply of her cup. "I might have known you'd found a prodigy. We have many similar tastes, you and I."

With such irreproachable approval, Thiervy became an instant success. On all sides, Mayport was besieged with questions. Unfortunately, they were all on the topic he was least prepared to answer. How had Thiervy thought of the thing, and how did he make it go? Mayport could only share their wonder and admiration as Thiervy rushed to replenish every cup.

Bonus Chapter: Endurance

Mayport found Thiervy on the *Process*. After so radical a success, her decks were his only peaceful refuge. In this way, it was easy to catch him relaxed and at his ease.

"You've made your mother proud," Mayport said. "You needn't put on that dismissive face. I know you've satisfied yourself, if only this once."

"If I've done so well, I shouldn't have to satisfy myself," Thiervy said. "I hope you've found me with that in mind."

Mayport hefted the basket he carried. "If you have a fire, we could roast these."

Thiervy peeked under the wet croaker sack at the oysters Mayport had brought. "It's certainly a start for what I need."

Thiervy managed the fire in the mess. Mayport set the oysters to roast. With beer and fresh bread, they made a luxurious supper together. They never bothered over plates, and threw the shells overboard when they were done.

"All this time, I wondered why you took such a risk," Thiervy said. "I dreamed this for years, but never began to make it real. What made you start such a thing?"

"I knew what you wanted," Mayport said. "I've known you longer than you realize. Some part of me thought 'Ah! This is the woman Thiervy wants to protect. She's the one he can't stand to see, for the pain of going away again.' It's wrong to come between a husband and wife, but your father is no husband. Least of all a caretaker for her. I think he won't miss her for a minute. You miss her all the time."

Thiervy shook his head. "I'm glad you didn't think it through. You might have realized what you were planning, and let convention be your excuse for failure."

"I've succeeded," Mayport said. "I don't need to find excuses, in this case."

"What do you need?" Thiervy asked.

Mayport turned to answer, to explain the fond fantasies that they could go on as they were. His words stuck in his throat at the sight of Thiervy by moonlight. Such a nature wasn't intended to stay fair or foul for long. His only hope was to weather the storms, and enjoy the peace as it came.

He took Thiervy by the arm and led him back down to the mess hall. Leading the way with impatient tugs and enticing kisses, it was easy to make Thiervy play along. Getting him naked was no trouble at all. He even stretched out on the table on request, without any sort of protest. Then, Mayport took up a jug of Thiervy's chocolate syrup, and found resistance at last.

"You can't expect me to hold still for that. It's too hot," Thiervy said, and started to sit up.

Mayport sat the jug between Thiervy's thighs with a bang. "It's not. No, never mind. I suppose it's too much to think you would trust me. Will you only wait a moment?"

He turned and marched out before Thiervy could argue. On the *Process*, rope was in abundance. He found some that had been worn smooth and pliable, and cut the lengths he wanted. When he came back, Thiervy was still sitting up on the table with his thighs parted around the chocolate jug.

He grabbed Thiervy's ankle before he could move, and looped the rope around it. After so much practice in their travels, the knots came easily to his fingers. He secured the ends to the table leg before Thiervy could quite believe what was happening to him.

Mayport kept his eyes on Thiervy's while he tied his other leg down. As he had hoped, but yet did not understand, Thiervy relaxed under the restraint. He lay back and stretched his arms out. His expression was a mix of vulnerability and longing that he only showed to Mayport. When the knots were fast, Mayport reached down to caress his cheek.

"Did he make you feel like this?" Mayport asked.

"No," Thiervy confessed. "I was always afraid. He knew what made me most frightened of myself. That was what he liked best about me. You make me feel safe, even like this."

"You certainly talk more, this way," Mayport said. He picked up the jug and began pouring thin streams of syrup over Thiervy's bare skin. He tried to copy Chef Gasteau's confident example, but was distracted by the curve and ripple of muscle before him.

He leaned down and erased his mistakes with his tongue. Thiervy sighed softly under each kiss. In this way, Mayport made the image a perfection, though his efforts were not. Curlicues and vines crept down Thiervy's chest, skirting the edges of his hair and outlining his nipples. The curves of his thighs bore narrow stripes, like the memory of rougher nights between them. Gently, he lifted Thiervy's cock and poured one more ribbon, carefully spiraling the stream along his throbbing shaft. Mayport stood back to admire Thiervy anew.

"I wish you could see yourself," Mayport said.

Thiervy stirred in his bonds. Mayport liked Thiervy dreamy, relaxed, and lost in his own world of pleasure. He leaned over the table and kissed again, this time to make Thiervy squirm and arch, straining toward every touch. With his passions thoroughly restrained, Thiervy had no choice but to endure Mayport's idea of a proper start to an evening alone.

Salt and musk and need blended with the sweet taste of chocolate. Mayport had grown indifferent to the taste of his exotic spice. In long licks, mingling it with his favorite flavor, it took on a charm he hadn't previously appreciated.

Thiervy obviously wanted to grab Mayport, hurry things along, and would have if he could. Equally, he had often professed a real pleasure in being unable to do any such thing. Mayport knew that desperate longing from trading places to try it for himself. Armed with this knowledge of prolonged desire, he took his time to savor each lick and kiss.

He leaned on his arms and got comfortable to lap at Thiervy's thighs. He had to ignore his own aching cock. In this way, the ropes worked on both of them. He was glad to be in his clothes, to keep his own impulses within his control.

Thiervy wasn't under any kind of control. As Mayport licked, Thiervy struggled against the ropes. His hips rose and fell in a steady rhythm. His soft sighs turned to demanding growls, then an urgent, wordless pleading. Mayport abandoned the stripes and plunged his mouth down Thiervy's shaft, slurping at syrup and salty precome. Thiervy groaned and thrust, trying to plunge his cock deeper into Mayport's mouth.

Mayport backed off a little, and planted his hands on Thiervy's hips. Even with leverage, he couldn't keep Thiervy down. Neither could he be expected to swallow all of Thiervy's cock. The heat of Thiervy's pulse burned against his tongue, and he sucked harder, locked in a struggle between reason and raw need.

Thiervy pumped harder, desperate for release, until at last Mayport sat up, gasping for air. "You're gonna kill me with that thing one day."

"Get back down and I'll try right now." Thiervy growled and humped at the empty air. "Go on. You know you love it."

Mayport chuckled, coughed, then laughed again. "You must be thinking of somebody else. I have ways of making you remember who you're with."

He got up and walked out of the mess, leaving Thiervy to his helpless position. He hurried to fetch the oil Thiervy kept by his bunk. Mayport found that ever-ready supply to be obscene, but made use of it anyway. He hurried back to the mess, but stopped outside the door. Thiervy was struggling again, and muttering through clenched teeth.

"Fuck me," Thiervy growled. "How hard is that to say? 'Mayport Titus, I want you to fuck me.' Just say it, you dumb bastard, before you lose your mind!"

Mayport almost laughed, but stopped the sound with his hand. There was no telling what Thiervy had endured when he was out catting around. Sometimes he came back with strange anxieties, hesitations over things he'd never worried about before. Of all things, this was the strangest Mayport had yet witnessed.

Mayport put the oil vial in his pocket, leaned against the corridor wall and waited. He could see Thiervy perfectly, but the shadows kept his observation obscured. More than anything Mayport ever did, Thiervy had to fight against what he did to himself.

Thiervy closed his eyes and shouted at last. "Mayport Titus!"

Mayport grinned to himself, but kept quiet.

"You'd better be on this deathtrap you call a ship!" Thiervy hollered. "You can't just *leave* me like this!"

Mayport heard the edge of panic in Thiervy's shout. "I didn't leave you alone."

Thiervy relaxed, and lay still on the table. "Don't do that. I can't stand it."

"I was right here the whole time," Mayport said. "I wouldn't abandon you so helpless. Anyway, you need me. I heard every word."

Thiervy shivered. "What are you gonna do about it?"

Mayport paced slowly across the room, watching Thiervy begin to twitch once more. He kept his hands low, out of Thiervy's sight, and poured out a handful of oil. He reached between Thiervy's legs and coated his ass with the fragrant lubricant. He took his time in opening and stretching Thiervy for the taking.

He thrust his fingers in, one or two at a time, withdrawing completely, then vanquishing that tense muscle once more. He stroked irregularly, now shallow, now deep, then sought out the tender place that, when stroked hard, made Thiervy howl with pleasure. Thiervy's cock rose up high and proud once more, straining to reach up to his navel.

"Fuck me!" Thiervy shouted at last. "Please, please, I need it! I want you, please, Titus, give me your cock..."

Mayport stepped away from the table, though he wanted very much to pounce. "Look at me."

Thiervy obeyed, though his eyes were at half-mast. Mayport stripped slowly, enjoying the focused attention burning in Thiervy's eyes. Somehow, Thiervy imagined that Mayport dreamed up all these exotic delights on his own. In fact, he had only to understand his lover, and the imagining was done for him.

He left his clothes in a pile by the table and got up to kneel between Thiervy's thighs. Thiervy watched hungrily as Mayport oiled his cock. The raw need burning in Thiervy's eyes was almost enough to make Mayport hurry at last, but again he had better plans for so delicious an opportunity.

Mayport stretched out on top of Thiervy, rocking his hips until the tip of his cock was pressed to Thiervy's ass. He might have plunged in, burying himself to the root. Instead, he thrust gently, sinking just the head of his cock into that hot, clenching passage, and withdrew once more. Thiervy whimpered and squirmed, trying to recapture Mayport's shaft. Mayport leaned in hard, holding Thiervy still for kisses, until he relaxed against the table again.

Mayport pushed his cock into Thiervy once more, not to claim, but to test the throbbing heat of his lover's body. Thiervy bucked, hips pumping to draw Mayport deeper. Mayport drew back again, hissing as the cool air caressed and soothed his burning shaft.

"Don't tease me like this," Thiervy complained.

"You love it," Mayport murmured, and kissed his mouth. "You can't hold still for it to save your life, but you love this."

Thiervy groaned in frustration, so Mayport thrust in again. He pumped his cock in and out, going no more than half its length, curving his back so that he tip of his cock scraped over that one sensitive spot on every stroke. Thiervy cried out, tried to lay still, but at last his body twitched and jerked, quite beyond his control.

Mayport withdrew again, and Thiervy complained, somewhere between a scream and sobbing. "We're not done, are we? You're not. I can see that from here. What are you doing? Come back!"

"Just be still," Mayport said, though he knew he was asking the impossible. "Trust me. Let me give you what you need."

Thiervy groaned in frustration, but tried to do as Mayport desired. He could not stop his own eager twitching. Mayport rocked slowly to pet all that passion-fevered skin with his whole body. He kissed Thiervy, reveling in the hunger his lover had for every touch.

Thiervy was not at all calmed by such gentle caresses. When Mayport pressed inside him once more, his whole body went tense. Mayport smiled at the struggle to obey. He could imagine the raw desperation pumping through Thiervy's veins, and all of it for Mayport.

He thrust a little deeper. Thiervy shuddered and shivered, but did not try to take control. With that capitulation, Mayport could enjoy his slow claiming as he sank in, inch by inch. Thiervy's body relaxed and yielded around Mayport' shaft, making his passage soft and easy, until Mayport was buried to the root.

Mayport lay still, feeling his cock pulse in answer to Thiervy's quivering. He took a deep breath to steady himself, then withdrew to the tip of his shaft once more. Thiervy made a desperate, pleading whimper, but held still within his bonds. Mayport kissed Thiervy's lips, then plunged in as deep as he could, all of his strength driving his shaft hard and fast into Thiervy's conquered ass.

Thiervy yelped, and his cock jerked between their bellies. Mayport drew back and thrust again and again, driving the full length of his shaft into Thiervy on every stroke. His shaft felt searing hot with raw vitality. Poised on the edge of blind pleasure, he poured out all his need into Thiervy, forging an immutable fusion between them with all the fire of his aching flesh.

Thiervy bucked and shuddered, his flesh pebbled, and he screamed. His ass clenched tight as his cock writhed and pulsed between them. Mayport heard his own howling as his control snapped. He pounded Thiervy's helpless body, even as his own passion tore through and out of him, branding them both with his mark of passion.

They lay together, senseless and gasping, until Thiervy made a weak struggle against Mayport's weight. Gathering the tattered shreds of his strength, Mayport sat up and set Thiervy free. He grinned, triumphant, when Thiervy drew him back down into a warm embrace.

"There now. Wasn't that the very thing?" Mayport murmured through tender kisses.

"You're the only one," Thiervy mumbled, sleepy already. "No other man ever could. They don't even really try."

Mayport stroked Thiervy's hair as he dropped off to sleep. Such a confession was worth the effort taken to draw it out. With it came the hope that one day, Mayport might be the only man Thiervy turned to for all that he desired.

Chapter Thirty-Three: Commerce

Missus Thiervy was lauded by all her acquaintances for having such a clever son to rely on. Mayport was graciously given half-mentions. After all, he had been wise or crazy enough to fund Thiervy's genius long before it was made apparent.

Costor was startled at being besieged on his vacation. He had any number of Confederate fellows trying to tempt him into their society. His prowess with finances was apparent to all. For the first time ever, he was caught absent a scheme with which to increase an investor's wealth.

He brought his despair to Mayport, who took pity on him with private intelligence. The voyage of the French smugglers had been funded entirely out of Mayport's pocket money. He was more than willing to share the risk, as long as he didn't ruin the men who involved themselves.

Costor was immediately grateful. "I can certainly find investors *post facto* for the shipments. Only, they'll ask for a piece of your company to boot."

"That's not for sale at any price," Mayport said. "This whole scheme could burst at any moment. I want to be the sole casualty, should that occur."

"Or the sole benefactor, if it doesn't," Costor said.

"Thiervy's my benefactor, and your child as fast as you can get me one to spoil," Mayport said. "I like the notion of being a rich uncle."

"You'll do a better job at it than that Jesse fellow," Costor said. "He's in a mess of debt ten years deep, and begging to go deeper."

"Thiervy might be named the heir of his nonsense, one of these days," Mayport said. "Should we help him out?"

"I won't lend to him," Costor said, final in his decision. "He's hardly aware of what's best for himself. Half these fellows are destitute, but too proud of being a master to ever give up and try at some other industry."

"There's got to be a profit in it somewhere," Mayport said, confused. "Why would they bother, if it's all rags and ruin?"

"I told you, it's pure pride," Costor said. "The costs of land and seed, the way the markets jump around when harvests happen, none of it's certain even when a fellow only has to pay hired hands. Taking on debt against labor that might never profit, and has to be housed, fed and occasionally recaptured? It's impossible. Now we've got ladies like our Bess who won't wear a stitch of cotton from down here, for fear some little darkie child was made to weep over her pretty dress. Things will change, but not fast enough to save that Jesse and his friends."

"Then do what you can to keep Thiervy out of it," Mayport said. "If it's the kind of trap you say it is, we're well off for ourselves without it."

"You look disappointed," Costor hazarded.

"I just..." Mayport shrugged a couple of times. "I thought there was more to it than that. They fought so hard to keep things like they are down here, I reckoned there was a reason for it."

Costor shook his head, once again bemused by Mayport's babbling. "I won't manage a portfolio that includes human beings as assets. Our bank would be shut down in an instant. I'm sorry to let you down, but that fellow disgusts me. It's not just those poor darkies. Something about him makes my skin crawl."

"Now you know why I wouldn't send Missus Thiervy back north on his say-so," Mayport said. "Something in him makes me the better choice of protector. It's that duty that makes me audacious."

Costor chuckled. "You've succeeded. Be satisfied."

"Not yet," Mayport said. "Thiervy depends on me. It can't last forever. You know his nature as well as I."

They sat in silence while Costor's fingers drummed to the beat of his internal abacus. He cleared his throat, looked embarrassed, but soldiered on in the interest of his client. "There are those who are very pleased to have the protection of a man who possesses the wherewithal to serve. My little Bess brags on it, in her way."

Mayport squirmed on his chair, but smiled proudly. "Maybe Missus Thiervy can see it that way. I don't think our friend ever will."

"I concede the point, but remember mine," Costor said. "Tell me what it is these local yokels want to buy. I'll find a lawyer to tell me if we should write anything down. It sounds like you're operating your purchasing on handshakes."

"None of this was my idea," Mayport said, hoping he sounded

innocent. "There's families all up and down the rivers looking for work. All I did was give some traps and maps, whatever they needed to get started, and off they went."

"Did you give them money?"

"Oh, sure," Mayport said. "Anyway, there's no guarantees. I might get my money back, but I doubt it. There's nobody else willing to go after what I want, so I took what I could get."

"When might you know if this was a profitable venture?" Costor asked.

"A day or two, perhaps," Mayport said. "I don't worry on that. I worry on Thiervy. These ladies want his machine. Won't that mean a workshop and metal and... things?"

"You mean to let him make these toys?"

"I wouldn't know how to stop him," Mayport said. "If he wants to take his crew in another direction, let him. I can roast beans faster than I can grind and press them. As for sugar, those swamp Frenchies down south of here have some scheme got up ahead of the Dutch wanting it with their lemons in summer."

"Sugar doesn't grow down there," Costor scoffed. "Those fools don't even know how to plow a field."

Mayport declined to correct Costor's ignorance, and so got him to fit the whole scheme in under miscellaneous expenses. Costor really didn't mind what his clients did, as long as it stayed in the black. Better, the narrow, shallow waters of the social pool in town flattered Costor's idea of himself as celebrated.

To that end, they all retired early to prepare for triumph. As promised, the city was beating a path to Missus Thiervy's door. The little cottage was too humble a destination for the parade. Mayport pleased everyone by packing up and taking over the townhouse of yet another failed plantation owner.

Until Thiervy had put in his request, Mayport had no reason to wonder at the grand residences. The locals called them by family names, according to who had built them. Costor told stories about landowners who had borrowed against labor, then borrowed to buy more when their crop profits hadn't covered the original loans. He put it all down as bad business and worse farming. Everything from rice to indigo had been tried in the Confederation. Nothing had yet proven equal to the value of a man's life.

The raw fiscal reality did little to change the habits of the locals. Just as the New Amsterdam fellows were mad to fund anything likely to sail east, the Confederalists were desperate to strike it rich as lords and masters of the fields. Their various proud assertions had nothing to make Mayport abandon his company and craft.

He chose a blue house with plenty of tall windows, sound in every respect. He then got out of the way while Thiervy indulged his mother. He had no idea what a lady's home was like, but was eager to find out. Bess and her sisters made themselves handy, to the delight of everyone.

While the ladies made the place homelike, the gentlemen got down to business in the outbuildings. Mayport was kept busy trotting samples to Chef Gasteau for grade and pricing. Thiervy insisted on setting up Mayport's workshop himself. Much as Mayport had profited with his cargoes, he was nothing like the steady fellow his little household imagined.

One afternoon, Chef Gasteau sat him down and very nearly put on a stern look. "You know quality and value by now. I've got all I need after the cocoa butter you sold to me. You'd do better to mind your own business and trust your own good sense."

Mayport hung his head. "I hardly know what that is. Little Bess is fit to be tied over her parlor cocoa running out. I can't suit her and Thiervy both."

"You can't suit anyone until you suit yourself," Gasteau said. "Bess has her parlor, Cully has his ship, Joseph has his shop, and his mamma got her home. What did you think to leave over for yourself?"

"I have Joseph, and Ma as a bonus," Mayport said. "There's no other reason to go on like I do. They've got no real idea that I'm no better than a smuggler and don't mean to change."

"It's a good thing you came back south," Gasteau said, now very serious indeed. "It's the only place left on Earth where a man can be a true gentleman. You'd better just forget all that Dutch nonsense and settle down."

Mayport shifted on his chair and tried to think of a reasonable reply. "At least I know I'll never harm your custom if I stay. It would take a lifetime to learn what you do."

Gasteau looked disappointed. "You're not trying to be a chef, young fool. I don't know what you are. Don't you even know why you started all this?"

"My father started this," Mayport said. "I had to see it finished, just to clear the debts he left behind. I've got something to show for it, that's true, but this isn't mine. If I ever do start up on something of my own, I imagine people will notice pretty quick."

"You sure made all his big talk into something real," Gasteau said, trying to be a comfort. "I'm glad you saw sense about your shipping operations. It'll save you a world of trouble and danger."

"It's not my shipping," Mayport said. "That's the whole point. The Process will do for running things up to New Amsterdam, or even further if Costor makes a deal. I have to move my own goods, so I imagine other fellows are able to do the same for themselves."

"It's more wisdom than your father had about it," Gasteau said. "He didn't trust anybody to do anything right. According to him, nobody could unless he was right there to make them."

"If he was alive, I couldn't do what I'm doing," Mayport said. "He would have fought me on everything and won. Who knows what I would have been?"

"You would have become like that Jesse," Gasteau told him, sharp and certain. "If I were you, I'd take an interest in myself. You're the only one you don't account for. I've said so twice, and you still don't hear me."

Mayport took his admonitions back home and dealt with the delivery of stock as he pleased. The quality was very fine, and in quantity to get his own mill turning. Bess had begun to crow about Mayport's chocolate from Amsterdam, which the local ladies thought had to be Dutch and therefore not half so delightful as what they called Thiervy's French chocolate.

He was glad to be stoking his oven when she came again to sweetly demand his entry to the parlor war. "You can't imagine how they try my patience! Just because your Joseph is a frog, that doesn't make his stuff a French chocolate! You'd think they were being ignorant on purpose!"

"Don't call his syrup 'stuff' to me young lady, or you can do without your so-called French chocolate, which honestly is Dutch as the day is long," Mayport said. "I've had them all, and Aztec too, and lump sweets from India. I've tried English milk bar just last week, and mean still to see what a truffle is. Gasteau's making chocolate that's pure white. I just dare you to argue with him about whether or not it's real chocolate, French or otherwise. You go on up to the house, picky child. I'll see to you by and by."

Bess obeyed, but looked shocked to have been scolded. Mayport was shocked to have spoken so, but liked less the nature of her badgering. He returned to his ovens and squared up once more to the challenge of roasting a bean fit to eat.

Once he settled into his routine with rake and paddle, treadle and press, he could be neither hurried or slowed. The beans made most of the decisions for him: how long to dry, how heavy to press, how fine the powder and pure the butter, all were beyond his control. He could only pay close attention to every detail along the way, and hope that fate would be kind.

Gasteau had been right about Mayport's eye for quality. He knew at a glance what stock had been exposed to sea or rainwater. No amount of French persuasion could make him unlearn from his own mistakes. Some men cursed him in the end, but Mayport found himself remarkably unwavering in his standards.

While he worked, he thought about Gasteau's worries. They were valid, for as far as they went. When he paused in his labors, he looked out at his home and wondered what else there was in the world for him to want.

Chapter Thirty-Four: Duty

Mayport started his day in a fine mood. He felt as full of merry tunes as Thiervy's crazy chocolate still. The sound of it going full tilt made him stop at the storeroom first, to be sure of their supply. With very little help from Mayport, a thin but steady trade in the stuff had become reliable.

His next important appointment took him out of the neighborhood and past his barber, though he longed to stop for a smoke. Further down the row, a Turkish fellow had fought a battle to revive his mamma's coffee, and liked Thiervy's machine well enough to pay money. Mayport stepped into the shop, breathed deep, and understood how the broad-smiling fellow had acquired such wealth.

He was met at the door with a cup of the legendary coffee, but the smile was not in place. "I don't mean to worry you, but I've been worried myself."

Mayport sipped his cup and made an appreciative noise. "I don't want you worried. How may I help?"

"There's a fellow in town," he said. "He's not from here. The way he talked, he's got to be from up north. I would have thought of you anyway, but he asked for you particularly."

Mayport glanced at the chocolate still, then raised an eyebrow. "Well, it's obvious that I've been around here. What did he want?"

"That's what worries me," he said. "He's after that nice Mister Thiervy's mother. I don't care to repeat the things he said, I'm a polite man. But between gentlemen, you take care of her."

"Of course," Mayport promised with a smile. "I think I know the very fellow you mean. I'll look into this immediately."

With his customer comforted, Mayport approved of the work being done and took himself out again. Thiervy was easy to find, up to his hips in an engine down in the belly of the *Process*. Mayport admired the view until Thiervy crawled back out of his first love and paid attention to his second.

"You're grinning like a fool," Thiervy said. "What's wrong?"

"Those men of yours are working harder than we are. Did you

find a place to send them lunch?" Mayport asked instead of answering. Thiervy frowned, so Mayport tried again. "Why would anything be wrong?"

"Just come out with it," Thiervy said, all impatience.

"I want you to make sure this thing will stay aloft, and your fellows can fix it on their own," Mayport said. "Captain Cully's almost ready to go north again."

"We can go any time," Thiervy said, waving a hand at the engines. "This is just maintenance, and it's done now."

"We're not going anywhere," Mayport said.

Thiervy looked startled, then embarrassed. "Why not? Have you got something else for us to do?"

"For now, I don't," Mayport said. "It might not be apparent to you, but we have responsibilities in this town now. Your mother's reputation depends on the fact that she is under our care."

"I'm sure you've done all you can," Thiervy said. "All right. I'll just keep to Cully's schedule and make regular hours. He said he wasn't going to wait for you to decide about the cargo this time."

"He's the captain," Mayport said, and shrugged. "He would know best. He'll have to make up his own mind about this vessel if I'm not around to do it. Your mother needs me."

"You mean, she will when I have to go," Thiervy said. "You never forget that I leave sometimes. Even though I could make a living on land now, and everything else you've done, you won't forget."

"You talk like I don't know you," Mayport said. "Maybe you should wonder if Cully wants you back on his crew."

Thiervy frowned. "Why wouldn't he?"

"I didn't really ask you about that, and don't mean to," Mayport said. "You'd be a fool to miss the chance, if he'll have you. One day, I'll make things so comfortable for you, you'll stick for good."

"You listen to Bess too much," Thiervy said. "What else about me needs fixing?"

Mayport looked him over carefully. "New boots. You've said you mean to, many's the time."

Thiervy nodded once, but didn't look satisfied. "Are you headed back to the shop? I could walk with you. I don't want to be down here when the heat rolls in."

Mayport was already drenched with sweat, and didn't want worse either. They made their escape by privilege of ownership but Mayport had to go see his grocer, the dairy fellow, and take a walk through the market before his day was truly begun.

"I don't see how you make money," Thiervy said when Mayport was done haggling with the ice monger. "You do no selling that I've seen."

"Never mind about that," Mayport said. "Your not-milk taught me a lesson, I'll admit. We brought it out of season. Some don't like it for the weather alone. We can't do much about the heat, you'll grant me that."

"I can see you're miles ahead of me already," Thiervy said, amused. "Shall I build something novel for you?"

"You might think of something once you see for yourself. I never know when your streak of genius will leap up and take us over," Mayport said. "For now, I must be the bearer of unhappy news. Er, unhappy for you. I'm thrilled."

"What?" Thiervy demanded, suspicious all over again.

"Your father has some fellows in town," Mayport said. "He may be here himself, I'm not sure. Several of our clients are concerned. One today took the time to tell me directly that we are being watched by unkind eyes."

Thiervy stepped back, perhaps seeing something unkind in Mayport's eyes. "What are you going to do?"

"Exactly what I promised you, so many years ago, if he won't see sense," Mayport said. "You are mine, fair and square. This business is mine. I won't be threatened and bullied as you were. It's better if he finds out the truth of me sooner."

"You never go without weapons," Thiervy said, halfway to excited already.

"I'm a lousy fighter," Mayport said. "I do better to avoid violence unless I really mean to go all the way. In his case, that's precisely what I mean to do. Your tolerance of him is the only thing that stops me."

"Let's go get some lunch," Thiervy said. "You get so cranky when you're hungry."

They went home for a cooling lunch. Bess was full of big talk, much of which Mayport had heard before. "Are you sure of yourself, my dear? I'm always your servant, but you've set yourself a challenge."

Bess pouted over her fork, then turned a sweet smile on Costor. "All I need is that stuff he makes you boys every night, but more of it and cold. I *can* have it, may I not?"

Costor looked embarrassed. "My dear, if you could only explain what you mean to do with it?"

"Our Mayport understands every word," Bess said, annoyed. "He only pretends he doesn't. I think he's jealous of me for being so clever and thinking of it first."

"Dear girl," Mayport said, when a beat gave him opportunity. "All has been arranged. You may ask our Mister Thiervy, for he remarked on my excess."

Bess blushed prettily and returned to her luncheon with a graceful murmur of thanks. The afternoon was devoted to her command, though Thiervy complained of the innovation. Mayport made the work go faster by using one of Thiervy's larger, but impractical, machines.

"I worked very hard to perfect that application," Thiervy said, annoyed with her demands.

"It's not our job to say about that," Mayport said. "Anyway, it's not my job to say. I let you do what you wanted, and you're satisfied. I can't stop people doing what they like, once they've paid their bill. She's a dedicated customer, and my friend. If she goes on being clever, I'll have to find an apprentice for the shop."

"Inevitably," Thiervy said. "Or one of us could become a scandal for the final time. I imagine you could get an heir for us very easily, if you tried."

"Even Uncle Jesse hasn't managed that," Mayport said. "In some areas, I don't mean to innovate. I'm simply incapable of living up to certain expectations. If I become the sort who can be responsible, an apprentice would suit me fine."

Thiervy shrugged a couple of times. "I have fellows who can run this thing better than I can. At least you'll have your afternoon free if you hire the labor for the work."

To Mayport, that was a very expensive free afternoon, but he hardly wanted to argue. The finer young sprouts of society had drawn around Bess and Costor as novelties. Their accents and reserved manners did little to pale their generosity and high spirit. Bess had found, at last! The haven of gentlemanly dance partners her home soil had never managed to deliver.

The heat of the day lingered long after sunset. The evening promenade of the neighborhood could hardly be put aside, regardless of the weather. The younger members of their little society were drawn to their door, ever attracted by Missus Thiervy's sense of hospitality. Then when the moist, waning hours threatened to stifle the convivial company, Bess presented her radical innovation.

Dishes of ice cream and crushed ice were offered to be smoth-
ered in the chilled syrup Thiervy had made famous. The company
was delighted. Each young man hurried to present a plate to the
sweetest girl he could corner. Mayport made his delivery to Thiervy
with discreet carelessness, though he dared a smug grin.

Thiervy tried the treat with mock skepticism, and was instantly
won over. Mayport brought fresh strawberries, and lured Thiervy
upstairs to his private den. On the window seat they enjoyed the
breeze, and fed on kisses as often as the chocolate. Thiervy pressed
Mayport back against the sill, unusually aggressive for so early in
the evening.

"We really must be careful," Mayport murmured. "At least
enough to draw the curtains. A bride would never endure less, nor
a gentleman attempt it."

"I forget more than my manners over you." Thiervy retreated
to the ice cream once more. "I can't understand what you mean
to do with your shop. One moment you're pressing cocoa butter,
the next, a lady's parlor novelty."

"I mean to do what's wanted," Mayport said. "Bess made me
see sense, though she didn't mean to. She's more interested in
thinking of her own ways to be novel, than doing what we tell
her. She's so proud of herself. I think there are ladies like her, even
if they don't speak up."

"So you mean to obey orders of our pretty little genius?"
Thiervy smiled. "It's a soft fate, and one you never imagined for
yourself."

"I might have had less," Mayport agreed. "I might lose what
little I have, for good reason."

"Make sure it's for a very good reason if you do," Thiervy said.
"It's a hard row to hoe, and no turning back once you go."

Mayport looked Thiervy over one more time, and again decided
his reasons were good as any. They finished their refreshment and
went down to enjoy the guests again. Thiervy was hailed as a genius once more, though he offered every protest.

Though he noticed nobody, more than one belle took a try for
Thiervy's attention. Mayport watched with helpless pleasure to see
how little they could move their prey. He knew that Thiervy sometimes wished he could be persuaded to fairer company, but it all
remained as wishes.

Missus Thiervy presided over the wild affair with matronly
tolerance. She remained unaware of the attention she had recently

attracted from up north. Mayport intended to keep her ignorant of notoriety unless circumstance forced his hand. Thiervy disagreed.

"I should tell her myself," he declared. "I won't leave her vulnerable, though I'm sure she's cautious enough. It's better for her to know there's danger."

"Be sure she understands everything if you put this burden on her," Mayport said. "There's no telling what we might come up against, trying to keep her where she belongs."

"I'm not sure I understand what you mean to do," Thiervy said. "You've never had much use for plain talk or common dealings."

"Your mother must be completely safe," Mayport said. "I've given my word on the matter, and don't mean to be a liar."

"You'll be a murderer instead," Thiervy said. "That's not like you, my friend. She's married, so there's at least one man who could come up against you."

"I can see that she must not rely on you to do the right thing," Mayport said, annoyed. "Even though you like thinking of yourself as a dutiful son, you only go so far. I can see my way to be dutiful and a patricide."

Thiervy stared at Mayport, shocked to the core. "I thought you had a sensible plan for all this."

"Maybe it's wishful thinking," Mayport said. "I'd be tortured if I never had the chance to say my bit. I can keep an eye out for years, trying to be ready when the time came."

"I hope he's that smart," Thiervy said. "He probably thinks of you as a spoiled eunuch. Anyway, he's a coward. He'd never come looking for a fight. Don't you worry what Mother would say if you go on like this?"

"I don't, not a bit," Mayport said, with a grin. "She never liked him in the first place. If the world was fair, your Uncle Jesse would have been married off north. He looks the sort that would have liked the rough handling."

"Maybe it runs in my family," Thiervy suggested.

Mayport laughed, but Thiervy had a point. He had come by his fiery passions honestly. They both had violence in them that made crossing them an uncertain thing. The filial duty Thiervy owed had saved his mother a world of worry. Mayport had no such duty. He laughed easily, and enjoyed his evening of good company and better entertainment. If this was the life he was willing to die for, he could do no better than enjoy it while it existed.

Chapter Thirty-Five: Desserts

Ma Thiervy was made to be more aware of her company, but for weeks had no other interruption. Mayport had resigned himself to the unseasonal seasons, and local customs that defied the days. Costor set the example of gentle indulgence, and she matched him merrily.

Mayport had known worse vices, and at last, it was only the fashion she had admired in her youth. Eager conviviality was a sight better than a lesser lady might have done. He followed her example by tending his business and readying himself to earn his keep without Costor's ready advice.

"They say a man can't run a business down here without abandoning all morality," Costor said, like a warning. He was having fun triple-checking his cargo manifest. "How do you intend to live?"

"Quite well," Mayport said. "That rumor is true, as far as it goes. It's impossible to have an honest business here. That's why I work with smugglers. Just make sure nobody up north thinks to wonder, and let 'em bid high."

"I didn't hear a word, do speak up next time," Costor said. "Anyway, the Dutch don't give a tin whistle for this Spanish so-called trade blockade. Back home, your goods are as sound as... well, me."

"One day we'll all see sense and go back to the old world," Mayport said. "Where do you suppose I would be sent? There's no telling how I got here."

"What a funny thing to wonder," Costor said. "You'd come back to London with me and the rest of the bank. Now, go tell Captain we're stowed right and tight. I have to make these chickens and ducks see reason somehow."

Mayport wished him luck and went on to report. "Cargo's stowed, Captain. How's the weather look to you?"

"She's turning fair," Cully said. "Can you stand still for ten minutes? I've been sending on to you about that Pilot Thiervy, and I want an answer, right now, to my face."

"Crew your ship how you like," Mayport said. "I know he's

sound and trustworthy, but that doesn't make him the only man for the job."

"I can think of a few who would be better," Cully said. "With all his options, he ought to make room for the juniors he's raised."

"It might take two or three of the fellows to replace him," Mayport said. "Just be sure one of them is open to persuasion, and you'll be right as rain."

"Did he tell you..."

"I did not ask," Mayport said. "I prefer my own, sordid version than the tedious details. Really, I hardly imagine it at all."

Cully seemed unsatisfied, yet reluctant to pursue the topic. "He hasn't asked to come back. I hardly imagined that he would."

"Did you do all that he asked?"

"Yes."

Mayport's mouth went dry, but his smile came like a reliable friend. "Yes. I imagine he wouldn't go twice in a row for that sort of thing. Anyway, you count it all too heavy. I have come away with another man's wife. No matter how noble my intentions, we must be practical."

"And watchful," Cully said. "I think I finally know why you ran here. Your Ma Thiervy would have gone anywhere if she'd picked."

"Maybe, but this place has done her some good," Mayport said. "I may go on west one day, settle in with the swamp French. They say I'd fit right in."

"You'd fit in with angels or alligators if it suited you," Cully said. "All right, you stay and help Thiervy be watchful. There's nothing so urgent as this to take you from port. I'll run Costor and his ladies home before they miss their precious season. Then you must face reality and understand that these little French cocoa runners think they have you over a barrel."

"I'm lucky to have you," Mayport said. "My father was wrong to distrust you. It is a relief to leave all this safely in your hands."

"We'll go again together when I come back," Cully said in an encouraging way. "India, if you like. You barely got a taste of the place. Ma Thiervy would like the markets."

"Or our prizes for her from them," Mayport said. "Don't forget your tribute from New Amsterdam, or she'll strike you from the kitchen list."

Cully laughed, and at last dismissed Mayport from inspection. Mayport looked on the *Process* with pride, only a little sad to know she would set out by night, and on a course he did not know. He did not linger at shops as he might have. Cully had the right idea. There was plenty at home to keep him occupied and handy at a moment's notice.

He missed Bess and her bright company the moment he stepped inside. The midday table was waiting for him, so he went in without changing his jacket. Ma Thiervy only smiled, where Bess' sharp glance would have sent him out on the hop.

"Is it possible that there may be peace at last?" Ma Thiervy asked. She tilted her head this way and that. "Silence! I thought it could not be bought at any price."

"I thought you'd had a lifetime of it back home," Thiervy said. "I like this soup. Thank you for remembering."

"I think we're all a little tired of excitement," Mayport said. "Anyway, Cully's to be off with the weather, and didn't ask you to crew. Now you don't need to think on that for a while."

"You do work miracles," Thiervy said. "Maybe you're right about the excitement. I feel like I could sit down and read for a week."

"Carry on straight ahead," Mayport said. "I have my days full making good use of your ready-made innovations."

"Very well. If my genius isn't appreciated, I shall sulk," Thiervy announced. "Don't expect even one little thing from me."

Thiervy made good on his threat directly after being fed, and blessed silence prevailed once more. Mayport endured the heat of the workshop until the last bean was rendered. There, boys with messages could find him without risking Ma Thiervy's patience.

He was outside washing his face at the pump when he saw the *Process* rise up and drift away. He was startled to see and recognize her at a distance. He longed with all his heart to change his mind and bring her back. Instead, he went up to his room and made a bit of fuss over himself for dinner.

To his surprise, Thiervy's idea of pouting was to make up lies from snipped-off parts of his reading. He delivered it all in the same somber, earnest tone as a gauge reading. Even Ma Thiervy couldn't catch him until he took an abrupt turn for the ridiculous and left them weak with laughter.

The others retired early, Ma Thiervy to plan her morning attire and Thiervy to devour more books. Mayport lingered in the parlor, enjoying the luxury of cigars and brandy and silence. He turned his chair to the open window, and watched the street come alive for the night.

Up the row, a brood of bachelors were having a fine time. Mayport hoped Ma Thiervy would soon be prepared to endure a similar row. He felt settled, and only wanted company to be satisfied with himself.

He finished his evening indulgences in time for the maids to set up their trays on the porch. He got up and went to sit with a glass of lemonade. His neighbors offered greetings, or stepped up to the porch to enjoy a glass with him. Thiervy came down to ask about a missing volume and stayed for the cookies.

The evening was no different than any other since they had settled at last. Thiervy drew company among the young neighborhood fellows. The young ladies came to call on Ma Thiervy, their timing coincident with the fellows who had their fancy.

Thiervy was noticed as often as Mayport was. Among their peers, they seemed driven by industrious nature to decline all attentions. If their guests wondered beyond that, it was to be grateful for two less competitors among the belles.

Mayport heard the cheerful violence of the bachelors evicting someone into the street. An indulgent chuckle went through the company as all eyes slid to ambiguous points of interest. The expelled man voiced his sense of injustice at length and full volume.

"They'll get the watchman called if they go on," Mayport murmured, but made no move to summon the authorities.

A few ladies used the commotion to gain escorts, and so returned to the promenade. Mayport went as far as the gate, and stood a moment to see what he could see. The street had gone too quiet for a drunken misunderstanding. Then, like a roach on the dinner table, a string of vile invective ruined the evening's tranquility.

"He's on the wrong street to find a streetwalker. Should we go have a word?" Mayport asked.

"Those young bucks will set him straight," Thiervy said, but sounded uncertain.

"Whore! Come out before I find ya!" the drunk bellowed. "You know what you get for hiding! You ain't too old to be a mamma again, so come on home! Whore! Don't make me hunt you now!"

Even the youngest boy on the street shouted down the fool. He found new curses for them all, and seemed genuinely startled at their stand for decency. The louder he yelled, the more Mayport heard of an accent he recognized.

"Go inside, Joseph," Mayport said. "Keep your mamma in, and

send a maid to run for your uncle and the watchman."

"What the hell do you mean?" Thiervy demanded.

"What I say, now go on," Mayport said. "You don't want her worried by a drunk."

Thiervy peered out at the fresh volley of threats and obscenity. His face went pale, and he rose from his seat, shooing the maids ahead of him. Mayport went up to the porch to keep an eye on the road beyond the garden gate. "I ain't going off to hide with the women, Mayport Titus. You're talking to the wrong fellow for that."

In the street, shouts of objection had become murmurs and a rush to get away from the senseless fellow. Mayport watched his unsteady progress, recognizing a familiar rage in a new shape. He leaned against the porch post as Mister Thiervy shouted insults and demands at the neighborhood.

"We don't allow that sort up in here," Mayport called out. "Why don't you go back up north where you belong, you damn fool?"

Mister Thiervy paused his tirade to peer blearily up the path. "Good God! You're Mayport Titus!"

"The very one," Mayport said.

Mister Thiervy looked suspicious. "You left out of here this morning. I saw you."

"That was my ship," Mayport said. "It goes as it must. This is my home, where you are trespassing. Go on home, or just away, before you can't go anywhere."

The warning did nothing to slow the beery assault. Mister Thiervy reeled up the garden path, peering up at the second floor windows all the while. "Whore! You get out here! I'm being nice! Come all this way to bring you home! You come on fast, and I won't be mean!"

"You shut your mouth or I'll shut it for you," Thiervy said, near to shouting himself. "I've done it more than once. We're not back home any more, old man."

"You turn around and go," Mayport repeated, low and tense. "There ain't nothin' for you here but trouble you don't want. You had whores aplenty last I saw of you. Go back to 'em."

Mister Thiervy laughed in his face. "Don't think I'm ignorant of you and your tricks. Money won't get you out of this one. You've seduced my wife, but I mean to have her back. Every law in the world is on my side, whether you like it or not."

Mayport knew his fury was burning in his eyes. Mister Thiervy laughed again, mocking and full of confidence. Mayport could think of one law that would stop him for good, and maybe that showed along with his temper.

Mister Thiervy hesitated in his hilarity and studied the house anew. Mayport drew his brace of pistols faster than his opposite could make a decision. All that drunken rage focused on him at last, but too late.

"I don't fight fair, Mister," Mayport said. "You need to understand where you are, and who you're talking to. I didn't seduce your wife, you damn fool. I took your son and mean to keep him. You want to stop me? Let's see if you're faster than a hot ball."

Mister Thiervy stood staring at Mayport's guns, some of the careless confidence petering away. "You're a damn fool to risk your life over either one of them. You ain't but half a boy anyway."

Mayport would have answered, but something howling and heavy flew past him on the path. Thiervy plowed into his father with all his strength, then drew back and struck, rocking Mister Thiervy's head again and again. Neither of them could check their momentum, and they slammed hard against the low picket gate.

Thiervy shoved with all his strength, making primal, triumphant sounds as his father cried out in pain. Mayport holstered his weapons and yanked at Thiervy's coat "He's hung up! Let go!" Thiervy kept up his attack until Mayport grabbed him around the waist and hauled hard to toss him aside. He grabbed the elder Thiervy by the coat and yanked again, then leaped back in case they decided on another round.

Mister Thiervy fell forward on the gravel walk, blood pouring from his back where a picket had torn cloth and flesh alike. The sound of his half-drowned curses drove a cold spike through Mayport. Mister Thiervy struggled to his feet, hardly slowed by his wound.

He swung at Mayport, wide and powerful, as if he expected no resistance. Mayport ducked and came up with a swing of his own. He cried out as his fist connected with the solid target of Mister Thiervy's jaw. Something gave under his hand, and Mister Thiervy staggered back once more, spitting blood and bits of white as he went.

"You get the fuck out of here while I'm still letting you live," Mayport heard himself command. "I always wanted to make your wife a widow."

Mister Thiervy looked around at the street full of people, none of whom seemed interested in taking his side. He wiped at his mouth, then laughed despite the pain. "You fools! Don't you know these two ain't natural? That woman this one calls a mother ain't natural. Why would a natural woman wander off from home? And he's one just like her, and worse!"

Mayport wanted to make good on his threat. More than one fellow on the street would be inclined to look away, as they had over the earlier jovial ruckus. He slid his hand back to a pistols once more, and then froze when he heard "Mayport, son, you stop this fighting now. I won't have it."

"It's your husband, Ma," Mayport said. "I made a promise about him, and I mean to keep it."

"He's leaving now," Ma Thiervy said. "Aren't you? There's nothing for you here, just as my boys said."

Mister Thiervy stared at his wife, expression a mix of longing and disgust. Her stone-cold stare never wavered, though he waited a long time for something that never came. One of the little boys took the opportunity to wing a stone over the fence and strike him on the back. He whirled, but the child had darted away. He snarled at the crowd in general, but most of the blind rage had drained out of him.

Mayport kept his hand on his weapon while Mister Thiervy made his choice. There was nothing to do but wait. Mayport had made all his choices long ago. At last, Mister Thiervy pushed the bloodied picket gate open and staggered away, this time bent with pain instead of liquor.

All the air went out of Mayport and he sat down hard on the porch step. His head throbbed, heart pounded, and lungs went along with the rebellion. He was lying there, weak and senseless, when Uncle Jesse splashed his face with water. "Get up. A watchman's coming, and I don't know who else."

"I... I..."

"Shut up, son," Jesse said. "Do as I say, just this once. You're in a world of trouble if you won't listen to me."

"Why are you here?" Mayport asked, still suspicious.

"You sent for me, idiot," Jesse said with a chuckle. "I came loaded for bear, but you done made a spectacle of yourself. Keep quiet, and you won't do the same to our Joseph."

Mayport endured hours of isolation in cold shock. The only sound in his head was the hollow hum left by the thoughts racing too fast to understand. He didn't know what he was waiting for, until Joseph opened the door and flashed a reassuring smile.

"I am so sorry," Mayport heard himself say. Joseph shook his head, and cut his eyes at the fellow who crowded in behind him. "Hello. I suppose you've seen what I've done."

"Mister Titus, you might want for a lawyer," the fellow said. "I'm the watchman, Oliver. I'm no easy man to bestir. You sure did attract attention."

"I'm so sorry," Mayport repeated, still lost in Joseph's steadfast support. "I'll tell you what you want to know. I doubt it's any secret."

"I understand that the Yank you pounded was your partner's father," Oliver said. "He's been heard around town making big talk about his wife."

"I can't pretend to be surprised," Mayport said. "In New Amsterdam, he's tolerated despite his character. He's no more than a shipwright, and no better than myself. Joseph's mother is a lady, sir. Even a rough fool like me knows it makes a difference down here. Up there, he did what he said he would, and nobody blinked. He had to come south to find a woman who would wed him at any price."

"That says a mouthful." Oliver blinked rapidly, then slowly sat down on the sofa. "You say he meant to carry her out of here, when she'd told him no? I know her father. What in the world gave him the nerve to talk like that to one of our belles?"

"He doesn't just talk it," Joseph said. "He's an honest villain, and has done everything he threatened. He came down because he means to do it again. I won't stand for it. As for wanting a lawyer, my uncle is already here."

"It seems the family means to protect her from him," Oliver said, still puzzled. "I don't dare begin to wonder how."

"He made Mayport Titus fear for her," Joseph said. "Nobody that knows our Mister Titus is surprised over what happened. My mother wanted to come home, so he carried her off away from that monster back to where she could be protected. It's a disgrace that we had to, on her very doorstep."

"I am sorry," Mayport said. "I'm not a very good fighter. I have to rely on weapons, when reason won't work. All of mine are deadly. My stock in trade is valued at something quite shocking, so I do well to go armed."

"Ah!" Oliver said. "I had wondered why you went about so dangerous on your own porch."

"It's a precaution," Mayport said. "I learned to do so on my voyages. I imagined if anyone came looking for trouble, he would be a stranger."

"Do you think anyone's going to come down in here to raise a fuss?" Oliver asked, licking his lips nervously.

Joseph hesitated. "I can find out, if you like."

"You ask yours, and I'll ask my people," Oliver said. "If it suits you, and you don't run off before we have some answers, I think we'll be fine. Mister Titus, get a lock for your stock and put those fool pistols away in town. Don't you know that's how accidents happen?"

"I'm sorry," Mayport said. "I will."

"If Missus Thiervy ever comes to me asking to go back to her husband, you'll have to explain yourself a little better," Oliver said like a warning.

"I'll try," Mayport said. "I don't think there's much else to say."

"We'll just see," Oliver said, and stood up. "I don't like mixing up in family problems. Don't nobody tell me the truth anyway. Y'all need to keep this out of the streets as best you can."

"Thank you," Joseph said.

As soon as Oliver had gone, Jesse brought Ma Thiervy, who rushed in and looked Mayport over for damage. "Good Lord, child! What in the world made you do it?"

"I'm sorry," Mayport said. "I didn't have much choice."

Ma Thiervy frowned at him, frustrated. "Now what kind of answer is that?"

"It's the one we're gonna get," Jesse said from the doorway. "Unless you want the dear creature in jail, leave it alone."

"Well!" Ma Thiervy stood in wide-eyed shock a moment only, then recovered herself. "What do you boys mean to do?"

"Sit still until Oliver turns us loose," Joseph said. "He wants to know if the boys back home are going to come down and start a war. What do you reckon?"

"They better not," Ma said, but sounded worried.

"It's all right, Ma," Mayport said. "We'll see about everything. You'd better go get your beauty rest."

Ma Thiervy looked at them all, still not understanding the truth of what her boys had done. Mayport couldn't make himself tell her he had almost killed her husband over his threats. He might have gotten less trouble from the law for burning him down instead of beating him. Still, he was glad she didn't have to face the full horror of his fury.

Jesse saw her to bed and made a short goodbye, offering not a moment of reproof. Joseph lingered at Mayport's side, quiet and thoughtful.

"I need to know if you're done with me over him," Mayport announced. "I'll fight against him with all my fire, but don't tell me to leave him alone. He's not gonna allow that."

Joseph stared at him, then stuttered to answer. "I guess I ought to just tell you the truth."

"I'm all ears." Mayport tensed all over, and his softest smile came out as a defense. He wasn't sure why Joseph hadn't yet skinned him on general principles. Nothing had made sense, after he had stood against that drunken beast.

"I know you cared about me when we were little. I thought you would grow out of it." Joseph looked away, embarrassed and shy. "You're tough as pig iron, no matter what you pretend. I knew you loved me, but I didn't want to imagine more than what there was. Even when you came to find me, I knew and didn't believe. No matter what you did, nothing felt real. Then, Cully and I..."

"Don't," Mayport said. "You do not have to confess to me."

"He did everything I asked," Joseph said, like he wanted to tell. "All the things you refused, he did. I used to think the man that would do that would love me to the bone."

"Captain Cully doesn't love anyone but himself," Mayport said. "I don't refuse your desires just to spite you. Men like Cully are easy to find, so go get what you want."

Joseph's mouth drew down to an irritated pucker. "I don't intend to ever do such a thing again. Aren't you listening?"

"I am trying," Mayport assured him. "I wish you would make more sense. If anything holds you down or back, you smash it all to bits. I don't want you to do that to me. I've been awful sometimes, but we've always played fair together."

"This is not a game!" Joseph cried. "Not to you! Was it ever?

All these years, was there a moment when you were insincere?"

Mayport's mouth went dry with a fear so old, he couldn't remember when he'd first felt it. "No. I always loved you. Sometimes
I didn't know that's what I was doing. It didn't matter. I did everything for you that I could think of. I'd still do anything for you. I
want to."

"That certainly seems apparent, on this of all nights!"

"Don't," Mayport heard himself say, pleading already. "Don't
make me run this time, Joseph, *please*, don't be angry tonight. I've
got nowhere to go!"

Joseph froze in mid-shout, and stared at Mayport all over again.
"What did you call me?"

Mayport ran the words in his mind again, and the fear spiked
deeper, surprising him with its power. He bowed his head, apologized, and gave up on making any progress. Thiervy loomed over
him, and lifted Mayport's chin until their eyes met.

"You look scared enough to cry," Joseph said, fascinated. "What
do you think I mean to do to you?"

The possibilities were endless. Mayport already knew a few
things about Joseph's temper, and didn't want to know more. With
all his heart, he wished for something he could understand out of
this man he knew so well.

Joseph leaned down and kissed Mayport. His lips softly teased
Mayport's apart, and he tenderly invaded with deeper kisses.
Mayport's body slowly relaxed from tense fear, and he whimpered softly. His whole body shivered, caught between sudden,
urgent need, and the instinct to flee far and fast before Joseph's
anger.

"Now, what did you call me?" he whispered against Mayport's
mouth.

"I didn't mean to," Mayport said, blushing all over again. "It
just... slipped out."

"It's alright," Joseph murmured, though he sounded amused.
"I won't tell the headmaster. It can be our little secret."

Mayport squirmed, embarrassed as the schoolboy he'd been
when this conversation had last taken place. Still, his instincts
hadn't changed much. "What do you want me to do?"

Joseph smiled, and seized him by the arm, got him up and
moving. Quietly, they hurried to the room at the top and back of
the house that Joseph had claimed for his own. Mayport's heartbeat
spiked at the thought of being allowed within.

Joseph locked the door behind them. "I wondered if you would ever visit me."

"You wanted quiet," Mayport said. "Solitude and silence, for when you're thinking and all."

"I didn't mean from you," Joseph snapped.

Mayport tensed, and didn't know what to do. "I... I'm..."

"Don't apologize," Joseph said. "If that's all you can think to say, just keep quiet."

Mayport nodded quickly, but Joseph didn't seem satisfied. Instead of trying to figure things out before they got started, Mayport retreated to the bed and began to undress. In the shadows of the darkened room, he couldn't see Joseph's impatient stare. Instead, he felt the heat of that gaze and could only imagine the annoyed frown that went with it.

Mayport started to prepare the bed, and then Joseph was at his back, wrapped around him, kissing his hair and neck. They fell sideways onto the bed. Mayport turned over onto his belly and squirmed eagerly under Joseph's weight, so familiar and comforting.

To his surprise, Joseph didn't pin him down and skewer him. He looked back, wondering what the holdup was. Joseph was staring at him again, perhaps had never stopped, but this was not in the usual, hungry way. Mayport turned onto his side and tried again, rubbing back against whatever part of Joseph he could reach.

Joseph chuckled, then wrapped around Mayport and held him still. "Is this how you like it?"

"What?" Mayport squeaked, surprised. "Yeah. Sure."

"You can tell me," Joseph said in an encouraging way. "I already know you're up for almost anything. How do you really like it?"

Mayport was suspicious of this sudden curiosity, especially at such a moment. Wary, he eased himself from Joseph's embrace and moved to lay back against the pillows. Joseph watched his every move, like a tiger tracking his prey.

Mayport couldn't meet his eyes. "Can we try like this? Maybe like when we were in that jungle? You never said what made you want to, but I liked..."

Joseph pounced, abandoning his strange hesitation. He devoured Mayport's kisses, stroked their cocks together even as he petted Mayport from shoulder to hips. Again, Mayport tried to turn over, but Joseph wouldn't understand.

Instead, Joseph slid an arm under Mayport's knee and spread his legs wide. His hips were hoisted high off the bed, pinning him under his own weight. Joseph produced some of his fragrant oil, and spread it over Mayport's cock, balls, thighs and ass. Mayport twisted his fists into the blankets, groaning and twitching as Joseph worked plenty more oil inside him. Strong fingers stretched and opened him, smoothing the way far more gently than he had known to expect.

Joseph pressed his cock to Mayport's ass and thrust but shallowly, easing his way inside. Never before had be been taken with such slow, deliberate focus on his cries of pleasure and desperate squirming. He whimpered and groaned, bucking this way and that, trying to work his way down Joseph's shaft. He stroked some sensitive place inside him against Joseph's cock and yelped, instantly frantic for more.

"You love it," Joseph chuckled, and thrust deeper to make Mayport cry out again. "Look how you wiggle!"

"Please!" Mayport shouted.

Joseph leaned in with all his strength, silenced Mayport with kisses and rocked him gently over his cock. Mayport let go of the sheets, reached to hold Joseph any way he could, clinging to every thrust, drinking up all his kisses and groans.

Joseph's breath broke down into low grunts, then half-feral growls. Mayport arched his back, whole body burning with pure need. His ass was stretched wide, stuffed full, quivering between jolts of raw pleasure as Joseph took him harder and made his whole body burn.

Mayport tried to find a way to rub his cock against Joseph's belly without slowing his thrusts. Joseph growled again, seized Mayport's shaft and stroked fast and rough. New pleasure collided with the rest and Mayport howled, helpless to Joseph's passion. He wanted to beg, offer everything, all of himself, but Joseph was already laying claim to all of him.

"I love you," Joseph said between clenched teeth. "I love you. I love you. I love you."

Mayport gasped, tried to answer, but his body shook and his cock throbbed in Joseph's hand. His ass clenched around Joseph's cock, pulsing with the waves of pleasure rolling through him. He bucked in Joseph's embrace, undone utterly by the strange new power burning bright between them. Hot seed splashed his belly, even as Joseph spilled deep inside him.

He lay there panting, trying to get up the strength to move. When he tried to rise, Joseph pushed him back down among the pillows. In the haze of delight, it seemed completely natural to let sleep take him right where he lay.

Chapter Thirty-Seven: Saunter

Mayport stuck to his agreement with Oliver, and waited for Cully to return with his ship. As the days passed, Ma Thiervy became more confident in his assurances. She rarely saw him spotting Mister Thiervy's spies, or his return-threat to their intrusion. She only thrilled to have an escort of stature, and trusted completely in his protection.

Joseph was more discreet and active in the way he watched over his mother. Semi-amused tales of fights near to legendary cropped up in every quarter. By Mayport's count, the father and son had fought a half-dozen times in every bar that had room to swing. In such a town as this, bars outnumbered horses, but so did the tall tales.

Enough was true that Joseph came home to be patched up every time he went out alone. "Don't baby me. They're trying to wear me down. I wish that Cully of yours would hurry."

"When did he become my Cully?" Mayport asked, all the while winding bandages over Joseph's ruined knuckles. "I don't know why you go looking for these fellows."

"I hate worse the sound of these dogs at my door." Joseph hung his head low, at last showing a little shame for the way he carried on. "I don't want Ma seeing me like that."

"You got a lot you don't want your mamma to see," Mayport said. "Keep wishing and she'll go blind."

Joseph snarled, then winced over his split lip. "I hope you have some idea where to go. Ma's worked up like you mean to show her the world. The nicest place you've yet seen is right here."

"Cully will do what I say if you won't pilot for us," Mayport said. "I'll carry her off like I did before, if you don't want to come."

Joseph kept his eyes down. "I don't care about Cully one way or the other. I assume that's what you're trying to not ask."

"He's the one who will want those kinds of answers out of you," Mayport said. "Anyway, I've got more trouble than his pride. If he won't go along, I won't care what you do to him."

Joseph laughed, and seemed ready to do as much damage as

necessary. Mayport worried about the wear and tear on the man himself. Ma Thiervy only worried about her adventure-to-be, and the wardrobe she hoped would be required.

They let her go wild, let every tongue wag and brag over the indulgence, feeling not a pang over the example she set. Mayport reckoned the town old enough to handle the shock. Madame Gasteau took a lead role in the affair, showing off her own sort of genius.

Cully returned at last, hoping for a rest on dry land. He found hospitality and expectation his only welcome. Joseph had fellows putting luggage on the wagon before the Captain had his boots before the fire. The two hardly spared glances to one another, much less kind words.

"I thought you meant to linger here awhile," Cully told Mayport, suspicious of the shift in climate.

"I would if I could," Mayport said with a sheepish smile. "The opportunities have changed somewhat, and my hopes with them. There are fellows enough here to mind the shop, and Uncle Jesse to mind them. We can afford to wander, and you promised me fun one day."

"Where do you want this fun?" Cully asked, all caution.

"Ma likes hats," Mayport said. "Let's go south and show her where all those feathers come from."

Cully frowned. "You're not thinking on birds, when you try to point me south."

"I don't know what you mean," Mayport said. He took a deep breath, relaxed and tried to look a bit bored. "The fact is, Mister Thiervy came down while you were gone. We haven't been run out of town because of him, but it's better if we up and leave for a while. I even have to tell the watchman before I go. Aren't you proud of me?"

"So that's what happened to Thiervy," Cully said. "I wondered who he was mixing it up with these days. You look too fit and fine to be taking his temper much."

"Are you coming or not?" Mayport asked, impatient with the flippancy. "Joseph will navigate if you refuse to stand your post."

"Who?" Cully asked.

"Joseph Thiervy," Mayport said. "I introduced you myself. Don't tell me you actually forgot what his name was. That's not like you at all."

Cully looked startled, then embarrassed. "If I had any influence,

I would refuse this plan. It seems I shall have to do my share, if that's the only way to make sure you'll come home safe and sound. South, well... there's Spaniards and swamp French, Natives, and I don't know what else. Maybe some farms survived. There's no law down there, and less profit in the place."

"Never mind profit," Mayport said. "We need a place to take Ma on an adventure. She's got no idea us boys are a half-excuse away from making her a widow."

"She'll only be as safe as you can make her be, with your own two hands," Cully said. "Back when the colonies were slugging it out with the King's Armies, that little bit of swamp went wild and never came back. This one Spanish fella sent two armies in, and maybe a quarter of the men came back out. They say the waters are full of monsters, and the people are on their way to being the same."

"That sounds like just what we want," Mayport said. "You ought to have lied to me if you wanted me to stay out of there. I won't force you if it's all that bad. You can stay right here, tease the maids, and let us young 'uns take care of our lady's honor."

Cully didn't refuse outright, but reserved the right to grumble. The *Process* lay full of goods that had been selected for a southwest run. The captain had meant to try some of the passages their French smugglers used for speed and secrecy. Instead, they ushered Ma Thiervy aboard and made certain of her comfort.

She had no idea of a working cruise, despite her husband's profession. She had rarely been aboard a vessel of any kind. The innovations that cropped up at every turn aboard the *Process* were both wondrous and entirely unremarkable to her. That her son had made the craft a marvel of comfort and simplicity seemed only what she expected of him.

Mayport intended that she would never know what misery had been endured to make their vessel so fine and proud. Cully had practice at being servile with Costor, but had gained no grace in the matter. Once Ma had her luggage in order, they struck out south looking for birds. The legendary flocks were known to Ma Thiervy as decoration alone. Joseph buried her in the ornithology of fashion, and her curiosity did the rest.

Mayport left his shop to Joseph's men, though he readily imagined Costor's protest. For, although they had heard boasting on a ship sailed by one man alone, even Joseph hadn't expected to go out and try. Between the three of them, they kept the *Process* aloft, if low and slow. A small, gloved hand pointed the way after bands of bright-plumed birds or curious clusters of trees among the vast, wet woodlands.

For himself, the Process finally lived up to all her promise. Joseph was in his element, confidence the badge of his pride. Their first port of call was the same shell-crusted beach they had visited before setting out across the mysterious gulf. Ma had long admired the little collection Joseph had brought home, and made herself a fortune of ornaments from the lonely stretch.

She spent many a happy hour in sorting through color, though she grew dismayed at the damage to her complexion. "I just can't mind!" she finally decided. "You have no idea what some women would give for these. It's too rare a chance. I've got to be prudent."

"Why don't we just put them like they are in cargo?" Captain Cully suggested. "You can sort them on your porch much cooler than this place. You wouldn't be the first among us to enjoy too much of a good thing."

Mayport blushed so bright it made his own sunburn ache. "I think we can trust that so fine a treasure would be treated well. Only, don't overwhelm yourself, please. I thought we were on a feathering expedition, but shells are very fine."

"I just can't bear to watch you boys shooting like that," Ma said. "You can come back and have your fun another time."

They imagined themselves quite isolated until one morning the breeze brought the scent of smoke from beyond the northern horizon. Their imaginations were all too vivid, and so they said farewell to the little cove of seaborne jewels. Once aloft, Cully cursed himself for an idiot as they saw the scope of the flame from above.

"You wouldn't think a place like that could burn," Joseph said. He trotted to and fro on the deck, wet mop in one hand and bucket in the other. "It's the smoke I worry on, not this little bit of grass ash. Better stay seaward just in case."

"That's a long way home," Cully observed. He coughed and spat, but adjusted their course as Joseph advised.

The smoke only thinned with the breeze, and showed no sign of stopping. Some friendlier coves looked full to bursting with refugees. Others were black and ruined, or surrendering all to the flame. Even far beyond the band of burning lands, the smoke made every eye run with tears.

They had only Joseph's reckonings to estimate their position.

Coast and sea alike looked hellish and alien. They ventured inland only so far as fresh water and food demanded. At last, Mayport realized that Joseph was frightened, and relying on his seaman's instincts.

"It's a good job we didn't bring any stock south," Cully said. "The Spanish won't like finding us around here, but we're not carrying contraband for once."

"I wouldn't do that with Ma aboard," Joseph said. "She's not to become a notorious lady pirate overnight of our carelessness. I'd be happy to handle the dogs if we could find them. Everything I've seen today is dead or sooted."

"They say they keep the lighthouses on this coast," Cully said, but sounded uncertain. "We might could miss them, when it gets thick in the wind. They might be gone, and not admitted it."

"We'll take Spaniards, French, locals for preference, anything but salvagers," Mayport agreed. "I think we're more likely to get to them, than they to us."

"Don't expect to find much before we get as far north as the Confederation line," Joseph warned. "Everything down in here is wilderness, and getting wilder all the time. I've heard of bandits getting hold of whole towns for themselves, and nobody to say boo about it."

"I've yet to see sign of a real town," Mayport said. "Those little villages inland have got to be gone, and no telling where those sly fellows fled. I'd reckon anybody with sense would run if they could."

"These people don't have any sense," Cully said, very certain. "There's storms here as bad as anything you've seen in monsoon season. They know about when they'll come, and stay right where they are. They're like rats, hide some, run some, and know which for which."

"Then we'll find where they ran," Joseph said. "I'm not above a little wise company if the harbor's snug and sound."

Chapter Thirty-Eight: Prodigal

"Mayport, you'll never believe it," Ma shouted from her position at the bow. "You've got your own town!"

"That seems unlikely," Mayport said, as calm as he could be. "We can go on north if you like. There's plenty of supply, good weather, and the sun hardly up yet."

"It's Sunday," she said, and dimpled like a little girl. "There's sure to be a church, and it's early enough for services. We could all do with being grateful, after what we've come through."

He could hardly meet such a request with his usual indifference. He let her go tell Cully while he went below to warn Joseph. "Your mamma wants for some preaching."

"Why's that make her mine all of a sudden?" Joseph asked. "Anyway, where do you mean to find a preacher, way out here?"

"Cully has found my pinhole," Mayport said. "All this talk of being afraid over inland fires, and he's brought us within sight of the place. If he thinks being mysterious will make me more curious, he's mistaken."

"I think he knows that by now," Joseph said. "You *are* curious, but you look scared, too."

"You've seen my father's idea of a big surprise," Mayport said. "Wouldn't you worry too? If there's nothing here, that would suit me fine. I was enjoying this as something to look forward to, and now I have to be suspicious."

"Damn your fate," Joseph said, not at all sympathetic. "Dress nice if you're gonna walk with Ma to church."

Mayport went to do as he'd been told, and they took up Ma's position with the spyglass. There was a dirty break in the mangroves, of grassy mud and slow, fresh water flowing out to sea. A couple of bird-chalked pylons stood showing the high water mark. Spanning their jagged tops, whitewashed boards showed the faint traces of the town's name, and his own.

Cully dropped the *Process* into the sea and sailed the low winds that could take them to harbor. He said not a word, but tidied up and led his passengers ashore. He glanced around, then set off down a boarded sidewalk as if he knew the very place they sought.

Even for so early in a lonely inlet, the town was still and quiet. Cully murmured to Ma, who clung to his strong arm as they made their way down the sleepy streets. Presently, they came to a pine wood building with a cross nailed to the door. Ma hesitated only a moment, then marched past the gates and began a tour of the little graveyard.

"Do you know your mother's maiden name?" Joseph whispered.

Mayport shook his head. "Costor might. She wouldn't be here. I don't think there was even a plot marked for either one of them."

When the preacher came to open the doors, he looked them over with a shepherd's care. They took their places as other families began to congregate. At last it seemed the little church was holding all the souls their town could boast, yet all sat silent and watchful.

Even the minister kept quiet, though impatience was writ on every feature. His cold stare time and again fell on three empty pews at the front of the room. Then the congregation jolted in their seats as a shout shook the air outside. Mayport craned his neck to see out the windows.

The street outside was the promenade for a phalanx of folks marching in ranks as they sang and shouted. Their military airs made the morning lively, but the congregation shifted and glanced around, all wariness. The troop of singers clomped hard on the stair, filed down the aisle, and came to rest at the empty rows. They sat as one, and fell as silent and still as the others had been while waiting.

Mayport kept to his usual Sunday habits, this time with better entertainment. Though the crowd up front was neat and clean, they seemed worn at cuff and collar. Their garments were outdated, but in a uniform way and made of new cloth. Even the littlest girl wore long skirts and sleeves, though the morning was warm and promised worse heat in the day. At the first prayer, the windows shook with hallelujahs.

The preacher could hardly make himself heard above the hosannas. While he delivered a few announcements, the front rows sat stone silent. At the first note of song, every throat opened with full volume, if little skill. His sermon fell into a quiet so still, it seemed to swallow up all sentiments. When he came to a hurried prayer, all hell broke loose until at last the preacher hollered amen. Mayport found himself keeping score between minister and assembly, though he blushed at his own idle amusement.

Ma Thiervy sat through it all with stone-faced patience. Among the adults she fit very well. Both Mayport and Joseph earned pokes for returning silly faces to the little boys, who had been equally chastised. The closing hymn of the morning came near to lifting the roof off the rafters.

"Well, it certainly is lively!" Ma said when she was allowed to smile and laugh once more. "Captain, what shall we do with ourselves? There's so much to distract."

"We can go on north with the wind," Mayport suggested. "This place looks as plain and toneless as the name they gave it."

"I don't mind having land underfoot," she said as always. Whether thatched village or fish-smelling backwaters, Ma Thiervy knew her place in the world. "Perhaps you can move some cargo if you wait a day or two. This is a real port, my son."

Mayport took her meaning, if not her hope. They lingered at the church stoop to watch the marchers make their exodus. He wondered if they went about so all the time, or if they put it on special for Sundays.

He had not long to wait for answers. He saw no more of the adults, but spotted gangs of old-fashioned children here and there. They went in quartets on their hurried errands and sang down any remarks that might be passed. Though the show seemed hostile, Mayport could only laugh at the childish bullying.

"All right," Mayport finally relented to Cully. "What is this place? I have come and seen. I do not understand."

"You haven't seen the half of it," Cully said, sounding excited. "You don't know it, but half this place is all yours. More than half, I'd reckon. Your father bought it off some chieftain, and sold parts of it to other fellows on credit. These fools came in from all over the place for cheap farms and good fishing. That's only to start. Your daddy..."

Mayport shook his head slowly, and Cully trailed off in his excitement. "I don't see what you're so worked up about. You're talking about a real estate fraud."

"Does this place look like a fraud to you?" Cully demanded.

"I'll have to look closer to know," Mayport said. "I know all about land companies out on the edges, where there's no kind of real law. Are you saying my father got mixed up in that, too?"

"You ought to be proud," Cully insisted.

"Don't tell me what I ought," Mayport snapped. "I don't want a whole damn town to my name! What would I do with it, even if it was mine fair and square?"

Cully looked surprised, and totally unprepared to answer so obvious a question. After a moment, he came back to himself. "Be grateful, like I said. Of everything, you ought to be able to look at this and know it's a real treasure."

Mayport looked around the town again, and then turned to Joseph. "Should we stay a while and see what we find, or run north this very day?"

"We could use a rest," Joseph allowed. "Ma got a taste for hotels somewhere along the way. Let's find a place for her, and look into this nonsense. I'm sure it's nothing we can't set right. You do look a little scared, my friend."

Mayport nodded slowly, then sent Cully to find a suitable place to host Ma. She and Joseph looked uncomfortable. At last, Ma spoke up. "I wouldn't have said to stop, but I thought the name was funny. Have I caused some sort of trouble among you gentlemen?"

"No, my father has, and him not here to answer for it," Mayport said as gently as he could manage. "I knew this place was here. At least, I've seen it marked on a map. I was curious, but didn't intend to satisfy myself in this way. If you'll go on after Captain Cully, I'm sure there's good fun to be found here somewhere."

When she had gone, Joseph leaned in a little at Mayport's side. "If I'd known, I would have shifted our course. It's a small enough place to skip."

"Cully knew," Mayport said, more bitter than he had intended. "I told you I could show you about my name on a map. I hope Cully's wrong. The accounting alone for a scheme like this could send me mad."

"I wonder if he had plans for bringing you here all along," Joseph said. "He kept a pile of secrets for your father. I still don't know why."

"They were lovers," Mayport said in as neutral a tone as he could manage. "I guess that's why he never worked up the nerve to seduce me. It would have been incestuous, at least."

"He went along with me the first chance he got," Joseph said. "I guess his reservations stop at moments when he's the one being seduced."

"You mustn't expect fellows to resist. If one could, he wouldn't be human," Mayport said. "Whatever this place is, Cully didn't keep it a secret from me. He flaunted it almost as soon as I found him in India."

"This does nothing to soothe my worries," Joseph said. "It's got your name on the sign, big as life. How can you be so entirely ignorant?"

"I must imagine that this was my father's wish," Mayport said. "There may have been a plan or reason. You've seen what chaos comes of my father's plans, so don't get excited all over again."

"If there's a tale for this town, the best place to hear it is over a drink," Joseph advised.

They went together down the boarded sidewalks of the main street in search of a bar. They found a little hotel first, and heard Cully haggling within. They hurried on before they could be spotted, even though a shingle hung for a bar on the premises.

To their surprise, they had a long walk to find the next watering hole. The sparsity of accommodation was remarkable. In even the smallest town, a fellow expected a variety of establishments in which to disgrace himself.

At last Joseph followed his nose. They arrived at an unmarked door, but Joseph was confident. He knocked, and a fellow opened the door to peek out. Joseph flashed a coin and they were instantly invited to enter.

Within, they found a cozy room, full of stale smoke and smelling of wood wax. Joseph led the way to a table and soon the man from the door had returned with foamy mugs and a traditional greeting. "Y'all ain't from around here, are ya?"

"Just came up from feathering," Joseph said. "Didn't have much luck on account of the fires. Ma wanted to stop for some preaching, but we might linger a while."

"Yeah, we seen ya," the fellow said, confused. "You seen them fools and stayed on. That's more than most sailors do."

Joseph tasted his beer, then made a surprised noise. "What in the world?"

The fellow laughed. "We got one of them cold compressors from across to the gulf. Come thick weather, we cherish anything cooling."

Mayport tried the innovation and was instantly persuaded. Joseph remained skeptical of the taste, but was fascinated by news of a new machine. "We liked to have never found this joint. If I didn't sniff hard, we might have given up and gone back to the docks as thirsty men."

"Them ones from the church started in on the beer halls a while back," the fellow said. "They had men come from the farm and get roarin'. Their headman said it wasn't the fault of him that did the drinking, but him that did the selling. They called us a temptation no man could resist, until we all pulled down our shingles."

Mayport boggled. "What kind are they, that they boss the town? I heard there was no real law down here, unless some Spaniards come along."

"There ain't, and no bank neither," the fellow said. "We got them out at Titus Farms instead."

Mayport flinched at the name, but met the man's eye a moment later. "That wouldn't be the farm of a Corey Titus?"

"Mister Miracle himself, as-was," the fellow said. "He's a good bit dead, but they keep on like he'll come back one day. There's a son off somewhere, but he don't give half a spit for this town. Never did."

"Where would this young Master Titus go, if he were to suddenly care?" Mayport asked with a gentle smile.

The man studied Mayport more closely, then stood from the seat he'd assumed at their table. "Titus Land Company, I reckon. Or out to the farm, if he was crazy. Only a fool goes in there of his own accord. Too many have gone, and never come out again."

Chapter Thirty-Nine: Entitlement

Captain Cully made no revelations to Mayport until after he had Ma settled and comfortable. Joseph pressed Mayport to demand a full accounting of him, under threat if necessary. The more he saw of the town, the more Mayport understood that no one man could explain the peculiar settlement.

In town, men owned homes and stores, ran boats out in season for fish, and enjoyed a very simple idea of life. The ships to port were fewer than the little boats that came from inland on the river. In due course, they found out his name, and the vessel he had revived. For some, his arrival was akin to a ghost ship dropping anchor.

Mayport helped Joseph square up the *Process*, then ran cargo as Cully made bargains. Among them all, Captain Cully himself drew the most admiration. He was able to revive old feelings without elaborating on the past which inspired such easy welcome.

In the evenings, Mayport poured over his copies of Costor's documents, fascinated as never before. In the aftermath of fiscal streamlining, he could understand the meat of the records. The frightened, childish, secretive part of him kept hoping he would find some previously misunderstood entry among them all.

There was no mention of the place, nor income and expense sitting inexplicable among the accounts. At last, Mayport grasped the lawlessness of the land he had found. No matter how civilized the people, this place was beyond the reach of any authority to hold a man responsible.

With a heavy heart, he finally sought the inevitable establishment among bright and lively shops. He expected to find a monument to dust and neglect. He found a neat shingle swinging before shining windows. Peering within, he found the expected cram-jam of goods, but in this case stacked neatly in symmetrical bundles.

He recognized the contents of the bundles as packets of paper. Where the offices of New Amsterdam had been relatively scarce of documents, this was a library all its own. He did not need to wonder long what hands had kept the place supplied and tidied.

While he stood staring, a quartet of farm children approached along the boardwalk. They saw him watching their progress and stopped on the same step. He saw a kind of wise wariness in their eyes. One studied him up and down while the others stole glances at their leader.

He might have backed off, but would not flee from his own premises. At last, the tall, green-eyed boy stepped forward and squinted at him. He looked ready to stand his place until he'd worn a hole through the back of Mayport's eyes.

"You that Mister Titus?" the boy growled, squinting harder until he must have rendered himself blind.

"You want me for something particular?" Mayport asked back.

The boy thrust a ribbon-wrapped bundle of papers out in both hands. "I reckon these are yours. I can carry them right to you, if you tell me where you stay."

"Bring them as you have been," Mayport said.

The boy hesitated, then produced a key and unlocked the door of the crowded storefront. Mayport made to follow. A small, strong hand caught his wrist and squeezed firmly. He turned to find a little girl peering up at him. He shook the childish restraint off and went into the shop.

The boy moved nimbly between the stacks. Their weight gave the illusion of solid walls. The whole archive might have slid and crushed them both.

"That's all there is to it," the boy said, and shrugged.

"Have you a key for me?" Mayport asked.

The boy surrendered his own, then went out of the shop again. On the sidewalk, the boy took an identical key on a string from around the littlest girl's neck. He closed the door and turned again to stare at Mayport. The boy looked relieved, and finally hurried away with his silent companions. Mayport unlocked the door again, went in and fetched the top few layers of the short stack. He closed up the shop once more and hurried away.

He did not know whence he fled until his feet fetched up at Ma's door. She let him into her parlor, full of self-satisfaction over her arrangements. The tea table was ready for company, though she knew nobody to expect. She laughed at his confusion.

"The Ladies' Social Aide means to stop in," she said. "I think Missus Smiggins worries over my habits."

"Let us hope it is only that," Mayport said. "I remember now.

You asked for me. My head was in a fog, after a little shock."

"Sit at the window," Ma said. "A full belly will soon set you right."

He made a place for himself in the light and laid out his bundles of papers. "Is it alright if I catch up on my correspondence?"

"Who in the world has written to you here?" she asked back, astonished. She shook her head. "No, of course not, my dear. You must be attentive."

"Yes, Ma. As to the correspondent, there's a farm here with my father's name on it. Did you know? Captain Cully's not much for keeping secrets."

"Why, son, we were driven this way by the fire," Ma said. "You really do imagine things."

"These papers came from the farm, but I have no idea who sent them," Mayport said. "I'm near dead with curiosity."

Ma quieted him with tea and cake. The distraction was completely effective. The parade of ladies began long before he could sneak in a little sly reading.

The mothers and young wives had a wealth of sharp stares for him, but no real use. He paid attention to the lively chatter, though the topic eluded him. There seemed no other purpose to the gathering, thus making the cake a necessity for his happiness.

Every mouth had reason for complaint. Most of it was pointed at "them wild ones at the farm" and the roving bands of children. At last, Mayport could contribute. "Why are they not in school like the other children?"

"Them at the farm don't send the boys older than ten," A grandmother said, glaring at her cup. "They don't send the girls at all. I guess some would say it don't make a difference to folk like us, down here in nowhere."

"It matters more, in places like this," Mayport said. "Was there some particular reason they decided to stop?"

"If anybody should know, it's Mister Joyce, Lord take him fast," the grandmother said. "Your Captain Cully should know all about the fellow. He don't come to town but on Sundays, and not always then. Of course, he doesn't make himself hard to find."

Mayport retreated from the exchange. Even Ma saw the cold spite that came his way. Pure ignorance on his past was no kind of excuse, even to him.

If the ladies had come seeking something particular from him, they went away disappointed. Ma was displeased as well. "They asked for you, and for what? I've never seen such a lot of cold fish in my life."

"Never mind," Mayport said. "They enjoyed your company and each other. I don't mind to be unpopular. I'd rather be diligent."

At last she let him use a table for his reading. The papers were bundled in order of days. Accounts always look orderly at a glance. He settled in to understand the extent of this neglected venture from his father's past.

The first report listed mortgage returns on most of the town. Whole streets were listed as assets. Mayport looked out over the town and wondered who would want to own so much of the tiny village. He didn't, but had to face facts.

The second packet listed more debts and the names of men and various profits. As he read the particulars, his temper began to rise. Worse than being left ignorant, his name was attached to usury of the worst sort. The scope of the operation left him breathless.

Though he didn't know it, he sat dumbfounded for the rest of his afternoon. Ma's call to supper disturbed him at last, but only to deepen his embarrassment. He went down to the restaurant without going to change his clothes. Of all shocking things, his costume was the least of it.

He hardly made a sound as Joseph and Cully took their places. The table was remarkably quiet without his own lively interest in his companions. He tasted nothing that he ate, and stared hard at Cully. Once more, he had reason to suspect that there wasn't much difference between Cully and Corey Titus.

He held his tongue until Ma had retired to her rooms. He invited his fellows to join him aboard the *Process* for brandy and cigars. Without comment, he handed his new documents to Joseph. There was a spark of recognition in Cully's eye the moment he saw the bundle.

Joseph read without comment, then folded the pages neatly and returned them. "I want no share in this. Don't bring this business under our partnership. It would be our final ruin."

"Are those from the farm?" Cully asked. He licked his lips, and forced a smile. "They haven't bankrupted themselves, have they?"

"They have not," Mayport said. "They've ruined my reputation for miles around, but they turned a profit doing it. If the father who borrowed of them dies, the son is made to pay."

"I've heard they do that way in England," Cully said like an excuse.

"If he doesn't pay, he works the debt off on the farm," Mayport continued. "All the while, mounting debt on his own account."

"That's a French notion," Cully said. "You look angry, dear boy."

"Haven't I been clear?" Mayport asked. "You know my feelings on these matters."

"Oh, they're not slaves," Cully scoffed. "It's a debt and must be paid. They do the same in India, have for..."

"I am not from India!" Mayport shouted. "Nor England or France, and neither was my father! I am concerned with what happens *here*! It is being done in my name!"

"Cut this loose," Joseph advised. "It's a racket. Slip out, go home, and..."

"Never own it?" Mayport glared at the documents. "I don't care how legal this is or is not. It's a violation of my integrity and I will not abide it."

"You should have brought Costor," Joseph said. "I don't know how to help you with a mess like this."

"Your friend has less ambition than I imagined," Cully said. "So do you. I've kept my trap shut all this while. You've sold away your legacy and ruined your reputation as a dutiful son."

"Were you blind to the circumstances?" Mayport asked, irritated. "What duty can I possibly owe, when this is the legacy? Have you any idea what this means my father imagined of me?"

"I thought this would turn your head back, at last," Cully said. "You're not half ready. You'll wish you'd kept that factory before long."

"That is something I will never wish," Joseph said. "It wasn't worth the work to salvage."

"You're both ungrateful, lazy cowards," Cully said. "Don't you see? Everything's ruined now. You've gotten rid of the finest treasures you'll ever know. You're just too young and green to see it."

Mayport looked at Joseph, and knew his treasures were secure. "I've rid myself of much useless claptrap, but nothing I regret."

Cully chuckled in a knowing way. "Just wait until you see the farm. You'll understand what your father intended, and wish you'd had more respect."

"I will never respect inoperable equipment and obscene waste," Joseph said. "No farm can change that. More, I won't profit from cold, calculated exploitation of this kind. You seem to have missed the point somewhat."

"Yes, I have," Cully said. "You've sold and destroyed the very bones of business that would have seen to you for life."

"A business can't see to anyone," Mayport said. "Neither can money. I know that better than anybody."

Chapter Forty: Re-purpose

Mayport did take Cully seriously, though the provocation to abandon him was extreme. Joseph and he went walking on the country roads to find this famous farm. On inspection, it was difficult to find a patch that was not part of the farm.

Despite Cully's persistent expectation, the little farmhouses and more frequent shacks were pitiful. Every field had its own crew laboring at the rows. By his own accounting, he was owed a percentage of everything he saw.

When at last he found the proper farmlands, he understood better Cully's arrogance. A regular French plantation had been established for sugar cane. In the distance he saw the lush green of jungle trees standing in perfectly-cultivated rows. His heart sank at the sight of it all.

"Good God!" Joseph swore. "He must have thought to mill all this himself one day. No wonder the scale of his operation was beyond all reason."

"My father was, of himself, beyond reason," Mayport said. He sat on a fence rail and surveyed the disaster. "I wish this didn't make a horrible kind of sense to me. It's embarrassing."

"Don't explain your father's madness," Joseph advised. "You might confuse yourself. Are we going on, or not?"

"Not," Mayport decided. "These ticks have their heads buried deep in my flesh. Let's do what we can about the fleas for now."

"I think Ma had some idea of sending your card around to the debtors," Joseph said with a smile. "She remains convinced that tea and cake does much to cure all ills."

"Beer and cigars are better for business," Mayport said. "What I need is a gentleman's club, and not one to be found."

Joseph didn't dignify his worry with a response. They made their way back to town and threw themselves on Ma's mercy, if not her actual luncheon table. Cully was absent, and Ma was annoyed.

"I sent him away," she said, when Mayport asked. "He came along wanting to get me on his side about something or other. I don't have the patience for money you fellows enjoy. What makes him think I'm fool enough to side against my own son?"

"What did he want you to say?" Mayport asked.

"He didn't get that far," Ma said. "He said you were fixing to throw away all kinds of money. I reckon he had the idea I'd make you stop."

"If he ever tries again, listen before you say no," Joseph said. "He might take you into confidence to get his way. It makes no difference. He's sea-wise, and that's about all. Once he sets foot on land, he talks like he's the preacher of Corey Titus."

"It's insubordination," Ma said with a sniff. "If I had a maid who did so, she'd find herself out of position."

"As well our Cully may, but first we must attend this unexpected business," Mayport said. "He knew what we would find here. It's not up to him what I do about it. Don't mind our hours, or worry over how we go on. This is a rough place, and no town for gentlemen."

"As long as you are civil in society, I'm satisfied," Ma said. "Only, don't take after any of these girls here. They're too simple to be uprooted and carried away."

"Yes, Ma," they both promised.

They neither had an idea to comfort Ma with the knowledge that no upstart daughter would ever come to plague her. Though she was aware of their commitments together, she still enjoyed her motherly precautions. If she had settled on marking every living girl as unworthy, it suited them handsomely.

They set off for their evening entertainment with Joseph in the lead. Mayport wondered at himself for being so unhappy with his lot. Any of his schoolfellows would have been proud near to bursting if they had been master of such a place. Whatever quality it was that made him so humiliated, it had long kept him apart from such society.

There were too many wary eyes and unvoiced suspicion to suit him, and never mind the profits. Joseph had made arrangements at Collier's Hideaway to settle the difference between Cully's expectations and Mayport's business standards.

To his relief, men in this town weren't shy. Collier himself had taken the head of the crowd, though he was behind the bar minding his own business. At first sight of Mayport, he came out with a jug of wine and a trio of glasses, then sat down at the table.

"You sure look like your daddy," Collier said. In his mouth, the remark was not a compliment. "I guess you came looking for your money."

"You truly have mistaken me for my father," Mayport said. " You'd be mistaken. There's only one Mister Titus you should worry on. That would be me. Since you brought up money, I reckon I should look to see if I'm owed anything. I hadn't wondered before."

Mayport found the account entry in the ledger, then opened his own account book to a fresh page. "Mister Collier, I see your brother borrowed in Spanish silver at fifty percent plus additional refinancing fees. He has passed away and left you this legacy, correct? It is attached to this establishment?"

"Like an anchor," Collier said. "That Joyce keeps coming up with bigger numbers, no matter how I try to get him off my back."

Mayport recalculated the entire history of the contract, though Collier made every show of impatience to hurry him along. "Your complaint has been registered. My condolences for your loss. If you please, he's not my Mister Joyce, and I do not care who knows it. I'd rather not endure that sort of accusation. In any case, he's made quite a lot of trouble for himself on my books. This account was settled long ago, by any standard reckoning."

Collier opened his mouth to argue out of pure reflex, then stopped himself and took a deep breath. "I've said that for years, you don't know how many times. There just ain't nobody to hear me say it."

"I'll find the land deed and have it written over," Mayport said. "It may take some time for me to discover if there are refunds due. Any records you have of your payments would help me in resolving that matter. I can't trust Joyce to have done the thing properly after this, now can I?"

"I wouldn't trust him to water a petunia," Collier said, still very angry, though not at Mayport particularly. "I could feel sorry for a boy like you, stuck with a fool like him to tend."

"It'll be the other way around," Mayport said. He smiled in a businesslike fashion, and Collier returned to his post, still confused.

He was not the only man disappointed of a fight. Some, he forgave as he had done to Collier. Others, he wrote off as impossible credit risks. A few had managed their treasures despite the oppression of Joyce's usury. The prosperous were few, and even those had some mark against them, somewhere in Joyce's books.

Mayport imagined that Cully would have been impressed with the job Joyce had done. The books were filled with imaginary money. Collier's Spanish silver had grown by five hundred percent in a few short years. Even a man of means would have been ruined at such rates. Only a fool could have dreamed such a scheme could return a profit.

He found himself resisting Costor's tutelage as well. Without any usury law to stop him, even that steady fellow might have reveled in Joyce's tactics. By the same logic, he could simply undo what had been so diligently, wrongheadedly wrought in his name.

Joseph sat by, watching the fairy gold fade away before his very eyes. "You're not rich enough to be so generous."

"Look at these people," Mayport said. "Do they look like capital men? I'm no thief, not even by proxy. What do I lose by admitting to one and all that this fortune is a hoax? My reputation? Father did that in for me very well."

Joseph refrained from provoking Mayport on the matter while he had work to do. Instead, he made himself busy plotting the town map. The drawing as it stood was hopelessly inaccurate for both navigation and accounting.

The Titus Land Company did brisk business on ink as Mayport re-calculated mortgages. He kept in mind the French principles of such an agreement, though the contracts had been written in English, and with Indian ideals. They might have been Egyptian, for all it mattered to many of the debtors.

That bit of nasty work in town gave him a little room to breathe. He did not expect nor receive any particular gratitude for what he had done. More than once he longed for the relative anonymity of a busy New Amsterdam street.

His own accounting would not let him seek that pleasant refuge. Though no legal body would hold him to this higher standard, he had another judgment to fear. His fellow gentlemen demanded, above all, that he maintain that first duty of solvent, sound business practice.

Joseph had been spared this particular and unforgiving education. His peers demanded a very different sort of integrity. With very little effort he could conjure up the morality tales of greed and ruin.

Despite his obvious libertine inclinations, he was rather conventional in certain respects. He did not believe a fellow's personal standards could relax just because law or lack thereof left him at liberty. He felt prepared to enforce his own principles on himself first and foremost. The cost in theoretical wealth simply didn't enter into the question.

The embarrassment in the village was nothing compared to the task he faced at the land office. Joseph's map was a good start to a bad job. The documents themselves stood more as an obstacle than useful records.

He made a halfhearted start on the task, with no real hope in his dilemma. No one man, regardless of skill or good intention, could possibly verify the accounts. His alternative was to go on personally reassessing each account as it was brought to his attention. Worse, the farm children would probably deliver a new, totally inaccurate bundle to dump on the pile each and every day. When Mayport mentioned them to Joseph, he looked startled.

"Where do you suppose they come from?" Joseph asked. "Just farm labor running errands? They don't resemble enough to be family."

Mayport pointed to the piles of paper. "They're indentured to me. It's disgusting, but true. They or their parents owe me this imaginary gold. Therefore, the children labor to repay the debt, while the rest of the family works land to feed themselves. It's worse than slavery. With this kind of scheme, they all have hope of freedom that will never, ever come."

Joseph glared at the papers. "Throw these out, please. Even if you were owed every penny, every hour of labor, every child marked down to serve, you would not take it. I know you better than that."

"I need the deeds," Mayport said, sounding hopeless even to himself. "I don't know where to look. Men have worked years to get them, so I should at least deliver that much."

Joseph went up to the front of the shop and started searching. "That makes no sense. How can a deed be worth the paper it's written on, if there's no currency, no township, not even a watchman here!"

"It must mean something to somebody," Mayport said. "I could care less about it. We do well enough for ourselves, so let's find them and burn the rest. There comes a time when a fellow must clean the slate, if he's to make any progress at all."

Chapter Forty-One: Assay

With the thought of having words with children, Mayport went to find a bakery on the way to the land office. Before the appointed hour arrived, he had bait for his trap in the form of cakes and milk. He had then only to lie in wait for his prey.

They came as they had before, but the children themselves had been replaced. Mayport smiled brightly and opened his accounting book. Every one of them went pale with fear. The eldest boy gave over his bundle, but both eyes were on the treats Mayport had left sitting out.

"Go on," Mayport said. The boys needed no further temptation. Once their mouths were gummed up with sugar frosting, he opened their bundle of papers. "May I have your names, please?"

"No, you may not," said the eldest girl with a prim sniff. The cakes had received the same disdain from her and the little girl.

"I'm Hank Tate," the eldest boy said. "That little fella's Frog Dunel. I don't know a thing about these two, or I'd answer quick."

"Very well," Mayport said. He turned to the accounts, found the two boys and transcribed them into his own ledger. "Ladies, you may go."

"We certainly will not!" the eldest said. "I know what's right and wrong. I ain't to let these two from my sight. They'll run off."

"Young lady." Mayport stared at her until she fell silent. "The gentlemen will be discussing business. It does not concern you. Furthermore, you would find it tedious. Go home and tend your knitting."

He got up from his little desk and shooed them away like the precocious darlings they ought to have been. They seemed startled to be treated as no more than children. He ejected them from his office with only a little squawking.

"Mister Thiervy will come directly," Mayport said as he locked the door once more. "Do either of you fellows know what you've been carrying down and piling up?"

"They come from Mister Joyce," Frog said. "He sends us to run all over the place with papers off to the home fields or to the sharecroppers. There's always a couple of housemaids to go along when we come to town, is all."

"I see that you're working off debt for your daddy," Mayport said. "I know the feeling, so I mean to switch things around some. Will you fellows run for me instead of Mister Joyce?"

"It's worth my skin to go back." Hank laughed without amusement. "Those girlies had it right. I mean to split out as fast as I can get away, and find a place with some kind of law. You don't look like the fellow who means to stop me."

"I wouldn't," Mayport said. "Run if you like. I'll give you copper to carry you awhile."

Hank looked suspicious, which only confirmed Mayport's assumptions about his own reputation. "You won't squeal on me to Joyce?"

"He'll send the dogs after you anyway," Frog scoffed. "Once he has you, it's for life. He don't know the meaning of forgiveness."

"I intend to teach him," Mayport said. "He's doing things my father's way, I suppose. That won't go on for much longer, but I need office boys right now."

Frog looked Mayport over, far too shrewd for one so young. "I want you to write it down for me, that I don't go back to Joyce. It's got to be written and both of us signed. Anyway, it'll give Hank a head start if Joyce don't see things your way."

Hank preferred provisions to money, and set out on his way. Frog kept his word, once Mayport wrote out his letter to carry. The boy's first task was to recite the names of every indentured child he knew. Mayport and Joseph used the most recent packs of papers from Joyce to track down the debts and forgive every one, signatures and all, as Frog constantly insisted.

That local legal advice was bought at the reasonable rate of cakes and less vital victuals. Once Mayport started turning the children loose, Captain Cully began to avoid him. He went so far as to change hotels without notice. Ma found herself quite at liberty, and flourished under the arrangement.

"He's a gentleman," she said, cautiously optimistic. "At least, he's an officer. That usually stands just as well."

"This ain't the spring cotillion," Joseph said, annoyed. "He made to stand for you, then left his post. He could find himself walking home for that trick."

"Now, keep your temper," Ma warned. "Mister Titus has taught me how he values a capable lady. I'm sure I will manage well enough on my own. I did very well when we first came south. Didn't I?"

"Yes, and will again here, as you say," Mayport said. "Only, you must not hurry to forgive Captain Cully. He's had ideas about me from the start. I'm only now starting to understand what he meant to make of me."

"He's not your guardian," Ma said. "He can't make you do anything. He's a hired man, if an unusually loyal one. He shouldn't make you worry so."

"I might have allowed his influence of my own will," Mayport admitted. "There's our Joseph to think of first, and your safety. Those influences must come before his intentions. He's quite disappointed, but it can't be helped."

"I don't pretend to understand men for a minute," Ma said. "Let him shift for himself at meals if he won't mind, then. He agreed to obey a young man's will when he accepted his position. A fellow of years should yield with more grace."

"Cully was a particular favorite of old Mister Titus," Joseph said. "At times, his loyalty has been a godsend. Unfortunately, that loyalty goes directly to old Titus. He has very little interest in Titus the Younger, unless it's to pursue the will of a dead man."

"I will attend to our captain if the moment arrives," Mayport said. "He won't want for company long, so there's nothing to pity."

There was plenty of work to keep Mayport distracted from Cully's rebellious little career. He expected that old acquaintances would fill Cully's empty hours. Instead, Mayport was surprised to find that the society offered the man was quite limited, and often enticed only by the pitchers of wine Cully could provide.

The season itself made few the leisure hours of the local men. Even store clerks had some bit of field or a turn to take on the docks. No man got on doing just one thing. Lives blended in a patchwork of occupations as the weather dictated.

Outside of town, pinewoods and palmetto scrub had been pushed back over patches of high, dry land. The soil revealed was thin and poor, but the fishermen had the solution to that. A fellow with a cart full of seaweed and fish offal could make his garden patch the envy of the row.

The land itself was not the property of those who tended it. Such arrangements rarely went well for the farmer. Mayport had

only to think of Ireland and his own Confederated cousins to understand the risks.

The method behind such widespread madness was writ large
and pinned to the land office wall. A map of May Port, not as it
was but as Cory Titus had hoped it would become. The outlines of
factories and warehouses, broad avenues and squares of shops, the-
aters, and fairgrounds were all marked in the allotments.

Joseph's freshly-rendered map was less than a tenth the size of
the land office map. To be featured on the new chart, a building
or useful lot had to actually exist. He gave no illustration of good
intentions, nor credit for what was merely half begun.

Within the town limits, Mayport had been able to unload many
properties that meant nothing to him. The farmlands were not so
easily untangled. Hunt though he might, he could find no mortgages for the tracts.

"That land won't never be for sale," Frog told him. "Some can
manage to rent. Most just sharecrop it, like my daddy does."

"What made him come here for that?" Mayport asked. "The
soil won't hold spit, much less a seed."

"He saw a picture like that one up on your wall," Frog said.
"He reckoned a fellow could get three crops a year if the weather
was warmer. A man like you would be surprised what sand and
fish can do."

"What's your daddy's crop?" Mayport asked.

"Strawberries for preserves," Frog said. "He cuts cane and pulls
peas for Joyce in the seasons. I guess he didn't add up right,
though. No matter how he does, he ends up owing Joyce more
every season."

"So that's how Joyce got you," Mayport said. "Your father
traded your labor."

"It's only been a few months," Frog said bravely. "I know some
that's been sent down for years."

"And yet they have not all come to see me," Mayport said. "Are
they afraid?"

"It ain't like they can just walk off the farm," Frog scoffed.
"They'll get an assload of rock salt, a whipping, or both, if they
light out early."

Mayport nodded slowly, trying to keep the horror off his
face. He rose and got his jacket. "Carry my books for me, Frog.
Bring the folding secretary, too." They went together to collect
Joseph from the Process. "Come on. I've put this off as long as I

can. You'd better bring an extra brace of pistols."

"What's he doing here?" Joseph jerked his chin at Frog. "You can carry your own goods."

"He wants to carry them," Mayport said. "Hurry up, my fellows. Mister Joyce is in for some unwelcome company."

"You ought to bring Cully," Joseph said.

"He might as soon fight for Joyce," Mayport said. "Now, look smart. Frog, go find a buggy to ride us out."

"What happened to your daddy's steam coach?" Frog asked.

"The same thing that happened to my daddy," Mayport said. "Run quick now."

Frog elected a tall, rattling, antiquated touring carriage as appropriate. Mayport relied on his best New Amsterdam wardrobe, though the heat was oppressive. Even he knew the ridiculous realities of his sudden appearance in such fashion, and relied on its effectiveness.

He tried to count the fields in green and flower. Perhaps it was cowardice that made him shrink from such responsibility. He could not take pride in what had been done, and there the argument ended for him.

Joseph took in the view with equal discomfort. "You know there ain't really a thing wrong with all this. In Europe, they'd give you a title for owning all this. Sometimes I wonder why you struggle so."

"This isn't Europe," Mayport said. "Nor India, where I bet my father got his ideas. I don't deny the profitability nor claim certain knowledge of right and wrong. Still, I don't mean to live a life that gives men reason to hate me."

"I bet my father would be surprised to hear that," Joseph said with an indulgent smile.

"That fool may hate me, but he'd better not cross me again," Mayport said. "I might not be a son under the law, but I know my duty to Ma just the same."

"You like the way she pets on you," Joseph said. "That's all right. It keeps her off my back."

Mayport wouldn't deny the fact, so he contrived to look pleased with himself. Joseph kept himself busy tallying the acreage. Though his cartography skills had been honed for a higher purpose, he indulged Mayport in his desire for a strict and accurate accounting.

Presently, they arrived at a whitewashed iron gate set between brick pillars. The carriage rattled its way up a limestone gravel drive that made a pale curve through the shade of live oak. They followed it to the farmhouse, which stood as proud and grand as its European ancestors. They stepped down before a broad porch stair. For a moment, Mayport hesitated.

"Go on," Joseph said, and nudged him. "It's all yours anyway. At least it's not up to the rafters in scrap metal this time."

Mayport went up the stairs and was spotted by a maid before they could reach the door. She made a place on the cool, breezy porch and saw them refreshed. In this convivial way, they were prepared for the arrival of Mister Joyce.

That renowned person appeared in rough canvas trousers and a thin, short jacket over a plain linen shirt. His silver hair was carefully combed, and his eyes sharp and accusing above his genial smile. "I had wondered when I would have the pleasure. There were tales even this far south that young Titus got rid of old Mister Cane. I never met the man, but know he was a hard one."

"He is paying for his sins," Mayport said. "I'm disappointed in you as well, Mister Joyce. I've been in town for quite some time, and yet you have not come to pay your respects."

Joyce laughed at the little barb. "I am happy to say I am innocent of all excess. You'll find no malingering here, my son!"

Mayport frowned at that familiarity. "Our Mister Thiervy will be helping me with the survey. Your accounting is mostly fiction, except for the number of debtors. I can't trust the survey my father left behind, or the administrator either. Don't try to impress me with cane and cacao. I know you're selling these goods to smugglers. I may have bought some myself. I wonder if there was a profit in it?"

"Yes, of course," Joyce said, obviously offended. "You'll find every penny just as it has been accounted."

"That is my fear," Mayport said. "My fellows will need tending, so let your staff know we'll be here for a while."

Chapter Forty-Two: Fortune

Frog was soon of Joseph's opinion about Mayport. "Don't anything suit you? If I had a pile of gold like this, I'd be one happy son of a bitch. All you do is complain, no matter what you get."

Mayport kept a sharp eye on Frog's reckonings as he complained in his turn. "It's stolen from men who worked harder than I ever did. I might not even be able to give it back."

"Even if you knew, they might not be here to give back to," Frog said. "You ought to worry on your own self, not a bunch of deadbeats. If those ones are like my daddy, they never did mean to pay back. Not in money, for sure."

"You think about as much of yours as I do of mine," Mayport said.

"Mine didn't leave me a lockbox full of gold," Frog said. "If you can't think what to do with it, I got ideas."

"You just learn your figures," Mayport said.

Frog was curious about everything. He helped Mayport so he could handle the coins, though math was involved. When he was tired of sitting still, he ran off to find Joseph. Once, Joyce had spoken meanly to him, and Frog tattled to Mayport. Then and there, Mayport reprimanded Joyce for the brutish management of the farm.

He might have turned the entire Joyce family out to the road. Certainly, he had paid for services rendered and owed nothing more to them. His first stab at reeling in the greedy fool met with stubborn resistance.

"I always did so to these young thieves," Joyce said. "It keeps the place workmanlike."

"Do you intend to continue in your position?" Mayport asked, stoic in the face of such provocation. "I guess you expect me to be grateful for all you've done. I'm not. My father had no idea of business, but I do. You've sucked like a leech on every man you could find, until you've made a fat monster of this company."

"You've got a smart mouth on you, boy," Joyce rumbled.

"You will address me as Mister Titus or sir, your preference,"

Mayport said. "My partner is Mister Thiervy, and our runner is young Master Frog. This is a formal business. If you can't behave like a proper clerk, I'll find someone who can."

"It's just the way we talk here," Joyce said. "You're smart and snooty, both."

"You meant to be insubordinate, and speak to me as if we are equals," Mayport said. "That will not be tolerated. Neither will bold usury. If you go on squeezing these tenants in my name, expect to be squeezed yourself."

"Maybe I ought to just go off," Joyce said, annoyed and threatening.

"Go on if you want," Mayport said. "I'll be just fine without you. Ah! You look surprised. Did you think I couldn't count to twenty with my boots on?"

"You don't know the first thing about how this farm runs," Joyce said. "Nobody does but me. If I was gone, it would fall apart in days."

"Graveyards are full of irreplaceable men just like you," Mayport said. "You're no farmer, nor a landlord worth spitting on. You're a slaver, even if you call it indentured service. My father was a fool to trust you, but then again, he was a fool every other way. You're no surprise to me, nor wanted. Do you mean to mind me, or take your family on a walk?"

Joyce managed to hold his tongue, though his unspoken words seemed to taste bitter. Mayport resolved to keep a close eye on him. To that end, he set Frog the task of passing judgment on Joyce, no matter what he did.

With a reliable spy on his side, Mayport could turn his attention to his own business again. Joseph had done his best work on the warehouses. The sheer volume of sugar would make the Process earn her keep, even if she never made it back to India.

Joseph turned giddy over dreaming of ships to carry their newfound wealth. "Let's make Cully stay here with Joyce. They were made for each other. We can run north to port and back in a few days. Ma won't mind."

"No," Mayport said. "I've got trouble to settle here, first. Besides, Joyce gets left alone too much as it is. There's no telling what he's up to when I'm not looking."

Mayport had settled on Frog as a temporary solution to Joyce. The boy had shown a fascination with Mayport's pistols. He outfitted the young hellion with an old-fashioned blunderbuss, and plenty of powder for practice. What the weapon lacked in precision, it made up for in versatility and raw stopping power.

Joseph looked on the proud child with amusement. "You'll spoil that creature, and fast. What's next for him? Lace collars and heeled boots?"

"A rifle, if I can get one," Mayport said. "I would give him pistols, but he's bound to duel at the first excuse. I mean for him to stand guard while we're working."

Mayport let Joseph worry, and went on with Frog as he pleased. With that sturdy figure about town, he let it be known that Joyce had no sway with him. Though they might have taken rooms on land, the *Process* made a quiet nest to share. Cully sometimes walked the docks, but did not venture aboard. He spoke to neither of them, even when they were obviously preparing their machines to be landed.

"How will you tell him he's not needed on this venture?" Joseph asked.

"Directly, if he asks," Mayport said. "The *Process* was his home. I hate to see him lose her over misplaced loyalty."

"He should give all his duty to you, or go his own way," Joseph said. "I thought he was your man to order. Instead, he's been doing what your father desired, all along. Until now, the two had been close enough, so it didn't matter."

"He may believe I can't do without him, as Joyce still believes," Mayport said. "I'll prove him wrong. If we do that much, I will be more than satisfied."

"I'm being entirely selfish," Joseph admitted. "I want you all to myself, for once in my life."

Mayport was pleasantly startled by this bold admission. It strengthened his resolve in the matter of Captain Cully. He delivered the decision in person, and got a beery harangue on all his faults. The changes to Cully's character did nothing to change Mayport's opinion.

Despite these frustrations, their preparations were made without real disruption. Mayport was very merry indeed, when Joseph's measurements came out in a pleasing fashion. They need not take on a new property to go on with their business. They only needed to evict the paperwork that occupied the premises they already had.

Steady work by daylight hours left him free to enjoy the amenities Joseph had bestowed upon their vessel. He drew a hot bath in the copper tub and made the washroom bright with oil lamps. A boy from the village brought a basket packed with a hot dinner, and went away with a penny for his trouble.

By the time Joseph came back from his rounds at the bar, he had good news and a fine mood to go with it. "I hadn't thought how long these people have gone without a business that pays regular wages. I've got fellows from all quarters interested in work. I made no secret that the labor would be hard, and the product pure vice to ship north. That only made them more confident in the venture."

"You sound surprised," Mayport said. "This place wasn't built by lazy fellows. You've worked hard. Come have your reward."

Mayport ushered Joseph into the washroom and took pleasure in helping him undress. The favor was returned, and together they sank into the heat of a much-needed bath. Their dinner lay on a table beyond the edge of the copper tub. Roasted beef and hot bread did much to cure their ills, and the water soothed the ache out of labor-tensed muscles.

They leaned back at opposite ends of the tub, legs comfortably tangled between them as they enjoyed their dinner. When Joseph was satisfied of their little feast, he moved to kneel between Mayport's thighs and enjoy his livelier treat. The sweet wine and heat of Joseph's embrace made Mayport feel drowsy, soft and safe as Joseph devoured his kisses.

His cock drew tense by degrees, as if slowly waking to the gentle press of Joseph's body. Mayport rocked his hips, stroking without urgency until he felt his lover's shaft respond to his slow teasing. His hands wandered up and down Joseph's back, then slid down to squeeze at his cock.

Joseph made a surprised noise, then drew back. He smiled down at Mayport. "It's kind of you to think of me, but that's not what I want tonight."

Mayport blushed over his mistake, and shivered when his cock throbbed urgently. "You've been so generous to me lately, and I want you. I should have asked if you had other plans, before I began all this."

"That's not what I meant!" Joseph looked angry for a moment, and Mayport tensed. They were so close that Joseph could certainly feel the response. His eyes went soft again, and he stroked Mayport's hair until he relaxed once more. "Good God, how long have I been cold and cruel to you?"

Mayport shook his head, even more confused than before. "I don't know what you mean. We've had lots of fun, just like always. What's got you so talkative tonight?"

"I think about you all the time," Joseph said, and leaned in for a few more kisses. "I've hurt you when I was angry, and not just with my words. You really don't care, do you?"

"You were only a boy," Mayport said, ever willing to forgive his lover's wildest impulses. "It's not as if I didn't know you could be violent. I've learned not to provoke you, and we get on well now. Don't we?"

"It was never your doing," Joseph said. He kissed Mayport's brow, then stared down into Mayport's eyes. "I don't like that you must fear me now. I mean to make you forget I was ever so vicious, and let you be... what you are."

Mayport shook his head. "I don't understand. I'm a sinner by anyone's standards. What I get for that is nobody's fault but my own."

"No," Joseph kissed Mayport's lips, as if to still the words. "You never did anything but try to please me. Even now, you're absolutely terrified that you've done something unforgivable. Look at this place, at me, and all I have. You did this all, trying to win my worthless heart. You've become an honest gentleman, trying to be the one man I can't resist."

"Is it working?" Mayport heard the question before he knew he meant to ask it.

Joseph didn't answer. Instead, he leaned down once more and poured all his passion into deep and hungry kisses. Mayport groaned with delight, glad that their little moment of hesitation had passed by without incident. Joseph slid his arms under Mayport's hips and sat back, lifting him up out of the water. He came to rest sitting on the edge of the tub, and held on with both hands to keep from tumbling one way or the other.

Joseph ducked down and wrapped his mouth around Mayport's cock. A hot, wet, sucking embrace slid down around his shaft, and he was buried deep in Joseph's throat before he quite knew what was happening. He could not thrust, but braced himself against the tub while Joseph's tongue teased every inch of his cock.

Joseph's groans of pleasure were abbreviated sounds as he sucked. With one hand he tugged at Mayport's scrotum, keeping him from his release. The other teased at Mayport's ass, prodding gently until the muscle relaxed and he could stroke easily, fingers seeking out that sensitive spot inside. Mayport yelped, shaken by the raw pulses of pleasure that burned through him.

Joseph let go of Mayport's balls and grasped his own shaft as he pumped his mouth up and down, gasping and groaning around Mayport's cock. With that restraint gone, Mayport lost all control. He rose to stand over Joseph, twisted his hands into damp hair and steadied Joseph for the taking. As he thrust in and out, his ass flexed around Joseph's fingers.

He leaned his head back, eyes closed, lost in the only love he had ever understood. All of his aching need flowed through him like the wildfire that had driven him to this place. The urgent heat of Joseph's mouth possessed him utterly, and he surrendered all his desire to that passionate demand.

His hips jerked and his cock throbbed, swelling with raw desire. They clung together on the edge of release, drawing it out between them until, breathless and beyond control, all of Mayport's lust broke free of his restraint. He screamed Joseph's name again and again as he pumped hot seed down his throat. Somehow, Joseph took it all, though his body trembled with his own release.

Joseph steadied him as he sank back down into the cooling water. They clung together, gasping for air and shivering with delight. The rise and fall of The Dutch Process rocked them gently in the copper tub, lulling them to sleep in the safe harbor of their home.

Chapter Forthy-Three: Swamplands

Frog stood attentively at the doorway to the land office. Within, Mayport was tossing financial records into wooden crates. In a nearby lot, he had built quite a pile of the useless paper.

"What are you planning on?" Frog asked. "You'll never sort them out if you do all that."

"I don't mean to," Mayport said. "We're having a bonfire. Run off and find sausages."

"I'll get potatoes, too," Frog said, ever virtuous in the matter of diet. "Mister Thiervy said to say he's got drovers enough to carry a mill or something. He don't talk sense."

"All right, run on," Mayport said, impatient with his task and all interruption.

He managed to box and haul out enough paper to clear room for the treadmill. When the drovers arrived, they pitched in to help without complaint. Many of them had reason to despise the useless pile.

Frog returned with plenty to roast. Mayport put a match to the documents and they shared a merry midday meal. A few drovers roasted fish and shrimp to go with the main course, and shared cool beer among themselves.

"What is it you're gonna mill?" a man asked Mayport. "Those were millstones, for sure, but too small to do any good."

"I got bigger ones up north," Mayport said. "Before I haul my goods out of here, I need to know what it's worth. There's no way to know with cacao, until I've made something of it."

"You're not gonna try to make that chocolate stuff down here, are ya?" Frog asked around a mouthful of sausage. "It's too hot to think. You'll die of heat stroke if you try turning even a little bitty mill wheel on your own."

"It's no worse than a field," Mayport said. "Anyway, I have to try it for myself. That Joyce is ignorant of everything but gold."

"I heard he was getting an education, late as it is," the drover said. "You didn't really send him to the orchards. Did you?"

"I did," Mayport said, very proud. "And about time, too. I can't trust a foreman who can't farm. It's too ridiculous."

The working men had a hearty laugh over Joyce's plight. Mayport was less easy. The more time he spent at the farm, the more he saw that it held secrets yet obscure to him. That Joyce had gone quietly to the field seemed proof enough that he had something hidden.

On Sundays, the proof was undeniable. The same ranks of marching folk came and went. He had not worked up the nerve to follow them home, though it seemed apparent they lived somewhere within his own lands. With Joseph happily occupied and the papers on their way to the Devil, Mayport invited Frog to go exploring.

In fact, he needed Frog to go in any case. The farm had no map. There were no land rights other than those written by his own dubious land office. With no boundaries or law restricting expansion, the farm had spread as Joyce pleased.

Live oak and slash pine rose up out of palmetto scrub for miles around the little port village. Where cane fields and cacao orchards ended, the forests began. Low, wet marshes pooled where the pale, sandy soil sank low. Cultivation filled in all the high, dry patches and was divided by wild lands.

He needed a guide to get from one tract to another. Frog carried his blunderbuss on one shoulder, and a gig on the other. Under the pines, not a breath of breeze stirred. Frog could hardly see above the palmetto scrub, but marched through the cutting branches at a quick clip. Mayport came behind with a bag full of clerking supplies and a loaf of bread tied up in a bundle.

"I don't know what you expect to find," Frog said. "There's nothing but shotgun shacks and them holy rollers."

"Do you think you can find them that march in every Sunday?" Mayport asked, anxious to find out all he could.

Frog turned in his tracks and scowled at Mayport. "You think I'm ignorant about you and Mister Thiervy? Nobody is, and most don't care if they ain't drunk. These fools out here care plenty. They'll flog a fella for just kissing, no matter who he lays it on. They say they came all this way to get away from folk like us."

"You like a kiss too, then?" Mayport asked, trying to make Frog blush.

"I like plenty, but I don't mean to die over it," Frog said. "There ain't no law to care if you never come out of the scrub land. For all anyone knew, gators might get us without a fight."

"I understand why you brought your gun. I have mine, too," Mayport said. "If we go to a gator, we'd better take a few with us."

"All right," Frog said. He sounded genuinely in favor of the idea. "Anyway, that's sugar and bean trees off to the west here. There's share crops all around, corn and peas and what have you. Them farmers are their own kind of crazy, but they'll let you live. These ones you're hunting don't care if a man dies, as long as they think it makes them something special to Jesus."

"Let's go on to them anyway," Mayport said. "What do they do with their land?"

"We'll know when we get there." Frog mopped the sweat from his face. "It's dog-killin' hot. Let's stop at the spring stove, since we're going that way. We can swim and all."

"I'm just following after you," Mayport said. "Go how you like."

With that being the case, they stopped off a few times when the heat got to be too much. Frog picked places to rest where his gig could be useful. He proved his name with a string of fat croakers to carry along. At the spring rock, they made a fire to roast the skinned legs. Frog seemed impressed that Mayport didn't shy of their swamp lunch.

The spring pool was deceptively deep and perfectly clear to the grassy, sandy bottom. Frog jumped in fearlessly and Mayport followed. The cold of the blue depths bit hard, and he came up gasping.

"You could store meat in this!" Mayport shouted. "Doesn't the sun warm it?"

"Not a bit, never," Frog said, laughing. "No matter how bad it gets, you can cool off all you want."

After a few moments of pain, the cold water began to feel good. Frog dove down and brought up seashells from the sandy bed. They wondered over how they could have come so far from the sea.

"It's not people," Frog said, all confidence. "They come right up out of the sand, and not just here. Down south a little, there's a castle of just shell bricks. I heard the Spanish dug 'em up and all, somewhere."

"This place is crazy," Mayport said, and tasted the water again. "It's sweet as sugar. Oysters can't have lived here."

"I never seen 'em in here alive," Frog said. "I'd roast 'em up quick if I did."

When they were rested and dry, Frog found another path through the palmetto. The heat of the day soon wore through the cool of the spring. Again, Mayport marched through a hostile land where the very leaves of the forest reached out and drew his blood.

The bright sunshine beyond the edge of the woods made Mayport want to draw back to the shade. He squinted hard but was still dazzled and half blinded. They went through fields of corn and pumpkin vines. Frog made a shortcut through a couple of acres planted up like a kitchen garden. A few shanties stood in a cluster. Beyond, a scrubland pasture had been split-fenced as far as he could see to the east and west.

They walked down toward the shacks without being troubled. They stood under the porch shade while women within made a fuss. Nobody ventured to greet them, or even come as far as the screen door.

Mayport sat on rough planks and looked the place over. Youths ran here and there, at farmyard tasks. All of them stared, but none spoke. At last, a tall, thin grandfather came out of the fields and hollered at them.

Mayport pretended he couldn't hear. The fellow came down to stand before the porch, squared up before them and planted his fists on his hips. "What the hell are you fools doing here? Get off this land!"

"Don't talk that way to Mister Titus," Frog said.

"I know just who he is," the fellow said. "Y'all don't know me but you're about to find out. Get up and go before you can't."

"Now listen," Mayport said, low and slow. "I will fly my ship in here and take this place to splinters if I want. I'd say you've got the wrong idea of me, mister. I came to see what you're doing out here. There's more than one who thinks you're up to no good on my land."

The man laughed in Mayport's face. "Joyce won't let you do any such a thing, young cuss. This ain't your land anyway, so you don't scare me."

"Joyce won't stop us or anybody else," Frog said. "You act right, or I'll see you drop dead for fun."

The fellow licked his lips, then glanced beyond the porch. Mayport spun on his seat and drew a brace of pistols. A couple of surprised men stood stock still, hands clenching chunks of firewood. After a moment, they moved together, raising their weapons as they rushed at Mayport.

His fingers squeezed on the triggers, fast and more certain than his own thoughts. Both men fell screaming of their wounds. Mayport dropped the spent brace and drew his second pair. Frog was screaming at the old farmer.

Mayport rose as a door on a distant shack slammed open. A troop of young men spilled out, most of them clutching makeshift weapons. They saw Mayport, the fallen men and blood. They stopped in their rush, scattering out over the yard.

"Good God!" one yelled. "He done shot Capiter and Lee! Run tell the girls!"

"I said lay the fuck down you dirty ol' buzzard or I'll do it for myself!" Frog hollered again. "I don't even need to aim! Mind me now!"

"You better do what he says," one of the boys called out. "I heard he's got Joyce jumpy as a cat in a barn full of rockers."

Mayport didn't dare turn to see what was happening behind him. The boys were young, nervous and strong-looking. A couple of them ran off. At the screen door, the women had crowded in to see the fallen men. He expected them to charge. They only looked excited and hopeful.

"Somebody better kill that bastard!" one of the wounded men hollered. "You'll starve a month if you don't move now!"

If anything, the boys looked less inclined to press the attack. A black-haired boy spat in the dirt, then said "You better just lay there and bleed. Nobody's set to mind you now."

From somewhere beyond the barn there came the sound of many feet. Dozens of young women came running fit to beat the devil. They made a circle around the wounded men. From his vantage point, he could see the men were afraid, as they had not been of the guns.

"Andy Lee, you better come doctor these two," a young lady said. "They're bleedin' out, I think."

"I can't do a thing," the dark haired youth said.

"Can't, or won't?" Mayport asked, more confused by the minute.

"Can't," Andy Lee said. "You ladies better pray for healing. I never saw anything like this before."

"Frog," Mayport said. "I want you to turn around and keep your muzzle on these boys. Count three."

They traded off fast, but nobody took advantage. He studied the wizened old farmer, who stood trembling with fists clenched.

All of the fury had drained from him in a few moments of terror.

He licked his lips then forced a smile for Mayport. "Maybe somebody better run on to town for the doctor."

"No point," Frog said, careless of the men who heard every word. "They ain't got hours to wait on real help. Did y'all think we came too scared to fight? You're a born fool, Verry."

Verry held on to his false smile. "Come now, Mister Titus. You were warned, fair and square."

"I took you at your word," Mayport said. "I meant to kill your fellows then. Slow and messy does as good as fast and clean. I think you better run off out of here."

"Don't!" one of the women shouted. "Mister Titus! Don't let him run! Just shoot him where he stands!"

"I didn't come out here to clean up your house," Mayport snapped. "All I wanted was to know who was coming in making a fuss every Sunday. What are you people doing out here?"

"Nothing." Every voice said the word at once.

"Whatever it is, it's worth killing over," Frog said. "Don't think we're stupid just because we act crazy as loons."

One of the women in the house opened the screen door and walked slowly across the porch. "I am carrying my husband inside to bed. Shoot me if you want, little devil child. I have a power protecting me that is greater than your weapons."

"I don't want to shoot you, lady," Frog said. "If I did, God hisself wouldn't stop the nails I got crammed down this thing. Make one mean move, and I'll prove there ain't either any such a thing protecting nobody around here. You little girls help if you want."

"I ain't helpin' them fools," one of the girls sneered. "I swore I'd never touch neither of 'em, and mean it."

"What do you say, fellows?" Mayport called over his shoulder. "Somebody speak up quick! Are you all set to watch these men die like dogs?"

"Been waiting for it," Andy Lee said. "I'm about to be old enough for them to run me off into the swamp. I'd rather watch this than go wrestle gators like my brothers."

"What about your women?" Mayport asked, though he didn't really want to know the answer.

"They're kept like chickens unless they go in to church with the men," Andy Lee said. "Anyway, you can reckon for yourself where all us kids came from. Don't none of these young ones want them, but they're not getting much of a choice."

Again, Mayport's hands moved faster than his thoughts. There was no moment of doubt. Verry looked surprised, then the double shot from Mayport's pistols punched through his chest and out the other side.

Chapter Forty-Four: Faith

The afternoon was a still and stuffy one for dying. Mayport stayed put on the porch, well with in earshot of the deathbeds within. Verry had been left where he'd fallen, a feast for flies that nobody came to care for. The courtyard was lively with a carpentry crew of boys no older than Frog.

The women went on with their labors, though now with a mildly festive air. One gang of girls had led an assault on the chicken flock, with an eye toward feasting. Nobody reprimanded Mayport. He felt in no way accused of wrongdoing.

His civilized instinct insisted that all must be reported to some higher authority. Nobody else seemed to feel the exercise was necessary. Frog's sharp glance had gained an edge of respect. Only the blood-caked dust spoke of the wounded and the dead.

Frog had been given a plate of corn fritters and honey, which he did not share. He watched the farm with his free hand on his gun. The groans and gasping that poured through the shack's window seemed to go entirely unnoticed, in favor of sweet bread.

"Um," Mayport hesitated. "Does this kind of thing happen a lot?"

"When there's a reason," Frog said. "Most folks act polite and try to get along. They've all seen what happens when it comes down to a fight. I don't know why these boys ain't killed you yet, on pure principle. It ain't natural."

Mayport agreed, though the facts were in his favor. Before him, the youths built three strong boxes from planed pine. Somewhere out in the palmetto scrub, another gang was hard at work with shovels. They were trying to make holes deep enough for graves, but not so deep that water would creep in before the coffins were set in place.

"There's some places in the world where I would have to pay a family in gold for a thing like this," Mayport said. "Is there such a thing as blood price in these parts?"

"Yeah, I guess so," Frog said. " I ain't for sure you're a bit obligated to these ones. We got no law, but everywhere in the world has landlords. Sometimes the old men cuss and swear they'll tattle to Cory Titus about what they don't like."

Mayport shivered at what such an idea implied about him. As the struggle on the deathbed grew more desperate, Mayport smelled floured chicken going into hot fat. When the boys finished their job on the coffins, they set up tables in the yard. Young ladies brought cloths and dishes fit to feed an army. One child went around lighting smudges that smelled of orange rind, in vain hope of driving the mosquitoes back to the pines. The mood turned jolly as platters and bowls were carried to the table.

The women in the house came out together. One mother waved Mayport on, impatient with his hesitation. From field and woods they came, forty or more in total. Among them were older boys, whom Mayport had not seen at work among the youths.

Mayport and Frog were put in among the other young men. He dared not ask what was to become of the men he had shot. The plans for them seemed all too apparent. The others were merely waiting for the right time. Frog didn't let anything spoil his appetite. When Mayport sat too long over an untouched plate, Frog kicked him under the table.

"Don't be rude," Frog said with a scowl.

Mayport picked up his fork. "I think I've already gone beyond rude today."

"Then don't make it worse," Frog said, undaunted. "You can't refuse a lady's table, even if you did just shoot her husband. Even I know that."

Mayport did as he was told. He felt as lost as he had in the bloodthirsty kingdom across the gulf. He studied each face as he ate, but only got curious stares back.

After the table was cleared, a little girl came and took him by the hand. She led him through the yard, and to a little sturdy pine wood cabin. Within, several women sat at their needlework in companionable silence. He hesitated at the door, frightened as he had not been by threats and violence.

The little girl tugged at him to make him move once more, then piloted him to a wooden chair. He took a seat, though was ready to leap out the window if he had to. Frog stayed at the door, nibbling at a wedge of buttered cornbread as he watched.

"I have to apologize for Mister Verry one last time," a lady said. Her eyes stayed fixed on her fancy stitches. "I am Myra Verry, now a widow, so I must thank you as well."

"You're welcome," Mayport said on pure reflex. "I hardly knew what to expect when I came here. I can't say I've figured things out very much. I wish one of you ladies would resolve my confusion."

They youngest girl among them giggled. "He talks funny."

"Hush," Myra said. "I expect Mister Titus came on some important business."

At last she looked up, eyes calm and steady as a stone. Mayport smiled, and she blinked rapidly. A pink blush bloomed on her plump cheek. She looked away again, but her fingers sat still on her work as if they had lost their place.

"I came because I thought that Verry was up to no good," Mayport said. "I usually say a fellow can live how he wants to. Somehow, folks have the idea I know all about this place. I thought I'd better come find out."

"You know nothing about us?" Myra asked, surprised. "Why did you come here, unless it was to pass judgment?"

Mayport hesitated, then hid behind his smile once more. "I believe I'd rather hear this story from you. What is this place?"

She smiled in her turn, a cold and bitter expression. "Why this is paradise on Earth. Can't you just look at it and tell? No snow, plenty of good, sweet water, no law to say what a man must do. The Spaniards ran out of here years ago. They only don't admit it over the water. Everybody that lives here knows we're on our own."

"You sound angry about that," Mayport said.

"Father Verry came to preach God's word to the Papists," she said. "He's a Confederalist man, or was. You're too young to remember, but men once fought to bring the Light of Christ to this land."

Mayport certainly did remember that misguided conflict. That border skirmish had been the last proud flex of Spanish bravado in these lands. They had pushed north as far as the Savannah river. There, they had stuck, and suffered a humiliating, slow defeat by disease, deprivation, and bad leadership. Confederalist soldiers had come home swearing they felt bad for shooting the bastards, toward the end. Their retreat south might have been pressed to the mangrove islands, but the swamps and mosquitoes did for them what the Confederalist soldiers hadn't.

"Did he come to found this place as a Confederalist charter town?" Mayport asked. "That's bold, for a place that's not on any charts."

Myra looked embarrassed, then took a deep breath and met his gaze once more. "There was supposed to be a charter. The men got up all kinds of papers and had businessmen ready to come for the opportunity. Father Verry came to minister, but this heathen town! They never did want to go the right way. I heard of preachers being run out of towns before, but I never thought it would happen to us. We had nowhere to go but the land grant your father wrote, instead of giving tithes."

"May I see it?" Mayport asked.

Myra brought a box, which contained gold coins, Confederalist notes, and a stack of documents. Mayport found the land grant, written out to Verry on plain paper, with few details. A small map had been sketched in, and a block of acreage noted. Other papers detailed mortgages to the land company on the very parcel that had been given. At the bottom of the stack, he found a copy of a town charter, though it bore no signatures or seals.

A list of officers was attached to the charter. His father's name was prominent among them. Captain Cully was titled Harbormaster, and Verry as Chaplain. There were no rules for election to office by the populace. By the writ of the charter, officers of May Port were appointed for life.

"It's positively medieval," Mayport said. "Why was this never signed? It can't be presented to the Confed College without ratification. They might still accept it, even after all these years."

"Your father withdrew," Myra said, triumphant.

"Why?" Mayport asked.

Myra looked disappointed, then turned her attention to her needlework. "I'm sure I'll never know. Now, Mister Titus. There's all my fortune in the world. Is it enough to keep a roof over us, or should we get off your land?"

"I want to examine these more closely," Mayport said. "I'll act as my own copyist, of course, and will make my decision upon due consideration."

She only nodded. Mayport took the pages outside to better light so he could work fast. He hardly had time to study the details of the contracts in his hurry. Frog watched his labors with idle curiosity.

"Does that pay well?" Frog asked at last. "Writing up papers and all. You sure do a lot of it."

"It does, about one time out of ten," Mayport said. "Honest farming is a more steady thing. Anyway, I can't eat a penny, no matter how I boil it."

Frog took this remark to mean Mayport needed feeding again. They feasted on milk, honey, and cold biscuit while Mayport finished the copy work. By the time they set out for home, the heat of the early evening had settled down heavy and wet.

"Did you ever hear anything about this charter business before?" Mayport asked as they struggled through the palmetto scrub.

"I heard one about a preacher that come to spite the Spaniards," Frog said. "That was before the new minister came and built the church. I guess the other one was Verry. He must have been run out of town, or else why would he have some of your papers?"

"What do you hear about Captain Cully?" Mayport asked.

"Before, I heard he was something special on the seas," Frog said. "Now, I hear he spends time at The Duck Tub pinching the boys."

"Was he ever the harbor master?" Mayport asked.

"Never had us one of those," Frog said, sound proud of the fact. "I don't know that we need one, for our little boats."

They made it back to town in time for the first round of beer. They found Joseph eating roasted oysters from a street vendor. He looked Mayport over, and seemed satisfied that he'd come to no harm. "Not much of an adventure then?"

"I killed three men out at the Verry farm," Mayport said. He shook his head slowly, still shocked by it all. "I expect they've been buried by now."

"Well, don't tell Ma," Joseph said. "I guess the town will hear soon enough. Why did you do it? You didn't used to be so easy with lead-shot law."

"I'm curious about that myself," Mayport said. "Let's go find Cully. He might know for sure."

They went to The Duck Tub, where the landed Cully made himself merry in good company. They found him lording over a table crowded with admirers, and squeezed in where they could. Cully hardly noticed them until someone asked for an introduction to the new lads.

Cully peered at them, then sat up straight with inebriated dignity. "These are my employers. I think I must ask you gentlemen for some privacy."

The company abandoned the table with transparent excuses. They were quickly absorbed into other lively tables where the wine flowed as freely. Mayport took a more comfortable seat and helped himself to food and refreshment.

"You look very businesslike, but you smell like a goat," Cully told Mayport. "What have you been up to, young man?"

"I went out to the Verry farm," Mayport said. "Frog knew right were it was. What do you know about that fellow?"

Cully tried to be cautious, but the wine was miles ahead of him. "He was a preacher. He came on with the first settlers, and meant to build a church, or so he said. He took a land grant, too, and never so much as nailed up a cross."

"Then you knew him," Joseph said.

"I wish I never had," Cully said. "He was a liar and a fool. He suckered your father, and the whole time your daddy thought he'd suckered Verry. He would have stayed a preacher, but the women turned against him."

"He must have done something," Mayport said. "The women out there today didn't seem much in his favor either."

Cully shifted on his seat, first embarrassed, then angry. "Well, I guess they might have a reason. Verry was down as chaplain. He brought his brother and a couple of fellows to help him get started. They all brought wives and kids. He was all right, to start. Then he scared a couple of little girls."

"Listen to me, Jebediah Cully. You tell me the truth of what happened," Mayport said. "You don't know half of what I got up to out there."

"He scared them," Cully repeated, but didn't sound honest. "The daddies warned him. I thought he would know better, after that. Then one of the older girls was found... hurt. She said Verry tricked her and forced her. The daddy wanted blood. Verry said he would marry the girl and make things right."

"You said he had a wife when he came," Joseph said.

"He did," Cully said. "He offered to marry the girl as well, since there wasn't a law against it. I guess women didn't appreciate a preacher that thought so. They ran him out, and the rest of his fellows for good measure. I thought he must have gone home, if I thought on him at all."

"You're a liar. You knew he didn't go anywhere. Why wasn't this charter ratified?" Mayport produced his copy of the document and showed it to Joseph. "They're all on here. All they had to do was ink and seal it."

"We had to wait for a new chaplain to sign," Cully said. "By the time he got here, your father was gone to have *The Couverture* built. It was supposed to be fit for what he imagined those plantations would produce. I guess he meant to come back one day and finish what he started. He said he would."

"But like so much, he never did." Mayport put the charter away. "Is this what you brought me here for? More cleaning up after his failures?"

"You just have to sign," Cully said.

"I've read some of it," Mayport said. "I don't know that I would put my name on such a thing. I'd end up a chartered landlord, and in league with a bunch of bitter, vicious old men."

"I can keep Verry from troubling you, if that's the worry," Cully said, all confidence. "That minister will still sign, and here's you to chair the board."

"I already kept Verry from troubling me, or anyone else, ever again," Mayport said. Cully stared in cold shock, and seemed to sober up in an instant. "My father's dead, and so is Verry. You're the only one left, Cully. You can bet your bottom dollar I'll never sign anything that gives you power. You might be a fair captain, but on land you're a monster."

Chapter Forty-Five: Retreat

The conversation with a drunken Cully had served to sober Mayport at last. In such a mood he had to face the warehouse at Titus Farms. Of all he had seen, those acres were a true wonder. The storage was full to bursting, much to his chagrin.

"He might have sold some and made a profit," Mayport complained as he strode the dusty building.

"He did," Joseph said. "You could find out for sure of our Chef Gasteau. He had to know about this place. Where else could he have been sneaking this stuff? Anyway, it's all written down. That idiot Joyce is proud of it."

Mayport clenched his jaw, furious all over again. His belly had been sour for days. He'd wanted shut of Cully for good, but there was nowhere for him to go. He kept himself busy grading the stored beans and selecting the best of the lot for shipment back to his own workshop.

Sugar and cacao he now had in abundance. It was more than his little shop on the Savannah river could process. Joseph made vague but reassuring promises about the shop, but could do nothing about the quality of goods. Time and again, he found whole lots of produce gone to hell in the humid heat trapped within the warehouse.

"It's not fit for New Amsterdam, that's certain," Mayport said. "I'd be ashamed to show such a thing to Chef, too."

"It looks like that crap they tried to sell you across the water," Joseph observed. "I wonder if these wild men around here have a taste for it?"

"I guess we could teach them if we have to," Mayport said. He called the grade "western brown-white" and gave up on claiming it for his own. "It would make more sense to send it off to those who know what it's good for."

"It's not all a loss then," Joseph said. "An hour ago you despaired of using the good quality you'd found. If you wanted, we could get us a wind-powered cargo and send Cully the long way around west. He's not too old to master a craft."

"West to do what?" Mayport asked, utterly confused.

"To sell, you fool," Joseph said. "South, then west, and across the water. They give gold for it. You wouldn't have to stir a step."

Mayport laughed at the idea, then later wished he hadn't. Joseph acquired a cargo and crew, ordered the load and had her provisioned of his own expense. When Cully balked, Mayport could only support his partner's decision.

Ma was most pleased by Cully's exile. "He's the very figure of a coarse seaman. I would rather no society at all, if he passes for an officer. If I told you the rumors, it would curl your hair and mine."

"I do not mean to see you suffer such a fate," Mayport said. "We'll be going north soon, to the Savannah river. I've gotten in over my head again. This time I need a lawyer."

"Why, we'll ask Jesse," Ma said, all confidence. "He was never so vulgar as to practice, but he handles all the family affairs."

Mayport wondered if he rated such consideration, but not out loud to Ma. Joseph was entirely free of obligation in the matter of the charter town. He might have gone to New Amsterdam for advice, but lawyers from there didn't count for much below the lines.

He stood mute as Joseph managed their northbound voyage preparations. Part of him felt he was running away. That same part suggested that he never return. The urge to follow his own bad advice gave him reason to be grateful for Joseph's businesslike attitude toward their venture.

He wasn't about to leave Frog behind, with Joyce in a regular lather over Joseph's decision. The boy had no intention of being forgotten. Joseph made no argument, but took over the boy's education at once.

By the time they were ready to sail, Frog had been drilled to the bone on the deck engines. He was happy as his namesake when Joseph ordered him to take the vessel aloft. There was not a moment's fear in the child, even as they climbed too fast and Joseph had to step in.

"I never knew math could do such a thing," Frog shouted above the roar of the engines. "I reckon Mister Thiervy knows something better to do with numbers than just add up the gold."

"I told you so all along," Mayport said. "Though the gold makes it go, too."

Ma had more sensible ideas about the menu, now that Cully had been ousted from the mess. Her preparations were simple to the point of childishness, but hearty and more suitable for a voyage. She was proud of her table, as she had never seemed to be when managing a flock of maids.

In this way, Frog was roughly deposited among gentlefolk. He sensed their pity on his rough ways, and resented their condescension. Ma had experience with resentful boys, and took on his case with her usual grace. He spent his days cursing like a veteran engineer, and his evenings mastering the skills needed to be allowed at Ma's table.

"I had to do your father so, when I was a young bride," Ma told Joseph. "He imagined there would be no difference between himself and the tony fellows, once he had money. Then he decided he only needed a proper wife. They sure taught him different, and my help came too late. I hope that won't be true of our young master Jean Pierre."

"Don't call me that," Frog grumbled. "I won't answer to it. If I could go back, I wouldn't tell you what my mother named me. I didn't know you would make fun of me, too."

"Call him what he likes," Joseph said. "I don't want him softened up one bit. I only wish he wouldn't dribble on the tablecloth."

Joseph got his way with Frog, right up until they arrived at their port. In a large town, Frog saw the real difference between poverty and prosperity. He took to washing his face and hands each day, and accepted a choice of clothing instead of his rustic costume.

He didn't give up on his blunderbuss, which gave Oliver the Watchman pause. Though Mayport had a gentleman's agreement about not carrying his pistols in town, Frog was no gentleman. When suggestions were made in the matter, he pretended not to understand.

Mayport wished he could feign such ignorance. News of his cargo made him notorious all over again. He put raw sugar up at the dry goods exchange, hardly aware of the local shortages. He was quite embarrassed of his profits, but not enough to refuse them.

Joseph's engineers were thrown from sloth to sudden expectation overnight. With the working prototypes to begin, they scrounged materials and took both mill and press to scale. The construction of such beastly machines required the acquisition of a proper factory, instead of the shed behind Mayport's town house.

Mayport was glad to have that little workshop all to himself. There, he had access to Ma's kitchen, and could be on hand in case of trouble. He couldn't put on a show of leisure as his peers did. He was proud, therefore, when he could imitate them in a different way.

He presented the documents from May Port in the relative comfort of Jesse's private study. As Ma had expected, the family privilege was extended to Mayport. He was embarrassed of the necessity, but knew Jesse as Confederalist to the bone. Each page of evidence was examined with professional care.

"So. Your father meant to make a town," Jesse said at last. "He would have done it, too, if he had remembered to sign."

Mayport shivered, but tried to keep a brave face. "I'm glad he didn't, then. I don't know the first thing about it."

"I don't imagine he intended to benefit you particularly," Jesse said. "He would have been king in all but name of this charter town. Some men think that's old wisdom."

"I don't," Mayport said, bitter and not hiding the fact. "It's a fraud, the entire scheme, but a very clever one. I've tried to undo this mischief. It's all quite beyond me."

Jesse folded his hands on his desk and studied Mayport anew. "Well, you sure aren't greedy. Any other young buck would be itching to get these papers signed and submitted before the sun set."

"Most men my age have the luxury of foolishness," Mayport said. "What I've got is responsibilities I don't want. I'm not cut out to become a soft prince of the land. I've seen what becomes of men who want such a life."

Jesse looked embarrassed. "You mean that wedding I sent my sister into. There's no need to be so subtle with your accusations."

"Your conscience accuses you, not my intention," Mayport said. "If you wish to confess your past, I will hear you as fairly as I can. Your sister has never breathed a word against the arrangement. Only of the man in particular."

"That only makes my conscience burn hotter," Jesse said. "At least you should know what I stooped to, since you've come for my advice.

"It was Father who met Mister Thiervy first. He came south to find a bride. The lowness of his character was apparent to me. I should have cared more, but I was just the kind of young fool you don't want to be. Father is a cotton baron, you know. I imagined I could make up for my carelessness when my fortune came by and by.

"So I assured my sister of Thiervy, and sent her to his side. She never doubted our judgment until she saw the bastards she must make her own sons. Father said she would be happy once she had a son of her own. God will never forgive me for how I got my nephew, or how I counted on his coming along."

"Joseph always hated his father," Mayport said. "I was a child when I first knew him for a monster. Meeting him has only confirmed that first impression. You might have intervened, as I have done."

"I thought I had," Jesse said. "I persuaded Thiervy to send Joseph down home for his schooling. For good or ill, he is my heir. I had something to say about him, even if I'd given up every duty to his mother. All that did was deprive them each of their only happiness. I shouldn't be surprised if he hates me in the same breath as his father."

"He's got his father's temper in full measure," Mayport said. "We all get a slice of it now and then."

"You do your best to make up for the happiness they missed," Jesse said with a chagrined smile. "Therefore, we must talk about your future, not my sins. Let me end by saying this: If the chance comes again on Confederalist soil, burn that Thiervy down where he stands. I won't let the law pester you over a family matter. My sister has a better protector than I. You must not be hobbled."

"Yes, sir," Mayport readily agreed.

"Now, as to your charter." Jesse took out a stack of long stock and chose a pot of ink. "I must assume you are displeased by a lack of elected officials. Certainly, you're of a democratic bent. The Confederation is a republic, and its charter towns something less. If the men of May Port want the right to vote, they will have to go north, where such things are offered under the law."

"But the charter isn't signed," Mayport said. "It could be written any way we liked."

"No." Jesse gestured at his law library with an air of finality. "The principles of a town charter are quite European in their ideals. Men who hold power must be able to maintain order, not flit away on a convenient breeze. The limits are quite plain. Authority goes to the man who owns the most land. Even by Joseph's reckoning and after your generous gifts to the villagers, you are that man."

Mayport shivered again. This time, he couldn't stop. "That's it, then. The people will have no say at all, regardless of my character. Neither will I."

"Just so," Jesse said. "But what have they to fear of you? Carelessness? Inattention? A failure of your duty? They suffered these things of your father and survived. You can't do worse than he did."

"He made a show of propriety. There was my mother and me," Mayport said. "I can't. I won't. I mean to have Joseph and nobody else."

"He might choose to be more conventional," Jesse said, smiling over Mayport's declaration. "If he doesn't, you could do just as you like in a charter town. Who could speak against you, if you're the sugar baron? Oh, they might chatter, but they couldn't stop you. It's better than what you'd find, even in libertine New Amsterdam. You might even set a fashion."

Mayport was struck dumb by so audacious a suggestion. Then, he laughed. "You've found the one morsel of bait that can tempt me. Even if I'm never a respectable man, at least I wouldn't be a criminal under my own law."

"A justice of the peace would be more suitable to sign than a minister," Jesse said. "One who can be bought and paid for, if you can find him."

"I shot the only preacher who might have gone along with this scheme," Mayport said. "I'll send for the other one, and see if I have a way to persuade him. Since it's a port town, won't we need a port master? I have the very fellow for it, much good may the office do him."

"You mean that Cully fellow," Jesse said. "He's been at your back from the start. What is it he wants?"

"Wine, boys and song," Mayport said. "He's willing to do without the music. You said bought men would be best, and he's paid for. I might as well get some use out of him."

"I see you intend to take my every word to heart," Jesse said. "You're talking about giving a man real authority. Of all those he could have chosen from, even your luckless father didn't consign you to Cully's care."

"There's also a case of the devil they know down there," Mayport said. "I only ask that you keep Joseph free of responsibilities in this matter. He must always be able to roam as he likes, with nobody but Ma to scold and rule him."

"I assume he must somehow gain all benefits as well," Jesse said. "Then you should marry him, as fast as this charter is ratified. There won't be a law in the world to stop you, once the town is yours."

Chapter Forty-Six: Anticipation

After his first consultation with Uncle Jesse, Mayport had drifted along on a heady fantasy. He went so far as to request particulars of a jeweler, in case his audacious suggestion was not rejected outright. His estimation on the expense gave him a small shock. It was nothing on the disappointment he felt after leaving the shop in a panic, empty-handed.

He got the feeling his state of hysteria was part of a widespread epidemic. He privately enjoyed the wild exuberance that lurked in the breast of similarly ambitious young men. Like no gold or jewel ever had, Joseph Thiervy inspired in him the unwavering need to possess.

The object of his desire remained oblivious to the fixations that Mayport endured. Only in their most intimate moments did Mayport allow a hint of his intentions. Joseph was appreciative and intrigued, but disinclined to pointed curiosity.

Their days were spent in happy industry of Joseph's choosing. Mayport had his skills tested in days-long time trials of new factory works. Frog dogged Joseph's heels, box of tools swinging in idle threat at his side. He was the object of some curiosity and much open speculation.

Someone suggested Joseph as a parent to the boy, and won instant contempt for his mistake. When eyes turned Mayport's way, Frog could only laugh. "I'm not a second like either one of them. Y'all got some funny ideas. I work for 'em, like anyone else."

The habit of tools or firearm soon established itself as sincere. Frog disdained the company of smooth-spoken boys with tidy knees. If he was no man's son in particular, he became everyone's little brother by default.

For Mayport, he viewed the workshop as an endurance event. While the crews for the machinery changed, his supervision was, of necessity, constant. He had no idea of bearings and pressure valves. Those who did had no idea of cocoa butter or the popular syrup Joseph had devised. Moreover, there was still a clamoring from up north over the cocoa powder he could produce.

All these ignorances had to be remedied and his own standards made clear. He might have despaired over his failures if not for Chef Gasteau. He freely offered opinions over their efforts. In his skilled hands, there was nothing Mayport could do to render his materials irredeemable.

"Consistency," Gasteau said for the full hundred. "Of all things, this you must carry with you everywhere. A consistent standard will make your name a proud thing, even in Europe. Obey me, and find out how for yourself."

Mayport savored a cup of Joseph's chocolate. "Still, I don't think it can be fashionable. That man's mind is all efficiency. He wants it sold off docks to fishermen, at less than a penny a cup. There are still men calling it medicine, too."

"Hush, you make my point for me," Gasteau said, disappointed. "All this variation will be the ruin of you. Make a choice, and focus on that one thing you have selected. Anyway, try again. I think you have blamed these innovations all you can."

In between factory runs, he occupied his own workshop for hours at a stretch, focusing on his timing and technique. Like Gasteau, Joseph required consistency and efficiency of operation. The time limits on the power used to drive the works made even their tests a profound self-indulgence.

"We have a sun boiler," Joseph complained. "It's tied up making that boat of ours fly. Or, as it happens recently, not."

"I have thought a hundred times how to copy it," Mayport said. "There's no telling who cut those lenses, or even how they accomplished such a feat. Power like that should serve a useful purpose, I agree. The question remains if this factory is useful or not."

"I don't mean to gut our lady," Joseph said. "I only wish her secrets were not lost on me."

"I wasn't trying to think of a way to take her apart," Mayport said. "The efficient thing would be to live as the whalers do. It's a dog's life. I've seen it. I don't want it for you."

Joseph looked started, then he smiled. "It won't be as bad as you imagine. For one thing, beans don't put up much of a fuss."

Mayport ducked his head down to hide a weary smile. He had avoided putting the thought into Joseph's head, for fear that he would like it too well. "You've done so much to streamline her. She really can go on a crew of four. As a home, she wants for nothing."

"These machines need a crew of their own," Joseph said.

"They're unforgiving like the tides and winds. Without human judgment, I wouldn't trust them for a second."

"You see my point exactly," Mayport said. "The Process would have to be rebuilt all over again."

"Don't talk like a loon," Joseph said. "I could fit up new gondolas here at the dry docks. There's a shipwright on every street. I'm just glad you thought of this here, instead of down south a ways."

"I thought of it first in New Amsterdam," Mayport admitted. "I liked living in the shop with you. If only it hadn't been stuck to the ground."

"Never mind," Joseph said. "First we make this factory work on the ground. Then I'll see one day if it can fly, too. If nothing else, we can cargo the works down closer to the plantation."

"I wondered if you would consent to go back there," Mayport said. "It's a limited society, as you mentioned. Anyway, my business goes north first, though not over the line. Your uncle Jesse means to go as far as Richmond, and advise me on my dealings."

"You're going to get that charter ratified," Joseph accused. "After all I said, you're going on ahead just like your father."

"I will attempt to have a charter ratified for that little town, but not the one you read," Mayport said. "I imagine I will make myself unpopular, but I mean to succeed. It is a crime that this was left undone. I do not speak in the figurative. There must be a remedy."

"Does that suddenly put me in business with the landed class of the Confederation?" Joseph asked. "This changes things somewhat."

"It's not as if I'm being ennobled," Mayport said, annoyed. "Not quite. In any case, no. If I got my way, we would be in something more lasting than business together."

Again, Joseph looked surprised. This time, with understanding came contempt. "Even if you fixed the charter like Verry wanted, you would never live to see the day."

Mayport frowned. "I'm glad I didn't bother to really ask you, then. I will live to see such a day, even if you don't want to be there when it comes."

Joseph looked away. "I can't believe you spoke to my uncle about such a thing. He ought to have beat the idea out of you with a stick."

"He thought of it himself." Mayport smiled down at his knees,

Chocolatiers of the High Winds

enjoying Joseph's cold shock. "He's going alone, to grease the wheels and play at formality on my behalf. Perhaps he knows best. I've never been much of a political man."

"I imagine Ma will go right along with him," Joseph said. "Be certain this is what you want. You might believe you wouldn't be a noble gentleman, but nobody will agree."

"I did not seek this power," Mayport said. "Tell me you can't abide it, and I will stop. We've got work enough to suit us without new responsibility as well."

"Go on being workmanlike for the rest of your life if you like," Joseph said. "I won't be the one to wish for languid idleness. You know who cultivated that taste in your father. You've sat at his table, many's the time."

"I prefer your mother's menu," Mayport said. "There's opportunity to exclude Cully from the chain of command, if not the wine cellar. You have your opinion about which he may prefer."

"Bold idleness won't wear well on him," Joseph predicted. "I imagine he'll enjoy it anyway. I'd pay a fair wage if even one charming boy could make him forget Corey Titus and the loss of a chance. Since no such miracle is possible, he's set you on the path your father chose."

"I'm writing an entirely new charter," Mayport said. "New statutes, new institutions, new officers, and entirely on its on merits as of this very day. I think that stands more of a chance than what Father and Cully dreamed up, then abandoned."

"What's in it for you?" Joseph asked. "I can see you've decided a lot by yourself."

"Your uncle helped," Mayport said. "He's angling to make an officer of you yet. If you mean to stay free of the place, it's him you must watch out for."

"And be more wise than you?" Joseph laughed without humor. "You've got nobody else you can trust to put his name beside yours. Is that what made you talk so crazy before?"

"There's Jesse," Mayport said. "He could sign as the justice instead of having a preacher. That town might do better if I didn't fool with it, but I feel I have a responsibility."

"You still haven't told me why you want to," Joseph said.

Mayport had, but Joseph hadn't given it a moment's thought. He shrugged and looked away. "I could at least change the name of the place. It's my name. I don't want to share it."

Joseph laughed heartily this time, going so far as to disturb his mother's peace. When told of the joke, she went flustered and deployed her fan. "My son! You would go so far over a joke? That's terribly extreme."

"What would you change it to anyway?" Joseph asked.

Mayport scowled. "I'd call it 'Joseph Thiervy' since it wouldn't matter a bit to you."

Ma laughed over Mayport's temper, and smiled brightly at her own amusement. "Perhaps a contest, or a ballot vote to choose? Those are always so popular with the young gentlemen."

"I would have to enlist a forum first," Mayport said. "I can't until there's a charter. I would put the question myself, if only I could. For all I know, the citizens will want to keep things as they are."

"If you're opening votes, maybe you should ask if anyone wants you for their lordship," Joseph said, still annoyed. "I can think of reasons why they wouldn't, and I would be happy to tell all about them."

"I imagined you would oppose all this," Mayport said. "And yet you don't insist that I stop."

"You'll be fine, even if you're called to answer for yourself," Ma said, and leaned over to top up Mayport's punch glass. "My brother is in up to his neck with our town fathers. They take to port for the whole of that crazy river your town sits on, where the feathers and seashells come from. You're not the only one around here who knows to make a profit of it all."

"Ma!" Joseph sat his glass down too hard. "What in the world have you done?"

"Made a profit, so there." She snapped her fingers under his nose. "You shouldn't be so hard on our Mayport. Nobody else will care what happens to the place if he doesn't. You should be proud of him. I've learned a great deal from his way of doing business."

"Go on then as you like," Mayport said. "I don't mean to stop your freeport running, if it makes you happy."

"If only your Frog would be my purchasing agent," Ma said, well into her fancy. "He knows the name of every piece I brought back. He comes and names them to show off, but thinks I'm too fine to know of such things."

"He's mine. I'm not sharing," Mayport said.

"He would be surprised to hear it," Ma said. "Anyway, I approve of what you're doing, even if my child is too willful to like it. You're right to let the lawyers do their worst, and stick to your shop. That's the only reason we tolerate such fellows in regular society. Now, put business away and see about your guests. You'll want all their good will, if Jesse has a moment's success in this venture."

Chapter Forty-Seven: Persuasion

Mayport hovered at Chef Gasteau's table, jittering with anticipation. For once, he wasn't dreading the opinions and advice. With the Chef, he was guaranteed excesses of both. This time, he truly wished to share what he had created.

Chef took his time over powder and butter. Each was tasted and held to the light. At last, the cocoa powder was pushed aside. "It's well enough for your Dutch drink, at least. The butter is very fine. Your standards have raised somewhat. And you say this is to be available in quantity?"

"For you, it will be," Mayport said. "The rest of the world must wait. I've done what you said. I mean to focus on the cocoa butter, and perfect my technique. There's no telling what it's good for. I certainly don't know. Somehow, I've found an affinity for it, though it's not what was expected of me. I think it would not be wise to speculate on my name and reputation, and so I mean to try this."

Gasteau chuckled. "You're not much your father's son. I know you will appreciate my thought."

"If you will have this for your establishment, its more honor than his name ever gave me," Mayport said. "This little craft came to me by your teaching, not by his empty promises."

"I will have it then." Gasteau admired the samples once more. "I think you must be sick to death of the taste by now. I don't remember a particular fondness for it, even in the beginning."

"A rest from it would do me good," Mayport admitted. "Alas, it can not be."

"Then let us make a fortune together," Gasteau said. "You've made your choice and found your focus, though I'm surprised at where you ended. Your father never had the first idea of standards and quality."

Mayport took his turn to laugh. "I have seen proof of that for myself, that's certain."

Gasteau shook his head, smiling over his student once more. "I understand his fondest wish will yet come to fruition. He boasted on his intention of making you a landed gentleman one day."

"I hope to remain a simple man," Mayport said. "I must put security ahead of my preferences, like everyone else. What would have become of me if I had tried to suit this world? Anyway, youth is on my side for once. It was the only excuse I needed for being unwed. Uncle Jesse has done the thing up like a proxy for a spoiled young fool. I suppose he is right."

"We need a young fool to dare such a feat as this," Gasteau said. "Only, don't sacrifice yourself for strangers who despise you. Treat them like you did that bastard from the north, if anyone dares to challenge you. Once you set foot on this path, you must be endlessly ruthless."

"Did Mister Thiervy stay long, once we were gone?" Mayport asked. "There were a few improbable vows made on that point."

"Your fellows ran his crew out of town when you weren't looking," Gasteau said. "I think you can not be careful of this man, though you might desire to be merciful."

"We've gone beyond that point long since," Mayport said. "He thinks I have no right at all against him."

"As you say, you're beyond that point," Gasteau said. "I have seen points of honor come to blood, but this is no such thing. You must stand for a man. Your elders have failed you once more."

Mayport laughed. "You mustn't speak of Uncle Jesse in that sly way. He works daily to give me the authority to keep Ma and Joseph from that fool. There's a kind of protection in that support."

"A coward's kind," Gasteau muttered. "And here's me only good for rowdy sons if it comes to blows again. You're right to rely on a lawyer's advice."

"He only says to wait about Mister Thiervy," Mayport said. "I shall. Now, for Ma I am sure you are able to the tasks she has set. I don't know how she means to keep the belles from fainting in drifts, but she will have her party or die."

"She will have all that she desires," Gasteau promised. "As for her child, you may soon discover what he wishes for. No man lives without desire. Don't pretend to me he's not the reason for all you have done."

Mayport kept that in mind as he endured hours in Uncle Jesse's company after his day's labor. The help was much appreciated, but the demands came in plenty. If they had been holed up in a stuffy office, laboring over the charter, Mayport would have endured his fate with more grace.

Instead, they made the beery rounds that the town had established as necessary. Endless acquaintances were made on basis of Jesse's introduction. Mayport had no idea of the impression he made upon these acquaintances, though worn-out and cowed seemed the likeliest image. Among such men he felt like a truant schoolboy. Their sons were among the scholars at comfortable universities. Several spoke Dutch or French to him, to impress their elders. Mayport tried to please, but his only instruction in language had come of adventure.

The proof of that education came late after dinner. When sons and junior partners were sent on their way to contemporary company, Mayport was kept back at Uncle Jesse's side. The society was no less merry, but a deal more challenging. Every man was curious about his interests in the wild lands south of the Confederation borders.

The chief complaints against Mayport were that he kept regular hours and didn't drink well. He had imagined himself quite accomplished in the latter pursuit. Sober seeming, steady Jesse knocked his wine back like an Englishman, and chided Mayport for his unsociable restraint.

Every morning, Mayport reaped the benefits of his relative sobriety. The samples he'd shown Gasteau were the product of long hours at hard labor. Even with machines to ease the backache, his business was not for the weak. Joseph's idea of a factory had suffered blows from reality. Nonetheless, his crew had performed every miracle they had promised.

Mayport would have stood on the treadle with the others if he had been allowed. Instead, he dashed here and there, watching the product of their labors. His sole responsibility was to make sure their efforts were not wasted.

Joseph kept command of the factory floor in his usual style. His workday was longer than any other man. Mayport wanted, time and again, to apologize for causing so much hard work. The pride in his men kept him quiet and made him try harder in his own efforts.

Gasteau had taken all the cocoa butter Mayport could supply. The powder went into colorfully labeled tins for shipment. "And where will all this treasure be going?" Joseph asked. "You did nothing to prepare your little village to crave your vice."

"I don't intend to," Mayport said. "Cully will catch up to us eventually. He can go north, all the way to New Amsterdam, like any other captain."

"You would send him along the Carolina coast?" Joseph asked, surprised. "It's a dangerous route, even in the best weather."

"Good captains sail it every day," Mayport said. "I can't have him below the line or by my side until Uncle Jesse has settled my suit for a charter. There's no reason to let anyone imagine I approve of what he and my father intended to do."

"You go on like making you a chocolate baron is some sort of crime," Joseph said. "You truly have not a moment's gratitude."

"I have made a baron of *myself*, though I don't look forward to the demands and duty," Mayport said. "They were long on promises and short on action. We've got no need for that down in the port, or anywhere else in this business. He may sail as he can, or seek greener pastures, but he will not influence that town again."

"I never thought you would give up on him so completely," Joseph said. "You went halfway around the world to find him in the first place."

"I did," Mayport said. "There was no way to know what I would find in him. Now that all is revealed, I have made my decision. I'm not cutting him loose. He's only lost his privilege of my trust."

"What if he repents?" Joseph asked.

Mayport yawned. "Alert the papers of a miracle. Anyway, we must have a half day today. Ma will want us neat and fresh for her party."

Their cozy drawing room was thrown open to the afternoon breezes. All the furniture had been re-arranged to make room for dancing. Instead of a formal table, Ma had adopted the buffet style of service.

The table was laid with delicacies from Chef Gasteau's kitchen. At the center of the spread stood a vase filled with what looked like lilies and white roses. On closer inspection, Mayport discovered that the vase was of blown sugar. The blooms were of some waxy-looking artifice.

"Couldn't we get the real thing?" he asked Ma. "You've gone to so much bother. I never imagined we would have to settle for wax flowers."

Ma laughed. "They're made of your chocolate, silly boy. Have one, and hurry on to change your clothes. Jesse's bringing all his fellows and means to show you off."

"I must make myself respectable," Mayport said, even as he selected a lily.

"Don't you dare," Ma warned. "You're no better than a young

adventurer of fortune. Show off for me, just this once."

Mayport had no choice but to obey. He soothed his nerves with the delicious flower, and wondered over its making. It tasted only faintly of its dark origins, and was otherwise creamy and smooth. He enjoyed the treat immensely, as it sparked no memory of his recent labors. He relied on the wardrobe Ma had assembled on his behalf from local tailors. On this of all days, he did not wish to look foreign and wild.

As the guests began to arrive, Mayport understood what game Ma and Uncle Jesse were playing for him. Absent were his rowdy engineers and the wilder bachelors Joseph had befriended. Despite the heat, lovely young belles had donned their regal finery to ornament his home. The lucky few bachelors invited came attached to their families, and on their best behavior.

The gentlemen so carefully courted by Jesse came in full number. Here, Ma could claim total victory. This social acceptance gave Mayport reason to hope that his machinations were achieving his purpose. Moreover, the town fathers quite monopolized his attention while his peers ruined the rugs with dancing. Mayport offered all gentlemanly comforts in his parlor. Though the occasion was a festive one, their conversation tended toward commerce of its own volition.

"We will miss your company," Mayport said to Jesse. "I've never been to the capitol. I don't envy you the adventure. I'm sure the natives there are less agreeable than some I've met."

"I would go more happily if I had any hope of success," Jesse said. "I've got a village to represent, right enough, and my good name. There's nothing else to support this application."

"What more could you possibly need?" Oliver asked. "They've chartered empty, wild lands to expand the borders. Your case should be a cinch."

"Those empty fields were founded by member cities," Jesse said. "We haven't got such a sponsor."

"Nor am I likely to get one," Mayport said. "There's no telling where I was born. I claim this nation as my own. Who knows if it will want to claim me in return? This little house is all I have to offer as my proof."

"Don't be so hard on yourself," Oliver said. "You've got more here than that. You pay your taxes like anyone else. I'm sure you have the wherewithal to acquire a sister city."

"I do need it," Mayport said, humbly and honestly. "I mean

well for that village, but I'm only one man. How can I possibly know how to manage? Crisis will come one day, and I will have nobody to rely on. Excepting my newfound uncle, of course."

Oliver chuckled. "Don't worry on that, young man. With Jesse comes the whole pile of us. Just move the border south, my boy. Everything you need thereafter will be provided."

Chapter Forty-Eight: Intentions

Mayport enjoyed his role of figurehead in all of Uncle Jesse's machinations. The position required little of him. He was only asked to withhold his objections on matters he did not understand. In this capacity, he failed on one account.

"I can't allow slavery," Mayport said. "Too many men, of all complexions, find themselves in debt to me. Such a law could be seen as a threat of action. I would be ruined by the sudden evacuation of debtors, if they were to panic."

"I see your point," Jesse had said, before the occasion of his departure. "I will explain the exclusion in a separate document, then. Perhaps the legislators will view the matter as presumed, rather than specified."

"Let them think what they like," Mayport had agreed. "Such a thing will never be tolerated, if I'm the one making the rules."

With that understanding, and letters of provenance from the town fathers, Jesse had set off on his mission. Ma was proud of her brother as she never had been before. For that pride, Mayport would have risked more than his own good name.

For Ma, Mayport and Joseph tried to be respectable. In public, they did all they could to disguise their private affection. In this effort, Joseph was far more successful. Though Mayport did all he could to restrain himself, his devotion became readily apparent.

He cringed every time he noticed his own mistakes in the matter. After Uncle Jesse had set out by steam coach to the capital, his nerves made him even less circumspect. That lone hope of a permanent commitment made him as eager as any other lovestruck young man. Every time he laid eyes on Joseph, he was gripped by the longing to press his proposal once more.

He returned to the jeweler's shop one afternoon, hoping that their prices would cool his impulse to something within reason. Instead, he placed his order and chose stones to be set in gold. The clerk was left in confusion, with so broad a setting selected under obvious intentions. That alone might have started rumors, had the shop not been long experienced in maintaining secrecy over affairs of the heart.

Only Joseph was close enough to realize the terror in Mayport's heart. One evening, long after Mayport had accepted delivery from the jeweler, Joseph could no longer ignore the nerves. Mayport had ruined the same page of accounting four times in a row, just because Joseph was lounging on his sofa.

"Come now," Joseph said. "If you can't tend your figures, let me help. I can add up as well as the next fellow."

Mayport blushed all the way to his hairline, and couldn't keep the annoyance out of his voice. "You're the problem, my friend. If you must lay about like this, you might be considerate enough to leave something to the imagination."

Joseph twitched the hem of his smoking jacket to cover his thighs, but his eyes never moved from watching Mayport at his work. "You're a fool to wear yourself so thin. Hire a bookkeeper, or one of Gasteau's boys to oversee the production line. Nobody does both jobs for himself."

"No gentleman does," Mayport agreed. "That's why the papers get so many good stories about embezzlement. As for the factory, Frog is coming along just fine. He likes shouting, so he'll do well when the time comes."

"Do you mean to apprentice that young hellion?"

"It seems that I already have," Mayport said. "He can crew the *Process*, and knows the standards for the factory. If we let him slip away, we're both fools. Men twice his age don't know a tenth of our business as he does. Law knows I can't get an heir the way your uncle did."

Joseph snorted at the mention of Jesse. "I have often wished I'd never been born. You better not expect me to thank him for his part in the matter."

"He's trying to make it up to you," Mayport said. "Just like I try. You're one hard nut to crack, once you turn bitter on a fellow."

"What do you mean?" Joseph asked.

"He's helping me in the hope that you'll forgive what he did to Ma," Mayport said. "We've made a couple of key omissions to that charter he's presenting up at the capitol. He knows he did Ma wrong, but can't undo the mistake. He's going to help me along instead, much good may it do him."

Joseph sat up on the sofa and stared harder at Mayport. "I didn't mean about Uncle Jesse. I meant, what makes you think I turned bitter against you?"

Mayport shrugged a couple of times, then looked down at his

ledger again. "When we were at school you hated me. You wanted to humiliate me, but once you had me naked and pinned, you found out I liked it. I guess it just took a while for you to like me, too."

"That's not how it happened," Joseph said, low and cold. "You know it wasn't like that!"

Mayport kept his head down. He didn't want to see what kind of rage he had provoked this time. "Yes, Joseph. Just as you say."

Joseph threw something at the wall, a pillow by the sound of it. "Fine! Tell me what you remember, then!"

"Nothing," Mayport lied in a hurry. "I don't remember much. It must have been nice. You were there, so it... just had to be..."

"Stop lying!" Joseph cried. "Tell me how it was for you. I want to know why you get so scared of me. It happens all the time!"

Mayport ducked his head lower. "I'm sorry. It was nice. You caught me out on breaking the rules one day, saying names wrong in English. I was still halfway thinking in Dutch, and I got confused because..."

The words stuck in his throat. Looking at Joseph Thiervy in a bad mood brought back all the best of his boyhood memories. Back then, he'd needed tutoring to learn 'Master Thiervy' from 'Professor Smith' and all the rest. He'd come to school unprepared and incapable of the simplest communication.

"I called you by your Christian name," Mayport said, still halfway apologizing. "I'd been thinking obscene things about you. I'd seen handsome boys before, but you... I got obsessed and stayed that way. In my mind, I called you Joseph, and imagined we were more than mere acquaintances. One day, it slipped out. That's when you took me back to your room. You made me feel so good, and after... we were friends, then. Costor didn't like it. He said you set me back in English by speaking like they do in New Amsterdam. Maybe he was right. I still talk wrong, no matter what the language."

Mayport glanced up to see if his confession had soothed Joseph's temper. The look in his eyes was still stormy, but had taken on that peculiar cast he did not understand. "You wanted me before I had you that first time?"

"Yes," Mayport admitted. "Maybe I corrupted you somehow. If I never came along, you might have turned out to be completely normal. Do you still hate me, for what you became?"

"No!" The sharpness in Joseph's voice made Mayport jump. Joseph got up from the sofa and stalked across the room, gaze fixed on Mayport like an eagle swooping for the kill. "No, I never hated you, not even back then. I might have hazed you at school, but I never disliked you."

Mayport nodded fast, willing to fault his own memory in favor of Joseph's version. "Yes, it was only hazing. Schoolboy pranks, just like that. I remember now. I really am sorry, that I made your life be this way. I want to make it up to you, somehow."

"You didn't make me this way!" Joseph's mood hadn't been soothed a bit by Mayport's agreement. "You weren't the first, for me. Was I really, truly the first man to touch you that way?"

"Yes," Mayport said, and squirmed on his chair. "You weren't the only one, but you were the first. I hope..."

Mayport stopped, words frozen on his tongue once more. Joseph leaned over the desk and cupped Mayport's jaw in that familiar, half-threatening way. "Yes? What do you hope? Tell me."

Mayport swallowed hard, heart pounding like it wanted free of his chest. "I hope you're the last. If I could, I would make you be the only one. I can't undo a moment of my history, but the future..."

His hand went to his pocket of its own accord. Numb fingers fumbled with the lacquered box, where he had hidden his gift. He held it out, hand shaking, and managed to get the lid open. Within, the ruby and diamond jewels gleamed in the gold setting. Fear and desire fought for shares of him, but he forced himself to finish his secret wish to Joseph.

"For the future, please, you're all I want. Everything I need, it's you." Mayport licked his lips, and tried on his smile that helped him in such awkward moments. "It might mean nothing to anyone but me. Please, Joseph Thiervy, if you will have me, I'll husband you for all my life."

Joseph let go his hold on Mayport's jaw. He plucked the ring from its box, and held it to the lamplight. His expression was all softness and vulnerability, hesitation, but no anger at all. Mayport held his breath. He'd been turned down without thought, the first time he'd dared to suggest such a thing. Trying again would have been more than he could have managed, if he'd thought about it beforehand.

Joseph slid the ring onto his first finger, imitation the fashion of belles who were spoken for. "Yes."

Mayport didn't remember standing. He might have gone around his desk, or over it, for all he knew. He wrapped his arms around Joseph, claimed his mouth in a hard, demanding kiss, and forced him back until they both fell on the sofa. He tore at Joseph's clothes, half-aware that his own attire was being attacked in equal measure.

Their skin made contact from chest to thighs, and Mayport groaned against Joseph's mouth. Their cocks were hard and hot as forge fires, quivering tense and trapped between them as they writhed together. Joseph wrapped his legs around Mayport and locked hard against his spine. The strong flex of muscle under and around him drove all reason and restraint from him.

Mayport got his knees under Joseph's hips, curving his lover's spine up and back. He thrust desperately, found an angle on Joseph's ass, and found his lover slick and ready for the taking. "Good god!" Mayport shouted, even as his cock slid past that clenching muscle. "Were you ready for me? Did you know?"

"I hoped," Joseph said through clenched teeth. He pumped his ass down, impaling himself on Mayport's cock. "Don't disappoint me."

Mayport laughed over his lover's wanton plans, and leaned down hard. Joseph writhed and bucked, legs flexing, trying to force Mayport deeper. His desperate struggles were beautiful, so Mayport held still to watch them. His cock throbbed with aching need, but he resisted his instincts until Joseph was sweating and breathless beneath him.

At last, Joseph fell back against the sofa cushions. His body relaxed, and Mayport snapped his hips forward, driving his shaft in to the root. Joseph yelped. Mayport chuckled, and pressed his advantage, He seized Joseph's shoulders, pulling him down, rocking him back and fort in time to his taking.

"Stroke yourself," Mayport said, breathless in his need. "Do it, let me see..."

Joseph grasped his own cock, pulling roughly as Mayport bore down on him. "Please, more, yes, please!"

Mayport rode harder, driven by the abject pleading that poured out of his lover. His body burned, a luxurious ache that sizzled through his veins. His pulse seemed to draw down low into his balls, tense and pounding with all his pent-up passion. He heard his own cries, one word repeated on every thrust.

"Mine, mine mine," he chanted, and pushed his body to prove his claim.

Joseph screamed, his ass clenched tight even as his back bowed up off the sofa. Mayport froze, clenched his teeth and held tight as Joseph shook and shivered. Hot seed spilled out over Joseph's fist, making the air fragrant with that familiar musk.

Mayport sat back on his knees. "Turn over."

"Wh-what?" Joseph panted, eyes unfocused as his body continued to twitch. "Seriously?"

"Now, Joseph," Mayport said, impatient over even this slight hesitation. Joseph's legs relaxed down, and Mayport withdrew. Joseph tried to turn over, but instead slid off the narrow sofa. He ended up on his knees, slumped over the cushions.

Mayport scrambled to curve over Joseph's broad back. He thrust into Joseph once more, reveling in his conquest. He wrapped his arms around Joseph's hips and seized his still-pulsing cock. Joseph groaned and whimpered, helpless as Mayport demanded more of him.

Mayport lay his cheek against Joseph's shoulder, and let his animal impulses take control. He closed his eyes, lost in the tide of his passion. He breathed deep, then turned his face to suck and bite at Joseph's neck. Hoarse cries were the answer he got, and renewed energy as Joseph began to rock under him. He thrust hard, deep, lost in his need to prove all that he could not say.

"Please, Mayport, please, I want it," Joseph panted against the sofa. "I love you, just you, please, just you, forever, please, I love you!"

That confession undid Mayport utterly. He shook from head to foot, convulsed with pure pleasure. His fist was slick with Joseph's seed, even as he pumped his own passion deep into his lover's body. Satisfaction like white fire rushed through him, and left him weak and satisfied in their embrace.

"I love you," Mayport whispered, and kissed Joseph's neck again. "No matter what else becomes of me, I will have you for my own. Never doubt me, Joseph Thiervy. I am yours, for always."

Chapter Forty-Nine: Deviation

What elation Mayport felt at Joseph's capitulation was soon lost in an agony of labor. Captain Cully arrived with a cargo of cacao from May Port. He also brought gold ornaments from his expedition to the western kingdom across the water. To Mayport, it was apparent that Cully expected gratitude, reward, and forgiveness for all his adventures.

Joseph had no patience for his initiative. The cacao needed processing, and had grown more expensive for being moved north. His plans for porting their factory works south was thrown off its timetable. The gold offset the overhead, but in principle irritated Mayport's sense of accounting.

For weeks, Mayport ran his factory at its hardest pace. The weather shifted for the worse, but he raced on anyway. The local tinsmiths turned an easy penny supplying him with packages for his powder. Meanwhile, Chef Gasteau enjoyed a spate of fashionability with his innovation in cocoa butter. Mayport knew the recipe to be a revival of lost confection. The town knew nothing of it, and awarded the chef all honors for its recent introduction.

As shocking as white, waxy chocolate was, Joseph's change of stripes went far beyond it. One afternoon, Joseph presented him with a sapphire ring fashioned after the broad signets that were still popular in the north. Mayport accepted the gift without hesitation, but wondered over the sudden treasure.

"I can kiss you whenever I like now, no matter who might see," Joseph explained. He spent some time demonstrating his point. "I have a ring. You're wearing it. If anyone tries to stop me, they'll regret it."

"You could have all along," Mayport said, and took another kiss.

"No," Joseph said. "There has to be a ring. It's a rule. I dare anyone to argue now. I've done it all just as Ma said. The ring is important, somehow."

Mayport only cared about the kisses. Joseph had more respect for propriety than he admitted. Even with the rings, he was as reserved as his peers, and more rational than some. Few of their acquaintances misunderstood their intentions. A few severed all association, but their loss was an improvement on the general company. Of all who understood, only Cully dared to disapprove. If Mayport hadn't been worn out to the point of impatience, he might have taken the rebuke with false grace.

"You boys are gonna be tarred and feathered," Cully said. "There's laws against what you're doing. I don't care about your private lives, but you're going too far. You make things difficult for those of us who are properly discreet with our preferences."

"You liars don't matter much to us," Mayport said and frowned over his wine. "Go on sneaking with the catboys you buy. If you've got something to hide, by all means, go on as you have been. I've got nothing to be ashamed of, least of all Joseph Thiervy."

"You're a criminal and a sinner," Cully declared. "Shameless-ness in such a fellow as you is nothing to brag over. Some men would kill you where you sat, just for breathing!"

"They can try," Mayport said. "I don't expect to be treated like a convict, like you do. It's never the sin men care about. It's lying, and pretending to purity, that causes all the trouble. Even if that wasn't true, I have no talent for being a hypocrite."

Cully looked shocked. "You've only been lucky, my boy. One day, somebody will call you down or shoot you down, for the way you carry on."

"You're the only one who's yet dared to say a word against me," Mayport said.

"I'd guess they're saying it where you can't hear," Cully said, and puffed up his chest. "That's how they do a fellow. Secrets, sneaking, and coming at your back when you least expect it."

"I will not live the way you do, expecting betrayal of every man because I have lied to their faces," Mayport said. He looked at his ledgers and made a decision. "You seem unable to reconcile yourself to that fact, so I will make it immaterial for you. This ruins some of my plans, but it can't be helped."

Cully laughed without humor. "You can send me as far away as you like. Maybe you think that charter will protect you, when the time comes. That Jesse fellow will have a fit if he finds out what you intend to do with it. He's hoed a long, lonely row, to be able to help you in this matter. His protection will disappear once he realizes you've got some scheme cooked up."

Mayport laughed back, all merriment and contempt. "He knows everything, and encouraged me every step of the way. I've heard sermons like yours before, Cully. It came from the mouths of men who wanted to restrain me in public and ravish me in private. I won't abide that kind of sideways shame. Especially of a man who can't sweeten the deal with even base pleasure. You may not have noticed this on your own: You have no influence over me. You have no right to dictate the terms by which I live."

"I have never tried to control you," Cully said, but couldn't meet Mayport's eyes.

"Then you must think I'm a cowardly child, unwilling and unable to accept responsibility for the choices I've made," Mayport said. "In fact, you owe me for coming to rescue you from exile. Go on as you please, if secrecy pleases you. I won't make the mistake of pitying you twice. As to what I endure for being who I am? I accept the cost gladly."

"You're so sure of yourself," Cully said, barely restraining his anger. "Your precious Joseph is a faithless fellow, and I should know! He'll abandon you if trouble comes. You'll see, soon enough."

Mayport set his empty glass down so hard the stem broke. "Even if you were right, I wouldn't hear such a thing out of you. I'm your employer, and never was anything else to you. How dare you say a word against my Joseph, when it was *you* who instigated that incident? It was no betrayal. I could have asked him to refrain, but didn't. If I'd said a word, it would have been to remind Joseph that fucking the help gives them funny ideas about what they can get away with in the company."

Cully looked shocked, then settled back into his chair. "I see I've offended you. It wasn't my intention to make you angry. I only meant to make you see sense and behave yourself."

That thin show of contrition meant nothing to Mayport. Not for the first time, he wished he'd listened to Ma when she'd suggested Cully should be dismissed. "All this makes me wonder how you got Joyce to release my stock from the warehouse in the first place. Did you say you spoke for me?"

"You're angry," Cully said, as if to soothe. "We'll talk again once you've calmed down."

"We won't," Mayport said. "You've misunderstood me completely. You may take that cargo vessel as your severance. I'll let you walk out with it, and your life. That's the end, for you and I."

Cully sat still and quiet, considering Mayport anew. "You can't. You need me."

Mayport frowned at the very idea. "It has always been the reverse, between us. I should burn you down where you sit, for speaking the way you did. You could have been important to me, but that you want so much to make me be the way you are. I assume you were special to my father, but I only have your word for that bit of history. For my future, there's no place for a man like you. I'll give you the means to support yourself. It's certainly more than you have earned, with your disturbing influence in my home and business."

Cully wasn't listening. "I'll run your cargo up north, and give you time to get over your temper. You've taken all this much harder than I expected. I thought you were a stronger man than one to break with a friend over hard advice."

Mayport saw then, how things might have been between his father and Cully. Cruelty followed by contrition and condescension might have defined their time together. With time and persuasion, the cold, judgmental insults might have been forgotten or ignored. For himself, he had made his decisions, though he hadn't expected to be tested this way.

He went to his desk and wrote out the terms of Cully's discharge. There was no need to consult with anyone over the arrangement. Joseph might not approve entirely, but neither would he reverse the decision. As the ink dried, Mayport counted out a stack of gold coins and secured them in a cloth bag.

Cully watched with a mix of horror and disbelief. "This is entirely without justification! You are making a mistake, my boy!"

"What employer could you insult, and get so generous a sacking?" Mayport asked. "If Joseph was my Josephine, you would never have dared. This is what you get, for denying him the respect he deserves. I intended to make up for the time you spent, abandoned in India, from the start. Here's the finish to that intention. Here's my signature to prove my sincerity. Take your treasures and go. You're a ruined man to me."

"You speak so innocently for a man with enemies," Cully said, but took the money and title.

"Let them come," Mayport said. "Come yourself, if you're among their number. You'll find out about the less gentle side within me."

Cully took his anger with him and left the house without a farewell to the others. Mayport took a fresh glass for his wine and stood at the window to watch him go. There was not even a backward glance from that sturdy figure to show a moment's regret.

Soft footsteps gave away Joseph's stealthy approach from behind. His arms came up around Mayport and held him tight. Joseph kissed his hair and nearly crushed Mayport with the strength of his embrace.

"I think we paid a small price to be rid of him," Joseph murmured. "I listened at the door. Cully's good at persuasion, and I should know. When he's around, I keep a close eye on you."

"Well, no more of that," Mayport said, and smiled over Joseph's caution. "He was never a moment's competition to you. As for what was between you two, it seemed only one of your many amusements. I never felt threatened or betrayed."

"He tried for both, and I should have told you," Joseph said. "I should have made you hear me sooner, about him. I have betrayed you that way so many times, the hurt must have worn off by now. Otherwise, you couldn't have endured this with such grace. I wonder what you will begin to imagine when I stay faithful to you? You expect to be abandoned with regularity, but now I must eternally disappoint that expectation."

"I won't mind if you still divert yourself now and then," Mayport said. "If you get lost, I'll come find you again."

"You would, but I don't mean to test you that way," Joseph said. "You've just proved that your kindness has limits."

"For you, limits do not exist," Mayport said. "Still, we're down by one cargo vessel and have a warehouse full of stock to shift. What to do? Hire a steam coach on the rail line?"

"There's a harbor full of cargo captains running the spice routes this very day, and every day for years to come," Joseph said. "Set your price and hire a broker. If your father had been that sensible he would have had his fortune, if not his adventures."

"I would rather be sensible," Mayport said. "Your uncle will have an easier time of my case if I seem somewhat established. Let's concern ourselves with our own business, and let the auctioneers do their worst. Have you persuaded any of your engineers to come south with us?"

"Not even one," Joseph said, and sighed. "I can't be surprised. Men of their skills and experience are needed where industry are in full bloom. They've done their part for us. I can't stand to keep them from the opportunities that come of it. They love their gears, I love you, and so we will have to do without them."

Mayport turned around in Joseph's arms and held him tight.

"I know you love your gears as well as these other fellows do. I'm grateful, that you've chosen me over those same opportunities they're offered. It seems you won't get much but a shanty town and a strange partner in the trade."

Joseph answered with more kisses, and held Mayport with all his strength. Never before had Joseph clung so. Now, contrary to all his public reticence, he poured all his longings into a bruising embrace.

After that moment, a new kind of fire sprang to life in Joseph Thiervy. He used his last weeks with his crew to finish off their stores of cacao. Then their factory machines were disassembled and stowed aboard the *Process* for shipment south. Mayport could only marvel at all that Joseph had prepared for their venture.

For himself, he was kept busy grading their products and dealing with the commodities brokers. To the last man, they tried to convince Mayport that his goods were nearly worthless. He let it be known that he would take a slow dollar over a nimble penny before he would sit still for a fleecing. When he made noises about hiring cargo on the steam coach line, the seaport auctioneers had a sudden change of heart in their valuations. That sparked a bidding war that was far beyond Mayport's influence.

All his profits were placed on account at the bank under his own name, but for Ma's benefit. He couldn't stand to take her from the society she found so peaceful, though there was a danger in her independence. His only recourse was to approach Oliver with a shocking proposition, and a heavy bag of coins.

"He will come," Mayport said, and paid his bribe in full. "Keep her safe, and let him know where I can be found. I'll draw a map. There's nothing else to be done with a dog like him."

"If she would accept her father's protection, I could burn that fool down myself," Oliver grumbled.

"Don't bestir yourself so on our account," Mayport said. "You have to live here, so your reputation makes a difference. If you can send him south by any means, I will be even more grateful. In ready money."

Chapter Fifty: Establishment

The Titus Chocolate Company became established in May Port with no fanfare. Joseph had already scouted the men he wanted for his machinist crew. He carried a book with him as a preacher might cling to his Bible. Within lay the collected knowledge from their experiments with the engines.

Now that the equipment was proven, Mayport's job was considerably easier. Frog had developed a taste for bossing his elders. He had his fun with making quality checks on the production line, and had only Mayport to answer if things went wrong.

The factory itself had taken over two buildings near the Land Company office. Both had been warehouses for a shipping company that had moved north some years before. Part of Joseph's work had been to weatherproof the structures. One held the production floor. The other resumed its existence as a storehouse, but this time for sugar cake and cacao.

The factory men were drawn from shipwrights among the townsmen. Mayport had responsibility for the supply line from farm to factory. He disliked the source of his labor, but had yet to find a way around the town's expectations. With Frog replacing Mayport on the factory floor, he had to face the logical conclusion about the farm.

He hitched a ride on one of the wagons on its return journey. The slow ride gave him plenty of time to imagine the worst. If Joyce had run off while Mayport was gone, the situation might have been less complicated. The man might have lingered on the expectation that the younger Titus would copy his sire's absentee habits. The best way to know was to go and see for himself.

Mayport dropped off the wagon at the gate to Titus Farms. He enjoyed the walk under the live oaks. He could see the nearest orchards, and tried to imagine himself as master of the place. The plantation house was lively with servants going about their labors. The porch was bright and colorful where belles and young gentlemen were gathered for refreshment. The welcome looked home-like, though it had not been arranged for his particular benefit.

Missus Joyce saw him mount the porch steps and cried out in surprise. Her shock was quickly disguised as excited pleasure. "Why, Mister Titus! What a delight! I never expected you would grace my humble gathering."

"My invitation must have been lost along the way," Mayport said, to hide his own embarrassment over his intrusion. "Indeed, I've come on matters of business, and only want use of the study. Please, continue. I don't intend to disturb your festivities."

"But you are here," Missus Joyce said. "I can hardly let a guest go without refreshment."

"In that case, I can be safely let go," Mayport said. "Since I am no guest in this house."

Mayport went past her party and into the cool hall of the plantation house. For the first time, he felt curious about the place. He might have gone on to the study, but instead wandered the halls, peeking in doors to see what he might find.

The Joyces and their daughters enjoyed an expansive homestead. Every formality had been observed. The public rooms were brightly papered and lavishly furnished. The library held a vast collection of volumes, though few seemed to have been recently disturbed.

He inspected the dining room and parlor, taking note of what extravagance his fortune had provided. On the second floor, he found a half dozen chambers, two prepared for guests and shrouded against dust. From the window of the rearmost guest room, he spied a little clapboard house set among a grove of cacao. He went downstairs and through the back yard to investigate the charming cottage in the shade.

At the garden gate he found a sign of green and white, bearing Joyce's name. Within, a kitchen and three rooms stood bare of furnishings. On the second floor he found four bedrooms with nothing but curtains in the windows. He made a few estimates of measures in his notebook, and set out at last to take over the plantation house study.

There he found volumes of household records, including a catalog of goods and furnishings. He was surprised to see a proper accounting of the place, but was grateful for the ledger. Satisfied on a few details, he turned his attention to reports from the field crews, and records of his warehouse stores.

Joyce came very late in the morning, made a surprised noise over Mayport, but did not disturb his work. A maid came along later with a rolling cart laden with lunch. Mayport was pleased to see that he had been accounted for by the kitchens, if not by Joyce himself.

A small table was laid and wine poured before Mayport closed his book and took his place to be served. Joyce joined him, but looked nervous. A valet served them from the platters, but seemed to have attention for the diners rather than his own utensils. Mayport tasted the wine and murmured his approval to soothe whatever worries were dogging the poor fellow.

When they were alone once more, Mayport maintained his silence. Joyce could hardly stand to keep still. He cleared his throat several times before he finally found his words. "I hope all is to your liking?"

"The meal is acceptable," Mayport said, low and slow. "Have you thought much about your position since we last spoke?"

"I have thought of nearly nothing else," Joyce said. "Missus Joyce has been instrumental in helping me to make better decisions. She cursed me for a fool over you. Of course, I should have expected changes with the arrival of our second generation. I would have served you better to listen, and comprehend, rather than trying to command as I have over these lands in your absence."

"You've been a faithful steward to my father's desires," Mayport allowed. "Some of his men have not been able to transfer allegiances to me. I trust your good wife does not allow you to foster such pride?"

Joyce laughed nervously. "You seem to know the lady well. Have you made her acquaintance?"

"I am close with a lady belle from the Savannah river," Mayport said. "I mean the mother of my partner. Perhaps your bride has been cut from the same cloth?"

"No, but nearly," Joyce said, shifting on his seat. "We come from Richmond. She insists on the customs of her girlhood, even out here in the wilderness."

"Do those customs include taking over the master's house, and assuming his role in the neighborhood?" Mayport asked. "I saw the foreman's house this morning. Were you there long, before this place became too tempting?"

Joyce blushed, and hid in his wine glass until he could speak without stuttering. "I think the change came as our daughters grew. They *are* belles, Mister Titus, or as best we can make them be out here without proper society."

"Intentions notwithstanding, you know you can't go on this way," Mayport said. "Missus Joyce will have to content herself with her place, as you will. She may be a belle, but she is not the lady of these lands."

"Do you mean to take up residence here yourself?" Joyce asked, as if clinging to some final hope.

"I do, immediately. The guest rooms can be opened this afternoon," Mayport said. "My partner's uncle and my representative will be coming here directly from the capitol. His welcome must be impeccable. He's a gentleman to the bone, and knows propriety like the back of his hand. Like your wife, he insists upon it."

"I see," Joyce said, unhappy.

"Come now, you must be cheerful," Mayport said. "He comes to bring me hope, and may have some for you as well. Captain Cully has disgraced himself for the last time. I will need a man to take his place among the signatures of the charter. I don't suppose you can make a harbormaster of yourself in a few weeks, of course. Still, you might do for a sheriff, which will serve just as well. We need a man on land more than a boat-watcher anyway."

Joyce went pale and breathless, staring at Mayport in cold shock. "Yes! My word, of course, if you like, Mister Titus. You might have given some small hint that... but certainly, that's no matter. I would be proud and faithful to serve the town in this way. So then, the charter has been ratified?"

"We will know when Uncle Jesse comes," Mayport said. "There is only a little time to prepare. The town and my business must be without reproach before I may assume these responsibilities."

"You may certainly rely on me," Joyce said. He wiped his mouth and stood in haste. "There is so much to arrange! I'll need my wife and all her cleverness, but the feat will be accomplished without delay."

Joyce did all that he had promised, though not without resistance from his women. Missus Joyce launched an effort to render Mayport's claim on his house a moot point. She set her eldest daughter the task of charming him into wedlock. Joseph noticed the attack, and enjoyed making a mockery of the young woman's endeavors. Mayport pitied her, but his kindness had to be given by coldly disregarding her childish seduction.

Despite that little intrigue, the plantation house was cleared of the Joyces. A room stood ready for Joseph, and another for Jesse. Thus Mayport thought himself well-prepared, until a stranger appeared at his door. Doctor Elias Oliver, cousin to the watchman of Mayport's acquaintance, came ahead of Jesse with word that their work in the capitol was nearing its result.

"I thank you for your trouble," Mayport said, after making the fellow comfortable in the library. "Of course, you must be my guest here. The maids will have a room arranged for you, though the furnishings are too feminine for real comfort. I had no idea the Oliver family had such particular interest in this matter."

"They don't, or of me," Elias said. "I came on account of my longstanding friendship with Jesse. We met again in Richmond just lately. He felt this place might need a good man of my profession, and sent me on to see if I liked it."

Mayport heard much in that gentle, reserved tone. He studied the fellow anew, and privately approved of him as a prospective relation. He could not fault Jesse for his choice, or hesitate before the apparent intention of resuming so charming a friendship.

"Indeed, we need all the good men we can get," Mayport said. "If you know Uncle Jesse as a friend, I would impose upon your help. I mean to welcome him as a hero, but I'm ignorant of his tastes. Perhaps you know what would please?"

Doctor Elias accepted the task, as well as the invitation to stay at the farm. His cheerful company lightened their anxious waiting until at last Jesse arrived by overland steam coach. By then the town was full of rumors surrounding a Confederalist lawyer, and the changes he would bring.

Joseph came with his uncle directly to the farm, for a proper welcome. All of their preparations were ignored in favor of Elias Oliver. Even insensitive Joseph saw what lay between the men, and the secret hope they had carried so far away from all that they knew.

"I'll just take these papers to the study," Mayport said, though the household had been expecting a day of festivities. "Elias knows the place well. I'm sure he will attend your every need."

Mayport took Joseph away from the table, and left their elders to moon and sigh as they wished. Joseph was dumbfounded, and needed strong wine to overcome the shock. He sat drinking in silence as Mayport read over the ratified charter. All was as he had hoped, though his personal tax burden would be something remarkable. He signed, and made changes to replace Cully with Joyce as a permanent trustee.

"So my Uncle means to take advantage of these lawless wilds, and of that doctor in particular," Joseph said at last. "I should have known his help wasn't entirely selfless."

"This place isn't lawless anymore," Mayport said, and fanned himself with the charter. "It's only that they won't be criminals here. I've made the law in that regard as libertine as old Verry might have wished."

"It's a good thing you shot him, then," Joseph said. "There should be limits to obey. You have the best intentions, but you're a singular fellow."

"Do you mean to change your mind?" Mayport asked.

Joseph looked down at his ring, smiled, then returned his attention to the wine. "I mean to have you, any way I can. These vows might be the only way to make things right between us. How else could you ever believe that I'm done with being a cold bastard to you?"

"It would take more than vows, to change the man you are," Mayport teased.

"Then by God, I will do more!" Joseph said, nearly shouting. He drew a calming breath before he went on. "We will begin with this, and I will do more. Only, let's not make a spectacle of this, please. We might be blameless under your law, but that's no guarantee that we've made ourselves respectable. I'm proud of you, and of us together. I can't endure ridicule from the ignorant and cruel men around us."

"As you wish," Mayport said. "No matter that we're private, people will find out. If I am ever pushed to do so, I will protect you with extreme prejudice. Since I've taken up a rather medieval responsibility, I intend to have and keep the prize I won by accepting this place."

They left Uncle Jesse and Doctor Elias alone for a long, lazy week before they made their little ceremony together. Jesse presided in his capacity as justice of the peace. They were all sad that Ma was left out, and kept ignorant of their private joy. That decision had been Joseph's to make. He had cared only for protecting her innocent ideals.

Mayport went along with any demand Joseph presented. Privacy, even secrecy, was very little to endure for such a prize. Once the vows were made, there was no turning back. He had won Joseph fair and square, beyond all others, and never need fear his loss again.

He hadn't realized how heavy that terror was until he laid it down. Joseph was insensitive, but his sincerity was unquestionable.

He would sooner have denied Mayport such a commitment, than to make one just for show. Even understanding that, Mayport didn't believe Joseph would go through with it until hours after the deed was done.

"Why did you marry me?" Mayport asked over wine, when they had retired to his rooms. "You didn't have to. I would have understood."

"This is a fine time to ask that," Joseph laughed. "You might not like the answer. It's too late to change things, if you don't."

"Tell me anyway," Mayport said.

Joseph savored his wine, and looked Mayport over has he had been doing all day. "Do you believe that I love you? Can you now harbor any suspicion that I'll slip away to play games with other men? Should you be tolerant, if I do?"

Mayport frowned over the questions. "I do believe you love me. But I'm asking why—"

"What about the rest?" Joseph prompted.

"I don't think you would have done this if you meant to go running off again," Mayport replied.

"Such a change, in so little time," Joseph said, triumphant. "I think you would fight, if anyone came along and made a bid for me."

Mayport shivered, but knew he would do worse than fight now that he could. "I'm your husband. If I become a cuckold, you may bet there will be blood over it."

"This is why," Joseph said, trying to be gentle. "I taught you that your love was not reason enough for me to be faithful. I made you believe your regard was worthless. It was a crime, to be so cruel when your love is so innocent. Worse, there was no way to prove I'd learned better and wanted to repent of my sins. You never have believed I could do any wrong. That's why you made yourself think I was still proud of how I have lived. I am ashamed of the things I've done to you. I could never make you understand even that much. Now I can. I have my whole life with you, to prove your love made a better man of me."

Mayport rubbed his eyes. His hand came away wet. He sniffed hard and looked away, embarrassed to show such depth of feeling to his strong husband. His chest only grew tighter, so he got up to stand at the window until it stopped. Joseph came after him and made him turn around.

"Don't, I'm a mess," Mayport said. He tried to hide his face against his sleeve.

Joseph forced his arms down and drew him into a strong embrace. He pressed Mayport's face to his chest and murmured against his hair. "Don't hide your tears from me, or your laughter. They're mine now, as you are. You must bring them to me, always. I won't abide the way you make yourself suffer all alone. Do you understand me, Mayport Titus?"

Mayport nodded hard. Then, even through the tears, he laughed. "Aren't I Mayport Thiervy now?"

"No," Joseph said, and kissed his hair. "I am proud to be Joseph Titus. Don't argue. I've wanted to be, for a very long time. I won't have you wearing my father's name, nor keep it for myself. We'll share what your father gave you, even down to the name."

Mayport nodded against Joseph's chest, then lifted his face up, silently asking for more kisses. Once they began, no power on Earth could have stopped them. There was something fresh and new in the quality of Joseph's taste. Mayport moaned, drunk on just the sweetness of his groom's lips.

Mayport pulled them to the bed, discarding their clothes along the way. Joseph felt soft and easy under his hands, leaning into touches and moaning, free as he never had been before. Mayport made him comfortable against the pillows and was quick with the oil Joseph had standing ready by the bed. Even that habit seemed endearing, where once he had thought the presumption bordered on the obscene.

Joseph wrapped his legs around Mayport's hips, urging him on. There was no resistance as Mayport slid inside, sinking himself in the welcoming heat of his husband's body. The kisses never stopped, and only grew more urgent as Mayport began to thrust. Joseph's legs locked across the small of his back, lending strength to the taking.

They writhed together, breaths and groans in unison, as warm pleasure built and broke between them, only to redouble once more. Mayport felt wild and strong, like the wind and tide, caught in the grip of something timeless and quite beyond himself. His body became a conduit for that power, and he poured it out into Joseph with long, slow undulations of his spine. His cock throbbed, but in a low and steady way, as if he might go on like this for eons and never tire of the delight.

Joseph bucked under him, thrusting his ass up and up again, demanding all that Mayport could give him. Together they burned, surrendering all that they once had held back. Mayport reveled in the passion, as the crucible of their love blended them together and made something new. Whatever pinnacle there might be to find, he felt he had begun there, and could only rise higher.

After his wedding, Mayport enjoyed a domestic peace he hadn't anticipated. Frog quietly usurped the lead position at the factory, then defended it with all he had. Joseph trusted the boy, beyond all reason. He went to town to play in his shop and endlessly fiddle with his creations. Otherwise, he occupied himself with plans for the future of the plantation.

Mayport made himself stay focused on the office work, from which neither Frog nor Joseph could liberate him. He had presumed that, without governor or judge, the townspeople would be used to settling things outside a court of law. Instead, he discovered that many had grown long on patience, if short on temper. Like the debts he had first found, grudges were handed down father to son. He was glad to have Jesse's help to organize all the disputes that were submitted to his desk.

"I think you'd better allow the dueling," Jesse said over a stack of complaints. "You'll never stop them doing as they've done all along."

"I don't mean to try," Mayport said. "They'd only go behind my back. But neither can I grant explicit permission on a case-by-case basis. I can't tolerate cold murder, which is what we'd get if we tried to stop this archaic tradition. Where did they get the idea that I would issue licenses for such a thing, anyway?"

"Men like to imagine that the law is on their side," Jesse explained. "The whole point of law is that it doesn't take sides. You could simply render yourself ignorant on these matters. You'd probably be inclined to prosecute all parties involved, if you were made to know everything."

"I understand the purpose of the exercise," Mayport said with a sniff. "Anyway, I have more important issues to attend. We're going to allow divorce the same way we handle marriage. That should even things out a bit. Won't that cause a ruckus? They've all been expecting one out of me."

"Let us not disappoint our expectations," Jesse said with a smile. "I think Elias will enjoy having a threat that will work on me."

"Be nicer to him, and he won't need to threaten," Mayport reasoned. "I'm more interested in the woods women, in this. Verry did a lot of marrying around here. I'd go hunting for the husbands like wild animals, but I don't have the time."

"There's plenty of sons who would do the work for you," Jesse said, still amused. "You could name a holiday for the occasion. It sounds festive."

Mayport was embarrassed of himself for laughing over so gruesome a suggestion. "I thought I would be a different sort of governor, but I'm the same as the rest. Men can get away with murder, as long as it's a murder I like."

"Just so," Jesse said. "The thing men care about most is the tax code. This place has a long way to go before it will look like a real town. How are you going to pay for road and port repairs before the weather turns hard?"

"If it was going to turn, it would have done it already," Mayport said. "It's not like you imagine. Frog said men expect to work straight through the winter. When the harvest is done, we'll shift crews around. By then, I'll know which men I can trust with responsibility."

"I'm sure Joseph will have plenty to say on the topic," Jesse said, very proud. "He's the one who travels these tracks, so he'll know best."

"You do a good job of keeping up with the gossip," Mayport said. "I wish you'd do the beer rounds for me. You've got the constitution for thirsty work, and I never did."

Jesse took Mayport's suggestion with pleasure, and began to set his own reputation in town. With him in circulation, the legal complaints slowed to a manageable level. Then, Mayport could let business be his foremost concern. The need for ready money showed itself in every shop. He was pleasantly surprised to be considered a reputable lender, despite the history he had in that capacity.

With Jesse and Joseph in town every day, Mayport never needed to leave his own land. The only inconvenience came from learning all his news secondhand. He was far away from the action, therefore, when his quiet life was once again unsettled by his past. Jesse brought Joseph home in a state of rage and blood.

"Who did this to you?" Elias demanded as he patched up the damage. "In this town, who would dare?"

Joseph wouldn't answer, but Mayport already knew the truth. He was grateful that Joseph had come out of his fight with his life.

He made the older men leave Joseph alone, once the doctor had done what he could.

"Don't let them worry you," Mayport said with false cheer as he settled Joseph in his room. "They don't half know either one of us."

"This is all Frog's fault, and he's proud of himself," Joseph complained. "He taught Ma to load rock salt, for the fun of it, and got her a little blunderbuss all her own. When my father came looking for trouble, she done gave him an ass full of it."

"Don't blame Frog for his good sense," Mayport said. "Your father would have hunted us down, even without that excuse. Be glad he's here. I'd rather this than him feeling he could keep after Ma. She ought to have plugged him full of tenpenny nails, but she's too much of a lady."

"I would have beat the life out of him, but Jesse fainted," Joseph said. "He's no man to husband a doctor. He can't stand the sight of blood."

Mayport leaned down and kissed Joseph quiet. "It's a good thing I don't have that weakness. You're too worked up to get any rest."

Joseph went even more tense, then grabbed Mayport with all his strength and dragged him onto the bed. Their kisses were savage, with Joseph in a fury and Mayport willing to go along. They tore each others' clothes to ruins, and soon their bare skin had worked its alchemy on Joseph's passion. He oiled up Mayport's cock, straddled his hips, and impaled himself roughly, driving a wild shout from both of them.

Mayport's back arched up from the bed, bent with the power of pure need. Joseph shoved him back down, and kept his hands planted on Mayport's chest. He rode hard, pounding his ass against Mayport's hips in a raw, carnal demand. The strength of his passion made them slide down the bed until Mayport braced his feet and grasped Joseph's hips. That did nothing to slow the maddened thrusting, but kept them from falling to the floor.

The bed thumped loudly against the floor and wall, but neither of them could care about the damage they were doing. Joseph jerked his ass higher and dropped down, over and over, until he was breathless and had to slow down. Mayport flexed his back again, shoved with his legs, and turned Joseph over in a rough tumble. Joseph cried out in surprise, but Mayport thrust hard, claiming his husband with all of his strength.

Fire sizzled through his veins, driving out all reason or restraint. Joseph braced his arms against the headboard, stretched out and arched his hips up higher. Mayport let him writhe and twist, riding Joseph's contortions until they were both running with sweat. The bruises and cuts Joseph had suffered seemed immaterial, and looked normal on him. Mayport leaned down to kiss and suck at those battle marks, as well as the scars from fights so long ago, only his flesh remembered what he had endured.

He seized one of Joseph's nipples in his teeth, bit and sucked until the flesh stood up high and hard like Joseph's cock. Joseph groaned, and reached down to stroke himself. For once, Mayport stopped him, grabbing his wrists and pinning them to the bed. Joseph moaned again, fought against that restraint, but not hard enough to break free.

Somehow, that halfhearted struggle struck Mayport as wrong. He withdrew, shifted his weight and turned Joseph over onto his belly. Again he grabbed Joseph's arms and folded them over the small of his back. He straddled Joseph's thighs and humped against his ass until he found that tight passage once more. He drove in deep, Joseph bucked, and again he was buried to the root in his husband's body.

Joseph strained against Mayport, worked his knees up under himself and tried to throw Mayport off. Mayport laughed, pounding wildly, trying to overcome all that muscle. Their sweat made it impossible to keep a solid grip, and Joseph sat up with a roar, tossing Mayport aside like a stallion who had tired of his childish rider.

Mayport tumbled aside, still laughing, but something feral was burning bright in Joseph's eyes. Before he could scoot away, Joseph had him by the hair and dragged him forward. He shoved Mayport's face down with one hand, and seized his cock with the other. Mayport opened up, took a deep breath, and hoped for the best.

Joseph drove his cock into Mayport's mouth, hardly caring about the awkward angle. Mayport sucked hard, licked fast and tried to get that throbbing flesh wet enough to manage. He could hardly be expected to swallow it all. Joseph kept his fist wrapped around the base of his shaft, and there, his consideration ended. He thrust into Mayport's mouth, spread his spit down, and thrust again until his whole cock was glistening and slick.

At last he let go of Mayport's hair, and let him come up gasping for breath. Joseph caressed Mayport's bruised lips with his thumb and chuckled. "Turn around."

Mayport shivered at that half-growled command. He turned on his knees and leaned forward onto his hands, then turned to look over his shoulder. Joseph seized his hips and yanked him backwards to straddle his thighs. Then he spread Mayport's ass and prodded with the tip of his cock. Mayport tensed, and stuttered "Maybe I should..."

Joseph thrust, piercing Mayport to the core. Mayport yelped and squirmed, whole body struggling against that sudden invasion. Joseph's hands clamped down even harder on his hips, holding him in place for the next rough thrust. He leaned down and bit at Mayport's neck, drove in deeper still, and began to rock Mayport to and fro, using the struggle to stroke his shaft.

Mayport whimpered as all the strength drained out of him. His arms slid out from under him and he pitched forward, half-hanging off the edge of the bed. His ass stayed high and kept moving in Joseph's grip. Mayport managed to get a hold on the bed frame and had no choice but to push back and try to keep up with what Joseph demanded of him.

Joseph wrapped a strong arm under Mayport's belly to hold him on the bed. With his other hand he grabbed Mayport's cock and stroked, hard and too fast. "That's it," Joseph purred, then chuckled low in his throat. "Just like that. Not much of a gentleman like this, are you?"

"Please!" Mayport screamed, but had no idea what he was begging for.

Joseph knew exactly what he needed. His passion was near to an assault, stretching Mayport from the inside, forcing pleasure that Mayport hadn't known his flesh could surrender. His cock jerked and danced in Joseph's grip. His balls felt swollen and ached with pent-up need. Within, the fire rose to a white-hot pinnacle that seared him to the bone.

Joseph's strokes stuttered, then redoubled. Mayport howled, lost in animal lust that broke through any memory of control. His cock flexed in Joseph's hand, and hot seed spurted as he quivered and shook, pouring out all his need, making the bed fragrant with all the love he could never express in any other way.

Mayport left the house early the next morning, long before the sun had risen. He did not allow himself even one kiss of his sleeping husband. He had every intention of returning, and claiming what was his by right.

He made his way to his factory and walked through, admiring the machines Joseph had devised and installed. They were nothing like the monstrous contraptions his father had created. Joseph had reduced the process to simple steps, and created engines to perfect each one. Frog presided over the production line, and lived in a set of rooms near the factory itself. No amount of spoiling could persuade the boy's return to Titus Farms.

It was he who found Mayport sampling the wares, and frowned with suspicion. "What are you doing here?"

"I own the place, don't I?" Mayport asked back.

"That don't answer," Frog said. "Don't act smart to me. I know you."

"Very well," Mayport said. He took an envelope from his pocket and handed it over. "You know where Joseph's fool daddy is holed up?"

"Sure," Frog said. "He made a ruckus, so everyone knows. He took up with one of Annie Cook's girls for the night. What's this? Bribes to get him out of here?"

"If such a thing worked on him, it would be," Mayport said. "You carry that to him, then come on back and run this factory like you want to. I've got to go inspect the *Process*."

Frog had more questions, but got no more answers. Mayport knew his town's habits, and obeyed them. While his letter was being delivered, he went to the docks and stood on the deck of the *Dutch Process* while the sun rose. He breathed deep, and tried to remember all the places he had been, and the people he had met, because of what he'd made of his legacy. Nothing broke his calm, or persuaded him from his purpose.

He breakfasted alone in the mess, and lay awhile in Joseph's bunk. The rocking of the vessel at anchor soothed him, as it had in distant waters and high altitude. If the fans had been turning, he would have been cool and comfortable all the day long.

As it was, the heat pooled below decks, and drove him from his drowsing. He moved only as far as the pilot's chair. The town had woken up while he lazed about. The harbor was busy with fishing boats, and the streets noisy with all sorts of commerce. He was comforted by the sense that all would go on without him just as it did on this very morning.

Through the spyglass he saw Joseph arrive to work. Even that seemed permanent, in ways Mayport couldn't feel for his own position. He looked at the levers on the deck, knew just how to launch the vessel, and finally understood how his father's efforts had gone so very wrong.

Fear clutched him. His mouth went dry, and his hands shook, then fisted on the edge of the pilot's chair. He leaned his head back and moaned quietly, lost in a surging passion that would have him up and out, fleeing south into the deep unknown if he had let himself move at all. He went tense until he was sweating with the effort to sit still.

He waited, fighting valiantly against the sudden desire for flight. Nobody could stop him but himself. That fact alone made him whimper with fear once more. Without limits, his options stretched before him in the darkness behind his closed eyes. To run away would be simplicity itself, with virtually no consequences that he would have to face. Like his father before him, he might be able to justify even his own cowardice.

He held on, hearing his heart throb and the pop of his clenched jaw. Slowly, the panic ebbed, drew down into his bones, and alchemized into something cold and familiar. When his hands were steady once more, he stood and left his beloved Dutch Process behind.

He walked past his factory without a glance. On the street, he saw changes of his own instigation. A few watering holes had hung out their shingles. Shops were being prepared to do business. He got a few greetings, but nobody tried to stop him and speak at length.

He only had to consult the map hung on the wall at his own Land Office to find out where Annie Cook lived. The plot was in a business district, and registered as a hotel. He needed very little imagination to realize what kind of business the lady was running. He admired her boldness, considering the way Verry and Joyce had kept the town locked down before Mayport had come along.

He went to the address and paced the block on the opposite side of the street. That same cold still sat at the core of his bones. He might have warmed himself in a shop, but clung to the chill within as the only thing that seemed real.

At last, the door opened and a woman of Ma's age, but with less fashion sense, came out onto the street. Mayport bowed politely as she passed. She stopped dead in her tracks. He blushed and looked away, embarrassed to have shocked her so completely.

"Good morning Mister Titus," the lady said. "Are you passing my door by chance?"

"I came looking for the senior Mister Thiervy," Mayport admitted. "It's too early for social calls, I imagine. I thought I should wait awhile."

"You'll do no good waiting out front," she said with a laugh. "Them that come in the street door leave by the alley. That Frog of yours came early with a message, but our guest is still asleep."

"I'm sorry if my boy was a bother to you," Mayport said.

Annie laughed again, but it seemed more of a habit than a true expression of her feelings. "I heard you were one for politeness, but that don't usually include me."

Mayport looked away, embarrassed all over again. "A gentleman is so to everyone, not just to those who can help him on in the world. I'll try to speak more roughly if that suits you better, Ma'am."

"Don't; I find your innocent attitude refreshing," Annie said. "Do I dare to wonder what you're doing, looking for trouble so early in the day? That Thiervy is nothing but, and this is your second time trying to get at him."

"It's better not to speak plainly about these things to a lady," Mayport said. "Anyway, I know where he is, and when he wakes, I'm sure you'll deliver my note. Then he will know where I will be. I assure you, he won't be a trouble to you much longer."

"You're a funny sort of governor," Annie said. "I think I like you. I was sure I wouldn't, but I've been wrong before."

Mayport smiled, but still couldn't meet her too-knowing eyes. "I'm glad you approve, Ma'am."

"Is there someplace you want him to go particularly?" Annie asked. "Other than straight to hell, which I can see without asking. Maybe I can be an influence on him."

"I'm sure you can," Mayport said. "I'd rather meet up with him down by the docks. Collier's Hideaway is where I'm known best. It won't be a difference to me if you can't work your magic, but I appreciate the offer to try. Am I keeping you from your business?"

"Not hardly. I'm only going down to see about replenishing the rum," she said. "I can't trust the maids to know quality, and that Thiervy has drank us dry. I guess I'd better make sure of his coin before we let him past the door again."

"That would be for the best," Mayport agreed, and tipped his hat. "A pleasant day to you, then."

She nodded once and walked on, as if they had never spoken. Mayport went down the block feeling a little lost until his feet took him to the Land Office once more. It was no such thing, these days. Instead of useless papers, it was used to house overflow of goods from the factory. Mayport wandered the rows of machines stored there, admiring their craftsmanship anew.

Once, he had imagined keeping his business small, using the little shop engines Joseph had devised for their New Amsterdam establishment. Now, those clever inventions sat gathering dust. Joseph had never complained of abandoning them. He cared only for his new loves, the full-scale versions that Frog presided over in the factory. His only complaint was that he hadn't yet perfected a method of harnessing the plentiful sunlight to completely replace the coal that powered his steam engines.

Mayport imagined himself as forgotten as the cocoa mill until Frog came in the back door with a basket. "You'll starve if you got nobody to feed you. I guess you really are a governor after all."

"I guess so," Mayport agreed. "Did old Thiervy send back a message to the factory?"

"No, but he's a coward," Frog said. "He came looking for trouble, sure enough. Maybe he'll get wise and run back where he belongs. Either way, this is no place for you to hide."

"I'm not hiding," Mayport said. "I'm waiting."

Frog left him to peace and quiet. From his seat he watched the town go about its business. Again, he found comfort in how little he was noticed. It gave him an idea of how much he could risk.

When the shops began to close up for the night, he saw to his belongings and went out into the street. Men crowded into their favorite watering holes and shed the ache of a day's labor. He passed slowly by saloon doors, listening for a certain kind of disruption among the merry chaos.

He found the accent he was listening for, and knew he owed Annie Cook thanks for her assistance. Collier's Hideaway was too near the docks for gentle custom. Joseph went there out of habit, having established himself among the patrons on his first day in town. The belligerent voice Mayport heard was similar to Joseph's, but not the right one to warm the chill he still carried in his bones.

He went in and quietly assumed a place at a table by the wall. Collier saw him, but restrained his usual, merry greeting. The barman came over with a pitcher and mug. "There's a fellow in the back, Annie Cook brought him here and gave me the high-sign to keep him merry. That one mixed it up with our Mister Thiervy last night. I wouldn't have let him in, but Annie mentioned your name. I guess he's still looking for trouble."

"It's found him," Mayport said. "I sent him my challenge this morning, but he hasn't answered."

Collier looked surprised and proud. "Well! I guess you're from around here after all! Don't worry that he's too much of a coward to stand up like a man. If you wrote out your challenge and he's still in town, that's good enough."

"I hate to mess up your nice place," Mayport said.

"Don't worry on that," Collier said, genial with so vital a subject. "There's plenty more sawdust where this pile came from. I reckon he's been running his Northie mouth about your Ma all this time. He's got it coming, so I don't blame you a bit for a mess."

Mayport smiled, then turned his attention to his mug. The taste should have been strong and rich, but might as well have been water. The cold patience in his bones seeped out, making his flesh numb while he waited. He kept his eyes on the back door of the tap room, while he gave time for word to spread of his arrival.

News must have trickled out to other bars, for the Hideaway filled up thick for so early in the evening. Mayport got lots of curious stares, and became the object of open betting. Otherwise, he was left alone. Any fellow who met his gaze soon turned away to avoid his cold regard.

At last, Mister Thiervy emerged from his private room. He was merry, but not as drunk as Mayport had imagined he would be. A couple of fellows were at his side. One asked Collier where they might find food, then led the way through the crowd and out into the street.

Mayport got up and followed, the crowd sidling away to make

322   Chocolatiers of the High Winds

322   *Chocolatiers of the High Winds*

a path. On the wooden sidewalk, he stopped and tucked his hands under his jacket. "Mister Thiervy! You come all this way. Don't you mean to say hello?"

Mister Thiervy stopped in his steps and turned around. "I've been looking for you, Mayport Titus. I assumed you ran off to hide in these woods! Didn't anyone warn you that I'd come to town?"

"If you were looking, you weren't trying very hard," Mayport observed. "I don't need any warning about you. I sent you my letter this morning. Did you bother to read it?"

Mister Thiervy laughed, all contempt. "You've been among the heathens too long, boy. Don't you know they outlawed dueling before you were born?"

"Maybe they did where you're from," Mayport said. "Down here, we're still heathen enough to allow a fair fight. Ain't that right, fellas?"

The crowd of men around him happily agreed to the fact. Mister Thiervy was surprised, and backed off a step. "What do you mean to do? Cross swords at dawn?"

"I'll take pistols right here and now," Mayport said, and slid his jacket back. "You want to say I got no reason or right?"

"You've certainly disturbed my life for the last time," Mister Thiervy said. "My wife and son belong to me, and I mean to take them back. A man can do what he likes in his own house!"

"This ain't your home," Mayport said. "As for how you did Ma, you're no kinda husband to be claiming rights. Maybe I could have let that lie, if you'd gone off peaceful. But now you come here and beat my husband to blood. I can't ignore that and call myself a man."

Mister Thiervy threw his head back and laughed. "You're a bold one! Hey, you rebel fools! Don't you know what he means? He's taken my son, and acts proud of it!"

"We know," Collier said from the door of his bar. "They're married. Our preacher has this verse about it all: Render unto Caesar that which is Caesar's. It's right there in the Bible, so we don't mean to fight the law. Now, ol' boy, you been challenged. What do you plan on doing?"

All the beery good cheer went out of Mister Thiervy and he studied the crowd anew. Most were merely curious, without a dog in this fight. Mayport knew they wouldn't really bother over the result one way or another. That indifference was worse in its way than open hostility.

"I think I'd rather swords at dawn," Mister Thiervy said.

"No," Mayport said. "Here and now, face me or run. Either way, you die. I won't mind to plug you in the back. We're beyond pride and honor, you and I."

The men around him scattered like spooked chickens at that announcement. Mister Thiervy drew, and his fellows did, too. Mayport's pistols were already out, his hands moving faster than his thoughts. The triggers felt smooth and easy on the draw. He kept his eyes steady on Mister Thiervy's, unmoved by familiarity or age, law or reason. His aim followed his focus, as always. He heard a half-dozen weapons or more shatter the evening air. Lead destroyed that cruel face in a hammersmash of blood and bone.

Mayport dropped his pistols and drew his second brace. One bully boy was down already, a leg reduced to raw meat, but he was still trying to aim his weapon. Mayport put a stop to that, and drew his third brace. Too late, because the other fellow had lost most of his chest as if struck from behind. Nails protruded crazily from the wound.

"Frog?" Mayport asked, but couldn't hear his own voice. His ears were ringing with powder blasts and pounding blood. Then the cold in him began to fade, and pain came crashing in. His legs went out from under him, and he fell in the dusty street. "Joseph!"

For terrifying moments he was alone with the agony. He could see nothing but the horrors he had created. There was time to wonder if he'd done enough to set things right. Then someone rolled him over, renewing the pain in his shoulder and thigh. His vision cleared a little, and he groaned.

"Wake up!" Joseph said, loud enough for Mayport to hear. "Tight now, hold on to me. We've got a way to go."

Epilogue

Mayport lay on his lounge, made comfortable by one of Elias' medicines. His arm was slung to his chest, and leg bound to heal. Elias had proven himself an able surgeon in retrieving slugs and stitching flesh, though he was unhappy with the necessity. It seemed best to show gratitude by obeying his commands during convalescence.

Joseph had turned himself into a nurse, going so far as carrying Mayport when he needed to move. He attended Mayport constantly, worried over fever and infection that was never allowed to set in. It was as if he had never seen Mayport at labor on the decks of the *Dutch Process* and had suddenly come under the impression that his husband was made of spun sugar. In the first day after Mayport's duel, he had sent urgent word to New Amsterdam, attempting to inform Costor of the facts before rumor could worry the poor fellow.

Costor's reaction had been to come south by steam coach and see Mayport for himself. Some shade of the day young Gasteau was lost had moved him to an abundance of caution. Mayport was touched to find their friendship could make Costor leave his comfortable home if his aid was needed.

He brought news of his newest treasure, little Rose Elizabeth Achely. Mayport and Joseph became godfathers even as Mayport struggled to overcome his wounds. They were all together when, at last, Mayport proved his fingers would still obey his will.

The view from his parlor window made him as peaceful as Elias' poppies. "We'll have us a corduroy road before spring. They're taking the pines down now, while the fields are fallow."

"So you've said, several times. I think that medicine is making you repeat yourself," Costor said with a smile. "I might come down again and open a real bank. Your ledger alone proves there's a need."

"You'd better try the summer heat before you decide to stay on," Joseph said. "This is the gentlest time of year. You've only seen this place at its best."

"I suppose you're right," Costor said. "Still, it's a sight better than New Amsterdam in winter. Perhaps I'll divide my time by the seasons. We could run a rail line here, if it wasn't on the south side of swamps and rivers."

"The river has its ferries," Mayport said, slow and careful because of what the medicines made of his attention. "We're getting all kinds of new people. I guess a banker won't be the worst thing that shows up to settle in."

Indeed, a few odd ducks had already found their place in May Port. The first pair had come from Annie Cook's establishment. Their profession ran contrary to their preferences. They had come humbly to ask if women were allowed the same rights together as men.

They had all been surprised to discover such ladies existed. Jesse went along, but only after exhausting all his protests. Under the law, there was no reason to deny the request. Since then, a few other marriages had been made in Mayport's drawing room. Some couples had traveled centuries of miles to get hands on a certificate, and came prepared to bribe all concerned.

Mayport was proud that his personal vices had come to cause these private joys. If they had even a fraction of his own happiness, they were counted among the luckiest of souls. Even laid up with his wounds, he felt his fortune was complete. Every glance at Joseph Titus proved the risk had been entirely to his credit.

"I haven't thanked you yet," Joseph said. "I wanted to find some other way, though it was more than my father deserved."

"Don't sound so ashamed," Mayport said. "It's a virtue, that you never turned patricide."

"Perhaps, but cowardice is no virtue," Joseph said. "Frog was the one who understood your intention. I didn't believe a word until you drew down right there in the street. I couldn't kill him. Frog's aim was truer than mine, even against his men."

"You saved my life," Mayport said. "I didn't think I would survive. Without you, I might have given up the ghost right there in the dirt."

"Don't talk about that," Joseph said. "At least, not until you're well again. I want to see you up and walking before I'll be happy."

"I will," Mayport said, and flexed his toes. "Not today, but eventually. Of course, you're making it tempting to delay. With you so attentive, I don't even need to walk."

"I'll bring anything you like. Do you want some cocoa?" Joseph asked, all anxious to serve.

Mayport laughed. "You know, most fellows court and flutter like this *before* the wedding."

"Never mind how backwards I am. I don't intend to stop," Joseph declared. "There's all sorts of tempting fellows around town these days. I won't leave them a trick to try on you."

"It wouldn't work, even if someone approached me," Mayport said.

"I don't care if they have a hope of success," Joseph said. "There will never be a thing any man could give, that I won't do with my own hands."

"Your hands are needed for more than my personal service," Mayport said. "Still, I enjoy it all too much. You'll spoil me beyond all reason if you go on so."

"That's precisely what I mean to do," Joseph said.

Mayport laughed, then winced as his shoulder twinged despite the medicine. "Marriage has certainly changed you. I've not heard a single word about heading off on the *Process* in all this time."

Joseph looked annoyed all over again. "You sit there, unable to walk, waking up from pain and nightmares every night, and wonder why I'd rather be home. I've never been so needed before in my life. This is my place, and I mean to keep it."

When put that way, Mayport didn't wonder at all. Joseph's reasoning also settled his own questions about how he could have killed a man in the coldest blood he had ever felt. Even with death on his hands, he was at peace with himself.

"You're both due a rest," Costor said. "I don't expect this domesticity to last the year, though. As soon as he can, our Mayport will start itching for adventures again. It's in his blood."

"Not mine, it isn't. You've mistaken me for my father," Mayport said. "Adventure was never my game. Neither was fortune. What I lacked, you've never understood, because you had it all along. This place is my home. Here, I have a family. There's nothing so tempting in the wide world as what I have right here."

The entire household worked tirelessly to keep him so content. Even Frog condescended to visit, though he made his little home in town. His fierce independence was only the mark left on him by his hometown. Among his peers, he was envied for his position with their new governor.

At dinner, he bragged in his taciturn way. "If I'd known what would come of it, I never would have helped you fellows. There's not a bar in town that will let me buy my own rounds. I guess they saw what I did, but that don't answer. Unless they're scared of me, somehow."

"I can't imagine why they would be," Elias said, all quiet sarcasm. "Everybody knows what's in your gun. For sure, it's not rock salt."

"Oh, I loaded it up special that day," Frog said. "Best not to tell anybody, though. They wouldn't believe you. They got a story all fixed up where the whole town gunned down an army of Northies that threatened our governor. You'd think I carried a cannon in my back pocket, the way they tell it."

Mayport laughed. "I'll have to go hear it myself, one day. It would be nice to know what I did."

"All I wanna know is, how did you figure out we were hiding to cover your back?" Frog asked.

"I didn't," Mayport said. "I knew I was about to die, but that wasn't enough to stop me."

Frog whistled, impressed. "You're not brave. You're crazy. That fool ought to have known better than to fight against crazy. There's no way to win, no matter how good a shot you are."

"At least his reputation is set in stone," Jesse said. "There's not a man in town that would go against him, now. It doesn't matter a bit that they know about his vices. He's got the one virtue that matters in a governor. He'll fight to protect his people. If they must, his people will fight for him. Young Frog himself proved that."

"I hope I never have to fight again," Mayport said. "I'm better suited to Dutch conquest, by trade and gold. My armory is full, on that account."

"May it ever be so," Costor said, offering the remark as a toast.

Mayport smiled over his table. At last, he knew what it was men dreamed of having for their own, when they risked everything to make a home. If he had understood sooner, he would not have been reluctant to claim his place

His prize was entirely original. It was his own, as he had never dreamed happiness could be. In Joseph's smile, he saw the mirror of his own contentment. With that honor, he owned pride and peace that could never be stolen away from him.

THE END

About the Author

H.B Kurtzwilde lives in the wet, sticky, mosquito-ridden depths of Florida. When not busily avoiding alligators, he scribbles out futuristic and paranormal fiction, as if this is any way for a grown person to behave. His works include Phoberia, Guide to Survival, and Sea Turtle Inn, among others. Drop by his Livejournal or his personal blog at hbkurtzwilde.circlet.com to say hello, or to make a donation in support of his artistic efforts.

Clasp Editions
Erotic Romance that is out of this world...!
From Circlet Press, publishers of eroic fantasy and science fiction, an imprint focused on love stories and relationships in the midst of adventure, magic, and the future.

Simulacrum, by Rian Darcy $6.99
In the virtual world of Simulnet, no one knows who you really are, making it the perfect playground for the imagination... and for a serial killer. Shaun's world turns upside down when a police detective asks for his help finding a murderer somewhere in the cyberspace sex clubs, ramen shops, and massage parlors of Simulnet. His partner on the case will be a prickly and enigmatic programmer known only as Lore. But as they search for the killer, Shaun finds himself wanting to know more and more about his partner. Ultimately the questions Shaun will need to answer most are the one's he asks himself, deep in his heart.

Princes of Air, by Elizabeth Schechter $5.99
The Raven-Goddess Morrigan granted two gifts to her nine sons: the ability to shift from raven to human form and to recognize their soulmates. But, even for demi-gods, the path to true love is far from smooth. The brothers have drawn the attention of a family of powerful mages who will stop at nothing to gain power. Each brother will be forced to make sacrifices to keep his mate alive and protect their land from harm.

Faewolf, by DM Atkins & Chris Taylor, $6.99
Faewolves, like werewolves, can walk among men. What happens when Kiya White Cloud, a young gay college student in Santa Cruz, wants one of these men enough to risk his heart—and his life? An m/m erotic romance from Circlet Press, Inc. [Warning: explicit sex, dubious consent, and rough scenes.]

clasp.circlet.com